Lovebird Escapes

Love of Power versus Power of Love

SHEKA TARAWALIE

The Book Guild Ltd

First published in Great Britain in 2022 by
The Book Guild Ltd
Unit E2 Airfield Business Park,
Harrison Road, Market Harborough,
Leicestershire. LE16 7UL
Tel: 0116 2792299
www.bookguild.co.uk
Email: info@bookguild.co.uk
Twitter: @bookguild

This work is entirely fictitious and bears no resemblance to any persons living or dead.

Typeset in 11pt Minion Pro

Printed on FSC accredited paper
Printed and bound in Great Britain by 4edge Limited

ISBN 978 1915122 704

British Library Cataloguing in Publication Data.
A catalogue record for this book is available from the British Library.

To Rose… For typing, and enduring, and loving… Locked up together, and by way of escaping from the harsh realities of the COVID 19 pandemic, we produced this…

To Family Church Saddleworth, for being the focus group throughout the process; to Holts Christian Fellowship, for playing a similar role; and to BB Scaffolding Services (North West) Ltd, for the special interest demonstrated…

To the publishers, the midwives…

To the unknown reader, who I would never meet…

To God be the glory!

Sheka Tarawalie
Oldham, Manchester, UK
August 2022

THE WORLD

Contents

Book One: Mother and Daughter 1

Book Two: Father and Daughter 177

Book Three: Son-in-Law 363

Book One

Mother and Daughter

"...We have escaped like a bird from the fowler's snare..."

1

For the past eight months, the British High Commissioner to Sierra Leone, Mark Fergusson, had not had time for his wife, Rachael. Tonight, in their North London home, he felt obliged. She indulged him, despite her inner mixed feelings, because a special day awaited them – as a family. They cuddled and snuggled and discussed…

All these months, Rachael had been wondering whether she would ever get her husband back. Because she was already losing him – somehow. Not that she feared he would have got trapped in the induced embrace of an African girl (she knew very well the stories of colonial and post-colonial love webs – or love triangles, as they called them in diplomatic circles – that got white men in Africa hooked from their wives by black girls 'using *juju*'; and she had read Graham Greene's *The Heart of the Matter*).

Rachael was sure – well, she believed – Mark did not do anything with other women beyond flirtations. She knew him more than any outside narrator ever would. She knew how he had always loved work so much – but not to the recent extent of being drifted away from his family. He had always been a good man – a good husband, a good father, who wouldn't want to tear his family apart. Nevertheless, Rachael had thought, one should never underestimate what fate could throw at one – what life could suddenly hurl at mortals.

So Rachael had kept wondering why Mark had religiously devoted himself to the seemingly hopeless cause of saving Sierra Leone: getting enmeshed in the affairs of a tiny West African country embroiled in a predatory political and military crisis – at the expense of his family. The excuse of cementing obscure pre-colonial family connections had never really convinced her – and it was no longer tenable. The other reason of staying behind to save his son-in-law (Son-in-law? Rachael had riled when Mark called him that), Stephen, trapped in the country's besieged capital city, Freetown, had been overtaken by events. It had become redundant and therefore a façade to her: it had been confirmed that Stephen had been killed; any otherwise hope was at best day-dreaming and a ruse. Mark's 'democracy saviour' posture was even more repellent to Rachael: she mused about why her husband would somewhat personally tote the responsibility of returning to power an overthrown corrupt African leader in the name of democracy. "And people have to be killed for that?" A confused Rachael once asked herself. And so she thought she was losing her husband to the whims of Prime Minister Ed McInroy.

She was disturbed. And just a couple of days ago, she got 'reliable information' from Liberia that Mark was having an 'inappropriate relationship' with a certain female Sierra Leonean journalist in Monrovia – 'working and doing stuff together' late into the night. Rachael would have loved to go there and prove it; but not now. She would confront Mark with the information; yet not right now.

For now, she had to bear it all – for the sake of their daughter and their grandson, both of whom she was coaxing out of miserable isolation. She only hoped and prayed for Mark. Well, she didn't really believe in prayer – as in praying. She only hoped and wished.

So tonight, in their bedroom in London, after discussing at length, Rachael's husband wanted to sound romantic – again:

"I've really been missing you," he said.

"Are you really sure, Mark?" she asked.

"You know I'm sure."

"And you are leaving tomorrow." It was not a question.

"The day after tomorrow."

"It's past midnight. So it's tomorrow."

He looked at his watch and wanted to say, "It's not yet midnight in West Africa," but he let it pass. He settled with: "Honey, you know I just have to go. I have no option."

She just smiled. And let it go…

He quickly added, touching her hand, "And, darling, you know we have a date tomorrow; well, tonight, because it's past midnight."

They burst out laughing…

***

Just a little over eight months ago, the Fergusson family seemed to have overcome its domestic troubles and appeared as a happy close-knit family – especially after the birth of their grandson, Joel – in the course of their diplomatic duty in Sierra Leone.

But then the coup changed everything. It was a messy affair, putting the country on the brink of an all-out civil war. As the most senior diplomat of the country's former colonial power, as the representative of Sierra Leone's current largest donor, the British High Commissioner had on his shoulders the responsibility of doing his best to resolve the political crisis. Another British High Commissioner might not have been more passionate. Mark Fergusson would risk his life and limb to get it done – to tell the soldiers that their place was at the barracks and not State House, and to back his words with action.

When it became more difficult than he thought, and the situation deteriorated further to a dangerous stalemate, he convinced the Foreign and Commonwealth Office to evacuate British citizens from Sierra Leone. Rachael was not happy that Mark was staying behind while she and their daughter Sarah and grandson Joel were evacuated back to Britain. Her only consolation was that she was inwardly happy that Joel's Sierra Leonean father, Stephen, was not coming with them as well. With time and being reconnected to her British friends and social circles, Sarah would forget about Stephen and move on with her life... was Rachael's wish. And – far beyond Rachael's wish – news came that Stephen had been killed in the war. She hadn't wished him dead – although "So sorry but so be it" was her immediate response to the news.

Somehow, it worked. It seemed to have worked. Mark committed the British Government to doing all it could to overturn the coup and restore the civilian government back to State House in Freetown.

Just that the mission had not been fully accomplished yet – the Sierra Leone coup-makers had turned out to be 'a very stubborn rag-tag army of fighters' resisting the international coalition led by the British. That kept Mark on the ground; but not enough to let Rachael return to Sierra Leone or go to meet him in Liberia as events unfolded.

But then just yesterday – by Sierra Leonean time; the day before yesterday by British time – Mark telephoned Rachael to tell her he was coming to London, having got directives from the Foreign and Commonwealth Office that the Prime Minister, Ed McInroy, wanted to see him tomorrow; or today, as the case might be.

The Fergussons were both happy for the news. They hadn't got the details of the invitation; but, to them, it could only be one of two things. Either he was going to be recommended for knighthood or to be relocated to another diplomatic station.

Any would be good, for Mark. But, no matter what it was about, Rachael saw it as an opportunity to present the case for relocation. Even if that was not the reason why Number 10 had asked him to come to London urgently, she was poised to prevail on Mark to present it to the Prime Minister – for family reasons. That Sarah, their daughter, of whom the Prime Minister was godfather, would only finally overcome the trauma of having lost her fiancé if they relocated to another station. Ed McInroy would understand, Rachael believed. Mark agreed.

So tonight, in their cosy North London home, it was a date with their pre-diplomatic life. Mark himself had been longing for it – buoyed with the joy of having to see the Prime Minister, his friend, in the morning. So, at long last, love was once more rekindled – Mark and Rachael were in each other's arms again!

So be it, Rachael thought to herself.

2

Mark Fergusson knew that, with all his love and passion for Sierra Leone, there was one man who possibly beat him to that – Prime Minister Ed McInroy. He was his greatest ally in this enterprise. If Mark was confident in what he was doing, if he had been able to convince Rachael to hang on just for a little while more, it was because the Prime Minister had fully supported him and backed every of his actions on the ground. To Mark, everything he had been doing was in accordance with the Prime Minister's rulebook. So a summons to Number 10 was a most welcoming development. He had great expectations.

* * *

Even before he became Prime Minister, Ed McInroy had been visiting Sierra Leone, which he aptly called his second home. For very good reasons. He was born there!

His father, Ed McInroy Sr., served in the Colonial Office during the Second World War and was based in Freetown as Special Assistant to the Governor. His mother, Samantha, while being a devoted housewife raising up two daughters, taught Latin and Greek three days a week at the country's premier university, Mount Aureol University. It was in the last year of their service to Sierra Leone that Ed was born. They left the country when he was eight months old. But that never deterred him from recognising the West African country as his place of birth. The stories told to him about the country when he became a teenager only buoyed him to want to visit. And once he got the first opportunity through a student-exchange programme with his University of Durham, he seized it. Since then, he had made it a point of duty to visit the country every year.

'I just fell in love with the place, and I have never met a more lovely and loveable people' had always been his justification for continued affinity.

So when he actually became Britain's youngest Prime Minister in a century under the New Order party, Ed McInroy's foreign policy was, among other things, tilted towards helping developing countries and safeguarding their nascent democracies – with Sierra Leone topmost on his mind, a secret he disclosed to his Foreign Secretary, Tony Lamb, as a matter of priority.

"Tony," Prime Minister McInroy had said after his first Cabinet meeting. "Our new ethical foreign policy is of the utmost importance to this administration. But as a friend and long-time colleague, I would like you to realise that no matter how bogged down we would be with domestic politics and major international engagements, Sierra Leone must be a priority in terms of aid and any other support."

Tony Lamb knew the background to this. He knew the Prime Minister had given him the position because he was one of few he could possibly confide in in such matters – personal matters webbed into public policy. The Foreign Secretary actually used the term 'wedged' afterwards when confiding in his Foreign Office lieutenant, John Coleson.

It was for virtually the same reasons that Ed McInroy had appointed Mark Fergusson as High Commissioner to Sierra Leone

– long-time friendship 'wedged' into politics to be sure of trust. Just that the Prime Minister knew Mark also had a personal relationship with Sierra Leone. But the new British High Commissioner had never been to the country before his appointment.

* * *

So, in London that morning of her husband's appointment with the Prime Minister, Rachael Fergusson woke up feeling like a newly wedded wife, with a glowing face, her round eyes brightening as rare sunrays pierced through the transparent window curtains into their bedroom that spring season. She smiled wryly: *it's just like yesterday.* She rolled on the bed, turned to Mark, who was still snoring, gave him a peck, and jumped off to the bathroom.

She did the private morning courtesies, and looked into the mirror to see a radiant blushing face, rolling back the years to the days before Sarah was born. Marriage was not a bed of roses, and it had taken its toll on her through the years. But there were those moments when she thought and believed that, with all its troubles, marriage might be worth entering into. And now was one of those moments for her.

She picked a hairband and tied her drooping hair before rushing to the kitchen to prepare breakfast.

Sarah was already in the kitchen, as was her custom ever since they relocated from Sierra Leone – coming to the kitchen very early to get a few things for her and her son Joel to have breakfast in their bedroom before anybody else came there. Today her mother was early. That was not surprising to Sarah, because she knew her father had just arrived yesterday from Liberia, Sierra Leone's neighbouring country hosting the overthrown government, and where the British High Commission had also temporarily relocated. And Sarah also knew that her mother was always dutiful about preparing breakfast for her husband – because Rachael liked breakfast chatter with him.

What was a bit surprising for Sarah, though, was the briskness with which her mother entered the kitchen with explicit joy written all over her face. She always knew it when her mother was genuinely happy – her smile could not be hidden. Sarah was a bit flummoxed about the overnight transformation. Could her mother have finally succeeded in convincing her father to abandon the Sierra Leone project and ask for a transfer? Or could her usually reticent father himself have told his wife that he was now willing to be the husband she wanted him to be?

Sarah was curious to know, but not so curious as to ask. What she knew was that all these months her mother had been complaining about her father having practically abandoned his family for a failed enterprise. And even when the message came through that he had been 'invited' by the Prime Minister to immediately come for a meeting to London, her mother was not excited about it.

"They may be planning to send more troops and arms to fight the rebels in Sierra Leone. This will never end," was how Rachael explained it to Sarah after revealing the news.

The only opportunity Rachael saw in it was that of trying to still talk her husband out of 'this entanglement'. Till last evening, after dinner, and before they said their various goodnights, Rachael was wearing a sombre face. At dinner, the father didn't say much beyond what they already knew about having been invited by the Prime Minister. Even when their son, Ben, tried to push him to say much, Mark had only retorted, "I am tired, Ben. I've had a long flight, really a long day. I woke up at 5am today, and I need to rest now before tomorrow's meeting." That was how they parted company last night – except that indeed Rachael had a brief brightness of face when kissing Joel goodnight, a fondness she had developed for her grandson, whatever the circumstances.

So mother and daughter exchanged a terse 'good morning', both still in their sleeping gowns – the mother in white, the daughter in black (it had become Sarah's favourite colour since she got the news of Stephen's death and relapsed in a world of mourning). Sarah got some cereal and an apple, poured some milk in her 'love always overcomes' inscripted mug (the only gift from Stephen that she had brought along from Sierra Leone), and turned for the door. She was already in the living room, heading towards the stairs, when, like an after-thought, Rachael called her daughter.

"What, Mum?" She did not return to the kitchen, but she stopped in her tracks and waited.

The mother came out of the kitchen and asked, "Did Joel sleep well?"

"He is still sleeping."

Sarah took another step to go when the mother said, "We'll talk after your dad has left for his meeting," in a sprightly tone and with a still-radiating face – in total contrast to her daughter's demeanour.

"I am here," was her parting phrase as she took the stairs to her room and found Joel still sleeping.

* * *

Rachael Fergusson, in the exuberance of renewed love and great expectations, had chosen what her husband would wear for the occasion, even down to the socks and shoes. The dark suit was the one for their wedding day; the white shirt was her gift to him on his birthday last year; the red tie was one of the presents her friend, Maria, gave him on their wedding day; and the socks and shoes were also a birthday gift from the man he was going to meet, his best friend and boss, the Prime Minister.

The Fergussons were all by themselves for breakfast as Ben, as usual, had left first thing in the morning for his university classes. Mark was now sipping the last contents of his coffee in their oval-shaped dining room, looking through the side window into the back garden, lost in wonderment. Today was the day. His mind raced back to Liberia, thinking of Sierra Leone's exiled President, Kargbo Ndomahina, and the intimate relationship they had carved for themselves through the hard realities of refusing to give in to the Freetown junta or give up power as time ticked away. It was not an easy job, having to do it for more than eight months with no clear prospects of winning, except the belief that the United Nations-imposed sanctions on Sierra Leone over air, land and sea were working, enforced by the Nigerian military and the civil militia on the ground. And the unequivocal support of the international community for the exiled government and its fighting forces was not waning. So now, with this pending meeting at Number 10, it was clear victory was in sight. Mark smiled. Thanks to UN Secretary General John Kirikiri. Thanks to British Prime Minister Ed McInroy. He would never thank Nigerian military dictator Mallam Musa Odofo.

Mark was still in a reverie when Rachael, in her flowing white sleeping gown, reappeared before him (not that she was not there all along; she was also initially drowned in thought) and took away the empty mug from him, and reminded him of the time – just being extra nice.

It was all smiles and kisses after the chauffeur, called by Rachael, came to the door and collected Mark's briefcase.

The journey from the North London mansion of the Fergussons to Number 10 Downing Street would normally take thirty minutes, traffic inclusive. But Mark was a very meticulous man, known for his attention to detail, promptness in duty, punctuality in every appointment – his Latin teacher at Exeter School had nicknamed him 'Punctualis'. His appointment was for 10:30. Mark left home at 9:30. "Always give yourself a waiting time breather of at least twenty minutes for any appointment," he had always lectured his son, Ben, who had imbibed his father's time-consciousness.

Mark was happy to see London again – his London, good old London – its usual bustling self as they navigated their way to Westminster. He had time to open his briefcase and re-read the UN's latest reports on the situation in Sierra Leone. One thing he had always told President Kargbo Ndomahina was that they were very lucky to have had John Kirikiri as UN Secretary General – being an African holding the topmost UN position at a time when results were needed on the African continent (the President knew better – because Kirikiri was his long-time friend). Mark was particularly interested in the document marked 'TOP SECRET' and signed by Kirikiri himself.

By the time he finished reading it, they were at Westminster. And then the difficult part: that short journey from the car park to the Number 10 door – the most famous black door on Earth.

Mark was a relatively shy man. And that's why, in politics, he had not gone for the jugular of being in the limelight as a mainstream politician seeking elected office or lobbying for a ministerial position. He had settled for the comparatively low-key diplomatic career, where one's public image was rarely at the centre of attention. And so, if it were left with him, if there were anything like an official back door alternative to entering Number 10, he would have loved to use it to avoid the ubiquitous cameras of the pack of journalists and photographers permanently stationed opposite the Number 10 door (whoever came up with that idea had ever since thrown spanners in the works of British politics, one politician had famously said). "If only they would mind their business or had something else to do or somewhere else to go," Mark vainly muttered to himself. The chauffeur heard him though. They reached the car park and he stepped out of the BMW to take the inevitable walk.

He kept a straight face, briefcase in hand, as he approached the door from the west end of the pavement in fast but measured paces. If his photograph were to appear in a London tabloid, let it be of the Mark Fergusson that people knew. He would not attempt to turn to the cameras, and was definitely not prepared to say a word in response to all their shouts about why he was there. As he raised the door latch and did a double tapping, the minute or so of waiting for the door to open seemed forever. His back was turned to the press but he could hear the fluttering sounds of camera clicks going on incessantly.

At last the door opened and Number 10 swallowed the image of Mark Fergusson.

The Prime Minister was waiting to see him. Mark was longing to see Ed McInroy, his friend, his boss…

3

Rachael Fergusson was particularly unhappy that her husband had only come for a very short stay. "The exiled President cannot do without me, Rachael, especially at this crucial final stage," Mark had told his inquiring wife when she pressed that he could stay longer. He had therefore scheduled that, after his meeting with the Prime Minister, he would only give himself this day to rest and then leave for Liberia.

Rachael thought that, after their lovely night and nice breakfast together, she had built a platform to try again to convince her husband to change his mind and stay for at least a week. So even as they stood at the front of their mansion, holding hands after the chauffeur had collected the briefcase, with smiles and all, she brought the subject matter again. Rachael's mind had swayed to what she thought was apparently pulling her husband away: late-night close-door 'escapades' with that Sierra Leonean female journalist in Liberia. *Could this African juju thing be actually working?*

But, good old Mark, he was quick to counter it with, "The Prime Minister would hate to hear such a proposal. And you know we already have a bigger proposal, the better one, as we already agreed," as he gave her another kiss.

So as Mark entered the BMW, Rachael closed the door behind her and returned to what had been her routine for the past eight months – taking care of her home, with especial cautious and conscious efforts to find the right words to say to her gloomy and unpredictable daughter, Sarah; and caring for her grandson Joel as much as she possibly could.

* * *

The Fergussons' daughter Sarah's life had been worse than a routine. It was a monotony. Actually, a melancholy! To this, Rachael Fergusson had committed herself to be an antidote; she felt bound to be a mental antibody to her daughter's melancholy – if anything like that ever existed. For the past eight months, it had become her preoccupation, her obsession. But it went way beyond that, in deep roots to Sarah's birth.

Whatever caused British doctors at the Royal Exeter Hospital to tell the Fergussons that their first baby, who turned out to be a girl, would be a boy, was still a scandal that stood out in the history of the hospital's once highly rated obstetrics section. For mothers not to naturally get along with their daughters was one thing. But when a thing as 'scientifically uncomplicated' as knowing the gender of a baby pre-birth got mixed up, and false hope was rammed down the throats of expectant parents to the last minute, then it was a most unnatural circumstance unwittingly setting the stage for a strenuous mother-and-daughter relationship.

Mark and Rachael Fergusson were not particularly choosy about the gender of their first baby. All they wanted was a baby: the first fruit of their unusual step of getting married on the grounds of the university where they met – Oxford. They didn't even discuss pregnancy, either before or during or after their honeymoon. They were just in love with each other, and committed to following this love wherever it led them. Rachael was teaching at the Exeter Sixth Form College, while Mark was working for the local council as a development officer. They even made it a point of duty to meet every lunch hour to pursue their instincts. It was a relationship that impressed the Exeter community – and Rachael was pleased and sure she had made the right decision in shunning her royal family connections for Mark's working-class status.

Rachael had gone to hospital on a totally different matter – she was having constant headaches – when she was told she could be pregnant. She confirmed it five days later when her cycle was interrupted. Not that it was unplanned or unexpected; for a couple who had been in a relationship since their university days, it was some pleasant sequel. Mark insisted on hearing it from the horse's mouth and accompanied Rachael on her next hospital appointment. And it was confirmed.

"And it's a boy." The words of Dr. Peter Robinson were unmistakable – they were like music in the couple's ears. They went home more than elated. And it would remain so for the succeeding months – as day by day they put the building blocks in place to usher in their bouncing baby boy.

The doctors didn't miss the date of delivery – though they didn't know the hour. Weeks before the day, the Fergussons went out on a shopping spree for the coming boy, whom they were going to name after their paternal parents: James Benjamin Fergusson – James, the father of Mark; Benjamin, the father of Rachael.

Rachael went into labour with a robustness powered by her expectations. The nurses couldn't have found a better ally in making their job easier. Mark – patient outwardly, impatient inwardly – pacing up and down the waiting room while intermittently reading blankly on the notice board, couldn't believe his ears when he was told the baby had come after just an hour. The only odd part was when he was told to go see Dr. Robinson first before seeing his wife and the newborn babe.

"Look, Mr Fergusson, these things happen," was how a crestfallen Dr. Robinson tried to pacify a clearly confused Mark after revealing that it was actually a baby girl and not the baby boy they had expected.

"These things happen these days, Doctor?" was Mark's rhetorical reaction. "In this day and age? All these months of telling us it's a boy? We are no longer in the Victorian era, where guesswork could be allowed in such issues."

"It was not guesswork, sir," the doctor continued to placate. "All I can say is, we are deeply sorry. This is beyond our understanding. We did everything scientifically correct to the letter. All the scans we carried out showed that it was a boy. I am a man who doesn't normally believe in miracles, but this is one. Let's accept it that way. She is a miracle child. A miracle baby."

The experienced medic, with twenty-odd years of service in the medical profession, having spent the last ten as head of the obstetrics department at the Royal Exeter Hospital, knew it would not be too hard to convince the father. His greatest fear was how to confront the mother with the news. He needed an ally in Mark. He got him – albeit reluctantly, understandably.

Both men entered the labour room just in time for Rachael to open her eyes, having fallen into sleep (induced by the nurses) immediately after giving birth. Her eyes met with Mark's. He was standing right in front of her at the foot of the bed. She was still weak and her right hand still had a syringe, though it was no longer connected to the cardiotocography.

She gave a broad smile, and Mark moved toward the head of the bed, closer to her, caressing her hand, with Dr. Robinson and the nurses waiting curiously.

"We did it, Mark," was Rachael's first expression in a soft low tone.

"Yes, we did, love. And thank you," he said, now clasping her fingers into his.

"Where's he? Where is our James Benjamin?" The most dreaded question in the room dropped like an arrow from the lips of the recuperating mother, piercing Dr. Robinson as if he did not expect it. He was ice stiff, unresponsive like a stone, cold and temporarily lifeless, sweating in a fully air-conditioned room. So the perceptive nurses wouldn't allow the medic to hear the mother's next question. It was better he didn't hear it, because it was directed at him. It might have made him permanently lifeless.

"Doctor, where is my baby boy?"

When it had become clear to them that Dr. Robinson was no longer his normal self (speechless and impassive to what was going on), two of the nurses had, just after Rachael's first question, unceremoniously escorted the doctor out of the room before the last question actually came out.

***

This was the strange way in which Rachael and Sarah came to be mother and daughter in this world. With all the pleas from Mark for Rachael to accept things as they had turned out, the nurses joining in pleading with her, she could not take it. She suspected foul play and accused her husband of not knowing better. She therefore insisted on using the recently discovered DNA testing (Exeter Hospital being among the first to provide the service) – "to prove that my baby is not a changeling".

"No, Rachael, we don't have to go down that route," Mark still pleaded.

"I will not leave this room until that is done."

"We don't need to. The baby is ours. She looks like us."

"I have said it. And I mean it."

The DNA test was carried out and the baby was theirs. To make it up to her husband, Rachael decided to name her Sarah, after her mother-in-law.

"I really love her," were the parting words she gave to the nurses as she cuddled "my little bundle of joy" with her signature broad smile – though she refused to ask about, or even didn't care to know what might have happened to, Dr. Robinson. "Let him clean up after himself!" she had told Mark in the car. The only thing she would later like about the medic was when she learned from her husband that Dr. Robinson had called Sarah 'a miracle baby'.

In her subsequent one-on-one conversations with Mark, Rachael liked calling Sarah 'our miracle baby'. And she did a lot of that last night and this morning at the breakfast table before her husband left for his meeting with the Prime Minister.

***

So when she closed the door behind her after Mark's departure, Rachael was prepared to have a bold, honest and mature conversation with her daughter about moving on with life. She wanted her daughter to put the past behind her, put Stephen behind her, put this black clothing behind her, and get her life moving again.

Ever since she had confirmed that Sarah was actually her daughter, Rachael had thrown her heart into motherhood, doing all that a mother could possibly do to bring her daughter up. She put her everything into it – even took an extended maternity leave to care for her 'miracle baby'.

Everything went on reasonably well until Sierra Leone changed everything.

And Rachael would always put the blame squarely on Mark's shoulders for making the choice of going to serve as British High Commissioner to that country. He could have been the British Ambassador to the USA, considering his close relationship with the Prime Minister. He would have even settled for a European country. She had wanted Mexico for the sake of her former university roommate, Maria. But Mark had deliberately chosen a war-ravaged West African country for very obscure reasons.

So Rachael always believed Sierra Leone was a mistake. If not, their daughter wouldn't be in this predicament now, as there would have been no Stephen in their lives. But then there would have also been no Joel. That's where Rachael was caught in a puzzle. She had never really liked Stephen, but she loved Joel to the uttermost.

And now Stephen was no more. Rachael's task – her current preoccupation – was to bail her daughter out of drawn-out grieving for him and move on with their lives. They had the consolation of Joel 'representing Stephen', she had argued. She knew it was a difficult task – she had been doing it from the very beginning with little or no success. But at the beginning, there was a living Stephen to run to or to think about reconnecting with; now, he was dead. Sarah must accept her fate and the prevailing circumstances, and move on. As parents, it was their duty to ensure it happened. This had formed the basis for most of the discussion between the Fergussons last night and this morning at their North London residence.

4

Joel had awoken from sleep moments after his mother entered the room with breakfast.

This was no new room to Sarah – though new in some ways, as things stood now. This was the room she had occupied since her teenage years after coming out of her GCSEs with flying colours, and her parents decided to surprise her with the 'self-contained apartment' within the house.

The Fergussons had bought the mansion through a mortgage during the second year of Mark's tenure as chairman of Exeter local council and had transferred there when Sarah had chosen London's Lady Margaret School for her secondary education. Mark had to leave the council to head a London consultancy firm partly owned by his friend, Ed McInroy's father. It was more a job to boost Ed's political ambition, as Mark devoted himself to devising strategies and writing his friend's speeches until they won the elections.

So Sarah's room, or apartment, had a master-bed, a study table with a matching chair, a bookshelf, a large wardrobe, a shoe rack, a Jacuzzi in the bathroom. It even had its own veranda with an outside chair and stool, overlooking the lush greenery of Victoria Park, from where she could also see almost half of North London.

Since her senior secondary school days, Sarah had made it a habit to have some meals in her room. Her mother didn't like that, but she got away with it with the excuse of having to do academic work while still eating and drinking.

* * *

But that life had ended when they left for Sierra Leone following the appointment of her father as High Commissioner. Sarah never wanted to leave Britain for Sierra Leone. "What for? Of all places?" she had quipped when first told. Rachael was in total support of that, though she had no solution as to how Sarah would live a life of her own with them in a faraway land – even as Sarah's younger brother Ben was now inevitably outward-looking. The once inseparable siblings were not as close as they used to be. And Sarah was daddy's daughter being doted on by Mark all the time – as Rachael would acknowledge. He was Sarah's security and her confidant. She had not got a boyfriend – or any time for that. She had not graduated from university yet, and so the prospect of going to a strange remote place called Sierra Leone, of which all she had heard was war and poverty, was a dumb and weird proposal: "Is it a wild joke?"

How Mark, with the assistance of his friend Ed McInroy, managed to talk Sarah out of that position and convince her about heading for 'a promised land', made Rachael further realise that no matter how much she tried, the father-daughter relationship was always stronger. She had solace in the fact that her own bond with Ben was stronger than the father-son relationship. But an outgoing boy like Ben, growing up so fast, would soon be lost to the embrace of a girl or to his peers and might not look back. Rachael always wished she would be closer to Sarah. But the more she tried, the more she found out it was not working – it even succeeded in sending the daughter closer to her father. How could

Mark and Uncle Ed have convinced Sarah that Sierra Leone's Mount Aureol University was equal to, if not better than, many British universities? And that completing her course there would still be a great, if not greater, achievement!

And this was what scared Rachael the most about Sierra Leone – the fact that Ben would not be coming, as he was just in his second year at university. She would be living in a place far away where she would always be outnumbered and outvoted by Mark and Sarah. But she accepted her fate and promised to do the best she could as a wife and mother, to make her home happy, for better or for worse.

When they left for Sierra Leone, therefore, Sarah cleared everything in her room with the belief that she would never come back here again. She was going to complete her university studies in Sierra Leone and thereafter look forward to a new future. Even when she had graduated and later returned to Britain, it would be to her own rented flat, she had envisaged.

She had actually already started fulfilling these dreams in Sierra Leone: she completed university, met Stephen, had Joel and left her parents' diplomatic residence at Hill Station for Stephen's apartment at Lumley. But the military coup shattered everything. British nationals had to be evacuated, and the High Commissioner's family was a priority.

* * *

Sarah still recalled the early morning loud banging at the gates of their Lumley residence by overzealous British military personnel based in Freetown. At the time, there was shooting everywhere, and it was so scary; more so for young Joel, who reacted in spasms at the sound of machine gunfire from trigger-happy coup-plotters.

Stephen and Sarah had thought it was some wayward soldiers or rebels looking for loot. He thought the anarchy that was befalling others had descended on his gates. He calmed a terrified Sarah down and went to peep through the window, only to see Major Robert Macarthy, the head of the British High Commission security in Sierra Leone.

"Thank God," was Sarah's sigh of relief after Stephen had said, "It's your father's men."

The evacuation was immediate and swift. Stephen and Sarah agreed that it would be in the best interests of Joel that mother and child left. Stephen would not go now, but would join them as soon as possible after putting arrangements in place for the continued operations of *The True Light* newspaper, of which he was Editor. He accompanied them to the helipad. He was holding Joel all through the trip, talking to him as if he was talking to an adult, asking the child to be a good boy to his mother, and promising to join him soon. Sarah was quiet throughout. Her thoughts were a pot pourri. She was leaving, but her heart was not. She had grown to love this place – the place where her great-great-great-grandmother had died and was buried, the place where she had found love.

Her parents were waiting at the helipad. Rachael was glowing as she took Joel from Stephen. "There is no time to waste," she had muttered. Stephen and Sarah hugged each other and, in the presence of her parents, and with all the security personnel watching, had perhaps the longest kiss they had ever had – with tears flowing from their eyes down their cheeks into their mouths, mixing with saliva and swallowed in transfixed embrace. The humming engine of the helicopter woke them up from their temporary, if not last, romantic nirvana. Mrs. Fergusson was now tugging the fringes of her daughter's dress away.

Mark Fergusson was also not going. The Prime Minister had asked him to stay put until the political ship was steadied in Sierra Leone. He brought smiles to, and a "thank you, Daddy" from, his daughter when he told her "April 17, the lovebird" was also being evacuated, as he briefly embraced her and gave her a peck. So both gentlemen stood by each other as they waved to their better halves while the helicopter took off from the Aberdeen helipad, overlooking the beach and the Atlantic Ocean. Mark asked his son-in-law to walk with him to the beach and have a drink. They would have their longest informal conversation so far.

* * *

The image that dominated the front pages of the local press the next day was that of the white daughter of the British High Commissioner kissing goodbye to her black partner, with the military chopper in the background. 'War Cuts Love Short' was how the Deputy Editor of *The True Light* newspaper splashed it on the front page, because Editor Amidu had taken time off work the previous day to see his partner and son off.

* * *

That was how Sarah Fergusson found herself back in her old North London room. She was at first very excited, knowing it was temporary, with the prospect of moving out to a rented flat the moment Stephen arrived. It was so for three weeks, as they had lengthy telephone conversations every day. Her mother complained about the telephone bills because Stephen would always make collect calls. It was a fortune to call direct from Sierra Leone to Britain using the telecoms payment booths. And, as things stood, Stephen couldn't afford regular calls. Mrs. Fergusson's pleas for less regular phone calls were not heeded, as Sarah didn't tell Stephen about her mother's complaints. So Mrs. Fergusson devised other means.

Stephen would always call around 8pm, London time – and, almost always, Sarah would have to be called from her room to take the call. But that particular night, Rachael wanted to put her complaints into action. She was watching television in the living room. The moment the phone rang and the operator placed in the collect-call request, Mrs. Fergusson responded that Sarah was not at home at the moment. Sarah was a bit surprised that Stephen didn't call that night. She did not ask.

The next day, Stephen rang and Mrs. Fergusson was going to pick it up when Sarah rushed down the stairs. "Why didn't you call yesterday?" was her first question.

"I did. You were out."

"I was what?"

"Someone answered the phone."

Sarah was mad at her mother.

When two weeks later the security situation in Sierra Leone deteriorated so fast that the whole telecoms infrastructure was disrupted – no one could call from or to the country – Sarah pointed fingers at her mother, shouting that "your dreams and wishes have finally come true".

The burden of guilt became weightier on Mrs. Fergusson when, another couple of weeks later, newspaper reports stated that Stephen had been killed. Her relationship with her daughter could not have been more strained. It was practically all but dead. She did her best to convince Sarah that – despite her initial opposition to the relationship with Stephen – she had come to accept it, especially after the birth of Joel, and that she had always only meant well for her. It didn't cut ice. Sarah withdrew into the deep recesses of her thought processes and into her room. She relapsed into wearing black, day and night.

* * *

Mark had already relocated to Liberia with the exiled President, and he was the one who had sent newspaper cuttings detailing

Stephen's death. When Sarah became inconsolable, Rachael had pleaded with her husband to talk to their daughter. He tried on the phone, to no avail. He had to specifically fly over to London for a week to put his house in order. That was over eight months ago. And he partially succeeded in reconnecting mother and daughter. They went out to a couple of restaurants as a family; he and Sarah alone went to the movies, leaving Joel with Rachael. Ben was in and out, without much to do with family matters – he was detached.

Sarah had only asked that she be allowed to mourn Stephen. But Mrs. Fergusson never thought it would go on for eight months. Their conversation was always brisk and terse, with no intention to open old wounds. But festering wounds had to be opened and the right medication applied if they were to be healed, Rachael believed.

Therefore, Mark's unexpected coming for his meeting with the Prime Minister had created that opportunity for Rachael. Last night, she had got her husband to commit himself; now she had a duty to relay the news to her daughter. Her only scepticism was how to go about it. She prayed she found Sarah in the mood; she had seemed to be in it during their short conversation at the kitchen door when she had retorted "I am here". Rachael hoped she was still in the same mood.

So the mother went to her daughter's door and knocked. After having her own breakfast, Sarah was now feeding Joel. She heard the knock but didn't respond. Maybe she was not in the mood anymore. Mrs. Fergusson knocked a second time.

5

The same 'TOP SECRET' document that High Commissioner Mark Fergusson was reading on his way to Westminster was the same document President Kargbo Ndomahina was perusing in his presidential office in Liberia. At this ripe age – and even before that – Ndomahina was a man who paid great attention to detail. He would read and re-read a document several times over, checking each paragraph, each sentence, phrase and word, ending with punctuation.

"People put words on paper for a reason," he would always say. "Every single written symbol has its purpose. And that purpose could be hidden in a thing as small as a comma. You have to look for it."

Save for the fact that he was in exile, President Ndomahina was still by and large the Head of State of Sierra Leone – he had famously referred to the Freetown junta leader as 'the foot of state'. Ndomahina was the President recognised by the international community, passionately led by the British administration of Prime Minister Ed McInroy and ably represented on the ground by High Commissioner Mark Fergusson.

For two years, Britain hadn't chosen an Ambassador to Liberia, since the retirement of David McCalister. The Foreign

Office had delegated the responsibility of overseeing the Liberian Mission to the British High Commission in Sierra Leone. And so when President Ndomahina was overthrown in Freetown and was whisked away via a British naval boat to Liberia, High Commissioner Mark Fergusson ensured the exiled President was safely ensconced in the residence of the British Ambassador in the posh suburbs of Monrovia. And then, within months, the British Embassy was quickly refurbished and transformed into Sierra Leone's 'presidential office', from where the President would perform his functions until his reinstatement. He was given all the paraphernalia of a Head of State: state security, a convoy of vehicles – of course flying the Sierra Leone flag. His pronouncements represented the 'authentic voice' of Sierra Leone to the international community. He was the one invited to conferences, including the UN General Assembly, the AU and ECOWAS. Virtually all embassies and consulates in Freetown had closed, some relocated to Monrovia. All diplomats based in Monrovia overtly recognised President Ndomahina as the legitimate President of Sierra Leone. He still held Cabinet meetings in exile. Even Parliament met at his behest in exile. All activities were bankrolled by the British government and its international allies.

Having been in power for sixteen years – and with his background as a former soldier, and afterwards a diplomat at the United Nations in New York – President Ndomahina was a highly connected man. His internal and external networks were 'a cobweb of political chicanery, subtle diplomacy, and military ruthlessness all hidden under the façade of his emotionless character', a description that got the editors of *The True Light* beaten up, arrested and detained, and their offices ransacked by police. That was what had kept him in power that long, as he had survived several coups (real or imaginary) and dealt with the perpetrators accordingly – some executed, some rotting in prison. His own Vice President and a journalist were among his latest victims of "death by hanging or by public execution for planning a coup," as pronounced by the President's handpicked judge for their trial. President Ndomahina was a political cat with uncountable lives.

Just that this latest coup seemed to have succeeded – almost succeeded. He hated any statement about him having been 'overthrown', even though he was in exile and his promise of returning 'very very soon' was becoming a derided byword of sympathisers of the Freetown military junta as the months rolled by. To President Ndomahina, the coup would only have succeeded if they had captured or killed him. And it would only be succeeding if he were not recognised by the international community. His networks always worked – they had helped him escape; they would help him return. With the sanctions and enforcement of the land, air and sea embargo on Sierra Leone and the huge military offensive being planned to dislodge the 'ruthless junta' through an operation to be spearheaded by his ally, Nigerian dictator Mallam Musa Odofo, President Ndomahina was as sure of his soon return as tomorrow's sunrise. He swore to his ancestors when assuring impatient exiled parliamentarians who were worried about "how the junta is killing our people on a daily basis".

That was why he was comfortably smiling while reading the document signed by his former colleague at the United Nations, Secretary General John Kirikiri. And that was why his thoughts were with Mark Fergusson, now on his way to see the British Prime Minister on the final preparations for the return of the exiled government.

So President Ndomahina had planned – unbeknown to Mark – demonstrations in Liberia to coincide with the High Commissioner's meeting with the Prime Minister in London.

"The people are tired with this two-prong approach of diplomacy and military pressure," he had told his Cabinet yesterday at a meeting called for the purpose of organising the demonstrations. "The British like too much of diplomacy. They don't know that these military boys can't understand soft language. The only language the Freetown junta understands is force. Force should be met with force. And the Nigerians are ready to do the job."

He informed his Cabinet that he had the full backing of Mallam Musa Odofo. He didn't have to say it because they all knew and saw it. The Nigerian dictator was the President's best friend, everybody knew.

"On some of the placards, make sure it is written: 'Only Nigeria Can Save Sierra Leone Democracy'," Odofo had told his friend on the line before the Cabinet meeting. It was more of an instruction than a suggestion.

"I will get them to also add 'Why is Britain Undermining Nigerian Efforts?'" a laughing, grateful Ndomahina patronised his principal. They were both happy.

"We are smarter than the neo-colonialists."

"We are smarter than the neo-colonialists."

And they hung up.

* * *

In the waiting room of the President's office were the organisers of the protests, his most trusted lieutenants: his party's Secretary General, Prince Bullet; the coordinator of the civil militia and general military activities, Major Mohamed Jambawai; and the head of inter-religious bodies, Munir Massaquoi. They had been waiting for two hours. But it didn't bother them. They had done what they had to do. Everything was in place. Everybody was ready. They knew the President was always busy.

He was now reading the UN document for probably the tenth time. He was just now cross-checking the signature of his former UN colleague. Ndomahina and Kirikiri did not join the world body at the same time. But once they met at the Department for

African Affairs and got to know they both came from Africa, they became instant friends. The Bugandan never saw any sense in his friend's subsequent decision to resign from the UN to return to Sierra Leone to participate in politics, "where only the ruthless and the brutal make it to the top in Africa". (Kirikiri had seen the naked brutality of politics in his home country before fleeing to the US.) On the other hand, the Sierra Leonean saw his friend with such intellectual capacity as dumb, to be "forever trapped in a bureaucratic machinery where an African will never make it to the top!"

They were both wrong. Today, one was the head of the UN and the other was the elected President of his country. And they had now reconnected with each other like never before. President Ndomahina looked at Kirikiri's signature keenly. It had not changed – the slide of the pen at the end. The President himself had changed his own signature – in line with modifications he made to his name – three times. It didn't matter. What mattered now was that all things were working for his good.

He all along knew his men were in the waiting room. He had kept them waiting for a long time not so much because of any special urgency to read the UN document, but out of his belief that a leader should always keep people waiting. For two things: to water down their anxieties and to get them to revere authority. He would call them in shortly.

***

By all means, the waiting room at the British-Embassy-turned-presidential-office in Monrovia was far bigger and more comfortable than the waiting room at State House in Freetown. While waiting, the three men were discussing the differences and making comparisons. Not that this was their first time being here. It was just their first time being here together. And to pass the time, having exhausted talking about the arrangements for the demonstration and the current "agony the people are going through in Sierra Leone under the yoke of the junta", they presently delved into admiration for the ambience of the waiting room.

"Those funny boys are in Freetown saying they've taken over the government. Which government? Can they compare their so-called State House to where we are sitting right now?" was how Maj. Jambawai inadvertently brought the comparison to the fore. "Look at this chair I am sitting in – it can buy all the chairs in that dirty closet they call a sitting room at State House."

Prince Bullet was more forthright. "Maybe they have already looted all the chairs and the carpets from there."

But the head of the inter-religious bodies, Munir Massaquoi, speaking in low tones, said: "I really don't know why we did not improve State House for sixteen years. It should be a priority when we return."

"I remember money was allocated for that three times, but nothing was ever changed and no one was ever held accountable," Bullet posited.

"The corruption was too much. Those Lebanese businessmen acting as contractors were too much. They and the civil servants, who I prefer to call evil agents, were more corrupt than the politicians. The President needs to clean the system when he returns," Munir ventured again.

"The British are ready to do anything the President asks them to do. Rebuilding State House is the least they can do. Even this very place was refurbished for him," Prince Bullet averred.

They were busy in the discussion when the women's leader, Mammy Kagboro, breezed into the room. She was not supposed to be in the meeting with the President. She and the youth leader had been tasked to rally round the women and the youths. They had brought the people out on the streets and had been waiting.

"The people have come out in large numbers. Can't you hear

the drums and the singing?" It was a rhetorical question. Her complaint was that the people wanted their leaders to come out and address them. They wanted to see and hear from their beloved President.

The three men were happy about the information and also knew that she had the magic wand of breaking protocols for the President to see them immediately. She had virtual unfettered access to him. "She is a mover and shaker," the President always said about Mammy Kagboro.

And it worked. All the secretaries and the security personnel knew Mammy Kagboro, whom they commonly called 'Mammy Queen'. She had the knack of electrifying a room with her never-ending chattering and loud laughter. She went to the security personnel manning the door to the President's office and asked if there was anybody inside with 'big papa'. When the answer was no, she immediately shouted: "Papa President, Mammy Queen don cam oh. All man don cam. All man don ready."

Within seconds, the President rang the bell summoning the personnel. The three men and Mammy Queen were ushered in.

* * *

Liberia's capital had become the hub for the Africa correspondents of major international news channels. And President Ndomahina used the attraction to his fullest advantage.

Ever since the President's escape to Monrovia and the international community committing to his avowed return, the foreign press couldn't have got a bigger and more intriguing story on the African continent. Journalists of all types descended on Liberia. A very small minority ventured into Sierra Leone. But with a blockade and ban on flights to and from Freetown, the eyes and ears of the Africa correspondents of the world media turned to Monrovia. And they were all present to cover the demonstrations

– they all planned to send a message to the world, especially to Britain, where Sierra Leone was currently being discussed in Downing Street.

Monrovia's central business district came to a standstill as throngs of demonstrators took over the streets. Offices were closed, trading suspended for the day, vehicular traffic disallowed except for essential services, a statement from the Liberian government declared "in solidarity with our Sierra Leonean brothers and sisters in the efforts to restoring the legitimate government and President of Sierra Leone back in Freetown". There was live TV and radio coverage by the state and private media.

The demonstration itself took the form of drumming, singing and dancing in a most debauched form: red-eyed youths and intoxicated women, some half-naked, chanted songs against the military regime in Freetown with the general theme of "returning to Sierra Leone soon to save our people from the brutal Freetown junta", as Prince Bullet put it when interviewed by Liberia's state radio.

But the international media was more amused by the messages on the placards: 'Britain, We Are Tired Of Exile', 'Stop Delaying Military Intervention', 'The Junta Only Understands Force', and of course 'Only Nigeria Can Save Sierra Leone Democracy – Why Is Britain Undermining That?'

The story had dominated the BBC World Service radio headlines since morning. The *Focus On Africa* programme had its correspondent not only describing how the ceremonies ended at the presidential office with President Ndomahina addressing the crowds, but also a one-on-one interview with him.

"These are spontaneous demonstrations from the people when they got to know that the British High Commissioner, Mark Fergusson, our very good and hardworking friend, is meeting with Prime Minister Ed McInroy in London today. All I can say is, Sierra Leoneans both at home in Sierra Leone and in exile everywhere, especially those here in Liberia, should know that the day of liberation is very near. The day of victory is here. I am returning to Freetown soon," the President's sonorous voice assured through the airwaves.

What was more topical later that day in bars and ghettos in Monrovia was, however, not reported by the BBC correspondent. In the course of the demonstrations, five 'infiltrators and collaborators of the Freetown junta' were sniffed out of the crowds by the civil militia 'high priests', dressed in dry animal skins and raffia-chained cowrie shells. Three were beaten to death by the mob, two saved at the last minute by women who vowed the already mercilessly beaten men had never even been to Sierra Leone. "But they look like rebels. They speak like rebels," was how event organiser Prince Bullet explained the mob action on state radio. "Those high priests can smell rebels."

Most of the demonstrators were people who had fled Sierra Leone; some had gone through horrific experiences of seeing whole villages and towns razed to the ground, themselves being the only survivors of their families. They hated anything that smelt like rebel or junta.

However, many in Monrovia knew that behind it all (what was reported and not reported by the BBC correspondent) was the hand of Femi Cole – "the engine of President Ndomahina", as she came to be referred to as in informal circles.

Radio France International and Radio Deutschland, however, though less listened to than the BBC by Sierra Leoneans, reported the aspect of the lynched suspected rebels.

6

Apart from the long hair and breasts, Sarah Fergusson looked exactly like her father, Mark: a small straight nose, a wide brow, squinty eyes, and a narrow mouth with an upturned upper lip; tall and walking with a sprint. But when she spoke, she had Rachael Fergusson's voice and brisk intonation – with a distinct fastness of speech that jumped over some syllables.

When mother and daughter were in a conversation, and the listener didn't see the speakers, it was difficult to make a distinction between the two voices – except if the discussion was intense, when the younger lady had a tendency to raise her tone. Mark Fergusson had once or twice got tricked on the phone by his wife, who pretended it was his daughter speaking. He had to devise a code for Sarah as one of their 'little secrets' to outwit the mother. Rachael got caught out and couldn't elicit the code from her daughter. She abandoned the scheme. It was fun then for the family.

But today was not a day for fun. It was a day to address serious issues affecting the family. Rachael was well prepared to have a mature conversation with her daughter. The matter should be handled once and for all. She wanted progress for her daughter and she would no longer dither about it.

That was why, after she knocked on the door for a second time and there was no answer from Sarah, Rachael decided to enter without seeking any further permission. After all, it was her house, and she was her daughter.

Sarah's reaction on seeing her mother was a mere "Oh, you are here." Rachael was not sure whether it was a question or an exclamation. The mother just took Joel from her daughter's arms straight away, together with the feeding bottle, rocking the bundle of joy safely in one hand while feeding him with the other.

"He seems to be eating a lot these days, this cutie," she ventured. Sarah merely smiled and rushed to the bathroom. When she came back, her mother had finished feeding Joel. "Could we go downstairs and talk?" Rachael ventured.

* * *

Sarah might be 'Daddy's girl' and the two might have had their 'little secrets', but Rachael knew she and her daughter shared the 'big secrets' of womanhood. She gave her daughter the motherhood she deserved. Even when Ben came later to balance the parental equation, Rachael didn't water down her attention to Sarah. When puberty arrived and the teenage years seemed unending, she kept on sharing her own personal experiences with her daughter.

Rachael's dignified personality was not only about being the wife of a diplomat; she was of royal blood. She was a member of the British royal family – a renegade member of sorts. She had royalty around her and was raised in royal circles. She would as well raise her daughter up with royal etiquette: from table manners, to appropriate dress, to use of language, to the company to keep, Rachael taught her daughter to remain within the bubble. She largely succeeded, until the Sierra Leone 'accident' happened.

What had happened had happened. It could not be undone. Now was the time to try to right that wrong. She knew they had

had very rowdy conversations before, especially since Sarah met Stephen. But now Stephen was out of the way. She wanted the way forward for her daughter. Sarah might have piercing, painful, even insulting, surgical responses for her – as before – but she was ready to take them, to absorb and handle them all.

As long as it was the route to moving on.

* * *

The living room was exquisite. Rachael might have chosen to marry outside royal circles for love, but she maintained royalty even in the looks of her home. Well-kept, flowery window curtains matching cosy settees in purple colour; a marbled centre-table matching whisky stools; and the Morrocan mulberry carpet creatively similar to the artwork on the walls.

The Fergussons liked walking around the house bare-footed. Mother and daughter had just arrived in the living room likewise. Rachael was humming a royal lullaby as she placed Joel in a crisp baby cot that she had acquired from the royal carpentry workshop. She lowered him gently into it with her daughter gazing at the bright eyes of Joel.

"Please don't listen to what we are going to say, my cutie," the grandmother joked to her year-and-a-half-old grandson, forcing a quick smile on Sarah, which she swiftly erased before her mother could notice.

Rachael would have loved to sit adjacent to her daughter. She would prefer a position where she would have a hard talk with Sarah without constantly having to look in her eyes. She would also want to express her motherly tenderness by occasionally touching her daughter by way of demonstrating her love, especially if the discussion became heated. But Sarah had quickly taken the snuggle chair that would cause her mother to sit on the sofa directly opposite, thereby having the conversation face-to-face.

"Well, here we are. Where do I even start?" Rachael rhetorically asked, tapping her thighs with both hands at the same time. Sarah just shrugged.

"I have thought it imperative that we should have this conversation." Rachael always tried to impress her children with the fact that she was not only a royal but an educated one too – despite having eventually opted to be the non-working housewife of a diplomat. And she could do this by expressing herself in educated English. Sarah knew this, and she merely looked blankly, still not saying a word.

"Sarah, my love, I know how hard it has been for you – well, for all of us – these past few months. They are the most terrible months of my life."

"Of your life, Mum?" Sarah interjected immediately. "Are we here to talk about your life or my life? Why am I here, in fact?"

"We are here to talk about life, dear. About our lives. About how life can be unfair, but how we can make the most out of life's fair side. We can be better than this, Sarah. You can be better. Getting stuck in one place, in one circumstance, can't take you anywhere."

"But, Mum, I can never forget about Stephen. That's impossible." The younger woman hit the nail on the head to stop her mother from beating around the bush.

"I know, darling, and that's why we are here to talk about it. It's been nearly a year since we lost him."

"You didn't lose him. I lost him."

"I know, my baby. But your pain is my pain. I may not be grieving as you do, but I am a tormented woman. No mother would love to see their daughter in the state you are in now. It pains me."

"You never liked him, Mum. Stop pretending."

Sarah was prepared to open old wounds, and she did it by looking her mother straight in the eyes. She was not shouting; she didn't even sound angry. Grieving these past few months had taught her many lessons, and she was now handling her mother as a mature lady would.

"Why would you hate someone just because of the colour of their skin or where they came from?"

This was a question Rachael had tried to answer in the early days of Sarah's relationship with Stephen. It had been drowned by circumstances ever since Sarah got pregnant and Joel came along, causing the grandmother to accept the situation as it turned out. But now – in this traumatic post-Stephen era – this question was back. It was not totally unexpected by Rachael – but what made her shiver within her bones was the serenity with which her daughter was asking it this time.

Back then, she had tried to dismiss her daughter as "being carried away by the presumptuousness of youthfulness". Rachael believed Sarah could not, on her own, think through what she was doing at the time, that it was not love but youthful emotions that drove her into the arms of Stephen. Rachael didn't change her mind even after Joel was born; but she was no longer openly opposed to the relationship. She supported it as a mother and grandmother.

And after they had arrived in London, leaving Stephen and Mark behind, Rachael tried to get her daughter into the old royal social bubble. She had wished Sarah could see reality and find love somewhere else, with somebody else. It was already topical within senior royal circles that Rachael's daughter had had a son with an African. But she wanted to right that wrong somehow by Sarah finding a British gentleman (there were many who would grab the opportunity of marrying any royal). But she discovered her folly when her daughter didn't budge, and the frequent telephone calls from Stephen didn't stop – until they were stopped by a string of bad news.

Sarah fainted on the day the news of Stephen's death was revealed to her. And she had been wearing black since she regained consciousness – eight months and counting.

"I don't hate black people. I don't hate Africans. If I did, I wouldn't have gone to Sierra Leone with your father in the first place." Rachael eventually found words to respond to her daughter's accusation.

"I am talking about Stephen here, Mum. You hated him. And that's racist." Now the young lady's tone was rising.

"I didn't hate him, Sarah. I am not a racist. My best friend is not white. Maria is Mexican."

"She is not African."

"Come on, dear, it's the same."

"It's not."

"They are both not white."

"But you prefer one to another."

"Not at all, dear. Joel is African and I love him so much."

That ruffled Sarah a bit – she didn't see that answer coming. Her adrenaline rose up. And then she found words on impulse: "You love Joel? What pretence! Joel, who you even wanted me to abort?"

This was much more than Rachael bargained for – much more than she could bear. She turned her eyes to the cot and saw the glowing eyes of her grandson as if he was listening to the conversation and himself accusing her. She collapsed.

At first Sarah thought her mother was acting, and she kept on talking. But when she could not get any response and there was no physical movement from Rachael, now sprawled on the settee, daughter rushed to mother's side.

"Mum, Mum, Mum, are you ok?" She held her by the shoulders and shook her desperately.

Rachael was unresponsive. Sarah called 999.

What she hated was having to go over what had happened after she confirmed to the operator that her mother was still breathing. She was asked to carefully roll her mother on her side with one arm under her cheek, to bend the top leg so that the hip and knee were at right angles, to gently tilt her head back, and lift her chin.

"What caused her collapse?" the operator said.

"We were just talking and she collapsed."

"Was she standing up and then fell?"

"No, we were sitting in the living room."

"And what were you discussing?"

"Family matters."

"Was it a pleasant conversation?"

"Family matters are always pleasant."

"Yes, but was it an argument?"

"It was a discussion."

"Did you say anything in particular to her?"

Just at that moment, Mrs. Fergusson sneezed.

"What was that?" the operator asked.

Sarah dropped the receiver and rushed to her mother.

"Mum, are you ok?"

She sneezed again. Sarah went back to the phone and told the operator.

"Ok. That's fine, she is resuscitated. Let her sit on the floor, with feet unbent, hands down, for five minutes. Then give her a glass of water mixed with a teaspoon of salt to drink. That should be it. If the situation does not change, call us back."

* * *

Sarah's growing maturity meant she could now read and interpret situations from different angles. She had serious issues with her mother, but she was willing to absorb new dimensions. She knew – well, she believed – that she had already lost her fiancé. She could not afford to lose her mother soon after, if she could help it. Even for Stephen's sake.

Stephen's memory lived with her, and that memory's most practical translation was their son, Joel. She had a duty to bring their son up in the best way possible. And the person who had been helping her most in achieving that was her mother. Despite her, Rachael had been an affectionate grandmother to Joel. At one point, she invariably expressed admiration for the black skin – well, for the mixed-race chocolate skin – of her grandson. In defence of her daughter to questioning royal relatives who visited her, she outrightly stated: "It was this same skin colour that attracted our great-great-great-grandfather to marry our great-great-great-grandmother. History is just re-enacting itself." She silenced them with the story, the source being the Queen herself. Sarah was not present at the time. Her mother had never said such things in her presence. But Rachael had said it in so many ways by cherishing Joel. And Sarah knew Joel had taken to his grandma as well.

Losing Rachael – or continuing to wedge things between them – as portrayed just now by her sudden loss of consciousness, would only make things worse for Sarah and Joel. The daughter's growing maturity pushed her into making the most of the circumstances in everybody's interest. She decided to let sleeping dogs lie. After all, it was her mother who had initiated the conversation. She needed to listen to what she would say. She was willing to listen more and talk less, if Rachael had recovered enough to continue with the discussion.

* * *

Mrs. Fergusson's recovery was as quick as her collapse. Finding herself in the arms of Sarah, and being helped by her to drink, was a most comforting experience. She had been longing for this for a long time. And now it was happening in an ironic twist of fate.

"Oh Mum, you scared me. I am so sorry," was how Sarah restarted the conversation when her mother started drinking the water on her own.

"No. I am sorry, darling. I love you."

"I love you too, Mum. Do you want to eat anything?"

"Maybe you can make me a croissant. Thank you, my baby." She nearly said 'miracle baby' but was quick to hold back her tongue from pronouncing the adjective.

She had just had breakfast and was not actually hungry. But anything to re-bond with her daughter was welcome. The offer was an opportunity. And while Sarah went to the kitchen, Mrs. Fergusson rose up and reconnected with her grandson. Sarah returned to find him in her arms. She was standing up, singing a lullaby.

"Oh Mum, you don't have to do that right now."

"I am perfectly ok." She insisted on holding Joel while having her croissant, now seated on the sofa with her daughter by her side. This was the sitting position she had desired for this conversation. And she made use of it as quickly as she could.

"Your father has finally agreed to leave Sierra Leone alone and return to us," was how she returned a hit on the head of the nail.

And it achieved its goal by the way Sarah reacted. "What, Mum, are you sure? You finally convinced him?"

"Yes, he agreed last night. We are moving to Mexico. You see, dear, we are doing all this for you. With all that happened in Sierra Leone, leading to us losing Stephen," Sarah had no intention to interrupt or correct her mother again, "we need to have some closure and move on. Certainly, Sierra Leone will always be in our hearts. And in fact, Sierra Leone will always be with us." And, looking straight into the eyes of Joel in her arms, she continued, "This bundle of joy is Sierra Leone." Sarah gave a smile, and Rachael knew it was a genuine one. She felt nudged to continue.

"You know how much I had grown to like Stephen. Yes, at first I had misgivings. But this was only natural. It was not any deep-seated dislike for him as a person. I only feared for what my daughter was going into. So I had to make my opinion known to you. It was not that I was trying to stand in the way of your feelings. No, I was not standing in your way in following your heart. I gave way when I saw the reality. But now fate has been cruel to us. We have to live with it. We have to live on. Let's live, my baby."

Sarah knew her mother was being economical with the truth, but she would stomach it. She still remembered the 'wardrobe experience' in Sierra Leone – the night she overheard the conversation between her mother and the American Ambassador's wife on the Stephen relationship. Rachael had even apparently forgotten about the telephone complaints and interruption after their arrival in London, when Stephen used to call from Sierra Leone.

But now Sarah was all too aware that it was unnecessary – and even dangerous – to interrupt her mother. She would at least allow her to recover fully. If her mother's talking was the therapy, then let it be. She would allow water to pass under the bridge. And Rachael maximised on the opportunity.

"I came to realise how loving and loveable he was, how much he cared for you, how much the two of you loved each other. You couldn't have asked for a better lovebird." She knew this would definitely bring a smile on her daughter, who doted on the little lovebird (named 'April 17') they had brought from Sierra Leone.

Mrs. Fergusson might have forgotten a few incidences about the Stephen relationship, but one stuck out in her heart no matter how hard she tried to forget it – even now, as she continued her eulogy. She had never come to terms with – and had always wanted to shelve and forget, and if possible erase from Sarah's memory too – the fact that she actually once told her daughter to do an abortion when Sarah was pregnant with Joel. She had tried to convince herself that she was not herself then – while at the same time, in reality, she still believed she only said it in her daughter's best interests. At the time, Rachael was truly convinced that her daughter had been charmed by 'African magic' or *juju*, as was bandied around in the diplomatic community in Freetown. And Sarah reminding her about that statement today only showed how she would have to live with this guilt. She was only now pacified that Sarah didn't agree to do the abortion, and Joel was here. But still Rachael refused to address the issue directly. She came close to the subject matter, but not so close.

"I know I had told you many things that I shouldn't have told you. Or let me say, I said things I needn't have said. And you have to believe me, Sarah, in many of those times I was not myself. I can't even recall some of the things I said."

Sarah just kept on nodding her head. She knew very well that, if not for anything, her mother had compensated with her undying love for Joel.

And, as if she was reading her daughter's mind, Rachael said, "Joel is a Sierra Leonean. We are forever connected to Sierra Leone for him. But I felt obliged to press your father to ask for a transfer so that we can move on – you can move on. We can't undo what has happened. You need your life back, Sarah. You are still young and you have a bright future in front of you. You should do it even for Joel. He needs a happy mother. He needs to be brought up in an atmosphere of joy. So, darling, please, when your father comes back, put on a bright face and tell him you appreciate his decision. He is really concerned that you have been constantly in this sorrowful state for all these months. You know what, he told me bluntly, 'I am not doing it for you, Rachael; I am doing it for my daughter'."

"Aww," came from Sarah.

"Do you know, he thinks that even his continued stay there – well, his stay with the exiled President in Liberia – was partly to please you? In the initial days, he thought maybe some information could have just popped up about Stephen's whereabouts, until he got the sad confirmation. However, he now sees Sierra Leone as his in-law country – our in-law country – on top of him being related to it on his own merit."

Sarah gave a deep breath and asked, "But, Mum, how sure are you about this?"

"He assured me he would insist on that during his meeting with your Uncle Ed. For family reasons. I'm sure that's something Ed wouldn't oppose."

"But I'm sure it will not be immediate."

"No. He thinks this whole issue of returning the exiled President to Sierra Leone will end in the next three months. He takes it as his pet project. And he would leave immediately after. He is going back to Liberia tomorrow. However, he is giving us a treat tonight. All of us – I mean all five of us—" she smiled at Joel in her arms "—will be having a family dinner at your favourite Ritz Hotel restaurant tonight."

Sarah was somewhat truly excited for the first time in months. Apart from going to the telephone booth on Sunfield Road to make her calls, this was the first time she actually had some event to look forward to in a long time. She insisted on still wearing black for the dinner though, despite her mother's pleas. Rachael didn't push too much; she was satisfied that Sarah had agreed to go. It was a major step forward.

7

Thirty or so years before all this, Rachael Wettin was a quiet, shy, unassuming, conservative introvert. As a schoolgirl, she had very few friends – if any – outside royal circles. She was the type that went to school for school. After school it was back home, and there was no time for extra-curricular activities. She was not even interested in school sports. The exclusive and elitist royal racecourses, where she normally escorted her grandmother, were enough for her. And here the socialising was from royalty to royalty. She had some lessons on horse-riding – and that was about it for her social life.

As the daughter of the fourth son of the monarch, Rachael was nineteenth in line to the throne. Whether educated or not, she was born privileged and would remain so. She was brought up to remain so. And she remained so to the satisfaction of the royal family.

Rachael's pastime was books. She read widely and wildly. She read more of adventure stories and historical novels that took her pliant mind to unknown places, fantastic spheres and unknown times. She was therefore far ahead of her peers in knowledge of facts. Her conversations were always authoritative, and that's how she became a favourite grandchild of the Queen. The grandmother loved knowledge – she loved knowledgeable people.

Sarah sat her GCSE, O and A levels, not as a royal who merely needed academic certification as an ornament, but as a dedicated student who wanted to put into practice the knowledge she had acquired over the years. And indeed she came out with flying colours, getting one of the best results at Lady Margaret School that year. This brought much joy to her parents as the *Monarchy Bulletin*, distributed within royal circles, picked on this unusual development in the royal family. 'Queen's Granddaughter Breaks Tradition, Tops A Levels Class' was how it plastered the headline across its front page.

Rachael became the centre of attention in royal circles, especially at dinners and other social gatherings – to the chagrin of the other grandchildren and cousins. Some avoided her company; some treated her with some disdain.

"I don't know what she is trying to prove. We, as royals, are only meant to be able to read and write. But she wants to make a name for herself," Rachael's first cousin Sophia said, while having a discussion with two other cousins over the recent storm of attention on her.

"She is Booker Washington's daughter," Victoria jested. "Maybe she wants to become the first royal Prime Minister of Britain."

"You know she has always been like that since childhood. She always wants to be seen as the innocent one, the crimeless one who does things differently. Let's see where her bookishness will take her. All I know is that she cannot overtake me in the royal line," came from Natasha, the first daughter of the Queen's first son.

But what would clearly ruffle the royal family was not so much Rachael's decision to pursue university education but her insistence to enrol as an ordinary student like anybody else, which meant staying on campus throughout the course.

After several secret consultative meetings over the matter, her parents decided to confront her. "You have really done us all proud, Rachael. But it is not advisable that you do this. To be a royal is to be different. You can follow your heart and go to university. That's alright. Many royals have degrees. Your father has a degree. I do have a degree. But please don't go down the route of staying on campus. There's so much bad influence there. You would meet all types of people there, and some who hate us as royals may try to hurt you," her mother, the Duchess of Lancaster, pleaded.

The Duke of Lancaster picked up from where his wife stopped. "My darling, Rachael, we are ready to put everything and anything at your disposal for your comfort and your safety. I can provide a chauffeur-driven car and personal security to take you to and from university every day. This is the view of the family; in fact, this is our decision. And your grandmother is in full support of this."

In conformity to her well-mannered upbringing, Rachael listened to her parents and never made any attempt to interrupt them. But when she responded, there was no way of mistaking her stance.

"I thank you for having been the best parents in the world. Thank you for what you have been doing and what you are still willing to do for me. However, I am now in a position where I can make my own decisions. As far as this university course is concerned, nothing can change my mind on it. I want to see more of the world, Mum." She was now turning to and canvassing her mother to understand.

"I want to see more of what I read in books. Please let me, please let me be, please let me go. I am just going to study and it won't change who I am. Nothing can change the fact that I am a member of this family, that I have royal blood in me. As for threats to my life, Mum, I don't see how I can be a target for anyone. I am not the next in line to the throne."

She said it with a softness of tone and an amiable innocence that any parent would not want to contend with. The Duke and Duchess succumbed to their daughter's perspective, with the father promising to make the Queen and the rest of the family understand.

To make the point clearer, Rachael opted for a university outside London.

* * *

Rachael Wettin quickly adjusted and got settled to university life at Oxford. No one could have helped her make it look simpler than her roommate, Maria de Sanchez, a foreign student from Mexico. Outgoing, outspoken, ordinary in all respects, Maria was the opposite of, perhaps the antidote to, or actually a complement for, Rachael.

It was none of their decision to live together. The Oxford system did it through an algorithm – with a view to making university life for students as diverse as possible. Rachael didn't complain when she found out who her roommate was. It was her decision to be a normal student and to abide by the rules. She believed there was not much to share with Maria, apart from the room itself. She was studying classical literature; Maria was studying politics. But she would soon find out the contrary.

Conservatism and liberal-mindedness were on a collision course, or perhaps a collusion cause. And it started with how things in the room were arranged or rearranged. Rachael wanted everything to be in the right place: photographs, books, shoes, chairs in their proper place, well organised. That was not the Mexican's way. Maria would drop books where she willed – even on top of Rachael's bed. She would move chairs around and would even use Rachael's personal belongings. Rachael would come back to the room and try to rearrange everything as originally placed.

But the day she found Maria wearing her slippers, Rachael decided to have a discussion with her roommate.

"Please don't misinterpret me, Maria. But I don't think it is right for us to exchange slippers. I have tried to understand everything else and you can see how I have been trying to put the room in order, but to use my slippers is a bit over the top," she gently told her with a pleasantness of voice that Maria had come to love from the first day they met as roommates.

The sudden laughter from Maria just displaced Rachael's mental order.

"It's not a laughing matter, Maria. It's serious."

"Of course, it's serious." She burst into a round of laughter again, now clapping her hands. "As serious as not wanting to sleep in the same room with me."

"When did I say that, Maria?"

"You don't need to say that. It speaks for itself. If you can breathe the same air with me locked in the same room, what is the big deal about wearing your slippers, Rachael? We are sisters now, Rachael, whether you like it or not. Our two lives are intertwined. Never sleep in the same room with someone you don't like." Another bout of laughter.

Rachael couldn't help but join in with the laughter.

"Yes, we are sisters now," she accepted. And she never would complain again about anything Maria did – even when she would one evening find her in her nightgown. One thing Rachael never wanted Maria to know about was her royalty. It was enough for her roommate to assume that her conservative attitude was "just the British thing" and nothing more.

It was in trying to hide this fact that she would allow Maria to lead her to the socialite world of the university: going to dinners, partying and clubbing. She was exploring the world, and as long as her main motive of getting a decent education was not submerged, she would sail along with Maria. They became very close friends

– perhaps the closest roommates on campus. 'We are sisters now' was their mutual relationship mantra.

It was through Maria that Rachael would meet her future husband, Mark Fergusson.

* * *

Mark was the epitome of the self-made British man, the grass-to-grace diplomat who defied the odds of his humble beginnings to stand out, to stand tall.

Mark was brought up in a run-down council flat in Exeter, over one hundred miles away from London, by a single father. His mother had run away with a Frenchman when Mark was three. A year later the tragic news came that she had been killed in a car accident together with her eloper in the streets of Paris. Mark's father, James Fergusson, tried to make ends meet by working during the day in factories while getting council benefits for his son's welfare.

Despite that, Mark proved to be a naturally talented and highly intelligent boy. By the time he finished primary school, he was known as the 'high-IQ boy' by his teachers. He seemed to have a basic understanding of every subject matter.

Even if he didn't have the full facts, he could always provide an answer that impressed. In a geography class, there was the contention as to whether the Earth was flat or spherical in shape. Most students were saying it was flat. "It is round," Mark said. His namesake teacher, Mark Myers, asked him to give a reason. "If it were flat, the sky would be static. I mean, the clouds would not be moving." The whole class clapped.

It was no surprise that he became the most astounding student in the transitional exams to secondary school. He was deservedly awarded the Queen's 'Disadvantaged Children's Meritorious Scholarship', taking full care of his education from secondary school to university. He sailed through effortlessly and was eventually admitted to the politics department of Oxford University, where he was a classmate of Maria de Sanchez.

It didn't at all start very well. Maria's talkative nature was a counter to, and on a collision course with, Mark's measured participation in class. She always wanted to present a counter-argument to every theory. Even if she was wrong, or knew it didn't make much sense, Maria would have to say something to the contrary. To her, this was the essence of politics – the presentation of alternative views.

Mark at first took it that way. But he would soon realise that Maria was picking on every of his views in a standoff that bordered on a criticism of British history and politics, especially regarding slavery and empire.

The whole class had to come to a standstill one day as Maria and Mark battled over ideas.

"Politics is evolutionary. What some people did during the days of slavery and empire is totally unacceptable today. But it was acceptable at the time. That was democracy at that time," Mark justified.

Maria delivered a punch in response. "As far as I am concerned, nothing has changed. Neo-colonialism is like drinking the same soup using a different spoon. The colonialists and *empirists* looked down on other people, enslaved them, and took away their resources. The same is happening today, using different methods. And the British neo-colonialists still bask in awards that talk about Officer of the British Empire. That's disgusting."

"Don't generalise it. Not every British man or woman benefited from slavery or colonialism, or benefits from the new colonialism you are talking about. There are deprived and disadvantaged families in this country who have suffered as much. People live on the streets in Britain. And these are white British people. But we have to allow society to evolve, changing the face of politics at every opportunity, step by step. That's how Britain evolved from Roman rule," Mark posited.

"Then you must first abolish the British monarchy, just as the Roman Empire was abolished," Maria exploded, sounding really animated and agitated.

Prof. Tim Bellingham, lecturer of comparative politics, had to stop the discussion there and then; not only because time was more than up, but because he was a conservative educationist – he believed in Britain's thriving monarchical democracy.

But, eventually, Mark discovered that Maria was a good-natured girl who just actually had a passion for learning, with a tinge of extra passion. Beneath her seeming aggressiveness was a desire to build bridges and acquire more knowledge. She admitted that Mark had an 'extra reservoir of knowledge' that she was willing to tap into, and she would not be shy about it. She therefore made a deliberate move to put that into effect. When an assignment was given on the evolvement of the European Union, Maria approached Mark and requested they met in the library for research and discussion. He acquiesced.

Soon their new friendship would be noticed by everybody in class, as Maria even moved seats to sit near Mark. Prof. Bellingham eventually referred to them as 'M.M & Co', and he put them in charge of organising the annual end-of-year dinner and dance for the politics department, to the acclaim of the whole class.

***

Meanwhile, the relationship between Rachael and Maria had been literally growing in leaps and bounds. Maria had told her friend virtually everything about Mexico: about her family, school days and friends; and she would even on occasion repeat the same haphazard personal stories, not knowing she had told them before. Rachael would only smile and listen – she had told her friend some stories in return, but nothing about royal connections. She liked talking about literary characters, and Maria loved it when Rachael compared her to Elizabeth Bennet of Jane Austen's *Pride and Prejudice*! Maria in turn got over the top to explain about her politics classes, and how she had been getting it hot with 'the boys'.

They would spend most evenings together and would sometimes jointly go to the library. Their bond had become stronger. It was therefore virtually impossible for Rachael to refuse Maria's invitation to attend the politics department's annual gig before the university closed for the year.

"I'm sorry, Maria, I have more coursework to submit for this semester, and I need to seriously work on it. I will attend next year," Rachael tried to persuade her friend while turning down the invitation.

"Is that reason enough, Rachael? I also have assignments to submit. Do you know how much I have told people about you? You definitely have to come. You can't do this to me."

"Don't take it that way, Maria, please..."

Maria cut in before Rachael could complete what she wanted to say: "Ok. Ok. Let's do a deal. Let's agree that you only come for one hour. If not, I'm also not going. And everybody would know that my best friend spoilt the politics department's dinner. We are sisters now."

Rachael gave in.

The wheel of destiny was dragging her to meet Mark. Obviously, Maria had been talking to each about the other. But she could not believe how rapidly the two blended after introduction. It was virtually love at first sight – 'the British connection', Maria would eventually brand it.

That night, there was so much to party for – as Rachael's coursework submission had actually been deferred to the re-opening of the next academic year. She dressed simply in jeans, low heels, and a white top. Maria dressed similarly, but she added a red scarf, "the Mexican way". Mark was also in jeans – as most students were anyway – and he had a long-sleeved flowery linen shirt. Maria introduced Rachael to everybody; and when she reached Mark, she just stated, "This is the Mark." And there was laughter all round, as they passed on to the next set of friends.

Maria, while busy with organising, had found a quiet corner, as per their pre-dinner deal, for Rachael to sit with a couple of other female friends. But soon she would engage the other two in activities, leaving Rachael alone at the table with a drink and snacks. But Maria kept coming back to check on her. She then brought Prof. Bellingham to the same table. He was the most hilarious professor Rachael had ever met, as he insisted that "a man is as old as he thinks".

Soon Maria was on the microphone calling the occasion to order. There would be speeches before the party began. "The politics department has to prove its mettle anywhere, any time," the professor explained to Rachael. "We rule the world, whether rightly or wrongly." He sent her into boisterous laughter.

The professor himself was one of the speakers, plus other lecturers. But the man who stole the show was the student president of the department, Mark Fergusson. Soft-spoken, calm, counting his words, but firm in his delivery, Mark spoke about "politics in our evolving world". He reached deep into the necessity for humans to have a ruling structure. He quoted Plato and Aristotle and some other hitherto-unheard-of philosophers. He even referenced Pope Paul VI in supporting his position that politics could be the best way to help humanity, if those in authority were honest, humanitarian and humane.

And then Mark's speech landed home in Britain. He did not mince his words on the evils of slavery. He minced them on colonialism.

"Colonialism by itself was not an evil thing. It depended on what you did with it. Britain itself was once, like it or not, a colony of Rome. The problem I have with the British Empire is that it did not do as much as it could to educate the majority of the people in the colonies. There was no deliberate effort in seeing that illiteracy was eliminated. Colonialism could have been used to redress the evils of the slave trade. But our nation, the leaders then, failed to seize the glorious opportunity."

The applause was resounding as his fellow students chanted, "Political Fergie, Political Fergie, Political Fergie." Rachael was enthralled, but she did not show any emotion.

"But all is not lost," Political Fergie continued. "Politics is a continuum. Later generations of politicians still have a duty to right the wrongs of their predecessors."

And then the here and now. "I know that we have had these debates several times in class, and we will continue to have them. Politics is not perfect. British politics is not perfect." Further applause, perhaps longer applause. "But the safeguards are there. The institutions that have been built are open to reform, to renewal, to revamp, even to overhaul if necessary. There are some who may want us to get rid of the monarchy."

This got Maria, who was now seated with Rachael and the professor, saying, "Now he is picking on me" with a smile.

"It is not a perfect arrangement, I must admit," Mark continued. "But it is an institution that has kept us going as a nation. In times of crises and divisions, the monarchy has somehow helped us to navigate through murky waters. And, on a personal note," Mark allowed the words to sink in, granting a few seconds of silence, getting everybody's rapt attention, "on a very personal note – call it subjective or whatever – I wouldn't have been speaking to you here today if not for the monarchy." Now he had got everybody guessing with his signatory temporary stops, before continuing, "Being the son of a working-class single father since childhood, my schooling would have been practically impossible if I were not a beneficiary of the Queen's 'Disadvantaged Children's Meritorious

Scholarship'. So, for now, without wishing to bore you, ladies and gentlemen, I stand with the monarchy, but I know that politics evolves as well. Thank you for listening."

The applauses and chants of 'Political Fergie' were deafening. Maria rushed to the stage and hugged Mark, practically dragging him to the table where Prof. Bellingham and Rachael were seated. She went back to the stage to declare the party formally open.

It was at that party that the foundation stone for Mr. and Mrs. Fergusson was laid. Maria felt cheated when she noticed that Mark was becoming closer to Rachael through the night. He had tried at first to dance with them in turns, but he gradually settled for Rachael. Maria was quick to describe it as 'the British connection' but she willingly and unreservedly supported the relationship once it became clear that the two were serious about each other.

They had gone away for the holidays thinking it was just the excitement of university partying. But when they returned for the new academic year, the affinity grew. And Rachael decided to reveal her royal self to both Mark and Maria. She did it in style. She asked Maria to invite Mark to dinner out of campus.

Coincidentally, on the appointed day, Mark was having a special guest on campus, his counterpart student president of the politics department of Durham University, Ed McInroy. The two universities had a long-running inter-departmental exchange programme. Mark had gone to Durham before for a similar occasion – speaking to colleague students on a particular subject. Ed was at Oxford for the same. And since his guest was passing the night, Mark asked if his friend could join them for the dinner. The ladies were happy about it.

Three years later, Rachael and Mark would tie the knot at St. Stephen's Chapel, Oxford, with Ed as best man and Maria as chief bridesmaid.

About fifteen years later, Ed McInroy became Britain's youngest Prime Minister in a century. And he decided to appoint his long-time friend as British High Commissioner to Sierra Leone.

8

"I knew it. I sensed it the moment you insisted on going to stay on campus. You were bent on bringing a scandal to this family," was how the Duchess of Lancaster reacted when her daughter first told her about Mark Fergusson. But what dumbfounded the whole royal family was not so much Rachael's rejection of all the wealthy potential suitors – including royals from Spain and Holland – but the fact that she 'stooped so low to hook up' with a factory worker's son.

The Queen showed some interest when the Duchess lamented about it. But the monarch refused her daughter-in-law's request to talk Rachael out of it. And when the young lady couldn't budge, the elder stateswoman publicly gave her 'unreserved blessings' to the relationship. There was, however, not going to be any royal pomp about the wedding. That suited Rachael and Mark's wishes anyway, as they had decided they would wed on campus in their year of graduation. The Duke and Duchess of Lancaster, out of parental moral responsibility, attended their daughter's wedding. But the rest of the royal family boycotted. Mark and Rachael were happy still.

The two people who worked hard for it to happen were Maria de Sanchez and Ed McInroy. To Mark and Rachael, those two were friends who stuck closer than blood relations. But perhaps the happiest man was Mark's father, James Fergusson. He was the only one dressed in royal apparel on the wedding day. Rachael was making a point when she bought the special 'royal' suit for her father-in-law through an outstanding royal stylist.

***

Ed McInroy came from a wealthy middle-class British family. Apart from his parents having both inherited landed property, they worked for the colonial administration and had retired with hefty pensions. Ed went to private schools and then to Durham University, where his mother started off as a lecturer – a trend she continued at Sierra Leone's Mount Aureol University.

Ed McInroy Sr. had always believed his son would become Prime Minister of Britain (the consultancy firm he co-founded and set up in London was primarily for that purpose). He said it as a joke to the colonial officials attending the christening ceremony of Ed Jr. in Freetown. And he had kept saying it to his son since he had ears to hear. And the son lived up to expectations. The son then worked for it – worked on it. Studying politics was a conscious effort at achieving his father's dream, which he had turned to his own dream. And he couldn't have found a better ally in fulfilling this dream than in Mark Fergusson.

They had met through their two universities' inter-departmental programme, but they carved out a relationship for themselves. The moment Mark had completed his speech at Durham University that day, Ed McInroy knew he had found his man: as student president of the politics department at Durham, Mark was his special guest. And he treated him to taste that evening, taking him to the best restaurant in Durham for dinner. They quickly arranged for a return presentation to be made by Ed, which coincided with the dinner date Rachael had requested with Maria and Mark at Oxford.

But it would be in later conversations that Ed and Mark discovered that their connection was more than an academic coincidence. They were destined to be together. They had a common denominator – Sierra Leone.

It was during the dinner talk that night at Oxford with Mark, Rachael and Maria that Ed told them he was going away for his gap year to Sierra Leone. Apparently, none of the others had ever heard of it.

"It's my birthplace," Ed stated, to the obvious surprise of all.

"How do you mean?" Rachael ventured.

"Just what it is. That's where I was born. And I have been looking forward to this moment. Our university has a long-standing exchange programme with the country's premier university, Mount Aureol University, which was set up by the British in the 1800s. My father used to work for the colonial office, and my mother lectured at that university. I was born there, but they left when I was just a year old." Ed delved into a lecture as the others got more interested in the details. He told them about the stories he had heard from his parents about the place, and now he was going to see it for himself. But one person that was terribly horrified with this news was Maria. She had thought she had found her own. She was just seeing him being taken away by an imaginary hand. The dinner fell flat in her eyes – though she still put on a brave face to the end.

***

Mark Fergusson was close to his father, by virtue of the fact that fate had tied them together in the absence of the mother. But the two were never intimate in terms of conversation.

As a youth, James Fergusson was very loquacious and outgoing. But ever since he lost Mark's mother, he became a very reticent man, never wanting to stumble into a conversation about his past – or about anything. He had even hidden all photographs of him and Sarah. Mark had tried to break through this reticence to ask questions about his mother or about his father's family, but he had always hit a brick wall. He never gave up trying to have a deep conversation with his father if the opportunity ever presented itself. He just believed his father needed to open up, at least for mental health reasons. Eventually, one thing that aroused the old man's interest was when Mark came from university one day and told him about his new friend, Ed McInroy, especially the fact that he was studying at a different university. James Fergusson loved the fact that his son was going somewhere – widening his horizons and network. Any time Mark came for a weekend, James always asked about how the two were faring on.

But James felt bad when his son came home one day and told him that Ed was going away to Africa for a whole year.

"Oh, that would seem like ages," he said, as he touched his son's shoulder. "But you would soon realise how time has wings."

"I know, Dad, but we are used to visiting each other now. It would be hard for both of us."

"I can imagine. Hope he is not going to Sudan. Too much fighting there."

"No. He is going to Sierra Leone. I don't even know where that is."

"He is going where?" the old man interjected in a manner that made Mark notice some kind of discomfiture in his dad. Whatever it was, Mark was not sure. But he assumed at first that maybe his dad had not heard the name of the country correctly, or it was not pronounced properly.

"Sierra Leone."

Before Mark could put his finger to anything, the old man had regained his composure enough to further ask, "You said your friend is going away for a year. But when exactly is he returning?"

This convinced Mark that it was more about a father trying to placate a disoriented son than anything else. He retorted, "He should be back here the first week in September next year."

* * *

James Fergusson had marked that down. And he bided his time. One week before Ed's return from Sierra Leone, he told his son he wanted them to have a conversation.

Mark was shocked. This had never happened before. Finally, he believed his father was going to open up. At last, he was going to know more about his mother – how they met, how they fell in love, what happened later for her to disappear from their lives. He didn't have anything against his father, and he wouldn't hold anything against his mother. He would be contented and pleased to just know the story and put it in perspective.

But when their discussion started, the first question turned everything on its head.

"So you said Ed told you he was born in Sierra Leone?"

"Yes, Dad."

"And you said his parents are still alive?"

"Yes, they are." Mark felt a bit drab.

"Maybe they know our story."

And now Mark's head started spinning, confused.

"What story, Dad?"

Mark sat quietly and attentively like a disciplined schoolboy as he listened to his father's narration.

He could hardly believe his ears – as much for the incredulous nature of the story as it was for his father's ability to keep it to himself all these years. And then the thought that perhaps – rather, obviously – this story would have never been told if he had not met Ed McInroy and they had become friends, and if Ed had not decided to go to Sierra Leone for his gap year.

Now his father wanted him to even be more intimate with Ed in order to pursue this story of his great-great-grandmother having died in Sierra Leone.

* * *

And Mark took the extra effort of meeting Ed at the airport on his return so they would have a chat while he was still fresh from Sierra Leone.

Mark asked many questions about the country, its people, its politics, its geography, its culture and much more. Ed tried his best to engage and give answers, but he was obviously tired and didn't – couldn't – say as much as Mark would have liked. But at least Mark was satisfied with what he had heard, especially with Ed saying he would remain connected with the country. Mark had got something to tell his father.

It would be a few weeks later that Mark would explain to his friend why he had asked all those questions on the way from Heathrow airport.

"I am as connected to Sierra Leone as you are," Mark broke the shell.

"You mean you were born there? Or was your father born there?"

"I think it's much more than that."

"I don't understand."

Mark took his friend through the story he had heard from his father: how, after the abolition of the transatlantic slave trade in the 1700s, British abolitionists founded a 'province of freedom' for freed slaves. It would later become Freetown, the capital of Sierra Leone. And that when these slaves were being taken back to this "new Jerusalem or new England or new whatever", according to the father, some white women went along with them. "One of these white women was my own great-great-grandmother."

Ed was gobsmacked.

"But what pisses off my father more than anything else is the fact that historians, or whoever is writing about these women, refers to them as prostitutes or mistresses of the former slaves. They were not. They were true lovers. They were following their hearts. She genuinely fell in love with this former slave after she had lost our great-great-grandfather at an early age. They couldn't get married here in the sense of the word because inter-racial marriages were taboo then."

"Is that so? I've never even heard about these women before. Never heard this story, Mark. That's really interesting. I'm sorry to hear."

This had put Mark off a bit. He'd thought Ed knew that much about the history of Sierra Leone. But he was happy he'd told the story to his friend. And he was already convinced that, no matter what, his relationship with Ed was sealed – they had a common path to follow.

"Is there a story about what happened to her?" Ed was now feeling some empathy for his friend, and showing an interest to know more. "What is the story? What did the old man say?"

"He doesn't know anything. Apart from a single letter that he said she wrote about six months after arriving in Sierra Leone, brought by some obscure sailor. And that was it. The family never got to hear from her again."

* * *

When Ed McInroy therefore became Prime Minister of Britain, he had no doubt that the best person to appoint as High Commissioner to Sierra Leone was Mark Fergusson. The only person who didn't see it in that light – and was truly disappointed in Ed – was Mark's wife, Rachael. To that point, she had never heard the story of her husband's great-great-grandmother. Mark had not told her about it.

9

The night of the dinner at Oxford's Mexicana restaurant was like an initiation ceremony to their quartet relationship. Maria saw herself being baptised into the secrets – some secrets – of British society; or into the secret of her best friend.

Rachael just wanted to reveal herself to her two closest pals, but then her boyfriend's newfound pal was also now her pal. She was dressed in silky green material, looking expensive. Maria thought it was all about having fallen deeply in love; Mark thought it was a way of being further induced deeper into the river of love. Ed McInroy's first comment on seeing Rachael was, "Wow, you are looking royal."

Rachael's heart skipped, thinking she had heard, "You are a lucky royal." When she responded with "Oh, thank you," her mind swayed. She expected Mark to get further on the issue of royalty (like 'yes, someone told me you are the granddaughter of the Queen'). But he merely retorted, "Really impressive." Her thumping heart cooled down with a "Thank you."

That's exactly why she had to get this dinner organised: to avoid the embarrassment of being found out before she spoke out. And as the dinner became light-hearted halfway through, with a few wine glasses gulped, she drew their attention to the subject matter.

"Lady and gentlemen." She started formal. "I decided that we should meet today for a very important reason." The clinking sounds of cutlery became silent, and the other three tried to pay attention – Ed and Maria were only half-attentive; but Mark was more composed, not sure of what was coming (He very well knew the local slogan that British girls were unpredictable – that they were just like the British weather).

"For more than two years, we have been together in harmony. Well, not you, Ed, but you have been a great friend of ours, of Mark's particularly, for a good while now; and that's good enough…"

Now that started sounding like a farewell speech, and Mark saw himself saying "What are you doing, Rachael?" but he didn't pronounce the words. His lips parted and closed again, then waited for what was to come. Sitting directly opposite her, Mark tried to make eye contact with Rachael, but her head was down. He restrained himself from using his foot to touch hers under the table.

"I came to this university looking for an education that would teach me life beyond the academic. And I am grateful to you two, Maria and Mark, for helping me on that path."

And now Maria also started thinking like Mark, not knowing the drift, but she intuitively responded with a sentimental, "Aww, my sister," and instinctively gave Rachael a peck. They were seated next to each other. Maria sat opposite Ed. She had arranged the sitting positions.

Rachael's emotions were now getting the better of her and she could not continue speaking in riddles. She could not control her inner being any longer.

"I just want you guys to know who I am. I… I… I am a granddaughter of the Queen."

Maria had arranged for a special room at the restaurant (the owner was her countryman), and clearly Rachael had timed it when the waiters were not lingering around. So no one else heard the dramatic chorus-like response of "What?" from the other three.

"What do you mean, Rachael?" Mark took the lead, and now their eyes met.

Rachael re-told the story and asked them to keep it to themselves, as she wanted to continue her studies as a normal student. Not that she really cared if anybody else found out anyway – the ones she cared about now knew.

* * *

Mark was obviously the more affected by these revelations. He definitely loved Rachael – royal or ordinary – but he was caught unawares by this. He quickly went into self-examination mode, questioning his ability to perceive – how on earth had he been dating Rachael all this while and not been able to notice that she was different? Why hadn't he ever noticed from the way she spoke? The way she did things?

Now he started to rewind their relationship to the beginning. Did he say something odd about the monarchy the night of the politics department annual dinner? After that, in later discussions, he had made his views known to her about British politics – and the monarchy. She had always sounded neutral. He had succour, though, in the fact that he had never kept secret his gratitude to the Queen for his scholarship.

But that didn't stop him from being bold enough – or gentleman enough – to ask some questions to his newly discovered royal lady. All four of them were now back on campus, on the corridor to the female hostel. Mark asked that he and Rachael be excused to have a quick chat in the room before he and Ed retired to the male dormitory. Left to themselves on the corridor, Maria was asking Ed all sorts of questions about what he was anticipating about the change of environment. She was inwardly disappointed that Ed was going away – she was always the unlucky one, she kept thinking to herself.

"Why didn't you tell me all this while?" Mark said as they closed the door behind them.

Rachael expected the question, "But I've already given my reasons."

"I mean you should have told me first."

"Perhaps I should have told Maria first."

"But I am your boyfriend."

"Yes, but she is my best friend. And I possibly couldn't have met you if not for her."

"Oh Rachael."

"What! Wouldn't you have loved me if you'd known earlier?"

As he said "Why not?" he drew closer and unwittingly pinned her to the wall by the door, and just kissed her.

* * *

After they got married, they made a decision to live a normal life. Mark got a job at the Exeter local council, Rachael picked up a teaching job at the nearby sixth-form college. Soon, Sarah Fergusson was born. Just over a year later, Ben Fergusson followed. Rachael withdrew from public service to become a full-time housewife to raise her children. After all, she had a constant flow of income through the royal fund.

Within ten years, Mark Fergusson became the head of Exeter local council. His diligence to duty and innovative ideas had paid off. He was especially sympathetic to – and created a special department for – immigrants. He had a particular interest in immigrants from Sierra Leone, ever since he heard that war was ravaging that country. He would visit immigration and detention centres to look out for the welfare of asylum seekers, and he tried to use his influence here and there – where it did not involve breaking the law – to get things fast-tracked for people from Sierra Leone.

* * *

Meanwhile, his friend Ed had gone on to study law and thereafter plunged into full-time politics. It was always going to be like that.

Though Mark was a good speaker, Ed was a natural orator. Mark was good at bringing out ideas, connecting them together and presenting them effortlessly. Ed's way of communicating those same ideas to an audience would be more dramatic, with the appropriate gesticulations, the necessary eye contact connecting with his audience. A politician's way.

They both knew their individual qualities, and they had all along complemented each other. They had stayed in touch all these years, with visitations here and there. Ed had his legal firm in central London, "where the action was taking place", as his favourite political justification. He had won his Durham constituency four years ago.

And Mark had to leave Exeter Council and relocate to London, having got their North London residence on mortgage at the time, for the primary reason of Sarah having opted for her mother's Lady Margaret School for her secondary education. This played into the political fortunes of Ed McInroy, who offered his friend the top position in the Ed McInroy Sr. consultancy firm four blocks from his Westminster parliamentary office. Mark drafted every of Ed's speeches – from Opposition to Prime Minister.

* * *

After they won by a landslide, far exceeding their own projections – they ran a blitzkrieg youthful campaign that attracted university students to the polls more than ever before – Mark told Rachael he was going to be an Ambassador. He had discussed it with Ed. Rachael was excited – if there was any political appointment close to royalty, it was that of a diplomat (with dinners and receptions and cocktails the order of the day – and of the night). Apart from that, she never wanted her husband to be in Cabinet in toxic British politics. She loathed the prying media always being on their backs. *Let us go away, start a new life, and live like royals abroad,* came to her thoughts.

"Is it America, Mark? The kids would love it. Or Canada? The other big one?"

Mark's silence ruffled, or rattled, her.

"You know, I would naturally opt for Mexico. Maria will be really happy."

When Mark mentioned Sierra Leone, it was like a mental thunderbolt struck Rachael's innermost being. Her face turned red. And she was forthright. "To where? For what? How can Ed do this to you? You'll go alone."

The rapidity of Rachael's words held Mark spellbound. It would take a lot of effort and the direct intervention of Prime Minister Ed McInroy to convince both Sarah (who was now already at Durham University) and Rachael to accept the posting to Sierra Leone.

***

When they arrived in Freetown, Rachael fell in love with the place. She had actually started falling in love with it before they arrived. Being the adventurous reader that she was, she had gone into libraries for books on Sierra Leone. She found out that Britain had a special relationship with this tiny West African country: it was a major slave post for British slave traders, and it was later the naval post for Britain in stopping the slave trade. It was the only former British colony established purposely to resettle former slaves – and it was among the very last in West Africa to let go of British colonial rule, and in a peaceful, negotiated way. That was really fascinating for Rachael – she was enticed to see the place.

But before that, when she still had her small doubts, she was good-natured enough to inform senior members of the royal family, including her parents, before Mark's appointment was made public. Her last iota of doubt was swept away by the excitement the news brought to her grandmother.

"I am really happy about that. You couldn't have asked for a better place to go to."

"But Grandma, that country is not stable. There is war there."

"Don't I know that? Perhaps you are being sent there to make it stable."

Rachael was mesmerised by the Queen's wisdom.

"You may be the one to get me to go there again."

"You've been there, Grandma?"

"Of course, the very year you were born – with the *Royal Britannia*."

***

Fresh doubts cropped up in Rachael's mind again as the aircraft was about to land in Freetown and she peeped through the window to have a view – dotted bushes and creeks and tin-roofed houses. But she quickly recalled having read that the airport was situated outside the city.

She was not impressed by the airport infrastructure. The building was obviously colonial; even the tarmac leading to the arrivals was rugged – though she could not ascertain how bad the one near the runway was because a VIP vehicle picked them up the moment they came down the staircase of British Airways 767.

But she started getting excited – nudging Sarah as well – when they entered the ferry to cross over the river dividing the airport area and the city. The last time Rachael was on a ferry ride was during school days when their geography teacher insisted on crossing the English Channel from Dover to Calais in France to determine the length of the area in practical terms. It was a first for Sarah, whose River Thames rides on private boats didn't amount to this experience.

Crossing the river, they were ensconced in a VIP compartment (air-conditioned) on the ferry. They were waited on by exceptionally friendly waitresses. The TV was mainly playing music videos, which drew Sarah's attention. But the monotony of it soon got her bored, and she could not keep up with her parents' conversation. Rachael noticed and suggested she and her daughter went out to the upper deck of the ferry to get some fresh air. They left Mark with the senior protocol officer who had been their guide since picking them up from the runway tarmac.

The driver, Brima, escorted Rachael and Sarah to the top deck. He was a friendly chap who spoke Krio in broken English, which Sierra Leonean humorists called 'Krenglish'. There were many other people on the open-top deck of the ferry. The wind was blowing. Rachael and Sarah's hair was being blown, to the laughter of the African women who mostly had their hair under head ties.

They walked to the front rails. Rachael was amazed with the captivating topography as the moving ferry brought the hills of Freetown nearer and nearer. She remembered reading about the Lion Mountains, and now they were right in front of her eyes. Sarah was also impressed, but nothing attracted her attention more than when she turned and saw the top parapet of the ferry, its name inscribed on it: 'Charlotte, the Black Queen.' She drew her mother's attention to it and wondered who this 'Black Queen' could be. "It could just be a name," Rachael quipped. When they asked Brima, he said, "Madam, we just call him Black Queen."

On landing at Government Wharf in Freetown's business district, they were siren-driven in flashlights through the streets to their official residence. Rachael particularly loved their new house – a mansion on top of the hills of Freetown. The protocol officer was quick to give them a brief history of the place: this was actually the former home of the British Colonial Governor representing the British monarch, and that the Queen herself spent a night in one of the rooms there with her husband, the Duke, when they visited the country many years ago. It was the guest room, but Rachael immediately instructed it be turned to the master bedroom where she and Mark would sleep.

***

Mark had no time to waste. He wanted to start work and deliver as soon as possible. After he familiarised himself with his embassy staff (who were there to receive them), he called the information officer to one side and asked him to organise a press conference at the house two days later.

"We normally do press conferences at the High Commission conference hall, sir. And that would be after meeting with the President," ventured John Davenport, who was regarded as the 'High Commission encyclopaedia,' for partly being the longest-serving official (having outlived three High Commissioners) and partly knowing a lot about Sierra Leone through his interactions with local journlaists.

"I am not here to do the normal. 2pm on Wednesday."

"Yes sir."

***

At the press conference, Mark appeared with his wife and daughter. He introduced them, and asked all the twenty or so journalists present to each introduce themselves – name and media house represented.

"I know you are all surprised that I have called this press conference at my house. Well, I am even constrained to call it that. I consider it a family meeting – a familiarisation meeting. I want us to know each other, and to work together for the benefit of this beautiful country. I wouldn't want you to see me as this ivory-tower British High Commissioner with a neo-colonial mentality. No, I consider myself a part of you, as part of Sierra Leone. I have a heart for this country, and I want to work for this country. I have introduced my family to you. Well, one member is absent here. My son, Ben, is at university in Britain and will one day visit. But I have introduced my wife and daughter in order for you to know that I am bringing a human touch to my position. I am not saying my predecessors have not done that – but I know they have never brought you as a group into this house." (There were nods and laughter from the press.) "So I don't want you to go and write in the papers 'New British Governor Arrives'…" (More laughter).

There were no questions; only a vote of thanks from the president of the local journalists' association, who invariably emphasised on the novelty of a British High Commissioner hosting them at his residence.

But there was no front-page headline that captivated Mark the next day more than the lead in *The True Light* newspaper: 'NEW BRITISH ENVOY IS A SIERRA LEONEAN!'

10

For a whole year, life went on well – as planned – for the Fergussons. Mark had entrenched himself into the Sierra Leonean milieu. He was not close to the government only; he also endeared himself with the opposition and, surprising to many, with the ordinary people. Britain being the largest donor to the country, Mark insisted that every pound of British taxpayers' money spent in Sierra Leone would have to be properly accounted for. He would visit remote villages as well as urban communities where British projects were being implemented. And in every move, he would carry the press along. He became a darling of the Sierra Leone media.

Rachael also did perfectly well in her own right. She could not help entertaining thoughts that made her feel as 'the queen in this kingdom'. After all, she was sleeping in the room where her grandmother once slept. Everything actually felt like royalty in Sierra Leone: she had maidservants at her beck and call; she had gardeners, security, a driver, even a personal assistant in case she needed anything written. And, as was the custom within the diplomatic community, by virtue of Britain's status as Sierra Leone's former colonial power, the wife of the British High Commissioner was the automatic head of the diplomats' wives' association. She was a queen.

Rachael handled the position very well – with her academic background, she was able to bring new ideas like meeting with the diplomats' wives once every month to plan and organise activities including dinners and fundraisers. She also engaged in humanitarian activities, introducing a scholarship fund for destitute children – paying school fees and buying books and uniforms for them. She hardly interfered in her husband's duties – except to ask peremptory questions on his general wellbeing.

Their daughter, Sarah, had found life even more interesting and perhaps more worth living in Sierra Leone. Two weeks after their arrival, they were taken on a conducted sightseeing of touristic sites around Freetown. Sarah saw the loveliest pristine white sand-covered beaches that she had never even seen in movies. She was gobsmacked to learn that the setting for the 1980s famous 'Taste of paradise' Bounty chocolate bar advert was one of these beaches, called Lakka. And, having always loved animals as a child, a visit to the gorilla sanctuary in the forests outside Freetown made Sarah feel some special attachment to the place. "Mum, we can live here forever. This is like paradise," she would later tell a surprised Mrs. Fergusson, knowing how Sarah had been fiercely opposed to coming to Sierra Leone until Prime Minister Uncle Ed intervened. Rachael only retorted, "You wish" with a wry smile.

And Sarah continued to ring that wish in her mother's ears when she started attending classes at Mount Aureol University. She fell in love with the campus scenery – the fact that it was built on top of a hill overlooking the city, the flourishing trees dotted all around and the friendliness of the other students. If Uncle Ed, the Prime Minister, had got it right in helping her choose his alma mater – Durham University – to start her university education, he got it absolutely spot on in convincing her to do her final year – as a gap year – in Sierra Leone. She loved it. And it became lovelier with the fact that other students from Durham were here to do their normal gap year. Though they were in their penultimate year, it was not hard for Sarah to cut friendship with them in a foreign land. And being the daughter of the High Commissioner gave her special attraction to others.

But Rachael's first stance against her daughter's wishes was when she put her foot down and insisted that Sarah would not be allowed to reside on campus like others. There was tension between mother and daughter, as the latter wanted to have a full campus life. Mrs. Fergusson was prepared to go the extra mile to thwart it and threatened to take the matter up with the university authorities. A compromise was reached when Mark intervened, allowing Sarah to stay longer on campus on Saturdays and to attend all social activities organised by her department.

And so, a year later, Sarah Fergusson graduated from Mount Aureol University with no major incidents. Except for one Saturday night when she extended the compromise by sleeping over at the room of her new friend from Durham, Juliana, after a departmental party on campus – to the chagrin of Mrs. Fergusson, who had blamed Mark for even allowing 'the daughter of the British High Commissioner' to be partying on Saturday nights.

But, all in all, the Fergussons' first year at post was brilliant. Until the day the woodworm and the lovebird came along…

* * *

The agreed plan of the Fergussons – after Rachael had succumbed to Mark's insistence on Sarah leaving Durham University to come to Sierra Leone – was that after the daughter's graduation, she would go back to Britain. And then Ben would visit.

Uncle Ed the Prime Minister had personally convinced Sarah to go to Sierra Leone when he asked her to "just do it to make me and your dad happy". Beyond that, Sarah didn't know the depth of this happiness for which she was being used as a vehicle. She knew about Uncle Ed the Prime Minister's attachment to Sierra Leone

– the stories of his visits there since his gap year, how he naturally felt it was also his home because he was born there and all, and how it was this desire to keep the umbilical cord connected with Sierra Leone that informed his decision to send his dear friend as his ambassador there. But Sarah never grasped how this would make her father happy for himself, if not for his friend. However, she had noticed that her father was exceptionally happy to be in Sierra Leone, not least during that house press conference.

After his daughter's graduation, and before she would return to Britain, Mark decided to do a special family dinner to thank her for accepting to come; and, above all, to come clean on the issue of his posting to Sierra Leone.

He rented a bungalow in the exquisite Lakka seaside resort for one night. He knew both Rachael and Sarah would love it. They had visited before, but they had never spent a night there. So they left home after Mark came from work early that Friday afternoon. They arrived at the beach in time for some swimming and running around, bumping into a few familiar people, especially ubiquitous Lebanese socialites and contractors whom Mark had known from various engagements.

It was a table for three in the evening, tucked away in an exclusive corner of the open-air dining hall at Lakka as the sounds from the sea waves mixed with the Calypso music in the background, giving a tranquil atmosphere of serenaded serenity. The dinner orders were placed by wife and daughter. Mark would always eat what they preferred – he was not picky when it came to food.

Sarah was now a graduate and was free to drink wine in the presence of her parents, Mark declared. But the daughter, while thanking him, respectfully said she was not prepared to use the opportunity on the first day given. Rachael burst out laughing, apparently bemused.

"You think I'll oppose that?"

"No, Mum, I just don't feel like it tonight."

They knew she had been drinking wine with all those bustling weekend activities at the university, but it was a home rule that Sarah would not do it in her parents' presence. And she had faithfully obeyed it. When they attended diplomatic dinners, they would only suspect she had had a drink from the offhand way she spoke; but they had never seen her with a glass. She devised and implemented a gulp-away-from-parents policy. At home, there were all types of wines imported from Britain that the parents and their guests indulged in all the time. But Sarah, though tempted at times, did not for once take any. So it was a bit of a surprise that she turned down the lifting of the restrictions.

"You'll see how I'll make use of it, starting tomorrow," she added, laughing. She settled for lemonade. Her parents had Brazilian wine.

After profusely thanking Sarah for making them proud parents – with Rachael intermittently interjecting with her own thanks – Mark decided to go straight to the point.

"I have invited the two of you—" he started.

But Rachael quickly tried to correct him. "*We* have invited her."

"Bear with me, darling," Mark debonairly said. "Well, whatever it is, we are here as a family. And I have something to tell you two that I have never told anybody else except Ed."

"Oh, Mark, don't do this," was the instinctive reaction from his wife. "Please don't ruin the night for me."

To Rachael, there could be nothing secretive that Mark would want to tell her in the presence of Sarah if not one that would get the daughter to ask the mother to forgive the father as husband. And the obvious secret would be an affair. Stories of diplomats and expatriates having affairs with Sierra Leonean girls were not in short supply. As head of the diplomats' wives' association, Rachael had found herself deluged with situations where she had to be counselling her members over the promiscuity that had suddenly overcome their husbands. Some did it with reckless abandon "as if Britain is an erotic prison where the one-man-one-wife rule was a punishment that should now be redressed in Sierra Leone," one bitter wife had summed it up. And, on a number of occasions, some wives had to pack and leave their husbands to continue in their new-found freedom.

"Freetown is literally free for them," Martha Tomlinson, the wife of the political attaché at the British High Commission, told Rachael when complaining about the escapades of her husband. Rachael had gone on to read several books on colonial activities relating to this issue – and she was amused at what a change of climate could do to white men. Many white wives had attributed this to 'African magic' or, as used in local parlance, *juju*. "My husband was such a faithful and devoted man until we came to this good-for-nothing *juju* land," Martha had cursed.

"Mark, please wait until it's just the two of us," Rachael continued her protestations at Lakka.

"But, Mum, do you already know what Dad is going to say?" was the question from the not-tipsy person at the table.

"I don't know… but… but I know," was the oxymoron from the mother.

"What do you know, Rachael? Please calm down. It is not what you think," Mark tried to pacify her.

But she could not be easily calmed. "So now you know what I think, Mark? What do you think I am thinking? I just think if there's anything you want to tell Sarah, you should discuss that with me first."

"You have a point. And I am sorry for that."

"There you go. You've started saying sorry already."

"I am saying sorry for your feeling slighted about my not telling you first, but not sorry for deciding to say it to you two together."

"Can't you hear how confusing you sound, Mark?"

Only when Sarah said she would leave the table if the bickering continued did Mrs. Fergusson calm down. "It's all up to you, Mark. Say what you may. I'm ready to absorb it."

When Mark finished speaking about his great-great-grandmother having come to Sierra Leone about two centuries ago with the freed slaves, and nothing else ever being heard from her apart from a sole letter stating she arrived safely, not only were the three at the table drenched in tears, but Rachael immediately threw herself into the arms of her husband with shrieks and words of consolation. "I am so sorry, Mark. I am so sorry this happened."

Sarah also got up from her chair and moved to her embracing parents, enfolding both in her arms, bending over to grasp a shoulder of each. For a while there was silence, the whole scenario sinking in.

"But Dad, you did not need to keep this to yourself all these years," Sarah broke the silence.

"Ed knew."

"I know, Dad, you already told us. But if I had known this before, you wouldn't have needed to even involve him in convincing me to come."

"Thank you, my miracle baby," Mark inadvertently said.

It did not register with Sarah, but it jerked Rachael, who interjected with, "Thank you, our baby, for your understanding."

Actually, Mark did not know why he had decided to keep this a secret from his family. It made him believe in the saying, 'like father, like son': James Fergusson kept it for a long time as a secret; Mark Fergusson merely followed in his father's footsteps.

After mustering some more strength, Mark said, "The frustrating part of the story is that I don't know whether she ever had children and grandchildren and great- or great-great-grandchildren here, where they are or what they are doing."

"Oh Mark," Mrs. Fergusson interjected.

"Yes, not to talk about where she was buried or what she died of."

"Oh Mark."

"Yes, at times I look at people in this country and I start to imagine whether they are not my relatives, whether they are not the great-great-grandchildren of Mary Fergusson."

"Mark, please calm down."

"So you see, I actually chose to come here. It was not for Ed's sake. Sorry, my dear Rachael, I had to turn down all your other proposals of going to a 'better' country."

"I understand, Mark, and I am happy you did it. Now I have a proper explanation for Maria about why you didn't choose to go to Mexico. She had thought it was still Ed's way of continuing to shun her." She tried to smile.

But Mark continued without reference to Maria; he was poised to put his point across in the way he had planned it. "I had to bring you guys here to have this fulfilment; especially for you, Sarah, as you are about to go back to Britain. Now you know you are not really leaving us in a foreign land."

Before the father could complete his statement, Sarah had got an idea flashing in her head. She wanted to please her father. She knew that if she left in a week's time as planned, her father's sorrows would continue in her absence. So why not linger around for a bit and do some soul-healing before departing? After all, there was nothing of particular importance she was immediately looking forward to in Britain, apart from basking in the splendour of being a graduate. She had not decided yet whether to work or to do post-graduate studies.

She released her parents from her grasp and went back to her seat. The atmosphere was now better, as all managed to force some smiles.

"Dad, I have an idea."

It was as if both parents were woken up from some slumber as they simultaneously asked, "What idea?"

"What about I do a six-month internship with one of the newspapers here before leaving? With this journalism degree, I think it would be an added advantage for practising in Britain if I also had some experience from here."

"Oh, Sarah, that sounds brilliant. Are you doing this for me?"

"No, Dad, I am doing this for me. This is our other home. It is my home too."

Mrs. Fergusson had misgivings about this idea. She had dreaded every moment that Sarah had lived in Sierra Leone, fearing a misstep or misguided move. And if they had managed to sail with her thus far, it was her motherly pleasure that Sarah was returning to Britain in one piece. She wanted her daughter to go back and join the race against time, the capitalist race. She wanted to state that internship in Africa was not something highly regarded by the British media – as far as she knew. But she didn't want to hurt Mark – not tonight. Not after hearing this hair-raising story. So she kept quiet.

***

With the niche he had cut for himself within the Sierra Leone media landscape, Mark would have had an easy sway in getting any editor to incorporate his daughter. Sarah would have been spoilt for choice. But Mark didn't proffer a choice. He chose *The True Light* newspaper.

It could have been due to that captivating front page after his first press conference, but it was much more. Mark had grown to love the paper for its editorial consistency, quality of English and in-depth reportage. Even in that first edition, the paper had a scathing article on British neo-colonialism: 'The new British High Commissioner purports to be in love with Sierra Leone even more than some of us. We hope it is not another charade. Let him step up to the plate and prove himself. We are watching you, Mr. British Sierra Leonean High Commissioner.'

And living up to the challenge, *The True Light* had been covering and monitoring every of Mark Fergusson's activities. They had gone ahead to do exclusive interviews with him. He had furtively remained guarded and never actually revealed why he was purporting to be so much in love with Sierra Leone, apart from what everybody already knew – that the new British Prime Minister was born in Sierra Leone during colonial rule and wanted the country to develop more rapidly than now. And Mark had ensured that among the three or four editors with whom he had created some special relationship (like always informing them of his activities and inviting them to special occasions and dinners) was the Editor of *The True Light*, Amidu S. Tamaraneh.

Mark believed Mr. Tamaraneh was one of the best journalists he had ever met – even by British standards. *The True Light* was the only newspaper that gave his maiden press conference the angle that caught not only his eye but also his spirit. All the other papers were merely doing routine reporting, according to him, with headlines like 'NEW BRITISH HIGH COMMISSIONER ARRIVES', 'NEW BRITISH ENVOY HOLDS FIRST PRESS CONFERENCE AT HOME', 'NEW BRITISH HIGH COMMISSIONER UNVEILS AGENDA'.

Beyond that, no other newspaper had tried to interview him. It was not only about *The True Light* being alone in asking, but he was impressed by the pressure he got to grant the interview. The Editor had insisted that they would not talk to a subordinate officer, 'because the press conference was done by the High Commissioner himself'. Mark succumbed two weeks later. The Editor himself conducted the interview at the British High Commission.

And Mark was impressed. The young Editor, Amidu, was affable and gentlemanly in his questions, even when piercing a nail into the High Commissioner's closet. He had pressed Mark hard on the issue of loving Sierra Leone.

"So you said you loved Sierra Leone?"

"I said so. I will also say so now, and will always say so."

"Ok. So you love Sierra Leone?"

"I surely do."

"How much?"

"Eh… As much as you can imagine."

"But that is vague, High Commissioner. How concrete is this love that you are propagating?"

"You will see it from my actions."

"Ok. You are just another British High Commissioner, but with a different agenda."

"If you put it that way."

"But that was not what you were trying to say during that press conference. You were exuberant; you were passionate, as if there was something extra."

"Yes, there's something extra," Mark found himself being dragged into a corner.

"What is it, High Commissioner?"

Before Mark could answer, Amidu had followed up with another question. "Were you also born in Sierra Leone by a former colonial civil servant?"

Mark felt the blood running up to his face and he turned red. This was clearly observed by Amidu. He was still finding the appropriate words when the Editor continued, "Do you also have a special relationship with Sierra Leone? I guess you saw our front page after that press conference. You virtually claimed to be a Sierra Leonean. Where is this love from, Mr. High Commissioner?"

"The love I have for this country," Mark eventually found the words, "is the love that the Prime Minister has for this country."

"But it is not the same, is it?"

"It is the same as long as I am his representative here."

"How's that? You don't have the same emotional attachment as he has. You are just doing a job."

"It's not just a job," Mark was pushed to say, and he thought he was crossing a boundary.

Amidu was readily pushing him to the other side. "If it's not just a job, then what is it?"

"You see, the Prime Minister has been my friend since our university days," Mark found himself involuntarily revealing. But he was satisfied that these were the words that came out instead of those lurking in the background competing to be revealed – about his own personal relationship to Sierra Leone.

"Yes," Amidu nudged on, giving Mark an opportunity to think quickly and continue with this revelation.

"That friendship has made me know him better, just as he has known me. I know how he feels about this country; he is very passionate about its progress. And so his choice of me to serve here was particularly deliberate. He told me to do all that is humanly possible to reflect his feelings on the ground."

"That is interesting."

"Yes, it's like your best friend going to another country and leaving their child in your care. I am sure you would take care of that child just as if he or she were your own. Wouldn't you?"

"Yes, I would," the interviewer now answered a question with a smile. Mark felt relieved, knowing he had not only escaped but had actually won.

Amidu gave the interview prominence on both front and inside pages.

And for the past one year, their relationship had blossomed at press conferences, dinners, project launches. Mark was sure his daughter would be in good hands in her internship at *The True Light.*

So when Editor Amidu got the call on the matter, he was flustered and felt flattered. When he realised how serious the High Commissioner sounded, he just thanked him profusely and thanked his stars as well. For Amidu, this was a providential stamp of approval from the most respected diplomat in the country. The credibility of the paper would be strengthened with its readership. The sales – and of course the advertisements – would be boosted. And he would be able to pay his reporters on time. Now he was beginning to understand how or why he had found himself in this denigrated and forsaken profession. There could be light at the end of tunnel.

* * *

Amidu and Sarah had met a few times, even if just briefly. The first time was of course during the maiden press conference of High Commissioner Fergusson. In the media pep talk after that press conference, Amidu overheard his male colleagues talking about how beautiful the High Commissioner's daughter was. He couldn't remember her face – his focus then had been on her father. The next time they met was about a month or so later, at a dinner organised by the EU representative in Freetown. Mark Fergusson attended with his wife and daughter, apparently trying to introduce them into the wider diplomatic family. This was after Amidu's interview with him.

Apparently, Mark had been talking about *The True Light* and its editor to Rachael and Sarah. So when they met at the dinner, he made it a point of duty to bring the Editor over to them and make a special introduction. Rachael had time to ask further questions, having apparently heard much from her husband and having herself been reading the papers. Sarah, after a brief 'hello', was off to join the young British High Commission officials at the other end. But not before Amidu confirmed with his own eyes the talk of her beauty.

They met again at the Mass Communications annual dinner the Saturday night that Sarah slept over at her friend's in the hostel. Amidu had been invited as an alumnus of the department.

In the course of the night, when he spotted Sarah, he went over to ask about her father. "He's fine," she said, without entertaining any further conversation, turning to her fellow British colleagues from Durham.

That was about it between Amidu and Sarah before Mark Fergusson threw this gauntlet of an internship.

***

About three months into her internship, Sarah asked her parents for an outing to the same Lakka resort they had gone to because she wanted to speak on a serious matter. Their obvious conclusion was that she was going to say goodbye in a special way. She had not really disappointed in her sojourn with them. And, as far as they knew, she had been doing well and enjoying her internship with remarkable breakthrough stories – the most prominent being the one on her great-great-great-grandmother, Mary Fergusson. She had got the foundation she needed and had unwittingly prepared herself for the British media even before she returned.

Sarah had proposed a same-day return to her parents – without having to sleep there as last time. Her mother's protests about the journey being too long on a rugged road to and fro on the same day fell on deaf ears. Sarah's explanation was that she had an appointment the next day.

"But the next day is Sunday."

"Yes, Mum."

"But it's a day to rest."

"Rest from what, Mum?"

"Rest from work. I mean, internship."

"But I did not say it's work. I have an appointment, Mum."

Mark Fergusson was not a man who liked unending banter without resolution. He asked his wife to agree to their daughter's request. "We can both rest all day on Sunday," he declared.

But perhaps what raised Mrs. Fergusson's adrenaline higher than anything else was Sarah's assertion that she would travel to Lakka on her own. They would only meet there and after dinner they would return home separately.

Mrs. Fergusson was now hysterical.

"What is the point, Sarah?"

"The point is that I have some things to do in town before leaving."

"But we can wait for you and all go together."

"Mummy, please."

"Please what?"

"Please, just let me be."

"Who is taking you?"

"A friend."

Mark Fergusson overruled the wife again.

***

The Fergussons did not believe in superstition or omens or a psychic interpretation of events. They were British. They were Anglicans – though they hardly went to church. But the events that bedevilled their journey to the beach that Saturday afternoon tested their faith – or their way of seeing a conflation of occurrences.

The first incidence happened just three miles after leaving Hill Station. Their vehicle had a puncture. It was surprising to Mark and Rachael because these were new tyres.

Fortunately, due to the absence of Sarah, who usually took the front seat on such trips, they had come along with one of their security personnel, who helped the driver change the punctured tyre. They had to spend some twenty minutes at a makeshift garage on the highway to repair it. Surprisingly, the real cause of the puncture would not be ascertained. There was a pinhole – which was patched – but there was no object, pin or nail, as evidence of the cause.

Mark and Rachael had planned some activities together before Sarah would arrive, and the last thing he wanted was for her to reach Lakka before them. He did not want another round of banter. He asked his driver, Brima, to go faster.

"Don't go beyond seventy," interjected Mrs Fergusson.

"Yes ma."

Brima was not only the best driver one could pray for, but also very loyal and committed. Mark was the third British High Commissioner he had served. His record was intact; he'd never had an accident. He had travelled with Mark up and down the country, and even to neighbouring countries, with consummate diligence and commitment to duty. He had never complained. He abided by whatever rules. He obeyed the wife just as the husband. So he would not go beyond seventy miles per hour, as the husband did not say anything afterwards.

In fact, Mark was now skimming through the local newspapers (he normally read the Friday papers on Saturday) while Rachael turned her face towards the thickets of the peninsula forests, lost in thought, her mind wandering away and wondering what her daughter could be up to. She had a latent feeling that it was not the celebratory farewell Mark was thinking about.

They were still on the paved segment of the road; and, before long, Mark's head slumped into his chest. His hands were still holding the paper, but it had dropped in his lap. Tired, he needed some sleep. Rachael was now in a kind of reverie. Her mind went back to the day Sarah was born and imagined how events would have turned out if she were actually a boy as had been initially predicted by Dr. Robinson.

And then, bang!

Mark was not sure what woke him up – either the loud sound or Rachael's shouts of "Jesus! Jesus!" But he could see the vehicle swerving and swaying from one end of the road to the other, Brima strongly holding on to the steering wheel, trying to put it under control.

"Brima, what is it?" was what Mark managed to spurt out.

"Boss, *duya* wait sir," came from the now profusely sweating driver as he manoeuvred from here to there, changing gears frequently.

Mrs. Fergusson's shrieks had halted and transitioned to shocked silence as she tightly gripped the shirt of Tony, the security personnel in the front seat.

About one hundred yards from where the collision occurred, having negotiated a curve, Brima managed to slow the vehicle down. He was driving at sixty-five miles per hour at the time of impact. He brought the vehicle to a halt by the tussocky grassland on the side of the highway. He opened his door, jumped out and started running in the direction they had come from.

Tony was enquiring about his bosses' wellbeing as Mark unfastened his seatbelt and took hold of a shivering Rachael. She muttered, "Oh God, what is this? What is this, Mark?" and melted in his embrace.

Tony ascertained they were not hurt, and he also now jumped from the vehicle and chased Brima as fast as he could.

There was chaos at the scene. All the passengers in the mini-van, locally called *poda poda*, had disembarked and were in some confusion. Some were hurt and sprawled on the side of the road, while those unhurt helped in a resuscitation effort. Some were standing near the vehicle talking disconcertedly about how it happened, or how they thanked their stars that they had survived, or about the carelessness of the driver.

Tony found Brima in a group of four standing in front of the *poda poda*, which had the bold inscription 'To be a man is not easy'. Brima was asking about the driver, and the passengers were insisting he had run away into the nearby bush.

"But why didn't you chase him?"

"How could we when we didn't even know what was happening?" said a self-appointed passenger spokesman.

"We were all shocked," said another, actually sounding shocked.

"We were telling him he was speeding too much, and he didn't listen to us," the spokesman said. "He said he had to do another trip in order to complete the master-money; if not, he could lose his job."

"Is that why he would risk all our lives?" Brima interjected.

"Not only our lives, but those of the British High Commissioner and his wife." Tony now came in after hearing enough.

The passengers were now further dismayed on hearing who was in the other vehicle. The spokesman immediately suggested they should scour the nearby bushes for the driver – because, after all, they wouldn't move until he came out. About four of them went on the search.

Only after they had left did Brima and Tony have a thorough look at the *poda poda*. The windscreen was gone and one side of the frontage was seriously damaged, with the headlights broken.

Meanwhile, another *poda poda* came by from the Lakka end and stopped. The driver and passengers were curious to know what had happened. And they were told.

"Oh Alimamy; it's Alimamy," the other driver gave out the name of his runaway colleague. All commercial drivers plying the same route knew each other. "He overtook me just about twenty minutes ago."

* * *

Back in the jeep, Mark and Rachael were consoling themselves that they had not been hurt. But neither of them knew what exactly had happened. They didn't know the impact had involved another vehicle. They only heard the loud bang and felt the impact. And now they felt reassured enough to step out of the vehicle and try to understand it all. The driver and security personnel had left without an explanation.

Mark and Rachael at first stood on the bushy side of the road, examining each other to ascertain there was no injury and no feeling of pain. They then moved on to look more thoroughly at the vehicle. Mark moved to the front but he did not see anything untoward. He drew Rachael's attention to it. She was also surprised. Practically, the jeep was intact.

"Whatever it is, we thank God," Mark said. "I wonder what Brima and Tony are up to. I am sure they've gone to look at where it all happened."

Rachael was going to say something, but was interrupted by shouts of "*Orpotho, orpotho*," coming from the other side of the road. They turned round to see three boys who continued to joyously chant "*Orpotho*, *orpotho*," waving to them.

Rachael was happy for the distraction and instinctively asked Mark whether he knew what they were saying.

"*Orpotho*. That's 'the white man' in Temne," Mark said with an air of extra confidence. It was all too familiar to him. He had tried to have a simplistic grasp of the elementary segments of each Sierra Leonean language in his extensive nationwide trips monitoring British projects while relating with the people throughout the past year.

The boys were obviously excited to see the two *orpothos* on the highway.

"How are you?" Rachael ventured a conversation, also shouting across the road.

"We are fine," the oldest among them connected, saying the words with such rapidity that Rachael only heard the 'fine'.

"*Usai una* come from?" Rachael switched into her basic mastery of the local Krio.

The boys became more excited as they burst into laughter. The youngest retorted, "*Orpotho dae* talk Krio", with more boisterous laughter from the trio. Rachael joined them in laughter now. Mark was so far a spectator.

Rachael had been good and fast in learning Krio from her domestic workers. Ramatu, the house girl, was her best teacher. Rachael could never bring her to respond in a single sentence of English. The driver and the gardener and the security tried to mangle English syntax here and there to communicate with 'madam', but Ramatu was always speaking Krio to her boss. Rachael's attempts to teach her didn't work; instead, Madam found herself being taught Krio by her housemaid, and she loved it. It was not hard to learn, after all – the greater percentage of the lexicon were English words. Rachael later found out that most of the diplomats' wives had learned some Krio as well. She flowed with the tide. And she had found it useful in her engagements even with government officials.

And now she was finding it useful in engaging three little boys on the highway to Lakka Beach. For a moment, the worries or imaginations over Sarah disappeared, the trauma of the accident was momentarily forgotten.

"We *commot* hunting," the youngest of the boys answered.

It was obvious. The boys were holding their catch. They had two grass-cutters and a squirrel – all dead. But what attracted Rachael immediately was a bird in the hands of the speaker.

"*Una* come make I see," Rachael called them over. Seeing that no other vehicle was coming, they ran across.

"How *una* catch them?" Rachael asked.

"Trap. We use trap." Now was the turn of the third boy.

"Ok." And she turned to the youngest and asked how he caught the bird. Trap, of course. "It's so beautiful. It's a parrot." Rachael drew Mark's attention. He was at first disinterested; but taking a look at the bird, he immediately realised it was not the traditional African parrot.

"Oh, it's a lovebird. It's the peach-faced one," Mark said with the certainty of having studied birds in secondary school and had extensive school visits to bird sites around Britain. He also knew Sierra Leone had a rich wildlife.

Rachael was now filled with emotion, her eyes glowing as she ventured to touch the multi-coloured creature.

"*Waetin una dae* go do with it?" Rachael further asked, drawing more laughter from the boys.

"We *dae* go eat am," the youngest said with glee. The thought of it made Rachael's face turn red, her heart beat faster. The thought of this bird being dead and eaten in the next moment made her feel sick in the stomach.

"*Una dae* sell it?" she did not know where the thought came from.

"Yes, we *dae sell am*." The eldest assumed leadership immediately, on the prospect of getting money for it. "Five thousand Leones."

She asked if they attended school. The answer was a resounding chorus: "Yes ma." She said she wanted to do a deal with them. And they became curious, with brightened faces. She told them it was good to hunt, and it was good to set traps for animals (there would be no other way for them to get meat), but it's not good to do the same to birds. "Birds are like our friends. We should not hurt them," she lectured the attentive boys waiting for the five thousand Leones.

She said, "I'll buy this one, but promise me you will never set a trap for birds again."

"We promise," they shouted in their shrill voices.

Rachael got their full names and the school they attended. She would later include them on the list of pupils she supported through her Destitute Children's Fund. She gave them one hundred thousand Leones and took the bird.

As the excited boys had gone a little distance away, the second one asked, "But why does Teacher Mallay always talk about killing two birds with one stone while *orpotho* says no hurting of birds?"

The elder boy was taken aback, and then he found an answer. "What we know is that we have promised not to kill birds. And we have got money. That's what matters."

"That's what matters," the youngest echoed.

"That's what matters," all three of them said in a chorus.

There was not a happier bunch of boys in Charlotte village for that whole month as they spread the news of how *orpotho* bought a bird from them for one hundred thousand Leones – which, at the time, was twice their headmaster's monthly salary. Their families were happy, and they became the topic of discussion for a whole month at Charlotte Mission Primary School. Teachers made reference to them in class, especially after their scholarships were confirmed.

At the scene, Rachael was not sure what to do with the bird. But the Classical Literature student in her had the better of her, as she caressed it with lines from 'Ode to a Nightingale': "Thou wast not born for death, immortal bird! No hungry generations tread thee down…"

And then she added her own lines:

"I know you are not a nightingale
But you are as much a nightingale
Much more than a nightingale
You are a lovebird
A *daylightingale…*"

Mark couldn't help but laugh out loudly.

The boys had merely tied a rope to one of the bird's feet, with the other end of the rope tied to a dry stick, so that even when not held, it couldn't fly away due to the weight of the stick. Her instinctive thought was to just release it and let it fly away to freedom again. But then this was a rare bird that she wouldn't want to part with so quickly. She could release it later. But then what if, when released, it fell into another trap? The thoughts were flowing back and forth in Rachael's mind, and she was going to ask her husband's opinion when they heard shouts from the direction they had come from.

Alas, they saw a crowd approaching. Tony quickly ran ahead to inform Mark and Rachael that the driver of the mini-van had been caught and was being brought to them.

"What mini-van?" Mark asked, confused.

"The *poda poda* that hit us."

"Are you serious? Is it serious?"

"No die sir, only driver get serious wound in hand."

"And they are bringing him here for what?"

Mark and Rachael had not been sure what caused the accident. Their surmises had ranged from thinking a stray animal was hit, or they had gone into a bad pothole at high speed, or they had hit another vehicle. This last guess was remote, because neither of them saw a vehicle coming before the impact (Mark was sleeping, Rachael was rapt in thought), and they did not see any evidence of an impact on the jeep. The front metal guards were very strong. The vehicle was intact.

And presently the crowd arrived, with Brima clutching the *poda poda* driver Alimamy's shirt. The latter had come out of hiding when his colleague driver joined in the search, shouting his name, telling him the other vehicle was carrying the British High Commissioner (*orpotho ka orqueen*). Alimamy had thought it was a military or police vehicle because it looked like one. And he had feared he would be mercilessly beaten up (as was normally the case in such situations), so he took to his heels into the nearby bushes without even checking on his passengers or what damage could have been done on the *poda poda*. He did not even immediately check on himself. It was in his hiding place that he saw pieces of glass stuck in his hand and blood flowing. The smashed windscreen had taken its toll. He could not continue to hide in such a condition. His driver friend's voice and message of assurance made him to come out.

"Why are you bringing him here?" Mark asked.

"Master, he drive us bad. He want to kill we," Brima responded.

"Ok. But he is bleeding."

"Master, don't feel sorry for *am*."

The passengers who followed along were just pleading for mercy.

"Just take his particulars and let him go get treatment," Mark instructed. "Time is not on our side." His thoughts now raced back to their appointment with Sarah. He was not even sure what time it was now. He checked. They were still within time, thanks to their decision to make the trip early – though their plan to have a good swim before Sarah arrived had now been thwarted.

On this final leg of the journey, nobody said anything to anybody. Only the intermittent flapping sound from the lovebird in the back chamber – as the little bird knocked its beak into the biscuits that Rachael had already provided for it – disrupted their rapt thoughts.

When they arrived, they went straight to the same table in the same corner of the restaurant where they had sat a few months ago. Sarah was not here yet. Just five minutes later she appeared, smiling all the way from the door as she greeted her parents and hoped they had not been waiting for long. She had apparently used the other road to Lakka.

"Is your friend coming?" Rachael asked after hugging her daughter.

"No, Mum, I said it's a family meeting as before."

"But you said a friend was coming with you."

"Yes, but not in the meeting."

"Ok, ok, that's settled," Mark passed his verdict.

And Sarah said she would have to leave as soon as possible because there was a story they were investigating and it was urgent that they followed a strong lead tonight.

"In the night? What kind of story is that?"

"Mum, you will read it in the papers."

"But why in the night?"

"Because we follow the story anywhere, any time."

Mark had to stop the bickering again by calling the waiter so they could take the order.

The parents had resolved not to tell Sarah about what happened on the way. They would only tell her at home later about the story of the three little boys and the lovebird. The lovebird would become Sarah's friend – as she would be the only one to try to teach it how to speak.

***

Having placed the order for the food and drinks, Sarah had resolved to go straight to the point. So she hit on the topic the moment they started eating.

"Mum, Dad, I am in love." She said it effortlessly, her face brightened.

Mrs. Fergusson dropped her cutlery with some food still in her mouth, obviously shocked. "In love? What love?" This was way beyond what she had ever imagined.

"Yes, Mum, I'm in love."

"What does that really mean?"

"I have fallen in love with someone."

Mark was normally able to control his emotions and would hardly express them. But this information, or the way his daughter had relayed it, tended to have shaken him. He had watched his daughter grow into maturity, but this was the last issue he was expecting to discuss with her at this time, in this place. Life was full of surprises. And they came whenever, wherever.

***

Mark and Rachael had noticed some changes in Sarah's social life recently. But they had put it down to the exuberance of having just graduated and now doing an internship in her favourite profession.

Mark particularly was more optimistic about what Sarah was doing – perhaps overwhelmed by his gratitude to the daughter for having taken the venture in deference to him for his great-great-grandmother. So when Rachael had recently raised concerns with him about Sarah's late-night escapades and coming home late, Mark justified it as a norm for journalists: "They are nocturnal beings." And he was not averse to his daughter going out – especially when she had found friendship with Celia, the American Ambassador's daughter.

They had their diplomatic and expatriate circles intact. Their company and acquaintances revolved around that. They had selected pubs and restaurants in Freetown. Mark believed Sarah should make enough relationships in Freetown before leaving for Britain so that those memories would always instigate her to want to come back and visit, even on her own.

"Such friendships are good and lasting. Look at my friendship with Ed," Mark continued in defence when Rachael said it was becoming too much.

But far be it from Mark's remotest thinking to expect such a topic that Sarah had just dropped before them. As far as he was concerned, she was daddy's girl. She was still that baby in his eyes – that innocent little baby. Miracle Baby.

Sarah had been very homely and dutiful throughout her school days and through university. She had big dreams about playing a part in the British media landscape – she wanted to be a real investigative journalist. She was focused on this; she had started proving it in Sierra Leone. And she was going to leave. She had only extended her stay because he told her the story of his great-great-grandmother. She did it to give him the necessary moral support. It was never in her plan to stay a day longer in Sierra Leone before he told them that story. Where had this love talk come from now?

***

Rachael had once or twice overheard Sarah and Celia discussing their social bubbles. And she could conclude that the German ambassador's son, Raphael, was doting on Sarah.

He had been making some moves, but they had met repeated rebuffs. Celia would laugh about it, saying that if the relationship succeeded, it would be the 'Maastricht treaty' – and Sarah would reply, "Which would never be signed."

But when Sarah presently spoke about having fallen in love, Rachael instinctively concluded that the 'German blitz' was succeeding.

She had never given it a thought. Now it was dawning on her that her little girl was becoming a woman, and falling in love was a natural phenomenon that unlocked itself at will. But, deep within her, Rachael had thought Sarah would wait to reconnect with the royal circles on return to Britain. She believed her daughter had always loved the idea of being a royal. Sarah had the supercilious looks of royal aura and she had acted it out perfectly in her school days (everybody commended how royal she looked in Westminster Abbey when she read scripture on Remembrance Day for World War II heroes in her teenage years), and all the way to university.

Therefore, falling in love with the German ambassador's son was not royal at all. What could have influenced her daughter to succumb? It could be peer group pressure. Celia, the American, was too outgoing for Sarah's comfort, Rachael had always believed.

* * *

Shock and consternation were written all over the Fergussons' faces when their daughter gave them the full details.

Mark was the first to respond. "Look, my baby, this is not something to rush into."

"I am not rushing, Dad."

"But have you tried to know him?"

"Yes, Dad, that's what I've been doing in the last three months, and I'm satisfied."

"Satisfied with what?" Rachael jolted in.

"I'm satisfied with him that he is in love with me."

"It is not love. He wants you for something else."

"What are you talking about, Mum? Anyway, I expect you guys to respect my decision. I am sorry, I will have to leave for our assignment."

"I would like us to have a thorough discussion of this issue at home," Mark implored.

"Dad, if I wanted it discussed at home, I wouldn't have asked you to come here."

Mark rose up and moved towards his daughter, lifted her up from her seat, and gave her a warm embrace. Rachael looked away, not even wanting her eyes to meet with her daughter's while in the embrace of her father.

Mark's face was turned toward the ocean view and his mouth was near her daughter's right ear as he said in slow whispers, "Follow your heart. Just be careful, my baby. I am always there for you."

If Rachael had turned that moment, she could have seen the lips of her daughter moving as she pronounced a similarly low-voiced, "Thank you, Dad."

* * *

As they trudged back to their vehicle after the departure of Sarah, holding hands, Rachael told Mark that she dreamt about a worm in a wood last night. "The deceitful, harmless-looking worm was eating into and damaging this beautiful wood. Now I know my daughter is that wood."

"Please don't over-interpret issues, Rachael," Mark consoled. "Let's go home and reflect on this matter."

"I was always against coming to this freedom-drunk country, where even dogs are free to roam about as they want. I suspected something like this would happen. You have brought this on us, Mark."

The husband did not say a word throughout their return journey. Even Brima and Tony realised that there was something wrong when Mrs. Fergusson kept on releasing sighs and gasps and shrieks, but without saying a single word throughout. Even the lovebird seemed to know what had happened. There was no fluttering from it on the return journey.

11

As the jeep snaked its way to the top of Hill Station, Mrs. Fergusson's mind was now made up – was now clear – as to the line of action to take. And she did not need to consult her husband on it. She would not trust him on this. She would not entrust this to him. She would go ahead on her own and call Ben. He could be the only one to talk Sarah out of this. And there was no time to waste.

* * *

Rachael's affinity with her son was exceptional. Not only did she feel compensated for the first false boy-child call from Dr. Robinson, but she felt fulfilled in Ben. Whatever it was that influenced women of her generation to crave the birth of male children – even if just one – was a powerful force.

Even as a teenager, in her peer group the sentiment was widespread. Was it a result of their own experience in society or had they inherited it? Or was it the way that society had juxtaposed itself? 'The pages of the history of the world are overpopulated with male characters' was something she had learnt from her secondary school history teacher, Mrs. Routledge (whom they nicknamed 'rock of ages' for still being a schoolteacher at seventy-five). Rachael agreed to a large extent, but thought she knew a few female characters whose stories overpopulated the pages of history. Her grandmother, the Queen, came to mind; but Rachael never countered her teacher's sing-song chauvinistic-world statement.

Inwardly, though, Rachael agreed with Mrs Routledge – the statement from the 'rock of ages' was borne out of experience, especially with a back-up justification: "Every mother wants to give birth to a king, not to another queen." And Rachael remembered that even her grandmother doted on her male children more. Perhaps that's just how society was. And Rachael was ready to toe the line. Even her being way down in the succession line to the throne was as a result of her being female: if she were a male child, she could have been fourth in line and not the pathetic 'umpteenth' she so resented.

So she wanted a male child as well – even if just one, especially the first. Why did women in the early to mid twentieth century still particularly fancy having male children? Was it also a way of exerting gender equality in humanity to remind the men that they couldn't have been without women? Or to square the equation of women also being in charge of men – even if these men were only tiny-tot versions?

She made conscious and deliberate efforts to ensure it happened. Less than six months after Sarah's birth, she was on the lookout already. She eventually convinced Mark into going for holidays to America. They spent two weeks in the sunshine state, Florida. She conceived Ben there; and got the services of an obstetrician as well – without telling Mark. She had lost faith in the British health system. She wouldn't want to see a repeat of Dr. Robinson's mistake – she couldn't gamble the possibility of meeting another Dr. Robinson. If these things were happening, they better happen in another country. She only informed Mark on their return to

Britain: that she actually went to see an obstetrician the day she had left Sarah with him in Florida to check into a hospital for a supposed overnight headache. And she had found "a good one."

She had made the decision that she was going to have her next child in America. She had a good lengthy lesson from the doctor on how to make sure it would be a son. She was surprised when Dr. Graham, a native Floridian, told her that Britain had the best obstetricians in the world, and she would get better advice there. Without revealing why, Rachael wouldn't have any of that. Dr. Graham accepted, thinking it was the craze about everybody else wanting to be American-related. He gave her hormone-boosting prescriptions.

A few months later, Rachael and Mark flew back to America with Sarah, and Benjamin Fergusson was born at Florida's John F. Kennedy Hospital.

That was the first – or rather the second – point of tremor in the relationship between Rachael and her daughter, as Sarah grew up asking her mother why her brother carried an American passport and she did not. It was just a coincidence, mother had always hushed daughter.

But despite that, though inwardly Rachael had this extra love for Ben, she went all out to prove to Sarah that she was loved as much. And any loophole was covered by Mark anyway, as he had his own extra love for Sarah, rather than for Ben.

Therefore, Sarah and Ben grew up loving and liking each other. They were brought up to do just that. They went to the same primary school, and their parents frequently took them on family trips around Britain and abroad (twice to Mexico on the invitation of Maria, who was now in an on-and-off relationship with a Jamaican fellow).

When Sarah and Ben became teenagers, the bond naturally became closer and deeper. They shared peer group secrets about secondary school. Sarah was at Lady Margaret School while Ben was at Westminster Boys'. They always had stories to share – about teachers, about pranks, about colleagues, and about academia as well.

With just a year and a half or so age difference between them, the bond continued even at university level. Sarah almost always came to London from Durham University every weekend, apart from in the holidays. Their affinity tightened. They went to most social events together and were nicknamed 'the sibling lovers' by friends – neither had an amorous relationship with anybody else before their father was appointed High Commissioner to Sierra Leone. And when the decision was reached for Sarah to go along to Sierra Leone, it was emotionally tough for both. It was the first time they were being separated for long – and by that far.

Rachael all too well knew the depth of her children's affinity to each other. She recalled that Sarah at age twelve had become so close to her brother that she had asked why a brother and sister could not live together for life. Rachael had promptly responded that that was not the way society operated.

"We need to expand our families and therefore go away as far as possible from our immediate families to make more families. And besides, God does not want it that way."

Sarah didn't say a word again. Her mother hardly mentioned God, but whenever she did to her children, she meant that she expected the matter closed. But in her remotest imagination, Rachael did not think her daughter would take the expansion of families this far. All the way to Sierra Leone! She concluded Sarah had taken her statement out of context. She would now do all she could to put things into context for her daughter.

***

After hearing from their mother, Ben gave himself two days to fully absorb and meditate on the matter before engaging his sister.

Rachael had told him that Mark was lukewarm on the issue. Naturally, Ben was reluctant to do it.

"She has a right to her choice, Mum," he had protested.

"But it is a wrong choice."

"How would you know, Mum?"

"Because I know."

"How?"

"This is not love, Ben, this is not love. This is lust. This is exploitation. This boy is deceiving her. There is a general trend here of African boys using marriage to white ladies as a route to a better life – to go and settle abroad. They always have their African women. After a while, they dump the white woman."

This was how Rachael appealed to the sentiments of her son, reminding him that, in the end, it would be the family that would suffer. But deep within her, her greatest fear was how she would become a topic of negative chattering within the diplomatic community in Sierra Leone, at royal dinners in Britain and beyond, if Sarah's relationship with Stephen materialised. If it worked. She did not want it to work.

"You are an American, Ben." She now patronised her son. She implored him to "deploy" his *Americanness* and "rescue" his British sister from "drowning" in Sierra Leone. Her history lessons from Mrs. Routledge ('the rock of ages') had come to mind – how America "rescued" Britain from defeat in the Second World War!

* * *

Ben was very measured when talking to his sister. Sarah was also correspondingly courteous. She was sure, after all the courtesies, that the matter would come up. She remembered her mother asking at Lakka Beach, "Have you discussed this issue with your brother?" and she had replied "Not yet." Two days later, she had not; and Ben now calling meant the news had reached him. Their mother had definitely wanted Ben to call on the same day, judging from how animated she was about the matter. But Sarah knew her brother very well. She knew Ben would ponder over an issue, weighing its pros and cons, debating for and against the topic, before responding. 'A slow but clear-cut position is better than a faulty hasty decision' was his mantra, even in academic work.

But the words that continuously rang in Ben's ears were his mother's repeated statement: "Daddy, please do this for me." Rachael sometimes called him 'Daddy' to remind her son that he was named after her dad. But Ben knew she almost always used it to put him in a corner.

Ben delayed for two days – causing a lot of anxiety for his mother – as he knew this was a sensitive matter for his sister. The provoking question their mother asked him – about whether his sister had first consulted him on the matter – also crippled his premonition to act faster.

Though they were separated physically, Sarah and Ben's sibling affection for each other never actually faded. There were frequent exchanges of envelopes and parcels of photos through the weekly diplomatic post. On top of that, there were at least bi-weekly family phone conversations. Ben momentarily felt his mother was right that his sister should have contacted him first before anybody else, the very moment she felt she was falling in love – or lust, as the mother had put it.

Ben knew how Sarah had come to the decision of staying for another six months in Sierra Leone – which had put a hold to his own turn to visit. She had told him of how she was enjoying the internship at *The True Light* newspaper: the editor was brilliant, the members of staff were professional (except for the ones she called 'the lay-bys and gossips' pretending to be reporters), and the practical part of the work was interesting. Ben knew about her ground-breaking investigative report titled 'Province of Freedom: 'White Prostitutes' were Not Prostitutes'. It had made the family proud because it had put their father's mind to rest with regards to their great-great-great-grandmother.

Ben knew Sarah had got new friends in the media in Sierra Leone. She kept telling him about her news editor, Edwina Campbell, a descendant of freed slaves who actually had her primary education at London's St. Augustine School, Forest Gate, and how they were becoming closer in and out of the job. But no hint of falling in love with anyone. Why would she go straight to their parents? What had changed? But he believed his sister always had a convincing answer. In their inevitable sibling debates, she did most times come away as winner. But Ben had always insisted that his interest was in the exchange of ideas, and not trying to win a debate.

And now, on the phone, he was still telling her how cold London was today when she decided to take the initiative.

"I know Mum has told you about my falling in love." They both burst out laughing.

"Ha ha ha, sis. I was the one who called."

"Yes, because lil brothers call big sisters for a purpose."

Another roaring laughter from both ends.

Rachael, ears all up like an antenna, heard the laughter from the living room. (Sarah had taken the receiver away to her room the moment she started talking to Ben.)

Sarah's explanation to her brother was simple and logical. They had both grown up loving each other, caring for each other, respecting each other; they had both eventually known that there would come a time when they would live independently of each other, when they could find love (she knew of Ben's newfound girlfriend, Michelle, whom their mother didn't know about) or when they would just mature and be drifted away from each other by circumstances. For her, the issue of falling in love was a very personal one that did not need any adviser. It was a matter where one would have to take full personal responsibility; one didn't have to blame its mishaps on, or credit its successes to, anyone else apart from the two parties involved. And the last thing she would want was to have issues with her loving brother.

"You know I used to tell you about the boys, even our royal cousins, making moves."

"Yes, I remember the moves by the Earl of Birmingham."

They both laughed again.

"That was because there was no feeling – or if there was some feeling, there was no falling in love. I had to prove it all by myself. I only tell you when I'm really sure."

"But you told Mum and Dad first."

"Yes, because that's the difficult part. You will always support me, Ben – or you would always trust my judgement. But even if you don't, or Mum wants you not to, trust me on this. I have made up my mind, or else I wouldn't have told them."

She ended up giving him a lesson on the history and future of multiculturalism or multiracialism – about it being a key to making the world a better place. She said both of them also had a moral duty to honour the memory of their great-great-great-grandmother, Mary Fergusson, who was married to an African in a most unlikely era in the history of mankind.

"I trust you, sis. I always wish the best for you."

Ben didn't bring up the thorniest part of their mother's complaint. Why couldn't Sarah at least have fallen in love with a white ambassador's son, or the German ambassador's son who was obviously head-over-heels for her? Ben was hearing about him for the first time from their mother. Rachael had even emphasised the issue of the maternal line of the British royal family having some German blood – though she was always bitter about Adolf Hitler. She would have been pleased with the German. Why an African? She was concerned about the manifest corruptibility of the Caucasian complexion that would forever be associated with her. She didn't hate Africans or blacks, but every race could – actually, should – keep to their lane in the racial divide while co-existing. No inter-racial relationships. Rachael therefore wanted Ben to use all of his convincing powers, backed by the soft spot that Sarah had for him, to present to his sister the disadvantages of making her children look different from all the descendants of the Queen.

But when Ben called back about twenty minutes after speaking to Sarah, it was to tell his mother that the best way forward was to allow his sister to explore and, maybe with time, reconsider her position. Sarah had returned the phone to the living room – Ben had tipped her that he was calling back to speak to their mother.

Downcast, feeling dejected and rejected, Mrs. Fergusson slept in the living room that night. Mr. Fergusson, alone and lonely in the big bedroom where the Queen had once slept, understood.

The first thing Rachael did the next morning was write in her notebook the name she had given to the parrot, the lovebird: 'April 17'. That was the day she got it from the three little boys. It was a day never to be forgotten. So she wrote below the name in her little notebook: 'The day I got a lovebird. Also the day a woodworm entered my home.'

She bought an impressively large cage for the bird from the neighbourhood Indian shop at Hill Station. And, not surprisingly, Sarah would – after being told the story – come to love 'April 17' more than everybody else.

12

Mark was also seriously concerned – emotionally interested, as every parent would be – about Sarah's falling in love. He knew his daughter very well. He studied her body language, the passion in her voice, and he knew she meant every word; he knew that it was coming from her heart (wrongly or rightly, he didn't know) about being in love.

She was in love with Amidu Stephen Tamaraneh. She pronounced his name in full in the opening remarks to her parents at Lakka Beach, but she would from then on keep calling him by his middle name, Stephen.

It was all now playing or replaying in Mark's head as he was being driven to work from Hill Station to his Spur Road offices that morning. He had, unwittingly, brought about the relationship between his daughter and Stephen.

He had always called him 'Amidu' or 'Mr. Tamaraneh' (which he found difficult to pronounce, so he would always prefer the former, except at formal occasions). He now knew what his middle name was through Sarah, and he was now calling him 'Stephen' – though Mrs Fergusson called him 'Amidu' or 'that boy' throughout the tense conversation at Lakka.

Mark knew Sarah had been a good teenager and that she was studious and serious. Her remarkable performance in her O and A levels, and the career she chose to pursue, caused Uncle Ed to strongly recommend she studied at his alma mater, Durham University – with no idea at the time how that would eventually lead to doing her final year (as recommended by Uncle Ed again) in Sierra Leone.

When he returned from work that evening, Mark came up with a plan: to engage Stephen on the matter. He wanted him, Rachael, Sarah and Stephen to meet and have a talk. But Rachael would have none of that.

"You expect me to sit with that boy to discuss our daughter?"

"Honey, let's try to manage this situation. Our daughter's emotions are involved here."

"There is nothing to manage. There are no emotions. This is mere adventurism that will scandalise this family."

"No, darling, calm down."

"I can't be calm and I can't meet him."

"Why don't we just go and listen to them?"

"You go and listen. It's your choice. It's a no-go area for me."

Rachael was trying to be tough, but she suddenly broke down, sobbing. Mark embraced her, calming her by patting her back softly-softly.

And then, with an emotionally charged and trembling low tone, she appealed, "Please, Mark, go ask him to leave our daughter alone. Ask him what he wants. We can give him a scholarship to go study in America if he wants, as long as he leaves my Sarah alone."

Mark merely said, "I'll do my best, darling." Brains charged, they slept in quietness, peacefully, that night.

* * *

Mark took two days before taking action.

When the voice of the British High Commissioner's personal assistant came through to *The True Light* telephone requesting to speak to 'Mr. Stephen Tamaraneh', the newspaper's secretary, Yainkain, was taken aback.

"We have only two Tamaranehs here, ma: Mr. Amidu Tamaraneh and his brother, Samson Tamaraneh," she tried to clarify.

"I am talking about the Editor."

"He is Amidu Tamaraneh, ma."

"We are talking about the same person."

It was that day that Yainkain knew her boss' middle initial 'S' stood for Stephen.

And Amidu was also surprised. Who was calling him Stephen apart from Sarah? Sarah had already informed him that she had told her parents about their relationship, and what their responses were. But what could have triggered a call from the British High Commission for 'Mr. Stephen Tamaraneh'?

The same Miss Caulker, High Commissioner Mark Fergusson's personal assistant, had always previously been cheerful and friendly whenever she called on behalf of her boss. Not that she was unfriendly today. She was just cold and withdrawn. The moment Amidu came on the line, Miss Caulker merely delivered a straitjacket message: "My boss would be happy to meet with you on Saturday at 8:00pm at the Lighthouse for a very informal meeting." It was more a directive than a request.

Amidu's involuntary 'Thank you' was halfway through when the line went dead. His questions remained in his stomach like a dog's dream.

He had a feeling – and it was so – that Miss Caulker made the call in the presence of the High Commissioner and just said what she was told and hung up.

***

The Lighthouse was an exquisite seaside restaurant resting on the lower belly of the estuary joining the Lumley Beach on the Sierra Leone segment of the Atlantic Ocean. It was one of the colonial legacies that started exclusively as a 'whites only' resort. The only Africans allowed there then were workers who had to carry passes or those invited, with special permits boldly hung on their necks.

After independence, the African middle class and politicians wedged their way through and overturned the 'whites only' tradition. But in actual fact, the majority of the restaurant's patrons were still white expatriates or investors, and Lebanese or Indian merchants. Its astronomically expensive menu naturally drove away the majority of Africans.

Amidu had been there before. It was a popular hub for government activities like workshops, seminars, receptions and cocktails. The Lebanese owner of the restaurant gave huge discounts for government activities in exchange for protection on many fronts. The ubiquitous presence of state security personnel as guards of the restaurant told the story in part.

***

Amidu didn't tell Sarah about his pending meeting with her father. He went as far as telling her he would be having a meeting with some chief executive that evening. He wanted to hear what the High Commissioner was going to say, and then he would know how to bring it up with Sarah. He had initially thought the father would inform his daughter, and Sarah would have brought it up with Stephen. He didn't hear anything about that from her. He realised the father would not want it known by Sarah just yet as well. It was a man-to-man issue.

***

Amidu arrived fifteen minutes to the time and was taken to a reserved room within the restaurant. Miss Caulker had called again earlier today – now her normal chatty self – giving Stephen details of what to say on arrival at the reception.

He admired the ambience of the place. He took out his signature miniature notebook and started taking notes while sipping from the water bottle he found on the table. He quickly put his pen and notebook back in his jacket pocket. He was in jeans: cotton traders' trousers and bluewash denim jacket, with a red lacoste t-shirt underneath.

Soon Mark entered the room. Amidu rose to greet him.

"Hello, Mr. High Commissioner."

"Please call me Mark," he said with a smile. He was also in jeans, with a white t-shirt, and sporting a baseball hat. "And from now on, I am calling you Stephen. It's easier." They both burst out in laughter.

"I'm honoured, sir."

"I said just call me Mark."

It was a light-hearted conversation – 'a deeply personal and honest talk', as Mark put it. The dinner was on him. It was interspersed with wine, making it more light-hearted. Mark drank more than the younger man. Stephen was merely sipping his wine at irregular intervals, listening to the issues his prospective father-in-law raised about Sarah's wellbeing, about her future.

Couldn't he say it without being tipsy? Stephen thought to himself.

Mark was going to order another bottle of wine, but Stephen politely said it was enough for him.

"Come on, this is Saturday night, Stephen."

"Sorry sir – sorry Mark – I have to go to church in the morning."

"Church? Are you religious?"

"I don't put it in my face, but I do go to church."

"I can't tell when last I was there or when next I will be."

"Did you tell your daughter about our meeting?" Stephen changed the subject back to the subject matter, with a feeling to say 'sir' or 'Mr High Commissioner' but not merely 'Mark', and ending up not using any. It was strange to him; it was un-African for a younger person to call an elder just by their first name.

"It's your duty to tell her, my dear Stephen," Mark said, gulping the last of the remaining wine in his glass.

Mark came away from that dinner believing there was reason to give Stephen and Sarah a chance to explore and test their compatibility. All he wanted was a commitment from Stephen. He didn't get it as much as he had wanted; but he was as well satisfied that Stephen kept deferring to Sarah as a special lady whom he would never hurt. He seemed sincere. Mark knew his daughter was also sincere. So Amidu's – well, Stephen's – commitment to explore without exploiting the relationship was good enough. Good enough to take away to Rachael.

13

Mark tried all he could to convince his wife that it was just a matter of time for them to know the depth of the sincerity in the relationship between Sarah and Stephen. But that was even what Rachael detested. She didn't want any 'matter of time', and she didn't want her husband to even refer to it as a 'relationship'. There was no relationship. It did not exist. It should not exist.

Though she was now calmer about it, she was not less zealous to stop it. She refused to give up – it was not in her nature – even when Ben was now apparently on her sister's side and Mark was talking about giving time to the relationship. She would still go it alone, a lone wolf out to fight for her daughter's rescue from a predator, to save a beautiful tree from a woodworm. She still had alternative methods to get that done.

Rachael's first resort was Sarah's friend, Celia, the daughter of the American ambassador. But Celia didn't have much to offer, as she said she and Sarah had not seen much of each other lately because the latter was too busy with her internship work. Celia told Rachael she knew about the relationship between Sarah and Stephen, and she didn't see anything wrong with it. Rachael didn't talk about race or racial difference, knowing the younger generation of Westerners had no clue what it was – didn't care what it was.

She pleaded with Celia to still find time to engage Sarah because she believed Stephen just wanted to use her daughter. Celia acquiesced, but on the provision that there was enough time for that. She revealed that her father had been transferred from Sierra Leone to become the American ambassador to Israel. They would relocate in a couple of weeks. Rachael, therefore, didn't find much succour in that.

She thought of contacting Uncle Ed, the Prime Minister, who had always been so influential in their family – who had, in fact, brought all this on them, according to Rachael, starting with the appointment of Mark, to convincing Sarah to come to Sierra Leone. As far as Rachael was concerned, Prime Minister Ed's personal affinity to Sierra Leone by way of birth far outweighed Mark's vague connection to a great-great-grandmother who left Britain for Freetown with freed slaves. But she knew how liberal Ed was, and matters were not helped by the fact that he was married to a British lady of Indian origins. It wouldn't have made a difference if Ed had married Maria, her Mexican university mate, who was even more anti-racist (or colour-blind, as Maria always put it).

Rachael's next option was what she called 'taking the bull by the horns'. She wanted her grandmother to be included. She wanted the Queen to know before she knew it from different quarters. Not only that. She wanted her grandmother to help.

* * *

Rachael's anxiety was not altogether misplaced, Mark had always conceded. Her concerns had some legitimacy in terms of the sociohistorical complexion of biracial relationships in Sierra Leone. Most of these relationships had ended in disarray. Rachael had enough data and stories to this effect. The continuing drastic economic conditions caused by bad leadership, war and poverty had made many Sierra Leonean young men (and women) always look for the quickest paths to survival – one of which, apparently, was to carve a relationship with some Westerner (in most cases, tourists) in order to have a way of escaping from Sierra Leone. Stories abounded as to how, say, a thirty-year-old Sierra Leonean man already married to a Sierra Leonean woman would pretend to be unmarried and get hooked to a seventy-year-old Western tourist lady just so that he could have papers to travel abroad. There was the story of one who actually used his consenting wife as bridesmaid in his wedding with a Norwegian lady. For survival.

With such stories, Mark further acknowledged, any woman in Rachael's position would fight the hardest to prevent their daughter from falling prey.

"But there is always the exception," Sarah had reminded her parents when Rachael raised the issue during their tripartite conversation at Lakka Beach.

"It's not an exception; it's a deception," the mother had stated outright.

And Mark understood. To a point! He took all into consideration. But then after meeting with Stephen, he made it clear to his wife that the best line of action was to observe the situation, while guiding Sarah where they could, if they could. She was of age. Mark had also reminded his wife that most of those involved in the sham greener-pastures marriages were uneducated and jobless. Stephen was an exception in that regard.

Mark also noted that in fact much of it was consensual: that, in many instances, love-starved or jilted past-marriage-age-in-the-West white ladies knew the reality of the situation in Africa but would turn blind eyes for a moment of bliss before life's dusk.

Rachael, in turn, understood. To a point, as well. Her husband was slowly but surely taking full responsibility of the situation. Or rather, the situation was gravitating towards his full responsibility.

He was taking the sails and following the wind. He would need his wife's full cooperation, not knowing how they would land. She agreed. She knew that any further show of outward animosity could only make matters worse. She was wise enough to know such could easily drive her daughter further into the arms of the 'waylaying Stephen'. She would cooperate.

While cooperating, she would – on her own – quietly operate her agenda. That's why she decided to seek the Queen's intervention. It should work. It was always going to be her last card – her winning card, she hoped.

* * *

It had been a while since they last spoke. But Rachael, by moving to Sierra Leone by the most unexpected of circumstances, had really brought joy to the Queen. It reignited their relationship and made the monarch relish how the wheel of fortune – or the dial of fate, as the grandmother liked calling it – was sometimes filled with humour.

The Queen's memories of Sierra Leone had been awakened. She had a soft spot for the country under the British Empire. Not only because Britain initially carved it out as a 'province of freedom' for the relocation of freed slaves, but because it was one of the last on the African continent to seek a total political break from the Empire. She was very hopeful for the country's progress at independence (even after independence, she continued as Head of State for well over two decades). There was hunger for education. And the new Prime Minister of Sierra Leone's wife was a white British lady. The Queen – or advisers acting in her name – played a role in making that relationship work. She remembered her trip to the country for the independence celebrations: the coterie of traditional dancers, the school visitations, the Governor's dinner night, and the diamond gifts.

The Queen was over the moon the day Rachael told her about having turned the guest room at Hill Station into their master bedroom.

"Your grandfather liked it more than I did," the elderly lady had said, sending her granddaughter into loud laughter. "It would interest you to note that we were in that very room during our African tour when we got the call from Buckingham Palace about the passing of my father, the King. I had to return home as his successor from that room."

"That's interesting, Grandma. No wonder I feel like a queen here," Sarah had patronisingly said, remembering what her grandmother had told her when Mark was appointed as High Commissioner to Sierra Leone.

Rachael was actually *the Queen* in Sierra Leone if what obtained at the Queen's Birthday dinner, annually hosted by the British High Commission, was anything to go by. It left no doubt in Mark and all the country's VIPs present (whether they knew the fact or not) that she was 'the royal' at the occasion. Rachael, dressed in royal apparel, read the Queen's speech, not the British High Commissioner, as was done by his predecessors – to which most guests associated 'a resurgent British quest for women empowerment'.

Since the Fergussons' arrival in Sierra Leone, there had clearly been a new royal focus on the country. Before now, ever since the 'Independence' party lost to the 'Republican' party in Sierra Leone, relations between Britain and its former colony were at best shallow. British politicians – and the Crown – were not happy with Sierra Leone's republican overzealousness after the opposition took over from the first Prime Minister's political party. The new Sierra Leonean leaders did not only throw away the British parliamentary system for an American-style presidential system, they even went to the extent of changing the vehicular traffic system from the British left- to the American right-hand drive. They were also accused of being too close to China and Russia at the height of the Cold War. They were communist sympathisers. These new politicians had even abolished the railway, uprooting the rail tracks, just to spite and get rid of the British company in charge. As a consequence, British moral and financial support to Sierra Leone waned on allegations that the new leaders were too corrupt, that sponsored projects never reached the intended beneficiaries – the people. The new Sierra Leonean politicians were heartless predators, as a British tabloid quoted Downing Street at the time.

But the taking over of Ed McInroy as British Prime Minister and the sending of Mark Fergusson as High Commissioner to Sierra Leone had completely changed the story. There was a going back to the old special relationship between Britain and her first African colony! A *Sankofa*: a retrieving of old ties.

The Queen herself did not find it necessary to visit again. She justified it. She couldn't now use the royal yacht *Britannia* that she had used several years ago to sail all the way to Sierra Leone. And she wouldn't now fly for several hours and then still take a boat or ferry or helicopter from the airport to Freetown. That was for younger royals.

And they didn't come in short supply. The heir apparent, the Prince of Britain (the Queen's eldest son), and four or five more royals had been making frequent trips to launch projects or reconnect with old ones since High Commissioner Mark Fergusson took over. The Queen Victoria Park, the Queen Elizabeth Quay, the St. George's Old People's Home, the Prince of Britain Secondary School, Leicester, Gloucester, Charlotte, Newton and Wilberforce villages (all colonial creations) got rekindled attention from the British Crown. Apart from that, the Duke, the Queen's husband, set up a special fund for the peace efforts and also directly supported Rachael's Destitute Children's Fund.

There could never have been a more British-focused attention to Sierra Leone since independence. All seemed to be going well.

But not now for Rachael. All was not going well. The Queen immediately noticed from the tremors in her granddaughter's voice on the telephone.

"What is troubling you, dear Rachael?" the experienced lady said in her usual calm and composed manner.

"It's Sarah, Grandma."

"Oh, my sweet Sarah, what has happened to her?"

Rachael was caught off-guard as to how to put it. All the words she had rehearsed on how to present the matter to her grandmother evaporated.

"She is naughty," she found herself saying.

"But you have always told me how good and well-behaved she is. She is such a blessing."

"Well, I don't think she is anymore, Grandma."

"Calm down, Rachael. What is the matter?"

Rachael was able to regain her cognitive powers and explained exactly how she had planned the presentation. The Queen was very attentive throughout. There was no single interruption until her granddaughter said, "This is the calamity she has put me in."

"What calamity?"

"I've just explained, Grandma."

"But she is of age."

"She doesn't know what she is doing, Grandma."

"But you chose Mark at a younger age than she is."

"Oh Grandma, the circumstances are different. I did not cross boundaries."

"You think so?"

"Well, I know Mark was from a working-class family, but we are of the same race."

"Oh, that?"

"Yes, Grandma. That's what people are saying."

"Does that really matter if they are in love with each other?"

"Why would she be the first to do such a thing, Grandma?"

"She is not the first, Rachael. I thought I told you before that the first Prime Minister of Sierra Leone married a white British lady," the wise elderly lady, one hundred and twenty years old and still sharp, admonished.

The Queen didn't like talking about Sierra Leone's first Prime Minister, Tuboku Metzeger. She was always very suspicious of the circumstances in which he died. That was one major, if not *the* major, reason for her personal loss of interest in the country for a while now. She had spoken to the Prime Minister the night before the third anniversary of Sierra Leone's independence (as she had still retained the title of Head of State), only to wake up in the morning to the news that he had passed away. The Queen was shocked. She hardly lent credence to rumours or superstition, but she leaned on the conspiracy theory that the Prime Minister was poisoned following a bitter struggle for power within his own party. She wrote Sierra Leone off. Until now.

"Y— yes, Grandma, but this boy is not a Prime Minister."

"Oh, dear, Mabel did not marry a Prime Minister as well. She married an ordinary man. Tuboku became Prime Minister years later."

There was some silence on Rachael's side for a while, in search of the right words and how to arrange them. "But Grandma, we are talking about the contamination of royal blood here."

"I've never known you to be passionate about royalty, Rachael," the well-versed Queen calmly replied. "Now, let me tell you, you are talking about something you don't know much about. So, let me ask you: what if you discover you have black blood in you?"

"How can that be possible, Grandma?" Rachael said, half-shocked, half-confused, by the Queen's equivocation.

"Well, that's exactly what it is."

It was now Rachael's turn to listen attentively as the Queen delved into a lecture of how her own great-grandmother was an African woman – or a black woman of African origins.

"We all have African blood through Queen Charlotte."

"What! Wow, Grandma."

"Yes; and there is a village in Freetown called Charlotte. My father named it after her. You should visit."

"I have been there, Grandma. We had a minor accident there and we got a lovebird from there." She narrated the story. Rachael's mind raced back to the day they arrived in Sierra Leone on the ferry, where Sarah had drawn her attention to the inscription, 'Charlotte, the Black Queen'.

***

Rachael could not have been more mortified after speaking to the Queen. Her cause was all but dead. Her last ally was gone to the side of Stephen and Sarah's relationship. It was now starting to look like a relationship would come out of this. But she still tried to convince herself otherwise – because, by the end of their conversation, the Queen had admonished her to "keep talking" to Sarah, particularly to prove how trustworthy Stephen was. The Queen also said Sarah might find out it was all folly – the wiser lady had actually used the word 'fun' – after returning to Britain.

Therefore, deep within her, Rachael was still not prepared to entertain this relationship. But, as things stood, she had no practical alternative. She would have to flow with the tide. Mark had told her he had got a commitment from Stephen. But what was killing Rachael inwardly was just the fact that this boy was going out with her daughter – and it was the hot topic of gossip within the diplomatic community.

There was nothing she could do about it now. The Queen had totally rejected the idea of speaking to either Mark or Sarah on the matter. Rachael was now counting how many more weeks – oh, it was still months – left for the internship to finish and for Sarah to return to Britain. But that meant Stephen and Sarah would continue to see each other every day. They were in the same office.

Rachael would bear it all; she would endure the temporary shame. Because she believed she would in the end be victorious – once Sarah was gone, she was gone forever from Stephen. Once she reached Britain, royalty would hold sway and expose her folly.

So once Rachael realised her divide-and-rule policy was now unworkable, she relapsed to that of assimilation. She suppressed her inner feelings and put on a compromising attitude. She became amiable again to Mark and courteous to Sarah. She would even ask her daughter how Stephen was faring on, though the latter never went beyond 'he's fine' or 'we are fine'. That only tortured Rachael. She never got the expected answer, like 'he's just another guy' or 'it was just a prank, Mummy' – the phrases Rachael received every time she had a dream about this so-called relationship.

It went on for a while and there was no incidence. There was peace at home. And Rachael became clearly jolly as the time for Sarah's departure drew nearer. She was now happy to see Stephen at their home. There was nothing wrong in talking to him, as long as it was a way of gently disentangling her daughter from him. It was a slow and meticulous process, removing a prey from the grip of an octopus.

Sarah was therefore a bit surprised when her mother told her to invite Stephen for a dinner she was organising at home for special friends. Sarah said her mother didn't have to do that; but Rachael insisted. The mother very well knew that even though she was hosting the dinner as a farewell for the American Ambassador's family, her daughter could boycott it and sneak away to Stephen if the latter were not invited. Sarah's absence would be a greater embarrassment; it was better to present a picture of what was already common knowledge than raise speculations of worse happenings within the family. Sarah's friend, Celia, would certainly be there, but Rachael knew that wouldn't matter much to Sarah if Stephen were absent. Rachael now knew – or thought she knew – the thought processes of her daughter, somehow. So she pre-empted her. Stephen was invited to the occasion. He and Sarah had a good laugh at the turn of events.

14

Mark noticed his wife's conciliatory steps and the atmosphere of managed peace within the home. He thought of cementing it. He came up with a plan: to invite his father, James Fergusson, to Sierra Leone, to coincide with the farewell dinner Rachael was organising for the American Ambassador's wife and family.

***

James Fergusson was a man of modest beginnings and had stayed modest virtually throughout his life. A change of fortunes or his son's change of circumstances could not erase his modesty. When he had found out the cost of the 'royal suit' Rachael bought for him for her wedding, James remarked that he would have got a better suit at a much lower price.

He had been a temperate man; his initial boyhood boisterousness tempered by his having to raise Mark up all by himself. By the time Mark reached university, James' view of life had been shaped into looking at the world with moderation, in modesty.

Once in a while, flashes of how life could have been otherwise came on James Fergusson's mind. He was a very outgoing youth brought up in the marshes of Exeter by his working-class parents. He couldn't go to university. He found a job at the town's supermarket after sixth form. He was full of youthful escapades until he met Mark's mother, Sarah. Then Mark came. Things became rough and tough when he lost his job six months later. Mark's mother almost immediately disappeared from the scene. The realities of manhood suddenly fell on and overwhelmed James Fergusson: raising a child all by yourself – as a man – was a cross that no other man should carry, he used to say when he ventured a word or two at the nearby pub after taking a pint.

If Mark's mother were around – or perhaps, even, were she only alive – things would have been different. Or if James had fallen in love again, maybe things could have taken a different turn. He tried to explore once or twice, but things did not work out. He was too preoccupied with investing his time and resources in bringing up Mark. All he wanted was for his son to be educated. He didn't want his son to be like him. He wanted his son to succeed in life. He was obsessed with this. And other women were not comfortable with that. He had made his choice. He would carry his cross alone.

By the time Mark moved out to university, James Fergusson had become immune to a life of exuberance, immersed in modesty. He did not buy new clothes for himself for many years. When he eventually realised he wanted some new ones after Mark went to university, James decided there was nobody to impress again. He would live a very private and content life for his remaining years on earth. So Mark was not much surprised when his attempt to move his father from the Exeter flat to a better apartment was rebuffed by the father.

"This is where I'll live for the rest of my life," he had told his son. "Your mother and I decided on it. It was here that you were born...Well, you were born in hospital, but this was where we lived even before you were born. And this is where I raised you up. So when I'm here, it's like I'm with my family, even in your absence," he had convinced Mark after his appointment as High Commissioner to Sierra Leone.

And now Mark knew his father would be excited about a visit to Sierra Leone. It was not altogether unexpected. James was the very source of Mark's Sierra Leone connection and passion. He was the one who told his son about their matriarch, Mary Fergusson, having been one of the white British ladies who got married to a freed slave and went on this fairytale expedition of founding a 'province of freedom' and never returned.

The original arrangement was that James and Ben would visit at the same time after Sarah had left following her graduation. But circumstances had changed. Mark had found himself in a situation. There were currents in the family.

James Fergusson could bring some moderation, some modesty, into the family, while at the same time fulfilling a reality he could only have dreamt of several years back. Ben couldn't come now while Sarah was still around – there would be no room. But James would be more than ok – it was in line with his modesty to stay in the boys' quarters, which was reasonably comfortable. Come to think of it, the boys' quarters in Sierra Leone were more exquisite than James Fergusson's Exeter flat, Mark brainstormed in a soliloquy. This was where the Queen's officials used to stay when she visited. In the colonial days, it was reserved for visiting senior officials if they chose not to stay in hotels – or if the Governor insisted. It had been serving a similar function when it became the High Commissioner's residence after independence. It was officially known as the 'senior officials' guest house', but the Sierra Leonean parlance of 'boy's quarters' had persisted and prevailed.

All that James Fergusson wanted was a reconnection with Sierra Leone. And Mark believed this was the time. Rachael thought so too. She had always had a soft spot for her father-in-law. Sarah was perhaps even more excited about the planned visit. At least they all agreed on this one thing – a strange thing in the family of recent.

And James Fergusson's two-week stay in Sierra Leone would be the most memorable adventure of his life. Perhaps it couldn't have been that memorable if he did not have a handy guide in Stephen. James' visit doused the flames and lit a torch for his granddaughter, Sarah, whom, carrying Mark's mother's name, he fondly called 'my wife'.

15

It was not only Mark Fergusson's insistence on calling him Stephen – in exceptional paternal deference to his daughter's wishes – that continued to ring in the ears of Amidu after that night. He had come away with too much to swallow at a go.

How could your girlfriend's father meet up with you to discuss your relationship with his daughter with such an open and frank approach? This was a culture shock for Amidu. Things didn't happen that way in his culture; there were layers of barriers and many rivers to cross before sitting face to face with a potential father-in-law at his hometown of Roboli. Could Amidu have fallen into a trap? Had he said too much? Could he even remember what Mark had made him commit to?

It was a confluence of thoughts. And they kept coming. Why would the High Commissioner elicit commitments from him? Why could he not elicit them from his daughter? Or why did he not get the three of them – together with Sarah – to meet?

Amidu already knew that it was just a matter of months before Sarah returned to Britain. They had already discussed it. They did not know where their relationship was taking them, they were not sure what direction it would take, but they felt between them that they were meant for each other. They had accepted the fact that Sarah would have to go and Stephen would have to stay in Sierra Leone and continue running his newspaper. Then things would work themselves out as they would.

Amidu already knew that Sarah's mother was sceptical – to say the least – about the relationship. Sarah had explained a bit to him about the Lakka Beach discussion and the subsequent maternal reactions. And for Mark to now have a direct conversation with him, to elicit commitments from him – however friendly it seemed – was bordering on the suspicious. It was a way of cleverly extricating him from Sarah. When they would be separated, distance could do the rest – an 'out of sight, out of mind' strategy by the parents, he thought.

But Mark looked very serious in insisting on calling him Stephen. What Amidu doubted – what was lacking, from his assessment – was the emotional attachment Sarah gave it, as if she had re-christened him. For the father to swiftly fall in line with the daughter's change from 'Amidu' to 'Stephen' was encouraging in the midst of the uncertainties that were flooding the editor's mind.

Unconsciously, or inadvertently, Amidu himself had now come to like the 'Stephen' name more. It gave him some air of freshness, as if he was being christened at an older age. It was now a bit confusing in the newspaper office: 'Stephen' was used by staff members when Sarah was around, but 'Amidu' was still used more often.

"What is in a name?" he had echoed his Shakespearean defence. "You can call me Amidu or Stephen, it's the same person," he told his staff colleagues at an editorial meeting, to cheers and laughter.

Back in his decrepit office, Amidu Stephen gave serious thought to the fact that there was always something new to learn in life. And there was still much more to learn in life. *We live to learn.*

***

He was named Amidu at birth for two reasons. It was his grandfather's name. In the culture of Roboli, firstborn sons were almost always given the names of their grandfathers, mostly from the paternal side. Consideration was given to the maternal side if the paternal grandfather was no longer alive. But, in some cases, men still gave their sons the names of their deceased grandfathers.

And Teacher Paul Tamaraneh and his wife, Rosemarie, had another reason for giving Amidu the name. In their tradition, the child given the name of a living grandfather would live and survive evil forces.

They had also – through the local church's custom – given their son the name Stephen. And his twin brother – who actually came unexpectedly late and was therefore a mystery to both parents and the native midwives – was christened Samson, in addition to the native name Amadu.

Amidu and Amadu were born one hour apart from each other. The Tamaraneh twins: the first to survive after three previous childbirth misfortunes for Teacher Paul and Rosemarie – three miscarriages. Their hopes were fading away until Amidu Stephen and Amadu Samson came.

16

The fame or infamy (depending on which side of the argument one took in Roboli) of the twins' grandfather, Pa Amidu Tamaraneh, was based on the story of an enterprising, outgoing, adventurous or wayward (or whatever they thought of it) young man who rejected the opportunity of being the paramount chief in his native land to go and fight in the white man's war – the Second World War.

* * *

The Tamaraneh ruling house of Roboli was almost extinct until the coming of British colonial rule. The rival Tikonko ruling house had been in control of the chiefdom's affairs ever since the immediate pre-colonial war, in which the Tamaranehs were defeated. Tikonkos had subjugated the Tamaranehs, who themselves had been in control of the chiefdom for two or more decades before their defeat in battle.

The tensions were building up again between the two ruling houses when the British Governor of the colony of Freetown extended 'protectoratism' to the hinterland, including Roboli. One of the first policies of Governor Leonard Barefoot was to ease tensions in all the chiefdoms on the issues of land and chieftaincy succession. He therefore introduced a rotational system for accession to the throne, so as to eliminate the continuing chieftaincy battles that were affecting the colony by way of trade disruptions and refugee influx. "When one ruling house knows that the other would also succeed the throne, there would be more fairness and less rancour. Vindictiveness would subside," Governor Barefoot was famously quoted to have justified the policy.

And it worked to a large extent.

***

Before the coming of the British, young Amidu – the grandfather of Amidu Stephen and Amadu Samson – was an obedient, hardworking son tending the farms and shepherding the goats and sheep of the family together with his siblings. He was the eldest son of Pa Amadu, the head of the Tamaraneh ruling house.

By the time Amidu became a teenager, he had joined five farming groups of young boys of Roboli, who came together to do rotational work on their various families' farms. The pooling of labour meant that greater work was done, resulting in greater individual yields – except for the lamentable year of the locusts, which many preferred not to talk about for fear of it repeating itself.

So Amidu was a pride not only to his parents but to the whole chiefdom due to his commitment to the farming activities that ensured families got enough produce to keep them through the rainy season.

They were busy working on their family land one day when a group of court messengers and other men suddenly arrived with one white man. They were surveying the land for the construction of a railway.

Amidu's father, Pa Amadu, was very angry. He had never heard of a railway. He did not know about a railway. He didn't even want to know about a railway. His protestations were not particularly about the railway – or whatever it was called. He was angry for the fact that, as the head of the Tamaraneh ruling house, the Tikonko paramount chief did not first inform him about it, or at least that the chiefdom court messengers were accompanying surveyors and a white man to his own farm. He could not have fought; he could not have asked his sons or the other group members working on his farm to fight. It would have been hopeless. They had heard what the white man did to Bai Bureh for resisting their rule. No one could fight the white man and win. What Pa Amadu believed was that the Tikonko paramount chief was using the white man to further exert authority over the Tamaranehs – to humiliate them and render them helpless. The old rivalry was at work all over again, even though the Tamaranehs had not overtly shown any resistance to the administration of the Tikonko paramount chief.

Amidu had watched his father reluctantly allowing the surveyors to do their work on his farm. The old man passed away a year later. But not before accepting that the railway idea was a good one. When they explained to him what it all meant, he wholeheartedly accepted it. And when work started a few months later, and manual labour was required in the construction, Pa Amadu urged his sons to work with the builders.

Pa Amadu's action was particularly buoyed by the fact that the new British District Commissioner had called the ruling houses to a meeting and informed them about the new policy of 'rotational chieftaincy'. After the Tikonko reign, it would be the Tamaranehs' turn. Pa Amadu went to his grave peacefully, knowing that the chieftaincy would come to his family – and that they wouldn't have to fight for it.

Invariably, after the old man's passing, the responsibility of steering the affairs of the Tamaraneh family rested on Amidu, the eldest son. Very soon, he would transfer most of his efforts from the farming activities to the railway construction.

On that day when his father protested and succumbed to the railway idea, he had chosen Amidu to guide the surveyors through the land. Amidu became very helpful and informative about all the surrounding lands (the boundaries, the names of trees, streams, rivers and ponds, swamps and upland) all the way to the next chiefdom. The white surveyor was impressed by such knowledge from a man who could not read or write. Though speaking through an interpreter – who obviously could not accurately interpret, but would pick a few words and pass them on to each – surveyor Bernard Fraser from the Royal Surveyors' Council expressed his liking for young Amidu.

Eventually, Fraser included this footnote in his survey report: 'the Tamaraneh family of Roboli would be useful in the field when constructing the railway'. So when the engineering work reached Roboli, Engineer Paul Hollingwood specifically asked for the Tamaranehs. That's how Amidu and his brothers came to be recruited to the railway construction work. And to be earning a shilling a day for that was great fortune for them.

While he still had interest in the farm as the eldest, Amidu gradually but firmly felt drawn more and more into the railway construction. He liked the activities: the movement of machinery, a crane moving a boulder, lengths of steel iron being fitted here and there. He wondered how human beings managed to make such things.

And, as the work continued, Engineer Hollingwood came to like Amidu's physical strength and his display of it. He would brush swathes of bushes in a relatively short time. While others showed signs of tiredness, Amidu was always enthusiastic. He became a regular railway worker; while his younger brothers were intermittent casual day labourers, putting more time into farm work.

Engineer Hollingwood felt obliged to promote Amidu to a foreman on the day they found a huge stone in the path of the proposed line of the railway. The bulldozer had broken down and Engineer Paul would have to send for mechanics to come from Freetown or from the south-east. That would take days and delay the work. Someone suggested that manual strength could get the rock out of the way. It looked an innocuous stone that would be pushed away by the combined strength of twenty strong men. But it turned out not to be a pushover. Engineer Hollingwood was going to ask everybody to wait for days until a mechanic would come, when Amidu came up with an idea.

"What about if we dig underneath the stone before pushing it over," he said through the interpreter. And it worked. Engineer Hollingwood felt mortified not to have thought of it in the first place, and immediately promoted Amidu. He was now a foreman, which meant he would be supervising his colleagues. But not only that, Amidu would have to be travelling to other parts of the country where the railway construction was going on at the same time.

It took him to other parts of the north, to the south-east, and to Freetown, the capital. He would always come back with fanciful stories of what happened where or whom he met when for his brothers, who had never travelled out of the chiefdom, just as himself a few months before.

Amidu would soon marry two wives in quick succession ('to represent me in the farm work', as he put it). The first wife, Mariama, gave birth to his first son, Paul, named after Engineer Hollingwood (who had ever since been transferred to Britain's Indian colony). He also named him Amadu, after his late father. But when he registered the child in school – adhering to the advice Engineer Hollingwood had given him – he only gave his name as Paul Tamaraneh (though they still called him Amadu at home).

So Amidu remained an itinerant husband and father, as his railway work took him from one place to the other around Sierra Leone. But one thing he always ensured was to return for a few days after receiving his monthly salary to meet his family's needs.

***

It was while he was doing supervisory work at Panguma, in the south-east of the country, that Amidu encountered Major Bartholomew Blake, head of a British military squadron. Major Blake and his men were on an excursion and they had apparently got lost in the jungles of Panguma when they bumped into these railway workers in the thickets. The handwritten map the squadron had was labyrinthine and was not taking them anywhere. Although Amidu was a total stranger in Panguma, it was always his intuition to study the terrain anywhere he worked, and he kept it as a mental record since he could not read and write. He did not only become handy to Major Blake and his men, but they thought Amidu's muscular features qualified him to be one of them. By the time he had walked them through the bushes to the main road, which was in the opposite direction of where they were heading, Major Blake made an appointment to see Amidu the next day at the town's military camp.

Speaking through an interpreter, the Major was blunt: they were enlisting and training men for the British forces, which were engaged in a big war called the Second World War. It would be good for Amidu to enlist. He had the requisite physique. The training was not hard. He should not fear, as the main job for the African recruits was supportive and not to be at the frontline of the hostilities. In addition, while he would be away or as long as he was in the Army, and even if something happened to him, the British government would take full care of his family, including paying school fees and all other educational obligations for his children up to university.

Amidu was very attentive, shuffling his feet here and there, as he sat under a tent with Major Blake. Suddenly, he heard the sounds of tramping boots, and then male voices singing:

"Go and tell my father, brothers and sisters
Go and tell my mother if she sees me no more
If I die in the battlefield
I die for the Crown
As every British soldier
Is fighting for the Crown."

The men were in rows, marching, singing. Amidu was captivated. He did not know what it all meant. But through these five or so years that he had been working on the railway construction, he had been able to learn a few English words and he was now mastering the Krio, the lingua franca spoken by many other Africans at the workplace. He might not know what the recruits were actually singing about, but he felt attracted by the symbolism that they were on a mission, that they had a noble objective. He always liked it when men came together to achieve a cause – as he used to do with the farming groups. He felt pulled to it. He felt it in his bones that this was what he wanted to do. Not the railway work anymore. He wanted to sing that song with the other men, marching in boots. He immediately gave his word to Major Blake with no compulsion, and no compunction.

But he needed to go and inform his family first that he was disengaging from the railway duties to enlist in the Royal British Army to go fight in the white man's land. Major Blake gave him two weeks. The Major also sent a telegram to the head of the Royal Railway Engineers to formally release Amidu Tamaraneh, as he was being drafted into the Royal Army. Men were needed for battle for the Crown.

It was on the third day of Amidu's farewell visit back at Roboli that the news came that paramount chief Tikonko had passed away. With the new British colonial policy of rotational chieftaincy having come into force, the leadership would now automatically go to the Tamaraneh family. And Amidu Tamaraneh, being the oldest surviving son of the family, was the obvious successor. The traditional lot fell on him. But, as per custom, it would take thirty days to go through the processes of mourning and performing ceremonial rites.

That did not dim the fact. The next morning, a group of elders had converged not only to discuss the funeral rites but the succession niceties. The elders agreed that Amidu's presence in Roboli at this particular time was a pleasant coincidence. They decided to go and formally inform him that he would be their next paramount chief.

* * *

Not that Amidu did not know. The chieftaincy succession was a possibility they had discussed ever since the new rotational law was enacted. Paramount chief Tikonko was getting old, and if Amidu lived to see the chief's demise, he was the next Tamaraneh paramount chief of Roboli. His father, Pa Amadu, knew this before he passed away. He had enjoined his son to take care of the family, with an eye on the chieftaincy. "And we are getting the crown without a fight. In that sense, the coming of the white man is a blessing. Though he killed our people at Kasse and humiliated Bai Bureh," father had said to son.

Now it had become a reality staring Amidu in the face. Just three days earlier, he had called together close members of his family and bade farewell. He had said he had found what he was looking for. Ever since he saw that group of recruits in Major Blake's camp – the way they marched and sang in symmetry – he believed he should be a soldier. He had told his family to keep it a secret until his departure, for fear of evil people working against it. Now, the death of paramount chief Tikonko was working against it.

The Roboli elders were therefore shocked when Amidu told them he had already made a pledge to join the Royal British Army to go fight in a big war in the white man's country. Some were not surprised though. They had seen the gradual drifting and eventual transformation of Amidu from a very traditional farm boy to an itinerant railway foreman. "Connecting with the white man is like tasting honey; you would always go for more. I knew from the beginning that we were losing Amidu to the white man. We have lost him," one elder later stated to the others in frustration.

That evening, Amidu called his two wives, gave them money, and explained that he just had to go away immediately. He would not sleep in Roboli tonight. He knew the elders had the potential to pile further pressure on him. But he had made up his mind. His family's needs would be met by the government. And he would be back in two years.

His immediate younger brother, Bai Kaffoir, was crowned instead.

This story of a man who ran away from the chieftaincy to go fight for the white man never died in the oral tradition of Roboli – in varied versions of fame or infamy, across the cultural divide.

***

Therefore, Teacher Paul (the father of the Tamaraneh twins, Amidu and Amadu – or Stephen and Samson, as the case might be) spent a huge chunk of his formative years, together with his siblings, without his father, Pa Amidu. But that did not diminish the fact that the Tamaraneh family was now ruling the chiefdom, and so all Tamaranehs benefited from the glamour of authority. The new paramount chief was the uncle of Paul and his siblings. But while Bai Kaffoir's own children stayed at court to learn traditions and customs, Paul and his siblings continued with the British school system in which their father had left them. Government inspectors frequently visited at home and in school to ensure everything was going on well with them, as they were on Royal British Army scholarship for the services of their father. But Pa Amidu's plan of returning in two years ended up turning into decades.

So the Tamaraneh twins – Amidu Stephen and Amadu Samson – grew up hearing lots of tales about their grandfather. The man himself told them lots of stories about his exploits in the Second World War: the battles in Burma and then in France to halt Hitler's advancing forces, his near-death experiences, how he thought he would never return; and then he told them the jolly stories in-between about how a white woman he met after the War didn't want him to return. "But I told her I already had two wives. She immediately ran away," Pa Amidu would narrate to the twins. "And if I had married her, I wouldn't have seen these lovely faces of my grand-twins." They would all burst out into laughter.

And Stephen and Samson believed that their grandfather made the right decision to fight in the Second World War. They grew up defending or propagating his patriotism and gallantry, especially with those medals of valour awarded to him for bravery. The Tamaraneh twins believed forgoing the chieftaincy was worth it.

"Ten chances to one, we wouldn't have gone to school if he did not make that crucial decision," Amidu once said to his twin brother.

"I am one hundred percent sure of that," Amadu mathematically responded.

They relished the fact that their grandfather's actions unshackled them from what seemed like a regimental obsession for the chieftaincy. "Let those who have taken it, take it. All sides are happy."

Maybe they would have appreciated their grandfather more if he had told them another reason for rejecting the chieftaincy. His own mother, Ya Dukor, had told him secrets about the chieftaincy, including that a paramount chief was usually pushed to his death by the sub-chiefs the moment he became seriously ill; that he would be decapitated immediately; and that being a paramount chief would mean that when she died he would not be allowed, as per custom, to be at her funeral. This had repulsed grandfather Amidu when he was still just a boy – and he had vowed never to become a paramount chief. What he was not sure of, when reflecting on the issue in his twilight years, was whether he could have been able to resist the Roboli elders' entreaties to become paramount chief if the railway had not passed through the Tamaraneh farm. As far as he was concerned, the spirits of the ancestors never wanted him to be paramount chief. And he was grateful for how it turned out.

17

Grandpa Amidu went to his grave not even telling this secret to his much-loved son, Teacher Paul. He believed actions spoke louder than voice.

He had returned to Sierra Leone much later than he had ever expected. The two years ended up being decades. It happened that the War took longer and was more destructive than anybody on either side had ever anticipated. Hitler had expected a quick run over Europe; the British had expected a swift robust victory. Neither happened. It became long-drawn-out. So the recruits had to be moved around.

From Sierra Leone, Grandpa Amidu's batch was first taken to Burma, and then to France. When the War eventually ended, he was among those demobilised to Jamaica. While waiting to be repatriated back to Sierra Leone, the British needed manual labour to rebuild London's battered infrastructure due to the German blitz. Amidu was one of those chosen to go in what became known as the 'Windrush programme'. He spent decades in London working in construction before finally returning to Sierra Leone.

One thing he was always thankful about was that his children had made good use of the education scholarship provided by the

Royal Army. Grandpa Amidu never stopped thanking Engineer Paul Hollingwood, 'the railway man', especially for his namesake, who had gone on to study at St. Augustine's College and had become a schoolteacher – the famous Teacher Paul.

And Teacher Paul had also endorsed his father's path when he broke tradition to marry a woman from the south-east. This automatically debarred him from the chieftaincy. As per custom, a man of Roboli would only be crowned a paramount chief if he was married to a woman from Roboli. Teacher Paul followed his heart at St. Augustine's College when he met Rosemarie from Tongo. It irked the Roboli elders, but Pa Amidu defended his son's decision. "I'm happy with my son's marriage. If it's palm kernel oil, then it should be truly black. Not half-black," he had relapsed in local adage to tell the critics that there was no turning back in the perceived rebellion of his family. They had decided to embrace 'the foreign'. And there was no half-way to it.

* * *

When Rosemarie started having miscarriage after miscarriage, the Roboli community was of the firm belief that the ancestral spirits' patience had been pushed to the limits, so they were angry and therefore punishing Teacher Paul. The elders came forward with suggestions of offering sacrifices to appease the forefathers. Teacher Paul stood his ground that he would not go back to 'primitive behaviour'.

"I am a schoolteacher. I am a model of enlightenment. What lesson would I be teaching my students? I will get a child when the right time comes," he had fended off the approaches.

Rosemarie had agreed with her husband. But she was a worried woman. She could not endure the taunting eyes every time she passed by, especially at the market. She believed people were always talking about her inability to have a living child. It had already happened three times. Time was going – and it waited for no woman. She was seen as 'this foreigner who has brought bad luck to the Tamaranehs'.

They had been married for five years. It became worrisome. She poured out her soul to her loyal friend at Roboli – her next-door neighbour, Mary, the local pastor's wife. Mary was a middle-aged woman and was many years older than Rosemarie. She had taken the younger woman as an adopted daughter and confidante since they had first known each other. Mary was perhaps, together with her husband, the only other person who openly supported and defended Rosemarie's marriage to Paul, apart from Grandpa Amidu. She had played a big role in organising the wedding.

* * *

Teacher Paul was never really happy about the close relationship between his wife and the pastor's wife. He was totally opposed to the influence of 'the white man's religion'. He was educated enough to know that religion was 'merely the opium of the masses'. He didn't want his wife to be drawn into it. But her constant recourse to this lady for solace or whatever was becoming a concern – he called it 'a nuisance'. As far as he was concerned, they did not need any external force, native or foreign, for them to have a child. It would be a natural biological occurrence.

Rosemarie herself went to Roman Catholic primary and secondary schools in the south-east before proceeding to St. Augustine's in the north, the only Catholic college in the country then. Back in school, she used to attend mass as a perfunctory – actually, compulsory – rite. When she came to St. Augustine's, she believed the duty was over and never attended mass again. It was here that she met Paul Amadu Tamaraneh (he had officially added the middle name of his own volition in secondary school), a very philosophical student who had attended government primary and secondary schools on the sole premise that 'learning is better than silver and gold'! Paul had gone to St. Augustine's purely in search of this learning without any regard as to whether the institution was run by a religious order or not. For him, all white men – be they British or German or American or whatever, administrators or missionaries – were the same: 'Colonialists or neo-colonialists or pseudo-colonialists: all exploiters, never explorers or genuine lovers of Africans.' He would always leave a caveat for white men like his namesake, Engineer Paul Hollingwood, who 'possibly are not real white men'.

"They came to our land and asked our people to close their eyes in prayer. By the time our people opened their eyes, the gold and diamonds had been stolen," Paul always mocked. "Institutions like St. Augustine's College were built from the change of the loot." That was how Teacher Paul came to be known among his peers as 'the free thinker'. He was neither in support of his Roboli traditions ("warped beliefs in ancestral spirits, instead of following modern medical approaches and science," he would say) nor an admirer of the white man's religion "which is manipulating the minds of the ignorant". He believed in education ("the one and only good thing the white man reluctantly brought along"). This was what he believed Engineer Paul Hollingwood had told his father, Pa Amidu; and this was what his father had passed on to him.

In their marital home, there was a big domestic dispute when Teacher Paul returned home one day and found out that Rosemarie had gone with the pastor's wife to a 'crusade'. The word itself brought avid revulsion from Teacher Paul. He knew what crusades were in history. He knew the details of 'the horrific part' of their history. He loathed crusades. His wife's protestations that the crusades – the ones in his history books and the one she attended – had different meanings never convinced Teacher Paul.

As far as he was concerned, the pastor's wife was indoctrinating his wife with the 'opium'. Pastors' wives were not the happiest of women, but they tried to make the happiest of other women. With their husbands busy with 'the flock', the wives tended to adopt this role of overseer of other women, especially the troubled. So if these other women were looking for consolation ('the opium'), they found it in the pastors' wives. At least that was how Rosemarie saw Mary, the Roboli pastor's wife.

Rosemarie then rationalised an opium defence, as she calmly and respectfully responded to her husband: "Yes, in fact it is the opium of the masses. Their leaders and politicians have failed them. It's the only message that gives them hope that all is not lost." And then she had appealed, "I think there's something special there that makes me want to go for more. I can feel it in me, Paul. Please understand."

She had felt more and more interested in the message of Mary and her husband and in their meetings. She explained that it was much more than the mechanical masses she used to attend in her school days. This was about a story she had never before heard, told in such a convincing way. She could feel some peace even in her nothingness. Teacher Paul himself started noticing some differences: Rosemarie showed less distress, less stress, as her face was glowing again as it was when they first met at St. Augustine's College.

Teacher Paul had resisted all pressures from family and friends to take another wife since it was apparent that Rosemarie would not have – could not keep – a child. But for him, having one wife was purely an economically sound decision, and not about any religious belief. So he had rebuffed all by saying that even if Rosemarie would not have a child, he was also prepared to remain childless. "There are lots of kids roaming around Roboli to adopt, if worse comes to worst," he had insisted. After all, he was happy about the great help his wife had brought to the other women of Roboli. Rosemarie had studied agriculture at St. Augustine's, and she only taught for a year in the same school as her husband's before she decided to form a farming cooperative with the Roboli women, combined with her duties as a housewife.

It took a great deal of time and effort for Rosemarie to get her husband to accept that she had found respite for her troubled mind. Paul seemed to have been convinced by his wife's differentiation of the 'crusades' afterall. She had argued that the crusades Paul was talking about were carried out by the Catholic Church and Mary's crusades were Protestant. "It is just prayer, Paul, it is just prayers. It shouldn't hurt you," she appealed to his senses – or his sensibilities. "It just makes me feel part and parcel of a community. I don't mind if I have no child, as long as you love me. Please, Paul, let me continue with Sister Mary's church."

Teacher Paul relented, before his wife wore him out.

* * *

It could have just been a 'natural coincidence', as the husband put it – or it could really have been 'a miracle', as the wife insisted – but it was following Paul's consent that the twins came, and stayed.

Just after a month, Rosemarie reported that she had missed her monthly cycle. The anxiety started all over again. All the previous miscarriages occurred within the first three-month period. When the third month had passed this time, the pregnancy was still there. Teacher Paul was excited. Rosemarie's 'crusades' continued unabated.

Soon the bump on her stomach started showing. And the Roboli rumour machine went into operation: Rosemarie could be pretending, she could be doing a cover-up; or, if it was there, it would end up just as the previous ones.

Sixth month. Seventh. Eighth. Ninth. This pregnancy was now for real.

* * *

The Roboli maternity centre was nothing but a polished mud house for traditional childbearing, for the women who ever bothered to come there. There was one nurse posted by the government to supervise seven of the same centres across the chiefdom. The real staff members were volunteer traditional birth attendants. They basically manually assisted pregnant women through the labour pangs. But the majority of the women in Roboli gave birth – indeed, preferred to give birth – at home.

* * *

Teacher Paul had always advocated that it was better for the Roboli women to give birth at the maternity centre than at home. He knew there was not much of a difference between the two in terms of service, but he said the fact that the maternity centre had a book where the date of birth was recorded was good enough. "This idea of telling people that they were born when such and such a farm was being cultivated or when such and such a chief was crowned or dethroned is archaic and untenable. How can a man like me keep guessing my age all my life? None of my children or those under my care will ever be subjected to such an anomaly," Teacher Paul had told a gathering of the parent-teacher association when he was now confident enough that his wife's pregnancy was for real.

He had been very supportive and more homely of late, especially since the pregnancy entered its seventh month. He would make frequent checks from the school to the house, back and forth, the two not far from each other. And he had noticeably stopped hanging out with friends at the Roboli roundabout, where they drank palm wine in the evening, 'in order to be near my lovely wife'.

And that evening of the ninth month when Rosemarie started complaining of belly aches, Teacher Paul said they should immediately go to the maternity centre. Thankfully, the roving nurse, Sento, was around. Two of the native midwives were also present. They had just helped in the delivery of two other babies. The moment Teacher Paul arrived, the focus turned on him. They knew how forthright he could be. But the women really liked Rosemarie, even though she was a 'foreigner'. They had been in sympathy with her for having been the butt of jokes, and now they were genuinely happy for her, hoping it would be for good this time. Besides, Rosemarie had tremendously helped the Roboli women in general in acquiring new agricultural skills. Through the cooperative, she had been able to secure the supply of farming implements, seeds and fertiliser, distributed to the women by the Catholic Relief Services. Rosemarie was actually loved, especially by the older women.

***

Teacher Paul had been pacing up and down the veranda of the maternity centre for about two hours – nervous, anxious, biting his nails, placing his hands on his head – when the nurse came out to tell him his wife had given birth to a baby boy. He raised a clenched fist in the air and said, "Thank God." He was himself surprised by his words, for he never associated human happenings with God. Not that he didn't believe in the existence of God, whom he preferred to call 'the Supreme Being'; he only detested the way men had made Him to be. "He does not interfere with or in our affairs. And we don't have to go about praying and praying and praying to Him. We are masters of our own fate," Teacher Paul would argue. But now he was saying 'Thank God' after hearing about being a father. Presently, he was surprised, if not a little bit disappointed, at himself for the pronouncement, which the nurse obviously heard.

Witihin minutes, they were discharged to go home. The news

had spread like wildfire in Roboli. By the time they arrived home, there were crowds waiting in the compound – fellow teachers, cooperative women and busybodies. All were congratulating Mr. and Mrs. Tamaraneh. They had barely entered the house when Rosemarie again complained of belly aches. They thought it was just postnatal pains. But Rosemarie started groaning. Teacher Paul rushed back to the maternity centre to inform the nurse and the midwives. They were taken aback. Nurse Sento decided to come and see for herself.

The experienced nurse discovered that Rosemarie was actually in labour again. The midwives were sent for again. There would be no time to take Rosemarie back to the maternity centre. The second child was born at home, about an hour or so after the first.

This was how the famous Tamaraneh twins, Amidu and Amadu (whom Rosemarie asked her husband, through Sister Mary's advice, to also name Stephen and Samson), were born.

And, suddenly, the good news had turned to bad news. Teacher Paul and Rosemarie had only succeeded in plunging themselves into a new scandal. In Roboli, twins were regarded as an abomination – they brought bad luck to a community. Women loathed bearing twins because they were prone to return to where they came from as soon as possible; they would die on their own if they were not gotten rid of immediately (and the elders of Roboli preferred the latter to avoid the wrath of the ancestral spirits). Nobody could remember any woman in Roboli that had ever bore twins and kept them alive. They all passed away – or were passed off – within days, after laborious ceremonial rituals. The general belief was that twins were sent by the ancestral spirits to look around the real world and return to report back to where they came from. They were spies and never meant to stay on Earth for long. Rosemarie had got a new scandal. Her status could have been better if she had not bore a child at all. But Teacher Paul vehemently rebuffed all 'primitive entreaties' from the Roboli elders to get rid of the new entrants.

***

Despite the scepticism and criticisms of the Roboli people, Teacher Paul had a strong belief that the twins were here to stay. He continued to condemn the primitive thinking about twins, saying that possibly many women had themselves passed off their twins for fear of the scandal. He and Rosemarie shared this belief. Their only consistent allies in this were Sister Mary and her husband. Teacher Paul couldn't help but succumb and acquiesce to Mary's comings and goings, offering prayers here and there – though he always excused himself from such prayers.

But Teacher Paul's strongest supporter had always been his father, the-over-the-moon-for-seeing-my-grandchildren Grandpa Amidu. He was a much more reticent man ever since he returned home from the War and Windrush (he pronounced it as one – *war-and-windrush*). He spoke very little and was reluctant to take part in any cultural activities, even when his younger brother, Bai Kaffoir, was now paramount chief of Roboli. He had always defended his son marrying a 'foreign woman'. Grandpa Amidu was always grateful to the people of the south-east for their hospitality when he was working for the railway, and for the fact that he met Major Blake there, leading to his conscription to the Royal British Army. He called the coming of the twins the icing on the cake. He told those who cared to listen that he had seen many sets of twins in Burma, in France, in Jamaica, and in Britain. "We even had twins in our platoon in India," he told the Roboli elders.

When the Tamaraneh twins were old enough to start schooling, Teacher Paul got them admitted. The elders told him it was a waste of time and money, as the twins would soon return to where they came from. Teacher Paul didn't listen to them. "My boys are here to stay," he had insisted, not really knowing where he was getting his confidence from, apart from his own father's practical experience, which he did not doubt.

And when the boys entered their teenage years and went on to secondary school, Teacher Paul's air of confidence could not be more profound. Roboli was confounded.

* * *

Teacher Paul and Rosemarie had long before decided on which name to give to their first child. There was no way of knowing whether it would be male or female. They agreed that if it were a boy, it would be Teacher Paul's father, Amidu; if it were a girl, it would be Rosemarie's mother, Safula – who was still alive. Teacher Paul's mother had passed away a year after Pa Amidu returned from the *war-and-windrush*.

Teacher Paul called it 'a mere coincidence with the dictates of tradition' in giving the name of his living father to his child. It was out of filial gratitude, not societal platitude. But inwardly, and in his discussions with Rosemarie, there was a tacit acquiescence to the belief that giving the name of a living parent to a child would help it survive.

So it was easy for Teacher Paul to give the name Amidu to Nurse Sento for the births records book. But when a second son came later, Teacher Paul was taken off-guard. He was never prepared for this. When Nurse Sento asked him which name to enter in the book for the second son, he just instinctively, if offhandedly, replied, "Amadu, for my grandfather; and it's also my other name." The pastor's wife was ever-present. Rosemarie consulted her again, as in the first instance at the maternity centre where they had given a second name for the first child – Stephen. For the unexpected second child, the pastor's wife recommended Samson. Therefore, in the register at the Roboli maternity centre (which would, however, later be burnt down to ashes by rebels during Sierra Leone's own war), the twins' names were written as Amidu Stephen Tamaraneh and Amadu Samson Tamaraneh.

In the first few months, it was easy to distinguish one from the other – Amidu was big, Amadu was small. But before long, there was a catching up in physique. After one year, they had become so identical that one was easily mistaken for the other. And when they grew up being almost inseparable, doing things together, dressing alike – and when you saw one, you were sure to see the other – their friends gave them the nickname 'AST Square'.

To reduce the confusion, midway in secondary school, the one decided to interchange his name to Samson Amadu Tamaraneh. So he became SAT. No more 'AST Square'. It helped a little bit. They entered Mount Aureol University the same year – Amidu studied Journalism, Amadu studied Accountancy. A few years after graduation, they had found employment in *The True Light* newspaper. Amidu would soon become the Editor; and Amadu, the Chief Accountant. On the staff list of the newspaper, their names were written as 'Amidu S. Tamaraneh – Editor' and 'Samson A. Tamaraneh – Chief Accountant'. It was nicknamed 'The Tamaraneh Paper', or 'the newspaper of the lookalike twins'.

Even Sarah Fergusson, the British High Commissioner's daughter, during her internship at *The True Light*, at first found it difficult to differentiate between the twins. But she would soon find a distinguishable feature – from the depths of love. And she sealed it by insisting on calling her boyfriend by his middle name, Stephen.

Sarah did not try to change the sequence in initials. But she preferred calling her boyfriend Stephen. It was her choice, her decision. And her father, Mark Fergusson, had also joined in calling him Stephen. The members of staff at *The True Light* came to terms with the new reality. And Stephen himself was adjusting to it – until he was taken off the scene.

* * *

And now, back in North London, Sarah's intense conversation with her mother had just instantly evoked deep emotions about Stephen. She found it hard to accept that he had been killed in the war in Sierra Leone. But her father had come with more newspapers as confirmation. She had to accept reality. Her father was presently meeting with Uncle Ed the Prime Minister to discuss their relocation to Mexico. Her mother had for the past few hours been telling her – had virtually convinced her – that it was time to move on without Stephen. That it would even be very helpful for Joel; that the little boy didn't deserve to be condemned to a life of sorrow and melancholy.

"It's time to move on, Sarah, it's time to move on." The mother had rubbed it in, with the certainty that her daughter no longer had a justification to continue in mourning.

18

That was how it was on that day in the Fergussons' North London mansion's living room. Mother and daughter ended up having something to look forward to together – a family dinner tonight at the Ritz Hotel. A table for four: Mark, Rachael, Sarah, and Ben; and a crib for the fifth, Joel.

Presently, Rachael and Sarah were waiting for Mark to return from the Prime Minister's office with the confirmation of their imminent transfer to the UK embassy in Mexico City. Rachael now planned to immediately make a phone call to Maria and break the news. Their university days came rolling back. Ed would finally be vindicated in Maria's eyes. If Ed had married her, he probably wouldn't have been Prime Minister today. Therefore, Mark also wouldn't have been Ambassador. And so these nostalgic expectations wouldn't have arisen. If Rachael was spoilt like a queen in Sierra Leone, she believed she was going to be spoilt more in Mexico with Maria around.

Rachael was almost lost in these thoughts when she was jolted back by Sarah saying, "Thank you, Mum."

"Oh no, darling, it's you that I should thank." Rachael came back fully to the present.

Sarah wanted to be nice and leave her mother in good spirits, in a spirit of reconciliation. She therefore replied in a soft tone, "Maybe you were right after all, Mum. Maybe I made a mistake, maybe I should move on. But trust me, Mum, Stephen was a good person. He loved his country. He loved me. There'll always be a place for him in my heart."

"Not only in your heart. There'll always be our Joel. So there's no mistake," Rachael aligned the conversation to suit her daughter as she gently handed the little boy to his mother. Sarah then told her mother that she would like to go for a walk with Joel.

As Sarah took the stairs to her room to change her clothes – from black to black – Rachael raised a clenched fist in the air. In triumph.

* * *

Sarah still had someone to consult though.

Whenever she wanted to talk to Andrew Decker, she would go for a walk to the nearby park with Joel. Those were her rare moments of going out – apart from the now-rarer moments of Sarah walking around the compound with April 17, as she talked to the lovebird, or tried to teach it how to talk. The walk to the park was more frequent these days. And Rachael had always liked that. It was by itself a sign of her daughter trying to move on. Though, for Sarah, this walk would always end in the neighbourhood telephone booth on Sunfield Road, to call the vicar.

* * *

The Fergussons – as Mark had confessed to Stephen in their discussions – were not a religious family. They were Anglicans by name, and perchance by tradition.

Mark had told Stephen About his connection to the Church of England (they had laughed over the editorial on Anglican priest Olumendi Metzeger). He had explained that virtually all British ('particularly Caucasian') people were Anglicans because the Church of England was a state institution. The Queen was both Head of State and Head of Church (facts Stephen already knew). "Once you carry Her Majesty's passport, you are directly or indirectly an Anglican, whether you recognise that or not, whether you like it or not. We all sing 'God save the Queen'."

Mark was baptised as a child, went to church for school-related programmes, but never went when he was at university until the time for his wedding with Rachael. Since then, he only went to church for other weddings or funerals, or when the royals were obliged to attend Westminster Abbey services to remember war heroes and the war victims, when Rachael was invited as a royal or royal-relative and he had to accompany her. And that was Rachael's way of life as well, except she was more prone to mention God in her conversations with her children. She said there might have been some exaggerations by some men, but there must be a God somewhere. However, she would not impose Him on her children. "The universe is too good to be an accident," was the farthest she could go in defence of God.

So the Fergussons raised their children on a philosophy of free choice, freedom, democracy, divergent ideas. Sarah and Ben were baptised as children just as their parents. And they followed the routine of their parents, as it were. Hence, Sarah was not religious at all. She had followed Stephen to church once or twice in Sierra Leone because he loved it – and, to her, church in Sierra Leone was also a social gathering for many people, being the only place they could meet with friends and family. But she could not keep pace, though she was not against Stephen going on his own – because that's how his mother had trained him and his twin brother, he had told her. Even when they had gone out on a Saturday night, the twins did their best to be in church on Sunday. They always had something to do there, either read the scripture or teach a Sunday school lesson, or the Pastor had given an assignment here and there. Sarah would use the time to listen to the latest R&B music. She and Stephen had had discussions on religion, starting from their editorial palaver, and she had heard him speak at times with passion and some devotion. She had half-heartedly listened, at times looking away. But she had kept some questions in her heart.

Only when back in London did she feel like asking him all the questions. He was not here now to answer. But there was Vicar Andrew Decker, she remembered. He needed to answer these questions.

***

Andrew Decker was the vicar who officiated the wedding of Mark and Rachael at St. Stephen's Chapel, Oxford. He was one of the royal vicars. That is, one of those vicars specially chosen by the Church of England to handle affairs of the royal family. They could be called upon at any time by the Archbishop of Canterbury to step to the plate whenever the royals needed them. Though Rachael's wedding to Mark was largely boycotted by the royal family (except her parents), it was her royal right to get one of the royal vicars to officiate at her wedding. It was the Queen herself who had recommended Andrew Decker.

Many years later, Decker, as vicar of Westminster Abbey, chose Mark and Rachael's daughter, Sarah, to read scripture on Remembrance Day. As a teenager then, Sarah had taken it as one of those perfunctory royal duties that were always assigned to a royal here or there. It was only now that she had returned to Britain from Sierra Leone, followed by Stephen's reported death, did she start to have the feeling that those words she had read on Remembrance Day resonated with some of the words that Stephen had said to her, for which she now needed answers. Andrew Decker was also the man she had consulted from Sierra

Leone through her father with regards to the editorial allegations against the Church of England in *The True Light*, to which she had taken great exception. She remembered he had added words of encouragement in the diplomatic dispatch.

Weeks after she, her mother and Joel were evacuated back to Britain, Vicar Andrew Decker actually visited – a visit that pleasantly surprised Sarah for its sheer coincidence just at the time when the questions were uppermost on her mind. On his part, Decker was doing the visitation as a pastoral function, both as the wedding vicar (and therefore obliged to offer counselling) and for the fact that the Fergussons were actually employees of Her Majesty's Government – as every government in Britain, no matter of which political party, was Her Majesty's Government. (Mark had once called it 'the royal misnomer of being Government and Opposition at the same time at all times'.)

It was while Rachael was in the kitchen preparing tea for the visitor that Sarah asked for his number, as she wanted to speak to him in confidence. The vicar acquiesced. He quickly wrote it down (he always had a pen and paper in his little 'armpit handbag'). He told her to contact him at any time. Collect call.

That was how Andrew Decker became Sarah's confidant. The Sunfield Road telephone booth had never known a more heart-pouring caller. She would tuck Joel on one hand – to be interchanging him from left to right and vice versa – while holding the receiver with the other. She poured her heart out. She told him her story – her stories about Sierra Leone, about Stephen, about Joel. She asked him whether the scripture he had asked her to read several years ago was true, whether he believed the words were true, whether this idea of the existence of God was not a made-up story; and she asked him why a man who loved this God would be killed in a senseless war just like that, leaving her in mourning and their son behind.

Andrew Decker had always found words of comfort for Sarah.

He was methodical, this old-time-religion priest. He was sure of God's existence; if not, he would have left 'this dull job of being a vicar' (which had caused muted laughter at her end – if only briefly). "But it is satisfying, even if through just listening to someone like you tell me a story I would never have heard at all. The words you read at Westminster Abbey are always true."

Sarah was not totally convinced, but she felt somehow pacified. Having someone to open up to, even if they were not answering your questions satisfactorily, was in itself a therapy. She felt drawn to him. She had found a Friar Lawrence in this of her own Romeo and Juliet tragedy. He was her escape route to some sort of reality. Sarah had once or twice thought of suicide – to go and meet Stephen wherever he would be in the beyond. But she had thought of Joel. Romeo and Juliet had no Joel, and her own Friar Lawrence had come after the relationship had ended – or had been ended. There was no way the priest would show her where to locate her Romeo. But he could probably help her find a way out of this psychological web.

And, after listening to her narration, one question he had asked that made her want to continue to speak to him was whether, deep within her, she believed Stephen was dead. She had immediately said 'no'. She had no reason for it, and then had added, "I'm not sure. I don't know." But that was how she felt, even if everybody else knew otherwise – what her mother had called 'a deliberate refusal to accept reality'.

It was in one of those conversations that Vicar Andrew had come up with an idea: for Sarah to give him the details of Stephen's family and hometown in Sierra Leone so that he could make alternative enquiries. Because, despite the military junta being in control in Sierra Leone, there was still a small contingent of British soldiers based there. They had been there for over a decade, both as a sub-regional base and to help train the Sierra Leone military. But they were trainers, and did not interfere in the internal affairs of Sierra Leone. However, as expected, the soldiers did frequently communicate with London from Sierra Leone. The Anglican Church was accorded the facility to transmit messages to Freetown for the Anglican clergy there via the British military. If he therefore had Stephen's details, he could ask for a favour from the British forces in Sierra Leone to cross-check with his family. Vicar Andrew had a good relationship with the British Army HQ in London, as the military also fell within the purview of the royal vicars. They were Her Majesty's Armed Forces. The top hierarchy knew Vicar Andrew well. Sarah was grateful and expectant.

Unfortunately, a report had eventually come back stating that all the people of Roboli had gone into the bushes at the height of the war. So Stephen's family could not be traced. Sarah was mourning over the dashing of this last hope when her father arrived in London and confirmed everything with the newspapers he had brought along – with Stephen's photo splashed on some of the front pages. Some had him and his twin brother. She mourned more.

But now, today, she had reconciled with her mother and had been convinced about moving on. She just felt obliged to tell Friar Lawrence – oops, Vicar Andrew – about this. He ended up telling her: "It is well with your soul."

***

When Sarah returned home from making the call, it was still only her mother in the house. Her father had obviously taken longer than expected. It was supposed to be a two-hours-at-most meeting. She had barely finished exchanging courtesies with her mother when Mark's car entered the compound.

The two ladies were excited and both rushed to the door with broad smiles. Interestingly, Ben was with his father. He must have picked him up from university to fast-track the celebrations,

Rachael thought – though the dinner was planned for the evening and Ben was supposed to be back home an hour before leaving the house. Ben alighted first, immediately followed by Mark. Surprisingly, there was no smile on either's face. What could it be?

Rachael read their body language but was not sure. Sarah was engrossed with playing with Joel in her arms, telling him, "Grandpa is here. Grandpa is here!"

***

Prime Minister Ed McInroy had accorded his friend the rare privilege of using the back door to leave Number 10 Downing Street. Mark was now not his normal self. He didn't want his present demeanour to be captured by those prying photographers waiting outside the Prime Minister's office. When his face would appear in the newspapers, let it not be this one in this present mood. He would choose not to answer their questions, but he wouldn't stop their cameras from clicking. They already had his picture when entering, may they never have one when exiting now. He had asked his friend for the favour – even if it was the last. And Ed had laconically retorted, "What are friends for?"

Everything was hazy: how the Prime Minister pressed the buzzer and an officer came in, got the instructions and escorted Mark through the back door. What was now vivid to Mark, though, was that he was being driven away from Number 10 for the last time. He wondered how to put it to Rachael. But he had the presence of mind to call his son first. He called the students' line of the university to say he was coming to pick Ben up. "I am calling from my car phone, and will be there in fifteen minutes," he had peremptorily stated. He felt it was better to inform Ben first, and then he would have an ally in confronting Rachael and Sarah with the news.

And, certainly so, Ben took it as a man, Mark thought. His

son's first response was, "These things happen, Dad. It's not new."

But it was a different matter altogether when Rachael and Sarah and Joel were now in front of them.

"Is everything ok, darling?" Rachael promptly asked as she met her husband halfway from the car.

"Yes," he offhandedly said. Ben just went to basics as he took Joel from Sarah's hands. And Mark told Rachael, "Let's go in and talk", holding hands.

But Sarah, not seeing what Rachael had seen, wanted to confirm what her mother had told her. The moment they entered the house, she quickly asked: "Dad, what time is the dinner at the Ritz?" Rachael tried to make some eye contact with her daughter because it was obvious that something was amiss.

Mark had no option but to answer, "I think we should cancel it, my dear."

Now Rachael quickly waded in. "What has happened, Mark?"

"It's a long story. I am not going back to Liberia." Everybody else was now silent, just looking at Mark as he slumped into his favourite corner of the living room settee.

"Ben, Sarah, would you please leave me and your dad at the moment?"

"No, let them stay. Ben already knows."

When Mark retold the story of how he had not only lost his job, but he was now the subject of a parliamentary sub-committee investigation for an 'illegal arms to Africa' deal, they all knew they had been plunged into turmoil.

He was going to be in the news for all the wrong reasons.

"That's why Ed called me back urgently."

"What is this, Mark? I can't understand. I don't understand. What is this, Mark? Is it a wild joke?" Rachael couldn't help herself. Sarah stood there transfixed, not making sense of anything.

Mark did not answer her questions. "Look. You all promise to trust me? I am asking you all to trust me. I am totally innocent and

I'll fight for my name. I'll fight for my family's name."

"But did you not tell this to Ed?" Rachael continued.

"I told him."

"Did he not believe you?"

"He said he did. But I have to prove it to the committee."

"But why is he sacking you then?"

"That's the protocol. He says I have to clear my name."

"Oh no. What are friends for?" Rachael echoed. But it was Ed's voice – those same words in Number 10 – that Mark heard. He just immediately stood up, left them all in the living room and went to their bedroom.

Book Two

Father and Daughter

"...the snare has been broken, and we have escaped..."

19

Perhaps the news shocked President Kargbo Ndomahina more than it did Mark. It was just that Mark received it in person – face to face, raw; he was a casualty of friendly fire. And also the President had a fallback position: the parallel plan with his colleague Head of State in Nigeria, Mallam Musa Odofo.

* * *

When Mark Fergusson had left his family downstairs, there was only one thing on his mind: to call and inform President Ndomahina.

Maybe the security officer permanently stationed at the front door of the President's office heard the shouting and thumping of the table by the President. Maybe not: because there were loud noises still coming from remnants of the revelling demonstrators in the waiting room. And, as Sierra Leoneans liked talking over each other in high-pitched voices and yet were able to continue in conversation, Sergeant Brima Thullah at times followed topics being discussed. That very moment – when President Ndomahina shouted after Mark broke the news – the lead organiser of the

Monrovia demonstration, party scribe Prince Bullet, was loudly boasting about how the large turnout of demonstrators had sent a clear message to the British government that the people wanted a military intervention in Sierra Leone now. So Sergeant Thullah was listening to that at just about the time his boss, the President, hit the table and shouted inside. If Sergeant Thullah heard the sound, he didn't show it – at least the secretary, Adama Saccoh (who had served the President from Sierra Leone to Liberia; she found her way from Freetown to Monrovia on her own immediately after learning about her boss' whereabouts) did not see any sign of that in his demeanour. But some security personnel hardly showed emotions on duty. They were professionals. The President's personal bodyguard was known for that – if not, he wouldn't have been assigned to the Sierra Leonean President by the Liberian Government. So, if Sergeant Thullah heard the President's shout and thumping, he didn't show it. And he never said.

President Ndomahina, after the first shockwave, somehow managed to compose himself to continue with the conversation with Mark – though hysterically.

"I am finished, Mark, I am finished," he said, while trying to recover from the shock. This was the first time the President was calling him by his first name instead of 'Mr High Commissioner'; and Mark noticed it.

"That's how it is," Mark retorted, sounding tired after recounting how the whole scenario unfolded – from his great expectations of receiving commendations from the Prime Minister to the sudden turn of events of being accused of having let the British government down, rendering his position untenable – that they had breached UN Security Council Resolution 1347.

Only then did it dawn on President Ndomahina what the last paragraph in the 'TOP SECRET' document was supposed to mean. The document was almost entirely devoted to the steps taken so far and the commitment of the international community to restoring back to Sierra Leone the democratically elected government currently based in Liberia. The document also made mention of the Banjul Agreement – an ad hoc peace deal by representatives of the exiled government and those of the Freetown military junta, signed in The Gambian capital.

The venue was specifically chosen by the UN for its deep-rooted colonial and post-colonial ties with Sierra Leone. The Gambia had been chosen and created during the European 'scramble for and partition of Africa' as a satellite state of the British colonial office in Freetown, with most of the official Gambian work force recruited from Sierra Leone; while Banjul became a holiday resort for colonial officials.

In the Banjul Agreement, both the exiled government and the Freetown military junta had agreed that 'the democratically-elected government will be restored in three months and the soldiers will go back to the barracks on a general amnesty'.

But the exiled government and its supporters had never taken that 'so-called peace deal' seriously. As far as President Ndomahina and his supporters – backed by Mallam Musa Odofo of Nigeria – were concerned, the Freetown military junta had just signed the Banjul Peace Accord in order to buy more time and consolidate itself in power. All the intelligence reports they were getting from Sierra Leone were pointing to that fact – there was no let up in the junta's repression: people were being randomly arrested, beaten, and in some instances killed. Although a UN special envoy recently visited the President in Monrovia and the junta in Freetown to elicit from each further commitment to the Banjul arrangement, both sides had never really trusted each other.

Some radicals within the Freetown junta were of the firm belief that they were being hoodwinked and would be eventually arrested. 'We better fight till the last drop of our blood in defending our territorial integrity than be arrested and humiliated before being killed', one senior junta official was quoted to have said, which the Ndomahina government had used to tell the world that the junta was just pretending to cooperate.

In fact, the Ndomahina supporters interpreted and openly said that all the so-called diplomatic moves were merely inducements to lure the junta into forgetfulness before the foreign soldiers would strike. Through the mobile radio station set up for the purpose, even government officials could hardly hide their intentions, while they parroted the fact that this radio station was donated and set up by the British government.

There was also no secret about British High Commissioner Mark Fergusson's role in securing the services of the private British mercenary company, Jungle Boys International, owned by the son of a former British Prime Minister. Therefore, as far as President Ndomahina and his team were concerned, the ultimate and unilateral plan of the international community was a military intervention to oust the Freetown junta. The Ndomahina supporters had only organised the demonstration in Liberia to fast-track the action; the weapons were already with the Nigerian soldiers and their civil militia allies on the ground. The airport, which had always been in the hands of the Nigerians (thereby preventing unauthorised flights from coming in), was used as storage for most of the weapons. And civil militia forces had already infiltrated the city. High Commissioner Mark Fergusson knew all this before he was suddenly called to London.

All the paragraphs in the 'TOP SECRET' document were fine – except that President Ndomahina was never comfortable with the terse last one: 'There are reports that all sides are breaching UN Resolution 1347, parts of which the British Government has agreed to address. Signed, UN Secretary General John Kirikiri.' Only now that Mark Fergusson had explained what had transpired between him and the Prime Minister did the full impact of that paragraph dawn on President Ndomahina.

"But what law have we broken, Mark? What law?" the President was now pacing up and down his office, handset held to his ear in one hand and the solid cast base carried along by the other. Now, Sergeant Thullah could hear the voice of his boss intermittently as President Ndomahina came close to the door at some points in his toing and froing. The bodyguard immediately realised the big boss was animated. "Resolution 1347 does not – ehm, should not – apply to us as the legitimate government. How can they put us on the same scale with these rebels who are not even fit to be called human beings?"

In his many years of working at the UN before returning to Sierra Leone, Kargbo Ndomahina was distinguished in his ability to understand ambivalent language. His colleagues had nicknamed him 'the decoder of equivocation'. Kirikiri had actually called him 'the talisman of diplomatic language' when he was asked to pay tribute to his colleague and friend at a UN ceremony for 'Ndomahina's linguistic clairvoyance'. When the Chinese couched their ambition over Hong Kong in a language written by their American-born UN Ambassador, it was Kargbo Ndomahina who recommended that the phrase "same language and same people" be changed to "people with similar speaking methods, and a close human-to-human co-existence". The UN Secretary General at the time, Kirikiri's predecessor, was impressed and promoted Ndomahina to Director.

But now Ndomahina was President. He was a politician – not in the business of decoding language, but in encoding it. So he had dismissed the last paragraph of the 'TOP SECRET' document as 'too much democracy-laden bureaucratic language not needed in African politics'. For him, the deed had virtually already been done: with the weapons and ammunition now in the hands of the fighters, the general consensus was that the operation would go ahead. Why would Mark Fergusson be sacked and investigated for that? And he suddenly remembered one of the statements often made by his friend and colleague, the Nigerian dictator, Mallam Musa Odofo: "Britain or no Britain, Nigeria will Save Sierra Leone."

President Ndomahina was not now as worried again as when the conversation started; he was not actually finished, after all. He was only now feeling sorry for Mark Fergusson who lost his job in the process. The President knew Prime Minister Ed McInroy would not have easily reached that decision; he knew how close the two were, and how passionate they both were about Sierra Leone. He empathised with Mark.

"But why an inquiry again when you have lost your job? What is it about?"

"Mr. President, we will have time to talk about this later. All I can say is, I wish you well. We know we did the right thing. And you know I am innocent."

***

Though she could not yet make sense of everything herself, Rachael tried her best to comfort her husband that night. She talked less but kept consoling Mark with courteous phrases like, "It's ok, my love", "It'll be ok, my dear", "It's not the end of the world", "We will be fine". She kept saying them until she fell asleep, her hand laid across Mark's chest. The husband remained awake for over an hour more, thinking and rolling back the years, from the time he met with Ed McInroy during their university days to the present. They both wished it didn't have to end this way. It didn't have to be this way. They didn't see it coming. That's life.

But before he slept, his mind came back to this morning. He was now recalling something that he didn't have time to think about when he was leaving the house for the Prime Minister's office. As he had passed by the cage of April 17 (the lovebird they had brought from Sierra Leone), the little creature had fluttered and flapped, releasing voices or noises as if it had wanted to say something, to tell him something. It was strange because this bird was not the talking type. Rachael had tried to teach it to speak like other parrots, but she was not successful. It was Sarah who was relatively successful in that; because she had grown to love it more than everybody else ever since she knew its story, and had devoted more time in domesticating it. Sarah succeeded in getting the lovebird to make a couple of repetitive noises, to everybody's applause. But not like what Mark saw and heard this morning. When they had to make the impromptu departure from Sierra Leone, Rachael was not keen on bringing the bird along to Britain and wanted to leave it at Hill Station. But Mark had insisted on taking it along as a surprise for Sarah (who was by then already living with Stephen) so that she would take it as some form of consolation because Stephen was not *yet* coming along.

"What was the bird trying to say to me?" he kept thinking. He wouldn't bring himself to the superstition of feeling the little lovebird would have known what the Prime Minister was going to tell him. "But would it have made a difference if I only stopped and looked at it?" he pondered. Only then did it occur to him again that the name Rachael had given the bird was April 17. Amazingly, today was April 17 – exactly two years after they got the bird. A lot had happened in two years. And this drifted Mark's thoughts to Stephen, remembering that it was on this day two years ago that their daughter had told them about her relationship with him. It was Stephen that stayed on Mark's mind until he slept.

***

The next morning, the British press was awash with the breaking news of the British High Commissioner to Sierra Leone, Mark Fergusson, having been recalled for an 'Arms to Africa' deal that breached UN Resolution 1347. A parliamentary sub-committee was going to investigate his role in the affair, and the Foreign Office could have colluded to break international law, the old-order-leaning media insisted.

This was not helped by the fact that the mercenary company involved was that of the son of a former Prime Minister, Sylvanus Attenboro. Jungle Boys International was just reeling from the scandal of an alleged botched attempt to overthrow the government of another African country. They were good at it, and they had been doing it. That was obviously what attracted them to Mark. And, as he insisted to President Ndomahina, he got approval from the Foreign Office to go ahead with the arrangement. The Sierra Leone arms deal had already been done before the Jungle Boys ran out of luck in Yugosobaland, with the mercenaries arrested (including Sylvanus Attenboro himself) together with some of their weapons. It took a lot of diplomatic rigmarole (some said an undisclosed ransom was paid to the Yugosobaland government) before they could be released on the intervention of the British High Commissioner to Yugosobaland.

Just a month later, another scandal involving Jungle Boys International: the Sierra Leone arms deal affair. Even the pro-government side of the British media showed no sympathy for Mark Fergusson. He was lashed for not understanding, or not making the Sierra Leone government in exile know, that UN Resolution 1347 clearly stated 'no party in the conflict should import arms into the territory of Sierra Leone' – which obviously included the forces fighting to restore the exiled government as well. Mark had overnight become a villain. All the work he had done over the years passed away with the night. This morning was all about the High Commissioner to Sierra Leone bringing Britain into disrepute on the international stage.

The headlines were as scathing as they were condescending: 'Britain Betrayed Abroad', 'Ambassador Sacked Over Arms Deal', 'British Envoy In Mercenary Mess In Africa', 'Parliamentary Sub-Committee to Investigate Rogue Ambassador'.

***

However, some thousands of nautical miles down the Atlantic in Freetown, it was a different picture altogether. In fact, it was the opposite: High Commissioner Mark Fergusson was a hero; the British media was wrong – meaning, the British government and the United Nations were wrong!

To the Sierra Leonean government in exile, plus its supporters in Liberia, on the ground in Sierra Leone and across the diaspora, Mark Fergusson had done nothing wrong. He was a man who loved Sierra Leone and democracy to the bones in one breath. All he had been doing was trying to restore the legitimate government of Sierra Leone, as agreed by the international community. This was the editorial position of most of the media houses in Sierra Leone and Liberia – which resonated across a continent that had been held hostage by coups and counter-coups.

***

Apart from the downside of not being in Sierra Leone in person, President Kargbo Ndomahina had all the paraphernalia of Head of State of the country – being hosted by the British in Liberia. Despite having been overthrown, President Ndomahina was the internationally recognised Sierra Leonean leader – in unison, in uniformity. And it was backed with action. All the bilateral and multilateral governance bodies toed the line. Embassies, high commissions and consulates relocated from Freetown to Monrovia. President Ndomahina was invited and feted at international forums. He attended the UN General Assembly, the Heads of State meetings with the AU and ECOWAS and the MRU. The World Bank and IMF supported him by paying his displaced ministers, members of parliament, and civil servants who had followed him to Liberia. The military junta leaders in Freetown were placed on a travel ban (save for belatedly allowing their representatives – but not the top five leaders, 'the big five' – to attend the Banjul peace talks). No wonder President Ndomahina had kept referring to the Freetown junta leader as 'the foot of state in Freetown' to cheers at these international conferences.

The only international agencies remaining on the ground in Sierra Leone were humanitarian ones like the Red Cross, *Médecins Sans Frontières* (Doctors Without Borders) and missionary medicos. They had become more active ever since the rebel soldiers started inflicting atrocities on the civilians and the bombs from the Nigerian Alfa jets started falling, with casualty figures rising along with the excruciating effects of the land, air and sea blockade. The prices of commodities were skyrocketing, as most Lebanese and Indian merchants also decamped from Sierra Leone. Even fuel was running out. When the military junta succeeded in surreptitiously constructing an emergency airport in the middle of the jungle using Ukrainian mercenaries (allegedly sponsored by the Libyan Dictator), it was not to airlift fuel or food supplies into the country, but to bring in weapons. The Nigerians got to know about it later, and the makeshift airport was bombed and rendered useless by the jet fighters. The Freetown junta became more than reactionary. It suspected almost everyone of being an informant. Journalists bore the brunt: some were beaten up for calling for civil disobedience, press houses were raided in search of 'stolen government documents', and five were locked up for days in a forty-foot container without food for writing about 'the foot of state'.

To that end, many journalists also left Sierra Leone – including the local BBC correspondent. The majority crossed over to Liberia and either set up their own news outlets or worked with the Liberian press. *The True Light* newspaper was not there. Editor Amidu Stephen Tamaraneh was missing in action.

* * *

President Kargbo Ndomahina succeeded in courting and cutting a good relationship with the media in Monrovia. Circumstances of necessity had made it easy for him. In Freetown back then, it was not so – he and the press were strange bedfellows, to say the least. His sixteen years in power had brought a lot of hardship in the country: unemployment was rising, school dropouts were increasing, public workers and civil servants, including teachers and nurses, were going for months without being paid, inflated contracts were being awarded to Lebanese conmen who shared the loot with the politicians with no work done.

And then a war had started. An hitherto less known former Army Major had started a rebellion, launched from 'the place where three countries (Sierra Leone, Liberia and Guinea) meet', saying he had come to liberate the people. President Ndomahina was caught unawares; the army was ill-equipped. The rebels claimed towns and villages. The media was very critical of President Ndomahina's leadership. He became hyper-authoritarian: journalists were intermittently and indiscriminately arrested and imprisoned either for 'not cross-checking with the government' or for 'incitement' or for 'releasing unauthorised information', or for no explained reason at all. Some had been executed as alleged coup-plotters. Journalists were a thorn in the flesh of the Ndomahina government. Editor Amidu Stephen was one of those leading the pack (he had been in jail for the umpteenth time).

That was the state of affairs that Mark Fergusson met when he arrived in Sierra Leone as High Commissioner. He intervened in a few instances to get journalists released from incarceration, and he prevailed on the government not to enact a bill that would have further empowered an already draconian Public Order Law, under which journalists could be arrested for anything. The proposed new law was going to add family members of journalists on the list of culprits.

The negotiations on the new Public Order bill were ongoing when a group of military officers drove all the way from the war-front to Freetown with their army trucks and Kalashnikov weapons to complain about lack of resources and low morale within the ranks. They said they were suffering strings of defeats and the civilian casualties were incalculable due to lack of adequate weapons – that the rebels were ten times more equipped than the military; they even saw white mercenaries among the rebels.

President Kargbo Ndomahina was incensed. The army had been under his thumb for the most part of his reign. He had foiled many coups – some clearly the figment of imagination, but still executions of the alleged coup-makers were carried out. Just a few months before, his own Vice President was executed alongside other civilians, including a journalist, and military personnel for an 'attempted coup', which was foiled before it was attempted, and the trial by judge alone lasted for three days. ("The state will not waste unnecessary resources on criminals," Information Minister Bai Sankoh had said on state radio.) The judge was President Ndomahina's cousin, Justice Bandaylay Ndomahina. And the public executions – 'to act as a deterrent to others' – were carried out at the beach, with selected spectators clapping, on the day the judgement was pronounced.

So many people in Sierra Leone feared the Ndomahina regime and could not talk. However, at the start of his administration, the President had not underestimated the importance of the welfare of the military in general: he had built a few barracks to house them and their families, he had ensured each personnel got a monthly supply of rice, and 'even if I myself will not be paid on time, the army must get their salaries promptly'. All the military top brass were his cronies, whom he appointed for very pedestrian and selfish reasons, certainly not out of merit. The Chief of Defence Staff was his first cousin.

On hearing of the mutiny, the President had immediately summoned a meeting of military chiefs at State House. He was really angry, to put it mildly. Repeatedly hitting the table during his address, he blamed them for not having their boys under control. He ordered the mutineers to be arrested and face a military tribunal. He was in the middle of his speech when gunfire erupted at the outskirts of State House. The meeting came to a sudden end when the ADC abruptly entered the meeting room. A coup was in the making.

The first person President Ndomahina called was High Commissioner Mark Fergusson. Using the back gate of State House, the special Nigerian forces stationed there (as part of the contingent sent by his friend, Nigerian dictator Mallam Musa Odofo), together with their Sierra Leonean counterparts, escaped with the President. On his orders, they drove him straight to the British High Commission.

* * *

President Ndomahina and High Commissioner Fergusson were not particularly friends. Ever since the topmost British envoy arrived and immediately called that maiden press conference before even meeting with the President, and without informing any government official, President Ndomahina had harboured misgivings about the diplomat. Tensions really rose to fever-pitch level (with low-level government officials talking about having powers to declare *persona non grata*) when Mark started implementing his reforms, especially not sending money directly to the government for British projects in Sierra Leone.

Mark did not personally dislike President Ndomahina, but the British diplomat had a mission to accomplish and he was not afraid of stepping on big toes. He oftentimes spoke openly about too much corruption in the government; he was concerned about

British taxpayers' money going into politicians' pockets. However, he was committed to the whole gamut of the democratic process. Therefore, to Mark Fergusson, if President Ndomahina were to be removed from power, it had to be through the ballot box – not by the barrel of the gun. He would not compromise that. Though he was personally against President Ndomahina enlisting Nigerian soldiers as part of the presidential guard, High Commissioner Fergusson was now not against them entering the High Commission compound with a petrified President Ndomahina.

From the High Commission office, he and the President were communicating with the military chiefs left at State House with orders to arrest the mutineers. The staccato of gunfire could be heard in the background. The desperately trembling voice of the Chief of Defence Staff was coming from State House about the boys being uncontrollable. The President shouted at him to do the right thing or face the consequences. The response the President and the High Commissioner got, to their utter dismay, was doors banging and boots stamping and discordant shouts and what seemed like sounds of scuffles… and the line went dead.

Late that night, President Ndomahina reluctantly agreed to be relocated to Liberia using a British naval vessel stationed on Sierra Leone waters for training purposes. The mutineers had succeeded in arresting the military chiefs. There was no resistance from the rest of the army. The Nigerian Special Forces guarding the President were too small to face the 'malcontents', as he called them. The majority of the Nigerian soldiers were stationed at the airport, too far away for a quick response. The British forces would not intervene; and even if they wanted to, they were also too small a force to carry out a successful job, according to their situation report.

There was gunfire all over the city. The President feared for his life. He left in tears. He and his quickly selected few were received in Monrovia by both Liberian government officials and British personnel manning the Monrovia embassy.

* * *

High Commissioner Mark Fergusson had organised everything. He had informed and got the approval of Prime Minister Ed McInroy every step of the way. Mark himself had been instructed to stay behind in Freetown to 'talk sense in the mutineers to see reason to abandon their senseless enterprise'. As far as the British government was concerned, the Sierra Leone soldiers had crossed the red line. They could make their protests, good. Mark was prepared to back them in getting the government to provide the required resources for their welfare and to prosecute the war. But they should not go on and overthrow the government. It was the military's seizure of the state broadcaster with the announcement of 'the overthrow of the Ndomahina wicked misrule' that broke the camel's back and made Mark contact Prime Minister McInroy for the evacuation of President Ndomahina to Liberia. But – Mark made it clear to the coup-makers – it did not mean Britain had accepted the Ndomahina government had been functionally overthrown. He told them the international community would not recognise their regime, not after a lot of resources had already been poured in towards the conduct of multi-party elections slated for next year.

So it was with faith in succeeding in these negotiations with the military junta that the High Commissioner remained in Freetown while he got his family evacuated a few days later. He had believed the situation would still be rescued, that it would be a win-win scenario, with President Ndomahina returning and the soldiers going back to the barracks or to the war-front, as it were. This was what he told Stephen on the beach after they had seen off Rachael, Sarah and Joel at the helipad en route to Britain.

* * *

Mark would soon realise the situation was never under his control. Nor did he ever know the whole situation at all. Just the morning after, the Nigerian soldiers at the airport started shelling the city with mortars. Jet fighters flew from Abuja to drop bombs at different locations in Freetown and other targeted sites in Sierra Leone. Mark protested. He said this would only worsen the situation. He called President Ndomahina to tell him that.

The President himself feigned not knowing exactly what was going on. He said the orders were coming from Nigeria, and that he had also expressed concern but got assurances from Mallam Musa Odofo that only military installations were being targeted "and there is no threat to the civilian population" – which was a far cry from what the High Commissioner was seeing on the ground. The President knew the High Commissioner was not on speaking terms with the Nigerian dictator. The British government did not officially recognise the Nigerian regime itself because the soldiers had refused to relinquish power there, having arrested and jailed the man who emerged as winner in an election that was mainly sponsored by Britain. The Nigerian soldiers were a bad example for the rest of Africa. Their actions could have even emboldened this new coup. Now their reaction to it was unacceptable to the British envoy. They didn't listen to him. The Nigerian shelling and bombing continued.

When there was no breakthrough on the way forward, the Foreign Office, on the orders of Prime Minister Ed McInroy, asked High Commissioner Mark Fergusson and all British civilian personnel in Sierra Leone to relocate to Monrovia. Once they did, the rest of the world followed. In a press statement, Downing Street made it clear that Britain was committed to restoring constitutional order back in Sierra Leone and that President Kargbo Ndomahina was its recognised Head of State.

***

Therefore, for the sake of a commitment to save democracy, High Commissioner Fergusson had to somehow be friends with President Ndomahina. They were now inevitably working from the same building in Monrovia – the President was occupying the upstairs of the embassy building, while Mark and his staff, plus those they met there, were working from downstairs.

The relationship therefore overflowed and resonated with the Sierra Leonean journalists in exile in Monrovia. Mark Fergusson, a darling of the press, created a media bridge with the Ndomahina government that once labelled journalists as 'enemies of the state'. The journalists still had an axe to grind with the President on that and on his failed policies, which some had insisted were directly responsible for the coup. But on the one point of respect for democracy, which Mark consistently and continuously pointed to them, they were willing to support the President's return to power. They were not particularly in support of him – they were in support of democracy, on the principle that he should only be removed through the ballot box. The journalists were therefore invariably in support of any means used to restore him back to power – including the use of force, or the use of mercenaries, as they were being updated.

For the British government – or rather the British Prime Minister, whom they knew and always hailed as 'a close friend of Sierra Leone' – to have relieved High Commissioner Mark Fergusson of his duties for doing what the whole international community had said they were committed to was not only the height of hypocrisy but the depth of betrayal, the Sierra Leone media intoned in chorus.

The newspapers went to town, denouncing both the British government and the British media for undermining and betraying 'a fine democratic hero like High Commissioner Mark Fergusson'. As far as the greater majority of the Sierra Leonean media was concerned, UN Resolution 1347 was unambiguous: it was targeted at the anti-government forces; that is, the rebel fighters and the military junta, not the recognised government in exile and the forces that were determined to restore it back to Freetown.

The headlines were unapologetic: 'British Betrayal', 'Britain Sells Our Birthright for Cocoyebeh', 'British Sell-out', 'Mark Fergusson Is Our Democracy Hero'. Some went to the extent of alluding that bribery (specifically with diamonds from the Freetown junta) had taken place through the UN envoy who recently visited both Sierra Leone and Liberia to emphasise on abiding by the Banjul Peace Accord.

One newspaper foretold what was to come: "We Will Go It Alone!" – sourcing officials close to President Ndomahina. And, ironically perhaps, the very radio station bought by the British for the restoration of democracy, was now at the forefront of denouncing the British government's hypocrisy, praising High Commissioner Mark Fergusson 'who is being scapegoated'. As far as they knew, all that the High Commissioner did had the blessings of the Prime Minister. Mark Fergusson couldn't have hired the services of a British mercenary firm, transported arms and ammunition to the Nigerian soldiers and got them distributed to the civil militia without the knowledge of the British government. It was all hypocrisy! The neo-colonialists never really wanted Africa to progress – President Ndomahina's party's newspaper had come out with axes blazing, spoiling for a fight.

20

Mark Fergusson's spirits would never be easily cowered. The boy who was raised in a council flat in a rough British neighbourhood by a working-class single father knew all too well that life could sometimes be unfair. But he also knew that life's storms could be weathered. It couldn't have been otherwise for him to have reached this peak. But this present storm seemed to be the most ferocious, most unexpected, the worst so far. Just as a man had laboured and sweated and clawed his way to the summit of the mountain, a sudden storm came and swept him away. He had to grab a tree trunk or hold on to a rock or somehow catch some rope. If not, he would soon find himself thrown down and fractured in the valley – if not dead.

Mark was ready to stand up to the storm – to weather it. He would not be like that fabled scientist who took poison on merely hearing about allegations of a 'sexed up' report about weapons of mass destruction. He must survive this as he had promised his family. But the news channels that morning didn't think so. Mark Fergusson was down and out.

The first major action he took that morning was call Monrovia (they had already heard the news) for all his files to be sent to him immediately, even before the rest of his belongings would be shipped back to Britain. He was determined to defend himself before the parliamentary sub-committee. He wanted to prepare himself well. He needed to read the files.

***

While waiting for the files, he now found all the time thrown at him for family. He was even the one cheering them up at breakfast that morning. "Well, here we are back again as a family for the foreseeable future." 'Except for Stephen', he wanted to say, but didn't. "It's an opportunity for us to care for and comfort each other," he said, decidedly looking at his daughter, Sarah, who was sitting directly opposite him, while Rachael and Ben sat opposite each other. Joel was in his crib. After breakfast, he asked Sarah to go jogging with him, while Rachael would look after Joel. Ben would be going to university.

***

One thing Mark terribly missed about Britain while away in Sierra Leone, and subsequently Liberia, was jogging. The two countries had no leisure parks fit for the purpose. He could not jog from his Hill Station residence in Freetown because the roads and pavements were too crammed and cramped and tight and dusty. What seemed an alternative was driving to nearby Lumley Beach and jogging along the coastline. But it soon turned out a weary process – not only for having to drive but there were too many distractions, which he saw as obstructions. Lousy fellows hanging around the beach would always disrupt to ask for money or he would meet a Sierra Leonean government official or an advocacy group member who would want to start a conversation. Mark abandoned the exercise. He joined the golf club where he came on weekends, but he stopped going there the day he saw Lebanese tycoon Amza Alie being feted by the same lousy beach fellows in the Teeing Area. He ordered a treadmill from London for home exercise. But it was never the same as the jogging he knew in Britain. The situation was similar – if not worse – in Monrovia, where all his time had been sucked by the continuous work towards restoring back the overthrown civilian government of President Kargbo Ndomahina. Watching from his car window around Monrovia, the jumbled roads and sidewalks gave Freetown a traffic pass mark.

It was not Mark's choice to abandon 'the Sierra Leone democracy project' to resettle back in Britain; but it was his paternal prerogative to go jogging with his daughter. Sarah herself was a bit taken aback when her dad made the proposal after breakfast. She knew her dad to be tough and resilient, but she didn't think he would demonstrate that so soon after what seemed the total collapse of his longstanding relationship with Uncle Ed the Prime Minister. She was going to ask her dad to postpone it, say that she was still mourning for Stephen and not in the mood. But Rachael read Sarah's mind quickly and had the quick-witted alertness to nudge her daughter to go with her father. "I'll also have quality time with my Joel," she had joined in, touching the crib that was standing by her side. After all, Sarah loved jogging too, Rachael knew very well. The daughter was very athletic at school and university at Durham. But, certainly for the same reasons as her father's, the jogging spirit had died in Freetown. It was buried when she became pregnant with Joel. And back in London, she had become reclusive and unsocial – except for those walks that led to the calling of Vicar Andrew Decker from the Sunfield Road telephone booth. And now her jogging spirit had been awakened by her father. She never dreamt it would come this early.

"Ok. I think that will make us all happy somehow," she summed up her acceptance.

For the next few days – while the father waited for the files from

Monrovia – this would be their routine. Two hours a day. And it yielded fruit – they had time to talk. The talk obviously centred on the 'Stephen phenomenon', as Mark put it to his daughter. Sarah was eager to hear it all first-hand as pieced together by her father.

21

By the time he had finished his telephone conversation with High Commissioner Fergusson, President Ndomahina was feeling far better than when it started. The thought that the arms and ammunition had arrived from Britain, the fact that he had an alternative deal with Nigeria's Mallam Musa Odofo who had always told him not to trust the British and the international community, and the fact that operational plans were already in an advanced stage, made the President believe that all was after all not lost without the British. But he also thought about what 'those crafty British' could be up to next. How far would they go? What further action would they take after withdrawing their High Commissioner?

So the moment Mark went off the line, the President immediately dialled his friend, UN Secretary General John Kirikiri. His initial instinct was to call his 'big brother' Mallam Musa Odofo immediately, but on second thought he decided he needed to speak to the UN top diplomat first. He needed the facts for a thorough explanation when speaking to the Nigerian junta leader. President Ndomahina wanted to get an insight into the details of what the UN or Britain meant by slamming the mercenary affair. How was it a breach to the UN resolution? Why didn't Kirikiri inform him about it when they spoke just two days ago?

But the UN boss was in a meeting and the President couldn't be put through, the UN HQ secretary politely told him. And the day's agenda was too full for Kirikiri to take any calls whatsoever. A dead end.

When President Ndomahina dropped the receiver, a whirlwind of new thoughts came rushing in. Would Mallam Odofo be afraid of a UN backlash? Would he pull out of their arrangement for fear of the British and the UN? But how would Mallam Odofo fear them now when he had defied them by remaining in power in Nigeria after he arrested and imprisoned the winner of the elections the international community had poured so much money into? No, Mallam Odofo was not a man who feared anything or anyone; he was the one who actually hatched the mercenary plan and got it executed. He had exchanged some of the diamonds President Ndomahina had been depositing with him for the arms, ammunition and personnel from Jungle Boys International. When the UN was planning a peaceful transfer of power from the military back to the civilians in Sierra Leone, the duo – Ndomahina and Odofo – were 'keeping a stick at the back of the door in case the neighbour's dog went mad'. But Mallam Odofo was a human being. He could change, President Ndomahina now thought.

'Stop thinking. Go back into action," he aroused himself. And the President's next step was to call his wife.

* * *

Mrs. Memunatu Ndomahina had relocated to the USA way before her husband was overthrown. She had found it convenient to be based there and be visiting when she could. Not of her own volition though. It was not an easy road to reach that decision – or, actually, conclusion.

They had been married for thirty-five years. They first met when Ndomahina was a second lieutenant in the army, while she was a schoolteacher attending the passing out ceremony of her own brother, who was Ndomahina's squad-mate at Bengeuma military barracks in the outskirts of Freetown. They would get married after Ndomahina returned from further training at Britain's Sandhurst Military Academy (where he first met then-Lt. Musa Odofo from Nigeria) and had become a full lieutenant two years later. Just after their third wedding anniversary, he was posted as military attaché to Sierra Leone's mission at the UN. Husband and wife used the opportunity to also study in the US, and Mrs. Ndomahina was also employed at the UN as a desk officer. It thereafter pleased the then-President of Sierra Leone, Daymia Turay, to retire Ndomahina from the military and turn him into a civilian diplomat at the UN as Sierra Leone's cultural attaché. Of his own accord, Ndomahina wriggled his way through the UN system and became a regular mainstream diplomat. He was hailed as a 'rising African star in the UN family', nicknamed 'the talisman of equivocation'.

Memunatu Ndomahina was therefore not happy when her husband first floated the idea of returning to Sierra Leone into politics 'because my people need me'. She had noticed a trend in that direction when her husband had lately got more involved with the Sierra Leone community in the US. He was being called from one meeting to another to 'speak to his people', and he was being feted here and there. But she never thought that would be a catalyst for a full-blown desire to go into politics. She believed they were alright with their jobs at the UN – with their only son, Kargbo Ndomahina Jr., away in Germany studying. But she would not resist for long. Throngs of Sierra Leoneans in the US pestered and prevailed on her to see where her husband had seen. She threw her hat in the ring when it became clear that President Daymia Turay himself, having remembered what then-Lt. Ndomahina did in foiling coups, had preferred her husband to lead the ruling party. And once she accepted, she didn't look back – until much later when they were already in the soup, in the pot.

Mrs. Ndomahina was in fact the first to tender her resignation at the UN. She went to Sierra Leone to lay the foundation for her husband's return – they had built a nice mansion up the hills overlooking the far west of Freetown and the ocean. Her husband returned to a well-set home a year before the elections. With Ndomahina controversially handpicked by the outgoing ageing President to be the sole candidate for the ruling party, Memunatu became more committed. She spearheaded a challenge and appealed to the female vote during the campaigns. Her husband won the presidency with a landslide – the results announced even before the counting went halfway. There was no other candidate. The Opposition was afraid to put up one – cowered by state-sponsored thugs.

It was all good for the Ndomahinas – or seemingly so – in the first eight-year term. But cracks came to the fore when President Ndomahina sought re-election. Though Memunatu Ndomahina enjoyed being called 'the First Lady', she wanted it to be seen as well. But her husband would rather not get her much involved in the campaigns this time; she would not be allowed to be travelling with him from place to place any longer.

Soon Mrs. Ndomahina would hear about an affair with a female TV reporter – that the newly-transferred State House reporter, Femi Cole (who once won the Miss Sierra Leone beauty pageant), was actually the President's girlfriend; that she was embedded in the presidency more for that purpose than for her professionalism. Gossipers had a field day in Freetown.

It wouldn't hide for long. The TV presenter's lifestyle suddenly changed after President Ndomahina's re-election. Femi Cole moved to a new palatial residence in the Spur Road neighbourhood just by the British High Commission. She had a brand-new BMW. And state security guarded her residence. The President usually came there in disguise at night. Soon the whole country knew there was a 'second lady' who travelled with the President in and out of the country as State House correspondent for the state broadcaster. It was no news to the Sierra Leonean media – it was normal. 'It's one of the sweets of African politics', one reporter had put it.

Mrs. Memunatu Ndomahina reluctantly accepted the fact after finding out that confronting her husband with it didn't change anything. It just made things worse for her. She merely asked to re-settle in the USA for health reasons. But she told friends she didn't want to create a scene, and she wanted to maintain her husband's 'respect in the eyes of the public'. President Ndomahina accepted. He could afford it. He bought her a mansion in New Jersey with a monthly stipend. Whenever he came to the US – whether for the UN General Assembly or other visits – he would come to his wife at New Jersey. She had only visited Sierra Leone once since, for the funeral of her father, for just two days.

Therefore, in the main, the Ndomahinas' relationship had since then mostly remained a telephone conversation. And it was not that regular – especially since President Ndomahina had been overthrown and sent packing to Liberia, where Femi Cole had also relocated with him (Miss Cole was among the selected few on the British naval vessel from Freetown to Monrovia that night). Effectively, Mrs. Memunatu Ndomahina's perfunctory conversations with her husband had been relegated to Sunday evenings – if he was not having dinner with friends.

***

So this call today was entirely unexpected and somewhat strange. Mrs. Ndomahina immediately suspected that there could be something more amiss than an overthrown President looking for old company. It turned out to be even worse than she had imagined. It sounded to her as an SOS call from the captain of a sinking ship: desperate, unintelligible, brisk, tense, terse, confused; the husband telling her about what had just happened in London and how he was trying to reach their old friend, UN Scribe Kirikiri, and couldn't. Now he was asking her to call Kirikiri's wife, Nana, who had always been Memunatu's friend since the UN days.

Mrs. Ndomahina wanted to ask questions, but her husband wouldn't let her. "Tell Nana to tell her husband to call me. Look, Memuna, if I go down, we all go down." He hung up, and the wife did not even hear the 'bye for now'.

* * *

President Ndomahina was now feeling exhausted – actually feeling dizzy – as he slumped in his chair.

The moment he pressed the buzz button and the bell rang outside in Sergeant Thullah's corner, the hangers-on in the waiting room came rushing to the doorman bodyguard to 'tell the pa we've been waiting for a long time'. They had been wondering why the President had not seen them for this long after a successful demonstration today, when normally he would immediately open the office and be buoyant with them. They had been checking on Sergeant Thullah intermittently, but he kept indicating to them that the President was on the phone.

Sergeant Thullah had hardly entered the office when the President shouted, "Let them call Dr. Ferenkeh for me". The sergeant was going to deliver the message from the waiting party stalwarts, but the President shouted again, even louder, "I said call Dr. Ferenkeh."

* * *

Dr. Mustapha Ferenkeh was the President's personal doctor. Like the ADC, and of course Femi Cole, Dr. Ferenkeh was one of the trusted few who left Sierra Leone with their boss on the British naval boat that night of the coup. There were criticisms from some sections of the press that, for the President to have monopolised the services of one of the very few doctors in Sierra Leone was 'an extreme act of selfishness'. But the government spokesman, Minister of Information Bai Sankoh (another of the chosen few on the British naval boat), had argued that the President's life had millions of lives hanging on it, and it was 'worth protecting to the fullest, even if Dr. Ferenkeh were the only doctor in Sierra Leone'.

The President had multiple health issues, the most notable of which was hypertension. He needed to be checked regularly and to be reminded to calm down continuously. Dr. Ferenkeh had advised the President that as a form of first-aid prevention, in circumstances that aroused adrenaline, he should silently count one to five before reacting. That advice flew out of the mental window when High Commissioner Mark Fergusson gave him the news. Now a confluence of actions and reactions had overwhelmed him. And he was feeling sick. He needed his personal doctor immediately.

While waiting for Dr. Ferenkeh, the President called his wife again to see whether she had spoken to Mrs. Nana Kirikiri. The UN top diplomat's wife's phone had been continuously busy, Mrs. Ndomahina told him.

***

When Sergeant Thullah emerged from the President's office, the waiting rabble were going to push their way through the door – as the usual practice was at a time like this – to cheer up the President and narrate divergent details of how the demonstrations had gone: the songs that were composed against the junta in Freetown, the insults that were hauled, who got more drunk than the others, the lynched rebel collaborators. But Sergeant Thullah quickly shut the door behind him, proclaiming, to their shock, "The Pa can't see anybody else now." They didn't understand until the sergeant crossed over to the secretary's desk and asked her to call Dr. Ferenkeh immediately. The doctor was just within the building. He had an office there.

* * *

While waiting for the doctor to come, though in a confused state, the President thought he should now call the Nigerian Head of State, Mallam Musa Odofo, and inform him about 'this strange British action'. He didn't want Odofo to hear it from somewhere else first – diplomatic news at times ran faster than current. He dialled Abuja. Mallam Odofo was in a longish cabinet meeting – President Ndomahina would have to call back in two hours, the Aso Rock secretary pleasantly said. He instinctively felt like asking if she knew whether her boss had heard any strange news. But she had hung up.

"Mary, mother of Jesus," the President muttered to himself, in his Catholic self – something he had abandoned ever since he ventured into politics. To him, the two could not go together – politics and religion were incompatible. Until now, when he said those words in his presidential office in Monrovia!

* * *

Before even Sergeant Thullah could knock on the door, President Ndomahina had pressed the release button opening the door. He had seen Dr. Ferenkeh through his video surveillance camera. And as the medical practitioner, who the Sierra Leone press had labelled as 'having the lean and hungry look of Cassius', entered the room, he was in no doubt that his patient was in a bad shape. The President was sweating profusely in the fully air-conditioned office.

"Are you okay, Mr. President?"

"I want us to go home."

It was not the first time that the President had used the back door – labelled 'fire exit' – to leave the Monrovia office. But it was the most extraordinary. In days when he only wanted it to be quiet or when he felt he had overworked himself and wouldn't have to add the burden of seeing hangers-on, or when Femi Cole needed him home, he would just inform Sergeant Thullah to tell the ADC that they were using the back door. Those in the waiting room would sort themselves out after they learned that the President had left. Today, the news from London compelled him to use the back door, together with his personal doctor.

He told Sergeant Thullah to inform the secretary to tell the party scribe to pass the information to the rest that Mark Fergusson, 'the hardworking and committed High Commissioner', was not coming back to Liberia – that he had been sacked!

22

Hearing the story of Stephen's demise from the horse's mouth had always been Sarah's craving. She had heard it through telephone calls and she had seen the newspapers. But a face-to-face conversation of how the father of her son became a victim of the war in Sierra Leone was always more desirable – hearing it from her own father was something she had always longed for. She wanted to fill the gaps in Stephen's story. The last time Mark was in London about eight months ago was primarily to console Sarah and try to mend fences between her and Rachael. There was no information beyond the story that Stephen was a victim of a Nigerian bomb. And Sarah then was not eager to know beyond that. She did not want to believe that. Now was the time to listen…

It wouldn't have happened now if, as had been planned, Mark had immediately returned to Liberia after his meeting with Uncle Ed the Prime Minister. *Things happen for a reason,* she thought. But she had concluded it was not right to raise the Stephen issue up immediately, because her father was also going through a harrowing time – having lost his job and his long-time friendship with Uncle Ed. But then Mark threw an early opportunity, somehow, when he proposed going jogging with her.

***

The last time Sarah saw Stephen was at the helipad in Freetown. And the last image that got stuck in her memory was when she was in the helicopter, taking off, and she looked through the window and saw her father and her boyfriend standing side-by-side waving, with Mark's right hand placed on Stephen's right shoulder. Tears had run down her cheeks. She didn't know if they ran down Stephen's as well. She wanted to know a lot from her father – what happened after their departure, how often Mark had been in touch with Stephen or vice versa before the whole fairytale-like story came to an abrupt end, leaving her an early widow.

***

Mark himself had been longing for the day when he would have time to give personal comfort to his beloved 'miracle baby'. He felt a burden in his heart to do this. He had spent sleepless nights on the issue in Liberia and had now been reminded of it in London by April 17. In more ways than one, Mark felt guilty that he had brought this calamity on his daughter. If he had not forged friendship with Ed McInroy, if he had not become a diplomat, if he had not accepted to go to Sierra Leone, if he had not asked his daughter to come along, and maybe if he had not tacitly given the go-ahead for her relationship with Stephen… If… if… if… If only; Sarah wouldn't have found herself in this web of gloom. But, he also thought, things happened for a reason. He remembered that his great-great-grandmother had also become an early widow after giving birth to his great-grandfather, and she thereafter got married to a freed slave from Liverpool and went away with him to Sierra Leone. Now his daughter was an early widow to a Sierra Leonean man. What a world indeed.

All he could do now was to find a way of facing the future, despite what had happened. His daughter was still young and she could turn the situation around in some way, in so many ways. He was prepared to talk her through it, where possible – as far as he knew it. He had been longing for that day. And it had come much earlier than expected.

***

When daughter and father had adorned their tracksuits (Sarah had a black one still) that morning and were ready to go out jogging, Rachael could not help herself but exclaim, "Oh, my twins." She brought some laughter to all – except perhaps Joel in her arms, who was in his own world.

But indeed Mark and Sarah looked like twins. They were the same height with the same face and both wearing baseball hats. With Sarah having folded her long hair into the hat, if one did not look keenly for the breasts, one would think both were men. If one did not look deep into the age lines on Mark's face, father and daughter definitely looked like twins. And mother didn't have to look into that – so all Rachael saw were her twins. But ironically, to Sarah, the humour immediately brought memories of Stephen and his twin brother Samson. But she did not show it. She laughed along. And off she went jogging with her father.

***

They didn't start off talking about the issue uppermost in their minds. It was more a question of rolling back the years in silence at first. This was what they used to do on weekends before his diplomatic appointment. Mark had, wittingly or unwittingly, created this special relationship with his daughter since her early age – and one way of expressing it was going out together for walks or jogging. Coincidentally and fortunately, Rachael and Ben did not fancy this type of exercise – they liked it indoors at health clubs. They had joined once in a while, but Mark and Sarah had made it a hobby. So the two were merely back to square one. They wished it was so; but it was not really so. At square one, there was no Stephen, no Joel. Sarah was not a mother in square one. Not a widow.

Just as they used to do in the past, they went out by the back gate, a shorter route to the park nearby, using the narrow path in the thicket of oak trees. They walked for a radius of two hundred metres without saying anything to each other – apart from Sarah initially drawing her father's attention to the sprouting daffodils that had come along with spring. They were silent until they came to the open field and found other people walking their dogs and jogging.

"Here we are again," Mark broke the ice, gesticulating with both hands at the expanse of the field. Sarah smiled. Child-like, she just started sprinting. Father-like, Mark followed. They used to go round this field six or seven times at a stretch. This time, just after the second round, Mark was tired.

"I am an old man now, Sarah dear. And you know, I've not been doing this for long," he said as he stopped.

"Come on, Daddy, at least two more rounds."

"You go, my dear, I'll sit here and wait for you." And off he went to one of the park benches. He watched his daughter continue running and realised how deeply he had missed this quality time all this while. Sarah also gave up after finishing that round. She came and sat on the grass by her father, despite him urging her to go at least once more.

"I don't enjoy it when alone," she justified, breathing heavily as she had actually increased her pace when she ran alone.

* * *

Back at home, Rachael was in reverie after playing with Joel for a while. She did not like the way things had turned out; but she did not entirely hate the outcome. She genuinely felt sorrow in her heart about Stephen's death. She knew she had initially been inwardly happy, after their evacuation from Freetown, about her daughter being separated from the 'woodworm relationship'. She had tried to like it for Joel's sake, and death was never on her wishlist for Stephen. But she accepted the way things had turned out without much complaint. It's the same feeling she had about Mark's situation. She had got her husband back – that was what mattered most to her. She wished he had not been sacked; it was her great desire to have been transferred to Mexico, mainly for Maria. But an eventuality that had brought her husband back to her arms in one piece was not altogether unacceptable. Rachael was on top of her world, singing lullabies to Joel.

***

It was Mark's suggestion to Sarah that they now used the other route to return home. He wanted to see the streets he had not seen for a very long time on foot. Of course, he had seen them whenever he was on official visit and had slept at his home. He had even seen them yesterday going to and from meeting the Prime Minister. But it was never the same as when he was on foot. He would have time to recognise changes in some houses or improvements on the pavements.

"Oh, there's a new off-licence here," he commented the moment they came out of the park to the main road on Colbert Lane.

"Yes, Daddy, it's been there for a while now," Sarah said. She felt emboldened to now start a conversation. "And how are you feeling after all this?"

"After all what?"

"This Uncle Ed issue."

"Never mind, darling. I'll deal with it. I'm ok. If not for it, we wouldn't be together right now."

It made Sarah laugh out loud. And in that instance Mark noticed the telephone booth, as they were now on Sunfield Road.

"Oh, this telephone booth is still here?"

"Where will it go, Daddy?"

"Well, everybody in this area now has a phone at home. Maybe it's needed somewhere else."

"Maybe it's still needed here by some people."

"You are right, darling."

***

They reached home all smiles. As they approached the gate, Mark asked, "And how about you? How are you feeling after all this?"

"What can I say, Daddy? Just like you, I'll deal with it. But it's not easy."

"I know, my baby."

"If only Stephen had survived," she let out.

"Yes, I know. His death is a phenomenon."

"What does that mean, Daddy?"

"Maybe let's talk about it tomorrow. We are already home. Let's go jogging again tomorrow."

Sarah felt somewhat excited. After the forced cancellation of the Ritz hotel dinner yesterday, she had something to look forward to again as an appointment. She had not had one for a very long time.

As they were about to enter the house, Mark inadvertently looked in the direction of the cage where the lovebird, April 17, was resting all by itself. This time there was no fluttering or flapping or noises from it. Mark just looked away without saying a word.

Rachael had seen them approaching and had come to the door with Joel still in her hands. Sarah remarked, "Hi Mum. You've been holding him throughout?"

"No. He was sleeping. He's just woken up now. But you guys are back early."

"I can't do it as before, Rachael," Mark said, adding, "I'll freshen up quickly and go to town. I need to do something there."

"What is it, Mark? You need to rest."

"I know. But I'll be quick."

* * *

It was more than a joyous moment when Mark returned about an hour later with a lovebird looking almost the same as April 17. He had driven to a pet shop and bought a companion for the lovebird. Rachael was gobsmacked and lost for words. She eventually said, "I never for once thought about this." Sarah just kept on chanting, "Oh Daddy, oh Daddy, you are one of a kind. This is so sweet."

With smiles and fighting back tears of mixed feelings at the same time, Mark said, "This is April 18, the day I started jogging again." All laughed again. Rachael gave him a peck. He had bought along a new cage with two compartments, a mesh separating them – each bird would be in its own room for now.

* * *

It would take another four or five days of father-and-daughter jogging to fully unravel the 'Stephen phenomenon' step by step, day after day. Mark tried as much as he could to tell the story in chronological order: how, immediately after the departure of Rachael, Sarah and Joel that day, he and Stephen left the helipad for the beach and had a long conversation over drinks; how they had spoken on the phone several times; how they met another three times (one of which was to watch a premier league football match: he knew Sarah would smile – and she did – because she knew her father and Stephen supported opposing teams and only watched together when they clashed; but today she did not ask whose team won); how suddenly things took a dramatic twist when the Nigerian Alfa jets continued bombing Freetown and communication lines got cut off; how Stephen had travelled to Roboli to see his parents and could not therefore talk before leaving for Liberia but left a letter for him; how he soon heard that a bomb fell on the offices of *The True Light* and 'killed some people, including the Tamaraneh brothers', according to the news on the radio donated by the British.

Mark said he was not sure whether the bombing of the newspaper offices was a coincidence or an accident. There were suspicions that they were targeted because *The True Light* was one of a few opposed to 'any illegal military invasion of the territory of Sierra Leone'.

In an editorial titled, 'Better to Jaw-Jaw Than to War-War', subtitled 'Making a Case for The Poor And Vulnerable People', *The True Light* had unequivocally condemned the coup and called on the junta leaders to bring sanity in the country and be prepared to go back to the barracks where they rightly belonged, asserting that Sierra Leone was bigger than any one segment of the society. The paper also, however, totally condemned the 'Nigerian gangsterism diplomacy' of using military jets to indiscriminately bomb Sierra Leone, calling Mallam Musa Odofo 'an unapologetic self-serving dictator who must be restrained'. The editorial called for dialogue as the only meaningful way forward in the interest of the poor and vulnerable: 'sitting round the table to solve our democratic anomaly is the only way forward from this quagmire'.

Mark said he discussed the editorial stance with Stephen and he believed the Editor was entitled to his own views – as that was the essence of democracy. "People should not be arbitrarily killed for their views," he maintained, now putting his hand on his daughter's shoulder. Though Stephen's corpse was never found, he added! Maybe mangled in the rubble. He didn't say that – he left it to his daughter's imagination.

And holding Sarah's shoulder even tighter, Mark said he thought his daughter was also now entitled to a new life – of looking to the future and concentrating on bringing up Joel in a manner that would have pleased Stephen.

"I'm sure that's what his spirit would want you to do." He didn't know where those words came from.

Sarah listened attentively throughout and only asked very terse questions here and there for clarification. The moment her father mentioned moving on, she knew he must have had a discussion with her mother on the subject matter. It then dawned on her that she could not continue to go against the tide: she would have to go with the wind into the future without Stephen. Now her father was in the same boat with her mother – and the reality could not be changed – it was of no use. Time for her to ride in the boat as well.

* * *

When they returned home from jogging on that sixth or seventh day, they found a package awaiting Mark. The files had arrived from Liberia. He therefore suspended his jogging routine to concentrate on his preparation for the parliamentary sub-committee hearing. Sarah said she was already enjoying the exercise and decided to go alone the next day. It was actually a trip to the Sunfield Road telephone booth to call Vicar Andrew Decker.

She recounted the whole story and rumbled over how life had been so unfair to her. The priest, in his usual calmness, told the young lady not to give up, as with time she would be healed or find answers to everything.

"I will never be healed from this," she lamented. "Not when I have a constant reminder in Joel. And even if there were no Joel, I don't think I would be healed."

"Yes, I understand the feeling. Well, you understand better how you feel; but still keep hope alive that there could be a better tomorrow, my young lady." (He never called her by name.)

Vicar Andrew went on to bring all types of biblical stories to pacify Sarah and to encourage her to go along with what her parents had prescribed for her.

And then Sarah asked, "But what about those words – the scripture reading – those words that you got me to read on Remembrance Day when I was a little girl? You had said they were…ehm… that they are true. How true are they?"

"They are still valid, my dear young lady. They are true."

"Why should I believe they are true?"

"You will ultimately find out they are true – usually not the way we humans expect, my dear young lady."

When Andrew Decker eventually went off the line, he felt the need to say an immediate special prayer 'to the One who knows everything' for this young lady's situation. She needed desperate prayers. She needed a miracle. He felt it in his spirit.

23

TV anchor Femi Cole was unofficially – perhaps even officially – the First Lady of Sierra Leone in Liberia. Sierra Leoneans already knew this back home, but Liberians and the rest of the world were only seeing it now.

***

Ever since Mrs. Memunatu Ndomahina relocated to the USA using health reasons as a cover, Femi Cole (the celebrated former Miss Sierra Leone and state broadcaster presenter) had slowly but surely taken over as the wife of President Ndomahina. She liked it when referred to as the epitome of 'beauty and brains'. However, the more radical wing of her critics – whom she called 'haters' – often described her relationship with the President as 'beauty and the beast'.

She had already moved into the presidential lodge in Freetown before the coup. She was of course the first on the list of five people allowed to go with President Ndomahina on the British naval boat to Liberia that night.

Mark Fergusson didn't like Femi Cole when he had heard about her relationship with the President. The British High

Commissioner snubbed all her attempts to interview him in Freetown. But, in Liberia, they had to work together. She was very influential to her peers within journalistic circles. The media loved her (she was one of them). The media loved beautiful ladies, the media loved celebrities – even if they had a potential to make them slip!

And once she got the opportunity to turn things around, she didn't turn on High Commissioner Fergusson for the Freetown snub. She turned it on its head to achieve her goal. She wooed him. And wowed him. Mark subsequently concluded that there couldn't have been a better person to work with in the enterprise of 'restoring democracy in Sierra Leone' – that if not for Femi Cole, President Ndomahina wouldn't have had the capacity to cope and coordinate. Put the personal on the side, Mark conceded, she was doing it with a passion for man and country: holding meetings here and there, fine-tuning the President's diary, arranging and conducting interviews. At the same time as being the 'housewife' of the President. She worked from home, which apparently became more like a 'mini State House' where Sierra Leoneans flocked daily in Liberia. Femi Cole found time for every group.

***

That day, Femi Cole was in the middle of a meeting with the Organisation of Sierra Leonean Women in Liberia (OSLEWIL – with the motto 'Yes, we will') in the hall on the second floor of the 'presidential lodge' in Grand Cape county in the suburbs of Monrovia when she heard the shrill sound of sirens from a distance. The police in Liberia – as those in Sierra Leone – hardly used sirens, even in emergencies. It was of no use; the roads were clogged, and to chase criminals using sirens was somehow fruitless. Ambulance drivers faced the same problem, but they used their own sirens anyway – perhaps to absolve themselves or their consciences from any blame if anything happened to the patients they were trying to rush to hospital in the unending traffic logjam. Fire engines and their poorly paid drivers, who often ended up nicking the fuel, were in the same category.

But soon the siren sounds were becoming louder and coming nearer towards the 'presidential lodge'. Such speed could only happen with visiting foreign dignitaries and the two Presidents (the exiled and the host) in Liberia. Traffic would have been cleared long before by traffic police personnel (who, like their Freetown counterparts, would be richer from unaccounted-for on-the-spot charges paid by drivers for unwritten traffic offences).

Femi Cole – whom some of the women were now unabashedly referring to as 'Mrs. Ndomahina' in their speeches at the meeting, either consciously or unconsciously – didn't know of any high-level foreign dignitaries in town. Her 'husband' would have told her. High Commissioner Mark Fergusson – who once in a while would be fast-driven with police escort and sirens when he wanted to hold blitzkrieg meetings with both Presidents separately on either side of the Liberian capital – was away to see the British Prime Minister in London. The Liberian Head of State, President Robert Lawson – an Americo-Liberian descendant of freed slaves – was also away on a private visit to Jamaica. And her 'husband', President Kargbo Ndomahina, was having a long day in the office following the successful demonstrations, as far as she knew.

Donning her trademark short skirt and a pink flowery top (pink being the party colour), Femi briskly left the meeting and walked towards the veranda facing the main boulevard – the click-clack sound of her high heels taking over the meeting briefly. And then she suddenly stopped, transfixed, on seeing the long convoy of the presidential vehicles and flashlights heading towards the house. The gate one hundred metres away had already been opened.

What was happening? Why was the President coming home earlier than he had said? Why hadn't he called her to let her know he was coming? Maybe 'Kargs' – as she nicknamed him – was up to those his pranks of surprising her by returning home without prior notice to 'just be in your company', when in fact he had either been consumed by jealousy for 'those too many young boys around' or by sensuality. She was not going to stop her meeting for any reason, she resolved.

The ladies themselves were surprised but their cheerleader, Adama Mankhantel (pronounced 'man can't tell'), instinctively chanted their favourite acronym: "OSLEWIL."

And they all, as always, shouted back, "Yes, we will."

"OSLEWIL."

"Yes, we will."

"OSLEWIL."

"Yes, we will."

By now, Femi Cole had asked her personal assistant to stay with the women, while she went downstairs to know what was going on.

Femi Cole didn't – couldn't – come back. The meeting was postponed.

* * *

President Ndomahina looked unmistakably poorly to her the moment she saw him.

"We are seriously sick, honey." Kargs muttered the obvious in a very low tone that Femi Cole had never heard before – not even when he was hushing her the night she discovered photos of a Chinese girl in his bag in Freetown and swore she would have to be part of any future delegation to China. And he always liked using the plural when he wanted her full attention. "We are seriously sick, honey."

Her first instinct was to ask, "What's going on?" but she instead settled for, "I see." Dr. Ferenkeh, supporting the President to walk, had immediately made eye contact with her, stopping her from asking any questions. She instead gave a supporting hand as well, as they walked with the President through the living room to the 'hospital' (a small room by the President's study, stuffed with his prescribed medication and a bed for his treatment specially designed by Dr. Ferenkeh).

The President had kicked off the shoes from his feet the moment he entered the front lobby, using one foot to remove the shoe from the other. He had walked in bare socks to the 'hospital.' He slumped into the bed immediately, and Dr. Ferenkeh automatically applied his stethoscope to check the internal workings behind the President's incessant perspiration. He discovered nothing beyond what he already knew: the President's condition was as a result of the confluence of events and the news he'd just received. His blood pressure was therefore very high. All he needed was to rest and calm his anxieties. The doctor recommended the valium pill, diazepam, to induce sleep, and he was just reaching for the medication shelf when the phone rang in the President's study.

Madam Femi (that's how everybody else around here was calling her), standing by the living room doorway adjacent to the study, was going to pick the phone. Suddenly, her husband mustered enough strength to mutter the words, "Don't pick it; bring it here."

"No, Kargs, you can't talk on the phone now."

"Yes, I can." He now rose from the bed.

"You are not well, my dear; you need to rest." She took a step towards the study.

"Ferenkeh, tell her I can," the President said with the finality of tone he normally used in Cabinet decisions – just that a 'wife' wouldn't recognise the import of such a tone.

He was expecting two very important calls, if not three. One was certainly from Mrs. Memunatu Ndomahina. The other was from the Nigerian leader, Mallam Musa Odofo. UN Secretary

General Kirikiri himself – his friend – might call back. Different thoughts rushed to the fore at once. That was enough to give him strength and alertness. He had therefore quickly pushed the doctor in the direction of the study with, "Ferenkeh, tell her I can." By the time Madam Femi realised it, the doctor was already on his way out of the office with the cordless receiver in his hand. He was the doctor. He knew his patient better.

President Ndomahina had feared it was his wife – well, his first wife – calling. Mrs. Memuna (that's how the domestic workers called her) had accepted the reality about Femi Cole living with her husband in the 'presidential lodge' in Monrovia. But she had wrenched from him an agreement to get 'the little girl' out of their business, as far away as possible. That meant whenever she called, it had to be him picking the phone, not Miss Sierra Leone. But the arrangement was for Sundays, between 5:00pm and 8:00pm Liberian time. Today was Thursday. Mrs Ndomahina might not have complained if Femi picked the phone today; but President Ndomahina did not want any room for the unexpected, if he could help it.

The female voice was unmistakable. Doubly fortunately, it was not Mrs. Ndomahina.

"His Excellency is on the line, sir." The Aso Rock secretary's voice sounded like sweet music in the President's ears.

It was now President Ndomahina's turn to dash with the handset from the 'hospital' to his office. He was excitedly shouting, "Yes sir, Your Excellency. Yes sir, Your Excellency," even before the secretary could connect him to Mallam Musa Odofo. As he quickly shut the door behind him, Femi Cole and Dr. Ferenkeh were left amused and bemused. From the study, with the speaker at the other end now in apparent conversation with him, the President loudly said, "Yes sir, Your Excellency, my big brother, sir"; and Femi immediately knew who had called – there was only one person in the world whom her 'husband' addressed as 'big brother'. She withdrew to the living room. The doctor stayed in the 'hospital', sitting and waiting on the bed.

When, nearly twenty minutes later, the President was still on the phone locked up in his study, his voice sounding hale and hearty, Dr. Ferenkeh decided to go to his apartment, which was just at the back of the lodge. He informed Madam Femi.

"Healing comes in different forms," he told her, as he slipped through the door leading to his backyard accommodation.

24

After offering a special prayer for Sarah that day, Vicar Andrew Decker still felt he should share the matter with his wife, Elizabeth, whom the boys at their parish church had nicknamed 'Old Mother Hubbard', for whatever reason no one exactly knew. He did not normally explain the affairs of his parishioners or whoever was under his pastoral care with her. He could recall he had only shared with her once before – in the case of the old widow who wanted urgent answers about euthanasia. That was over thirty years ago – way before Sarah was born.

Once again Vicar Andrew felt this was one burden he should share with the woman he normally called, in good times, 'my better half, Lizzy!' He asked her if she remembered Mark and Rachael and their wedding at Oxford. He always did this. But Old Mother Hubbard's dementia was not that bad. She scolded him for constantly thinking her memory had become so blank that it needed some jogging. He asked her if she could remember Mark and Rachael's daughter, Sarah, 'the one who read Scripture on Remembrance Day'.

"What happened to her?"

"Nothing really wrong, but not so good."

He released the burden…

***

When Sarah left the Sunfield Road telephone booth, one thing was clear: her last defence had been broken. No matter how she felt, it was time to move along with the tide. In some ways, she felt let down by Vicar Andrew. Why would he not do more?

At least Friar Lawrence gave some potion to Juliet. That was beyond mere words. Why did Vicar Andrew not give me a potion to drink and become unconscious and wake up to find Stephen lying by my side? Even if dead. So I could also drink from his poisoned chalice.

That night, Sarah didn't – couldn't – sleep.

She lay in bed as Joel peacefully slept in his cot and she pondered and wondered over her life. How had she found herself on the wrong side of history? Why would she become the black sheep of the family? An early widow? It was all her fault, she concluded. *Mea culpa.* She should have listened to her mother. Or maybe she should not have extended her stay in Sierra Leone in the first place. Or maybe she shouldn't have listened to Uncle Ed the Prime Minister who convinced her to complete her university education in Sierra Leone.

"It's all my fault," she said loudly as she lay in bed, her back to the mattress, watery eyes to the ceiling. "Yes, it's all my fault." She broke down, sobbing, tears now fully flowing from her eyes.

And then this sensation cropped up again in the midst of it – the sensation that her mother had referred to as 'a false hope against all the evidence. The dumb feeling, contrary to the facts, that Stephen could be alive'. To Sarah, there was actually no evidence that Stephen was dead: the body was not found; no pathologist proved whose mangled bodies were buried after the massacre. The news had always been that a Nigerian Alfa jet had dropped bombs at *The True Light* offices and Stephen was believed to be among the fatalities, together with his twin brother. The bodies couldn't be identified.

Sarah was first in shock, and then in disbelief. Why would life be so unfair? A young man who had such a passion for his country, who loved his profession, who loved helping others, shouldn't just be snatched away like that. Was that fair? Was God still there? These were the questions she used to ask Vicar Andrew.

And today he had again blandly told her that she would eventually come to know that those words she read on Remembrance Day were true.

It had happened at Westminster Abbey, the most famous church in the world where Kings and Queens who ruled the largest empire the world had ever known were crowned, wedded and buried.

She was then a thirteen-year-old, dressed all in white, at the very Westminster Abbey in London, in the presence of the Queen and all other royals and the Prime Minister and ministers and the war veterans; and her name, Sarah Fergusson, was called, and she went to the dais; and there was pin-drop silence in the cathedral, only her voice could be heard, as she read them, the words, as asked by Vicar Andrew Decker: *"I am the resurrection and the life. Whoever believes in Me will live, even though he dies."* All eyes were on her. Only her footsteps were heard walking back to the pews to sit between her father and brother, who sat next to the mother. Those words lingered – had always lingered – since that day at Westminster Abbey.

As she now resolved not to contact Vicar Andrew again on this issue – for it was as good as dead – her thoughts now turned to the personality of Stephen, deceased. She shuddered at the mere thought of it. She rolled back the short melodramatic years of their relationship.

25

The stories, or rather the rumours, were not in short supply – in fact they varied in degrees – as to how Femi Cole got hooked with President Ndomahina.

Some said the lady's father was a colleague of the President's in the Army; that when Femi Cole was a child, he used to jokingly call her 'my little wife'. And that when Ndomahina returned from the UN into politics, he looked for his former friend, found out that he had passed away, and then asked the mother for his 'wife'. When he was shown the grown-up Femi Cole, he couldn't believe it. He had never imagined that his little wife was the famous Miss Sierra Leone he had been admiring, doubling as a TV broadcaster.

But then the other story said Ndomahina was part of a UN delegation to Sierra Leone for some research on the falling standards of education in the country; and that one of the institutions they had visited was the Institute of Public Administration where Femi Cole was a student. She had asked many questions during one of the sessions; Ndomahina asked her to see him. And then one thing had led to another.

Yet, another rumour stated that they had never met before he became President. She went to cover an event at State House and was introduced to the President by the Minister of Information, Bai Sankoh, who previousy worked with her briefly at the state broadcaster. The next moment she had been transferred to State House.

Sierra Leone was a country of rumours. And they could be created out of nothing. You believed them, you were damned; you didn't believe them, you were out of touch. They used to say there was no smoke without fire; but in Sierra Leone, you would find out that the smoke was actually a mirage. Which of the stories about the Femi Cole relationship with the President was true, nobody knew. Maybe none even was true. But what was true was that she was now the unofficial wife of President Ndomahina. And she was in charge of their home in Liberia.

***

Dr. Ferenkeh had left Femi in a confused state. He had given her the full story of what he believed was the cause of the President's illness: that it had to do with the news he had received from London about High Commissioner Mark Fergusson's dismissal, putting the whole project of the President's return to Sierra Leone in jeopardy. No wonder the call from Nigeria's Mallam Odofo was so relieving, because it had apparently brought back some hope and revived him. That's why before the doctor slipped away by the back door, he had remarked, "Healing comes in different forms."

Now left alone in the sitting room – as her 'husband' was still in the study continuing with the telephone conversation – Femi Cole absorbed the full import of the scenario. She had been part of the 'return project' from the very beginning. There was too much at stake as things stood. She started looking at the odds: a permanent life in exile. She had been very vocal and would not dare return to Sierra Leone. The junta boys would tear her to pieces. And presently she was thinking about her personal fate, even in exile.

President Ndomahina had the option of relocating to his wife in the USA. And she, Femi Cole, would be left in the lurch.

This was disconcerting, to say the least. She was in a quandary.

But she realised she could do better than just ruminate. So she resolved to forget about the future – at least for now – and act in the present. She decided to do what she so often did – tiptoe to Ndomahina's study door and eavesdrop on the telephone conversation. She wanted clues and inputs that would inform her next course of action. She removed her stilettos, left them in the sitting room, and stealthily sprinted towards the 'hospital', from where she further tiptoed to the study door.

She found or heard President Ndomahina in a spell of laughter. She shook her head, not knowing what had dramatically changed. The laughter subsided, as he was apparently listening to the Nigerian Head of State on the line. Another burst of laughter, with, "Yes sir, yes sir, you told me this is what it will have to come to." Femi Cole became more curious and now leaned on the wall, pushing her neck forward and pressing her ear to the door – as she did at times when Ndomahina spoke to Mrs. Memunatu in low tones during their intermittent weekend calls.

"Yes sir, you told me I should never totally trust them."

Silence.

"Yes sir, I remember very well. These neo-colonialists are only interested in their interests."

Silence.

"Yes sir, you had told me to always have a back-up plan, sir."

Silence.

"I cannot be more grateful, sir."

Silence.

"I know, sir. I'm happy you insisted I should include that part in my speech to the UN General Assembly. They can't say we did not tell them."

Silence. Femi Cole was now enjoying the drift.

"Yes, sir, our project is very much alive. You are blessed, sir."

Femi Cole had heard enough and believed the conversation was drawing to a close. She quickly tiptoed back through the 'hospital' to the living room. She felt a bit relieved and now craved for a thorough explanation of the cycle of events. She decided to go change her outfit to home clothes. She picked her shoes up and was climbing the stairs when she heard the door opening and her husband calling, "Honey, honey." She immediately raced back with, "Yes, honey. Dr. Ferenkeh has gone to his apartment."

"I'm not asking about a doctor."

"What is it? Is everything ok, honey?" she pretentiously asked. She dropped her shoes again to face her man (that was actually how she called the President when speaking about him to other women: 'my man').

He now wore a broad smile. "Everything was not okay. But everything is okay now. I guess Ferenkeh told you about what happened."

"He didn't have time to tell me much. He said the High Commissioner has been withdrawn."

"Not only withdrawn but they want to put a big case on his head. These British people."

"But why? Mark was a good man."

"I know. Anyway, that's not the point now. That's no news again. I have the big news." He had a way of keeping her in suspense to make her come closer. And then he continued. "The fact is that Mallam Musa Odofo has just assured me that, British or no British, we are moving in."

"Wow."

"Yes, honey, the deal is done. I need to drink some champagne. Please get the ADC to invite all my Ministers and Members of Parliament and the others on your usual list here tonight. We need to re-celebrate the celebration that was cut short earlier today."

Femi Cole knew how ruggedly determined Mallam Odofo

was in President Ndomahina's 'back to Sierra Leone' project. She knew Mallam Odofo hated the British (whom he always called 'neo-colonialists') with a passion: 'Why do they still want to tell us how to run our affairs?" was his mantra. The British were the only ones standing in his way to more absolute power; he was clinging on to power against their constant pressure and demand for the release of the democratically elected President of Nigeria and a full return to civilian rule. She knew about the several midnight meetings and about some of the deals.

"Never doubt Odofo," President Ndomahina said.

"Never doubt Odofo," Femi Cole echoed, but just to herself.

26

Sarah's eyes were now tear-free in her North London room. She was still in the same position in bed, as her thoughts dwelt more and more on Stephen. She gradually accepted the reality that they would never see each other again. Not on this earth – maybe some day in the land beyond the sea, that land that's fairer than day, which he used to talk about during his metaphysical moments.

The fairlytale had ended, she now concluded.

* * *

And what a fairy-tale it was. Not merely in the sense of the inter-racial nature of their relationship, or the mutual robust rejection of any force that stood in their way. But in the very manner in which they fell in love with each other. 'The most unlikely characters of a bedfellow becoming the most compatible partners of racial diversity', Edwina Campbell would later write about them in a personal poem she only showed to her friend, who in turn showed it to Stephen. She entitled it, 'Colour-blind: My Boss and My Friend.'

***

On that first day of internship at *The True Light* newspaper, Sarah was given a welcome note by the secretary signed by the Editor, Amidu S. Tamaraneh: 'For Ms. Sarah Fergusson, Internship Schedule and Details', written in some scrubby, hardly legible handwriting. The secretary asked her to report to the News Editor, as the Editor was not in at the moment.

Sarah met the News Editor, Edwina Campbell, a charming, happy-go-lucky, bubbly 'Krio' girl. They would later become friends, as Sarah was intrigued to know that Edwina was a descendant of freed slaves who still had a traceable family tree in Britain. And when Edwina knew the story of Mary Fergusson, the great-great-great-grandmother of Sarah who travelled from Britain with the freed slaves, she used to joke, "Maybe our great-great-great-grandparents rode on the same boat on that journey from London to Freetown. Our friendship can therefore not be some mere coincidence." This was a joke that Sarah used to tell her brother Ben a lot on the phone – and about Edwina's amiable nature.

***

Later that day, when Sarah found out that the Editor was in his office, she told the secretary she wanted to see him. She was told he was busy. She came a second time.

"He is still busy," the secretary pleaded.

"He is busy for how long?"

"I don't know, madam."

"I am not madam. I am Sarah."

"Ok, madam."

"Call me Sarah."

"Ok, Sarah. He is busy, ma."

"Don't add ma. Just say Sarah."

"Ok, Sarah. I am Yainkain. Editor is busy."

"Right. Tell him I need to see him."

"Ok. Give me five minutes. I'll call you."

Sarah went back to the News Editor's office and engaged in a chat with Edwina, who would from time to time pop out to bring in a reporter or another member of staff for introduction to the new intern – not without ending each with "She is the daughter of the British High Commissioner," which Sarah didn't like but endured.

After about twenty minutes, there was no message from the Editor for her to see him. She came back to the secretary, "Yainkain, you said five minutes."

"That's exactly how to pronounce my name. Good."

"Ok, you said five minutes, and now it's past twenty minutes." That was one big lesson Sarah would learn in Sierra Leone: that when people said 'five minutes' or this particular time, they didn't mean it – even those at State House.

"Oh yes. Is it already five minutes?" Yainkain asked rhetorically, raising her left arm to look at her tight-fitting wristwatch briskly.

"Can I or can I not see him now?" Sarah raised her voice to a level that reached the Editor's ear.

It was not the greatest of offices. It was actually a cubicle. What separated the Editor's office from the secretary's was makeshift cardboard, which meant that even normal talk in the Sierra Leonean manner could be heard from within each side of the divide. So Sarah's raised voice just meant that it reached the level of Yainkain's pitch. The secretary was talking in the normal Sierra Leonean way and therefore the Editor could hear her voice, her part in the dialogue – if he paid attention to it. Sarah's raising of her own voice meant the Editor could also now hear the other participant in the conversation. It was a different voice from the many others he had heard from that cubicle.

Shortly after, the door opened behind Sarah, who was standing facing the secretary's desk. She turned to see Stephen – well, at that time, better called Amidu. He was dressed in a robe-like African attire. She recognised him immediately. Though they had only met a few times before, all in the night – once at the university at the journalism department dinner and a couple of times at diplomatic cocktails, she remembered talking to him briefly at least once in those occasions. But he was a crusader journalist who did not only report and analyse the news, he made the news as well – when the CID came looking for him for his 'anti-government' writings. Sarah had seen enough of his picture in the newspapers not to immediately recognise him again in daytime.

"Oh, thank goodness. Mr. Editor, can I see you for a moment?" she instinctively said, sounding a bit irked.

"Of course, please come in," he said with a wide smile as he opened the door wider with one hand and beckoned her in with the other. She didn't smile. She kept a straight face as she entered the office. She noticed that she was slightly taller, then she smiled. They were obviously in the same age bracket. She didn't like the scruffy office at first glance.

"Please take a seat. I guess you received my welcome note," he said as he lingered and waited for her to sit first.

"Is that the way to welcome me? This is my third time of trying to see you."

"Is that so? I'm so sorry."

"The secretary kept telling me you were busy."

"Ok, yes, she always says that. Don't mind her."

"Anyway, I wanted to just tell you that I am not a normal intern. I mean, I am not here in a bid to actually fulfil an academic requirement."

"Yes, I think I know that."

"Well, so you cannot expect me to go by that schedule in your welcome note," she sniped again.

"But your dad told me you wanted a normal practical experience."

"Yes, I know that's what he told you. What I meant by that is to work in a very flexible environment. I am doing it for him and not for myself."

Sarah explained. Amidu listened, but he was surprised she could open up on family matters so much so soon. In Sierra Leone, you didn't meet someone for the first time and summarise your family history to them, for whatever reason – except under duress. He had never before heard family stories from his staff – or colleagues at work, as he loved calling them – except for funerals or birthdays or weddings. That taboo was being broken by Sarah Fergusson right in his office, and he was amazed. But he didn't show it.

"So you see, Mr. Editor, I am just hanging around here to keep my father – your friend –" (she was smiling broadly now) "happy."

Just that moment, the office door opened. Sarah, sitting with her back to the door, turned only to see another Amidu entering the office. She turned straight again to see the Editor sitting there in front of her. She quickly turned her head towards the door again. And he was still there – the other Amidu, with the same wide smile. *Is it magic?* quickly flashed in Sarah's perplexed mind. Just that the other Amidu was dressed in a suit, without a tie.

Amidu immediately said, "Oh, Mr. Tamaraneh, you are back already." This only further confused Sarah, who recalled that her father had frequently referred to the Editor as "Mr. Tamaraneh." *Then who is this other Mr. Tamaraneh again who looks exactly like the Editor?* Sarah quickly pondered.

"Yes boss," the new entrant said. Sarah would later learn that they interchanged these courtesies as they pleased, calling each other 'Mr. Tamaraneh' or 'boss' in the presence of others. In private, they mostly called each other 'my bro'.

Presently, the Amidu in the suit said, "Oh, Sarah is here." She was going to melt as he walked straight to her. "I am Samson. I am the accountant here."

"Oh..." she exclaimed.

The Editor immediately interrupted with, "He's my twin brother."

"Oh wow, you are twins. Nice to meet you, Samson."

"Nice meeting you too. I knew you were coming today, but I was away to the bank."

"Oh good. He didn't tell me where he went this morning," she responded, pointing at Amidu, as all three of them burst into laughter.

Samson added, "He's like that."

Sarah knew she had to leave now. She had told him what he needed to know about her so-called internship: she was going to have more time for herself and with her diplomatic community friends, with the tag of an intern, wrapping up her stay in Sierra Leone, ready to return to her good old Britain.

Amidu escorted her to the door, opening it for her. He told the secretary, in her hearing, "Allow Sarah to see me any time she wants. She is in the category of Samson, Edwina and Thinking Pen."

***

For the next three or so months, Sarah didn't make use of the 'privilege' accorded to her. She didn't come to see the Editor. She didn't need to see him. Maybe they briefly met once or twice in the lobby or on the veranda and exchanged pleasantries, and he enquired whether she was enjoying her internship (whatever she had made it to be). She, not even knowing now which of the twins she was talking to, always gave brisk answers in the affirmative and in a hurry – "Yes, I'm fine."

As far as the office was concerned, Sarah had found the perfect mate in Edwina, the News Editor. She loved working with her. She loved talking to her – especially for their great-great-great-grandparents' stories. They were not only working together but they had started hanging out. Sarah was interested in writing stories about freed slaves or the slave trade itself. They visited the former slave ports in Bunce Island, Banana Island and Bonthe Island. They toured the port where the freed slaves first landed at King Jimmy wharf and the Cotton Tree in Freetown. They jointly wrote stories, which they bylined 'By Edwina Campbell and Sarah Fergusson'.

So Sarah didn't need to see Amidu until the day the Editor wrote an editorial about a Sierra Leonean Anglican priest who had divorced his wife of forty years to marry a young lady twenty years his junior. The editorial somehow took a swipe at the Church of England as a whole. Sarah didn't take kindly to that. She came to the Editor's office brandishing the newspaper. But she sounded courteous when talking to the secretary.

"Hi Yainkain, is he in?"

"Yes, let me tell him."

"Remember, he told you I could see him at any time." Sarah said it in the manner of the British police when they wanted to arrest you: very low tone, but with committed resolve. She ignored the secretary and entered the Editor's office.

***

Sarah couldn't have looked for a better lecture on the history of the church or the history of her own people – as she later put it to Vicar Andrew Decker. And the cubicle of the office of the Editor of *The True Light* was the last place on earth she had ever expected to get such a lecture. There, in that shabby office. In there. And the cardboard wouldn't have prevented the secretary, Yainkain, from hearing parts of the lecture. She was already curious the moment Sarah breezed in. So her ears were wide open.

***

The editorial was titled, 'Even the Church Cannot Save Itself: Only One Can'. But it was not even the main editorial. It was in fact the third in a row. *The True Light* had adopted this policy of multi-editorials in every edition. So in this particular edition, the lead editorial was actually a sting on the government of President Kargbo Ndomahina. It challenged the government on lack of commitment in prosecuting the war, as there were reports that three more villages in the Pamehun district had fallen to the rebels 'due to lack of adequate resources for the military, while ministers live a lavish life with fat Lebanese contract kickbacks'. It was titled 'Politicians Swimming With Blood Money'. While writing it, the editors didn't rule out a visit from the Criminal Investigations Department. Editor Amidu was used to it now. He had been locked up three times at the main Freetown prison and dragged to the CID countless times. They used to call him 'the jailbird journalist'.

The second editorial was an appeal to community leaders in the slum areas of Freetown to take sanitation seriously and mobilise their people to improve their environments. Its emphasis was 'not to rely on the central government all the time, especially as the rainy season is approaching. Because, at the end of the day, it will be the ordinary people and their children living in these communities who will die, while the children of politicians are going to private schools in Europe'. It was titled, 'God Helps Those Who Help Themselves.'

Therefore, Sarah's editorial – as Stephen would later turn the issue on its head in a joke after they fell in love – was just a three-short-paragraphs treatise on the clergy. It took a swipe at the Anglican Church in Sierra Leone for 'advertently or inadvertently following the footsteps of the origins of the Church of England, the mother church' through the action of the resident priest of St. Henry's Cathedral in Freetown. 'The action of Priest Olumendi Metzeger (once seen as a local beacon of hope) against his wife

– a dutiful comely lady – just points to one thing: that humans, irrespective of their status, even if they hold the keys to the gates of heaven, are still human. Men need to depend on God – He alone can save – and not depend on another human for their salvation.'

Therefore, when the cubicle door flung open, Editor Amidu's instinctive thought was that the CID had come for him again. He was, as usual, going to pick his jacket up and avail himself, when he suddenly stopped. There were no 'white' officers in the Sierra Leone Police – rather, the force had not upped its lapdog game to the extent of incorporating 'non-native people' into its ranks in post-Independence Sierra Leone. And they had never before used female officers in criminal operations. Female officers were too timid, too warm-hearted. Amidu looked properly.

And it was Sarah.

* * *

Once inside the cubicle, she dumped British police methods.

"What is this editorial attack on Britain all about, Mr. Editor?" Sarah asked in a high-pitched tone as she closed the door behind her. Not that she didn't notice that the 'attack on Britain' occupied a very tiny space in the editorial column, but she knew the picky press officer at the British High Commission read them all and would not hesitate to confront her on the derogatory writings of her newspaper. John Davenport had from the beginning expressed dismay in learning that Sarah was doing her internship with *The True Light,* which was 'so anti-British'. The paper itself had always pronounced its stance as 'unapologetically anti-neo-colonialism, but never anti-West. We believe in mutual respect of the sovereignty of every nation'. This was a stance Sarah generally accepted and respected. But in this editorial, she had clearly seen an anti-British strain. She felt hurt. And she wanted to know why the Editor had done this.

***

She had the lecture of her life, she later conceded to Vicar Andrew.

And now, as she lay in that bed in North London in this trance-like recollection, taking her back to those days, she briefly came back to herself and felt the loss – a huge loss, not only to her, she believed, but to Sierra Leone, maybe to the world. *For that was huge potential gone too soon in Stephen.* She thought about his parents and where they would be at this time: the last information she had about his family was from Vicar Andrew via the British military network, of Roboli having become a ghost-place as the war had intensified. *Life can be so unfair,* she thought.

And then her mind was transported again to that day when she confronted Stephen – Editor Amidu – on his 'anti-British editorial'.

***

Stephen had tried to sound pleasant as he responded to Sarah's question with another question. "What editorial attack, madam?"

"Please don't 'madam' me. Why does everybody here call everybody else 'madam', or 'ma', or 'boss'?" Sarah exploded.

"Because this is Sierra Leone. That's the way it is here." He tried to joke.

"That's the way it is here. But it should not be rubbed on some of us. Just because the dove is flying with pigeons doesn't make them all pigeons."

"Of course, but they are all birds."

"But not of the same feather," she insisted, adding quickly, "Anyway, I am here to know why you wrote this," (she threw the newspaper on the desk), "especially when you know I am here."

"I'm sincerely sorry if any of our writings affect you in any way. But your being here will not change our editorial stance."

"But this is about my country. This is about misrepresented facts about Britain in the newspaper the daughter of..." She hesitated. She didn't want to say it as she didn't like being called that, but she believed she had to say it to get Editor Amidu understand the point, so she continued. "The newspaper the daughter of the British High Commissioner to Sierra Leone is associated with."

"So what is the bone of contention here, Sarah?" He stressed on the name so she would understand the correction to 'madam' had been made, while still sounding calm and a bit confused.

"Look, Mr. Editor, or Mr. Tam... Tam... Tamar... Tamara..."

"Call me Amidu."

"Ok. Look, I am not a religious person. I don't go to church. I am not even sure if God exists. So, I really don't care what bones of contentions you have with your priests or pastors. But please, when you do that, stick to your people. Don't draw in the British people with baseless innuendos." She was also now speaking as the mass communications graduate that she was.

By this time, Stephen had moved from behind his desk to where Sarah was standing in front. He asked, "So what are these baseless innuendos?" and added, "Please have a seat."

Sarah for a moment didn't want to sit. "I am... I am not..."

"Please, please Sarah, let's talk this through."

She walked past him to sit in the only chair in the cubicle apart from his own.

The office still looked the same as she had seen it a few months back: desk splattered with newspapers and magazines, the small black and white TV on but without sound, the dusty window curtains half open as a stack of past editions of the paper blocked the other half of the window.

"You don't know the baseless innuendos?" she asked as she sat.

"There are no baseless innuendos in there."

Sarah said that if a priest of the Anglican Church in Sierra Leone had left his wife to marry another woman, it did not warrant the editor to 'baselessly bring in the Church of England'. She re-emphasised her non-religious upbringing, but said that all the priests she knew in Britain were decent people; that the law in her home country was 'one man, one wife', not as she was seeing in Sierra Leone. She now lifted her voice a little bit higher as Editor Amidu sat on the edge of his desk.

"Have you never heard of 'for better and for worse, till death do us part'? Why these baseless innuendos about your Freetown priest following the footsteps of the Church of England?"

"That was not what was written in the editorial. It stated, 'following the footsteps of the origins'... Underline that, *the origins* of the Church of England."

"But it's the same thing."

"Not really." Editor Amidu got off the desk and walked back to his chair. He leaned towards his drawer and brought out a book. "Have you ever read this?"

"What's that?"

"A book. *An Anthology of Oliver Cromwell* by Philip Riley."

"Never seen it before. Never heard of it."

Just that moment, the Deputy Editor, who preferred being called 'The Thinking Pen', knocked twice and opened the door. Editor Amidu quickly retorted, "Thinking P, Please give us some time. I'll call you when I'm done." The door was closed again; and Amidu took his time to respond to Sarah's queries.

He told her about what caused the Church of England's split from the Catholic Church; about King Henry divorcing his wife and ending up marrying six wives in total.

"Those are unwittingly the origins of the Anglican Church, which the Sierra Leone priest is now maybe inadvertently following. There is absolutely nothing anti-British in the editorial. And I can categorically state that, yes, the Church of England has largely shed off that image. The present monarch, the Queen, has played a great role in turning things around. Powerful and rich as she is, she has stuck to one man all through her life. If she were an American, it would have been a different story."

Sarah laughed out loud.

Having succeeded in achieving that, he continued, "But the origins are different from the now. And this Sierra Leonean priest knows about those origins. So I don't hate Britain, dear Sarah. I may have misgivings about some parts of their colonial legacy in this country, but at least it is because of them that we are today publishing a newspaper in English."

Sarah wanted to say something but then kept quiet again.

"If I were anti-British, you, Sarah, would not be sitting in this office right now."

"What does that mean?" Sarah snapped.

"It means I am not anti-British," he laughed.

She smiled a bit. "I am not really convinced."

"And by the way," he said when Sarah got up to leave, "I do believe in God. I believe He exists. And I do go to church."

"Really?" Sarah was apparently taken aback. "Journalists don't normally do church."

"Well, I do. I am first a human being before being a journalist. And I know – like everybody does – that I will leave the stage one day."

Sarah left the cubicle mortified, though with some reservations. Soon, office rumours would state there was great animosity between the Editor and the new intern. Whether they had come from the secretary or from the Deputy Editor, who had lingered longer and overheard the high-pitched voices, it was hard to pinpoint. But the rumours fuelled. Sarah would later recall that 'some staff backbiters' had told her that Stephen thought he knew more than everybody else. They turned out to be government spies surreptitiously planted in the newspaper. They disappeared the moment the relationship took a new twist.

***

It was Joel's cry that jolted Sarah back to life – rather, back to reality, back to her bed in North London. It must be midnight. This had been the pattern of the child since they came to London – crying at exactly midnight. But doctors had assured it was normal. She was now used to it, sleeping between two halves of a night, waking up – or being woken up – to give milk to the crying Joel, who within ten minutes would fall back to sleep till the morning. She would have preferred Joel skipped this particular midnight. Her thoughts – or were they not more than thoughts? – then raced back immediately from father to son.

Only then did she realise that she had neither slept nor changed to sleeping clothes.

She quickly jumped from the bed to the cot and picked Joel up. After she had given him the milk and he had calmed down, Sarah looked at her son and saw the eyes of Stephen staring at her. The boy was a spitting image of his father. *This is exactly how Stephen must have looked like as a baby,* she thought. Just that Joel was of mixed race, having the chocolate complexion of half-white, half-black – called *malatha* (mullato) or 'half-cast' in Sierra Leone.

Sarah had always known Joel looked like Stephen; but this midnight there seemed to be an enhanced father-and-son uniformity in the eyes, in the looks, in the way he looked at her. Her son's eyes did not only look now like his father's, but Joel was actually giving her that same look that Stephen gave her that night when he said, "I love you." And presently, instinctively, she just retorted, "I love you too." A few minutes later, the boy was asleep again. The mother also thought she could sleep now. But she still couldn't.

The difficulty started in choosing which colour pyjamas to sleep in. Still black? Or change to another colour now? She had already accepted it was time to move on. Circumstances had prevailed.

* * *

Ever since the news of Stephen's death, Sarah had donned black, even with her pyjamas. But now she had agreed with her mother, urged by her father and endorsed by Vicar Andrew, that it was time to move on. There was no need to hang on to the past. One could not change the past; though one should acknowledge the past. If you did not, it could come looking for you – as it was doing to her just moments ago. But she could not continue to hang on to the past. Stephen was gone, for good. The thought still sent some shivers into her. But at least she could still see him in Joel – those eyes tonight. But her life should not remain static, as her parents had exhorted. She was turning a new page.

But, for tonight, she decided to wear black pyjamas again. For the last time – the last night in black. Maybe tonight Stephen might appear to her in a dream. Sarah was always astounded that, with all her intensity of mourning for Stephen, she had never dreamt about him. If he could just appear or just tell her something… But nothing. She had even wished he could come to her as a ghost. She didn't really believe in ghosts – the whole world would be filled with ghosts – but she had read somewhere that ghosts did appear to some people. Now, tonight, she just hoped and wished she could see Stephen's ghost to put the matter to rest.

So, now wearing the black pyjamas, Sarah opened her balcony door, switched off the light and stood on her veranda in darkness. She imagined Stephen's ghost coming to her and talking to her. She stood for a while. Nothing. She went in again and closed the door. She walked to the cot and had a look at her son again. He was fast asleep. This time her mind raced to Joel's origins, to how the child was actually her decision and not really Stephen's.

* * *

When Sarah had come to the conclusion that Stephen was the guy she wanted, she took the bold and courteous decision of informing her parents about it. But she didn't know the road would be as bumpy as it turned out, especially the roadblocks from her mother; but there was no less pressure on Stephen from his Roboli relatives to not take 'the extreme road of wanting to marry a white woman', as one elder had put it. She dealt with both in one blow: Joel.

She had initially agreed with Stephen that they would wait until they saw where the relationship would lead them, even as they were committed to each other. But that night of the farewell dinner in Freetown for the American Ambassador's wife changed everything. Sarah singularly decided to go for the jugular – have a baby with Stephen.

When she told her mother a month or two into the pregnancy, Rachael was more than enraged. A storm was unleashed. She decried her daughter's 'thoughtlessness and recklessness', denouncing Stephen as 'a leech preying on opportunism'. There and then, she asked Sarah to abort the pregnancy.

Mark had then travelled with President Kargbo Ndomahina to a London conference organised to mobilise support for the war effort, as the government had committed to conducting free and fair elections the following year. He returned home to find that his daughter had left the house and transferred to Stephen's. His entreaties for her to return home, even with the pregnancy, fell on deaf ears. Sarah had made up her mind to have the baby as an independent woman.

Things eventually patched up during the later stages of the pregnancy. Rachael gave up the resistance and accepted the relationship. She was with her daughter in hospital when Joel was born. Despite everything, she paradoxically liked being called a grandmother. Sarah was also happy that she could leave young Joel with her mother at times. Things were like that until the coup occurred in Sierra Leone and they had to be suddenly evacuated to London.

Tonight, in her North London room, Sarah looked back to this string of events regarding Joel and didn't regret her decision – it was not a fault; he was not a fault; there was no fault, after all. If not for him, perhaps Stephen would have totally been eliminated from her life. Now the memories would linger, but she had to move on. She also felt she owed her father an obligation of not giving him more misery. Mark was trying to come to terms with his job loss, friendship loss, and pending case with the parliamentary sub-committee; the daughter felt she had a duty to try to pacify him by showing she was ready to move on with her life. She was wearing black pyjamas for the last time. Tomorrow morning, she would appear light-hearted and sprightly in a white dress to cheer her parents up, she decided.

But now, as she lay in bed trying to cajole some sleep, the words of Vicar Andrew hypnotised her: "They are still valid, my dear young lady. They are true… You will ultimately find out they are true – usually not the way we humans expect…"

Yet still, no dream. No ghost. No final goodbye from Stephen. She now had to move on. And then a brief tawdry thought came to mind. *Whatever might have happened to the fantastic companion Stephen used to talk about? Aslan.* But that was not really important to her now. She would just have to follow the advice of her closest relatives and move on.

She eventually slept – even if just briefly – in the wee hours.

27

President Kargbo Ndomahina ran the affairs of Sierra Leone as a 'family business – or at least on cronyism with reckless impunity', as *The True Light* had put it in an editorial in another edition. For all his sixteen years in power, state machinery was operated 'on the basis of *usai den tie cow nar dae e dae eat* (a cow grazes where it's tethered) – a saying coined by his political godfather, the former President, justifying corruption in offices'.

In fact, that was how or why Kargbo Ndomahina was handpicked for the job. There was absolute power in the hands of the former President. When he became old and almost blind, he believed the only way of protecting himself was handing over power to the man who had safeguarded his political ambition and presidency in its infancy, Kargbo Ndomahina. A ruthless party thug sprung into the military, Ndomahina was the man who unearthed coups against President Daymia Turay and got many people executed. He had himself become so powerful that, after doing the dirty job, the President decided to send him far away as military attaché to the UN. Still, the President didn't want Ndomahina to continue having influence in the army, and changed him to a civilian diplomat at the UN. But in old age,

President Turay believed bringing back his protégé to succeed him was the best security for his retirement. After all, he was his countryman – they were from the same chiefdom.

The President's decision was final. The party executive endorsed it. It was a pseudo one-party state. Elections – foregone elections – were held. Kargbo Ndomahina was the sole candidate. That was how he became President Kargbo Ndomahina of Sierra Leone.

The state of cronyism continued. President Ndomahina's brother, Swarray Ndomahina, was the head of the government's special security squad, sponsored by the party's main financier, Lebanese tycoon Amza Alie. The Finance Ministry was run by the President's cousin: millions and billions were being disbursed for electricity, but blackouts were the rule in 'the darkest city in the world'. Public sector workers went for months without receiving salaries. Only the military and the police got prioritised 'for security reasons'.

When a rag-tag group of rebels emerged, saying that the only way to end this inhuman cronyism and the downward economic trend was to get rid of the Ndomahina regime by force, it was initially dismissed as mere banditry. Soon it ballooned into a full-scale war. The soldiers at the war-front started complaining about lack of resources. They wrote to their military bosses and to the special security squad, which was actually in charge of the whole security network of the country. Nothing much was done apart from promising to look into the issues raised. Months passed; the military lost ground and suffered losses. The civilian population got caught in the middle.

So on that fateful day when a platoon of about thirty soldiers left the frontline with a few trucks and some weaponry, they said it was 'to make our concerns in public'. Just as the President was busy sternly addressing the military bosses at State House on the very issue, the mutinous soldiers arrived at the gates of State House. There was a bitter argument. One thing led to another, and a trigger-happy special security squad personnel opened fire and shot dead one of the leaders of the mutinous soldiers, Lt. Marouf Kabia. The group responded. That was the time the Nigerian soldiers came and whisked the President away, using the State House back door, to the British High Commission. Then things got out of hand, and he had to be evacuated to Liberia.

The soldiers took over the country with little or no resistance from the rest of the security forces. Their leader sounded breathless on radio, as if he had run all the way to the studios. He counted his words: "We have today taken the bold and patriotic action of overthrowing the kleptocracy of the failed and selfish Ndomahina government to save our country, save our people and bring peace to our land… This is the richest country on Earth. Yet, we are the poorest people in the world. We are last in the human development index, last in any good thing. We don't deserve this… Where are our diamonds going? What about the gold, the bauxite, the iron ore, the rutile? We have been living a nightmare in paradise – except for the megalomaniacs and the kleptocrats of the Ndomahina regime… We will bring them all to justice…"

Captain Matthew Thomas had gone on to detail the woes of the society – including the fact that Ndomahina himself had said that education was a privilege and not a right when waves of students had embarked on strikes for failure to pay teachers. No good health facilities, no good roads, no tap water and on and on and on. He even said they knew – though he did not name – where President Ndomahina had been sending diamonds for safekeeping, 'when the ordinary man cannot afford a square meal a day'.

The people listened with caution. Ndomahina had been good at foiling coups. He was good at comebacks. But the news quickly spread that he had left the country and had arrived in Monrovia. Some sections of the population therefore began celebrating openly – until the Alfa jets started the air strikes and the country was effectively blockaded by Nigerian soldiers. President Ndomahina made a broadcast from Liberia, saying he would return to power 'very, very soon'.

On hearing that, the Sierra Leonean soldiers became more repressive, harassing and arresting suspected informants of the former government, banning demonstrations, proscribing free speech beyond the Public Order Law.

* * *

Though British High Commissioner Mark Fergusson had opposed the coup, facilitated President Ndomahina's escape, and stayed behind in Freetown to tell the coup-makers to 'immediately go back to the barracks', he was also totally opposed to the 'arm-twisting military brinkmanship' of the Nigerian leader, Mallam Musa Odofo. The diplomat had famously openly said, "The Nigerian dictator does not have the moral as well as the legal grounds to protect democracy." High Commissioner Fergusson had therefore reluctantly relocated to Liberia when there was no breakthrough. He grudgingly shared an official building with the overthrown President in Monrovia 'only for the sake of democracy'.

Once in, High Commissioner Fergusson played a key role in galvanising international democratic support against the military junta in Freetown. President Ndomahina's 'friendship' with UN Secretary General Kirikiri made things easier. In their collaboration, High Commissioner Fergusson was also key in opening a dialogue with the Freetown junta. Junta representatives eventually participated in and signed the Banjul Peace Accord, setting out a transition period for the junta to peacefully hand over power back to President Ndomahina within three months.

It was High Commissioner Fergusson's idea to have Banjul as the venue for the peace talks. In his justification, he had not only delved into the history of The Gambia as having been specifically created as 'a province of Sierra Leone' by the then-British colonial government, but that the British had actually ceded some Sierra Leonean land up north to then-French Guinea in exchange for the Gambia River strip, then surrounded by French Senegal. He said that in contrast to the troubles plaguing the African continent, The Gambia had stood out as an oasis of political peace and stability since independence.

"The Gambia does not have any minerals but the government has created a strong economy through just groundnut exports and the tourism sector, which is far smaller than Sierra Leone's tourism sector. Sierra Leoneans have, even before the war, been migrating to The Gambia for greener pastures. How odd. Maybe, holding the peace talks in Banjul would irk the consciences of the warring Sierra Leonean factions to learn from the Gambians, whose own little-educated elite had all been schooled in Sierra Leone."

Kirikiri was thoroughly convinced by the High Commissioner's argument, hence the Banjul Peace Accord. But neither side trusted the other. The Freetown junta's demand that 'multinational armies, not just Nigerian forces, should play a central role in supervising the peace process on the ground' was taken with a pinch of salt by President Ndomahina – and was never going to be accepted by Mallam Musa Odofo. In fact, it was the Nigerian dictator who had actually hatched the idea of hiring a private British mercenary firm to supply arms and ammunition to the pro-Ndomahina forces.

High Commissioner Fergusson, who had thought it was Ndomahina's initiative, was at first opposed to the idea. He said he had a good impression of the Freetown junta leader during his initial negotiations in Freetown, and he believed the army would hand over without the use of force. He also thought the Freetown junta's demand that the Sierra Leone Army should not be disbanded was 'a legitimate and constitutional one': "If that idea at all should be toyed with, the Nigerian Army must never try to take the place of the Sierra Leone soldiers. A multinational force should be in charge until a new Sierra Leone Army is trained."

This had only tormented the duo. President Ndomahina and Mallam Musa Odofo believed High Commissioner Mark Fergusson and the rest of the international community did not know the true intentions of the military junta: that 'the foot of state's foot soldiers' had signed the Banjul Peace Accord to hoodwink the international community and buy time to consolidate themselves in power. Therefore, for Ndomahina and Odofo, the only way to remove the Freetown junta from power was through the use of a superior military force.

High Commissioner Fergusson only agreed to the idea of hiring the private mercenary firm at the back of two justifications. He was shown aerial pictures of the Freetown junta having breached the blockade by landing a plane full of arms from Kiev at an airfield that was hurriedly constructed by Ukrainian engineers in the jungles of Sierra Leone. Then the Freetown junta had brutally quelled a 'bring back our democracy' demonstration in Freetown, killing at least twenty people, wounding several others, and arresting many more. Though High Commissioner Fergusson stressed that diplomacy should be the top priority in resolving the crisis in Sierra Leone, he thereafter never ruled out the military option. It was a conditional clause in the Banjul Peace Accord.

Meanwhile, as far as the Freetown military junta was concerned, High Commissioner Fergusson was working hand-in-glove with President Ndomahina, even though the diplomat himself kept saying in public that his support was purely for democracy and not for the President as a person. To the junta, it was a farce; there was no difference: the British had escaped with President Ndomahina; the British were housing the overthrown President in Liberia; the British had been flying him to international conferences as the legitimate President of Sierra Leone, the latest being the United Nations General Assembly. In sum, the British and their allies had been bankrolling the whole government-in-exile machinery. The Freetown junta had cooperated with the High Commissioner up to signing the Banjul Peace Accord, but they were still always suspicious of him.

***

When the Freetown junta therefore heard about the sacking of High Commissioner Mark Fergusson and his being subject to investigation by a parliamentary sub-committee due to 'the illegal supply of arms to the territory of Sierra Leone in breach of UN Resolution 1347', there were cautious celebrations at State House in Freetown.

The country was in a quandary. Blockaded by land, air and sea – and the Ukrainian-built airport having been immediately bombed by the Alfa jets and rendered useless – the country was effectively at a standstill. A Ukrainian ship that tried to offload rice at the quay after stealthily berthing at night was prevented from depositing its cargo and forced back immediately by incessant artillery shells and air strikes from the Nigerians. Fuel pumps had virtually run dry, with few drums being smuggled from either Liberia or Guinea at exorbitant prices; basic commodities were almost out of stock in the markets; most people resorted to walking due to the virtual cessation of public transportation.

The MSF spokeswoman in Freetown called it 'a silent humanitarian catastrophe, with people, especially women and children, dying from hunger, lack of basic necessities, terror from combatants on the ground, and bombs dropping anywhere'. The local BBC correspondent (the new one, as the original reporter had fled to Monrovia when a junta spokesman said he was biased in his reporting) called it 'a grim, ghastly, ghostly and garbled situation'.

The Freetown military junta was obviously running out of options. The Nigerian military jets were a constant reminder of that. The junta leader had reiterated to the visiting UN envoy their commitment to the Banjul Peace Accord, while at the same time underlining their concerns, which needed to be addressed before the handing over in three months.

The removal of High Commissioner Fergusson, particularly the slamming and apparent shaming of the exiled government for the alleged breach of UN Resolution 1347, was therefore welcomed by the junta. 'It is a pointer to the fact that the British government and the UN are serious about a peaceful win-win outcome to this imbroglio,' junta spokesman Ibrahim Barrie had stated in a signed press release. Though it quickly added, 'The people's misery under the harshest of conditions and the affront to Sierra Leone's territorial integrity by Nigeria are continuing unabated.' They welcomed the departure of High Commissioner Mark Fergusson, but they would prefer a lifting of the sanctions as a matter of priority, the Freetown junta stated in their press release.

President Ndomahina's office in Monrovia quickly responded with a statement: 'The foot of state in Freetown is making unnecessary demands that clearly point to the fact that the military junta does not want to give up power willingly. They are just pretending to be willing to abide by the Banjul Peace Accord. If the sanctions are lifted, the junta will be emboldened to continue in its recalcitrance. We are willing, ready and able to stop them in their tracks. The dehumanisation of our people must stop now.'

The Freetown junta leaders knew, from their intelligence, that President Ndomahina had always leaned and relied on Mallam Musa Odofo more than on Mark Fergusson. So things were not the way they seemed. Both parties never trusted the process. While a President-Ndomahina faction believed he should be restored at all cost even if chickens remained to be ruled afterwards, a powerful faction within the military junta wanted to cling on to power even if only vultures eventually survived.

28

Sierra Leone's national lamentation at this time left no place untouched. Roboli could be worse… or rather, no less.

Ever since they broke the record of being the first twins to survive at Roboli, the Tamaraneh boys, Amidu and Amadu, were apparently poised to be some death-defying set. Year in year out, they defied the odds. In the third year, they almost succumbed when a wave of smallpox wiped out more than half the child population of Roboli. The twins were infected and severely ravished by the disease, but how they survived what became known as *da tu da Gbap-Rohng* (the plague of April) still remained a mystery. On top of that, in the course of growing up, at least one of them survived a bout of malaria, a snake bite, a road accident and drowning.

Teacher Paul and Rosemarie could not have been happier the day their twins started going to school. When the boys went on to attend the secondary school where he taught, Teacher Paul didn't give specific preference or ask for favours from his colleague teachers for the twins. He let them go through schooling as everybody else. But they soon proved their mettle anyway. Teacher Paul was so proud of his boys and boasted about them using one of his favourite African proverbs: 'an orange can only bear an orange, not a lemon'.

In and out of school, the Tamaraneh twins became famous. They were in the school's trophy-winning football team. They also liked watching Indian and Chinese movies on Saturdays at the matinee shows in the nearby town of Rombantha. They were also very creative: their childhood years were celebrated at Roboli for using sticks and ropes to make toy cars and bicycles. At the same time, they were doing well at school and soon passed their external exams for entry into university.

Word would soon spread – who started it, it was hard to lay a finger on – that the Tamaraneh twins were not ordinary, that they had special intuitive and supernatural powers, that they didn't even need to study hard to pass an exam, that they were not even studying, and that they could even foresee the future. Roboli was awash with strange and mystical stories about Amidu and Amadu. And Editor Tamaraneh's in-and-out-of-jail escapades with the Ndomahina government for his journalistic writings fed the rumours of his nine-lives-of-a-cat attribution at his hometown. He was simply invincible – the Roboli rumour-making machine churned out.

***

Going to Roboli on an average day and asking for Stephen and Samson would hardly yield results; no one knew them there. Ask for Amidu and Amadu, even a child would locate their house. Those were the names given to them by their father, Teacher Paul. Throughout their formative years, they were called Amidu and Amadu at Roboli. The first time the names Stephen and Samson were publicly pronounced was during the christening service at the local church, which Teacher Paul had reluctantly attended after it required the intervention of Pastor Dumbuya, the husband of Mary, Rosemarie's friend, 'for the sake of the children'. That day, the pastor called them Amidu Stephen Tamaraneh and Amadu Samson Tamaraneh.

Since then, not much was heard about Stephen and Samson. It was always Amidu and Amadu, as far as the people of Roboli knew.

Through *The True Light*, the editor and accountant were recognised as rising stars who had brought fame to Roboli. Their ageing paramount chief great uncle, Bai Kaffoir, was also proud of them. But it had sometimes caused him to regret not having sent to school his own children, who lurked in traditional vanity, as he realised in his twilight years. He had passed away fully knowing that the chieftaincy would not immediately directly go to his children but back to the Tikonko family, in line with Governor Barefoot's chieftaincy/ruling house rotational policy. Bai Kaffoir had also ruminated that if he had sent his children to school as his elder brother Amidu did (though Amidu had the reputation of having rebelled against tradition by abandoning the chieftaincy to go and fight in the Second World War), there would have been greater certainty of the future of his progeny, as was the case for his famous great nephews, Amidu and Amadu.

But – with the harsh political and military interregnum that had befallen Sierra Leone – if Bai Kaffoir were alive today, he would have rued that thought about the twins. The whole of Roboli was overwhelmed by the fact that the legendary story of the Tamaraneh twins had ended in tragedy.

* * *

When *The True Light* newspaper was in circulation, the rebel war neither reached Freetown nor Roboli. But the atrocities in-between meant there were serious dangers in traversing from one place to another. Villages and towns between the two were ransacked and at times razed, leaving behind a trail of death and destruction. The army was overstretched. There were frequent ambushes on the highway. It took a lot of risks with military escorts to travel within the country – at times ending fatally. A helicopter service was brought in by the President's Lebanese friend, his party's chief sponsor, Amza Alie, at a killer fare. The affluent, the diamond-and-gold magnates, and government ministers of course, used it to move from one point to the other. Selected government journalists sometimes benefited. The private media did not have an opportunity. They often had to rely on the disjointed stories of escapees from 'behind rebel lines' to know what was going on. Or through the telephone booths in some towns – of which Roboli was one.

Teacher Paul and Rosemarie had kept in touch with their twins during those cut-off moments by using the pay-phone every Saturday. It continued that way even after the coup against President Kargbo Ndomahina. Even though the military junta had claimed to have worked out a ceasefire with the rebels following the 'overthrow of the corrupt wicked regime', ordinary citizens still found it unsafe to travel ever since the exiled President announced that he was on his way back with the full support of the Nigerian Army. Everybody knew how close the former President was to the Nigerian dictator, Mallam Musa Odofo. Most resorted to civil disobedience, either in defiance of the military junta or in fear of the bombs or due to the unavailability of basic resources or just the general air of uncertainty, with clouds of gloom hanging over the country.

One reason given for one of the several arrests of Editor Amidu was libel against the President – *The True Light* had written that President Ndomahina deposited chunks of diamonds to Mallam Musa Odofo, with pictures in Aso Rock to support the story, six months after the President's inauguration. After two weeks in prison, the editor was released without charge. Now that the bombs were falling in Freetown after the overthrow of President Ndomahina, and the Nigerian media was asking about who was paying for the war effort, but Mallam Odofo keeping usual sealed lips, the pieces seemed to be falling in place on the veracity of the newspaper story.

And when the Nigeria-enforced land, air and sea embargo started biting Sierra Leone, the full extent of the doomsday picture dawned on the inhabitants. The literal caught-between-the-devil-and-the-deep-blue-sea (Freetown was located on a peninsula semi-circled by the Atlantic Ocean): the military junta was ruthless; Mallam Odofo's military was faceless. Neighbours became suspicious of neighbours. The country was crippled. In their hiding places, for fear of rebels or soldiers or *resols* (rebels looking like soldiers), townspeople and villagers also had to use palm fronds to conceal the plumes of smoke that came from cooking, so that the Nigerian jets would not mistake them for rebel camps. In a bush at Robanka, fifteen miles from Roboli, twenty civilians were killed when a bomb was dropped there. Roboli was deserted too. Just two bombs dropped at the police station– wounding four people, two of whom later died – were enough to cause everyone to run into the bushes to live just a little above animals. It was a moment of misery. It was at this time that rebels entered Roboli and burnt several houses, including the maternity centre.

On top of that misery was more misery for the Tamaranehs. Well, actually for Teacher Paul and Rosemarie. They got reports that a bomb was dropped at the newspaper offices of *The True Light* and that their twins, Amidu and Amadu, were among the fatalities.

A Roboli native businessman, Alieu Kondoh, had brought the news. Alieu was once a schoolmate of Teacher Paul's. He was commonly known as 'Vascular Bundles' for his notorious likeness of the subject matter during biology classes. He would later drop out of school to take over his father's merchandise business. He became successful – more so during the war.

Alieu Vascular Bundles – like a few other native businessmen – was well-known to both the army and rebels, as he paid them to safeguard him, using bypasses and detours to do his trading between Freetown and Roboli. He made a fortune out of excessive profiteering. He would take palm oil and other native produce to Freetown while he brought soap, salt and other 'valuables' to Roboli. Alieu Vascular Bundles told the newspaper-office-bombing story with the authority of someone present at the scene. He told of the mangled bodies that were found and the unceremonious burial. But his story varied, depending on who he was telling it. At times, he would say he was told by the twins' fellow journalists. "But whatever it was, what is certain is that Amidu and Amadu have been killed," he underlined when at one time someone reminded him of his double accounts. He had made sure he came with a copy of *The People's Voice* newspaper, which had the lead headline 'Tamaraneh Twin Journalists Slain By Nigerian Bomb', with pictures of Amidu Stephen and Samson Amadu Tamaraneh. Alieu Vascular Bundles – who over the years had developed or adopted a condescending attitude towards education – knew his friend, Teacher Paul, had always liked details and evidence since their school days. So he had brought the evidence.

Alieu Vascular Bundles – always ostentatiously dressed with matching gold or gold-plated chains and rings on at least three fingers of each hand, plus gold-plated front teeth – actually ended up meddling into all types of businesses during the war. And he was adroit in what he was doing. He became a conduit for Lebanese merchants in gold, diamonds and even arms. He built a fortune out of that, and eventually had his own private bodyguards that moved with him everywhere. His network of wholesalers and retailers was unending, in his own words. 'I have vascular bundles of connections' was his favourite saying – continuing with the schooldays' nickname.

***

So even in their hiding places, where everybody else was dejected, Teacher Paul and Rosemarie became rejected. The old family infamy came back into play. The rebellion of Grandpa Amidu (running away from the chieftaincy to fight in the Second World War) had come back to haunt the Tamaranehs in the midst of their misery. The family of Bai Kaffoir, who took over the chieftaincy, were now contented and boastful that he never took the Western education route. Teacher Paul and Rosemarie's relationship also came under the gossip spotlight: why did he marry a 'foreign' woman? Furthermore, his son had over-emulated him by having a relationship with a white woman – in total disregard of their customs. So now that Alieu Vascular Bundles had brought the news that the twins had been killed, most Roboli people believed it was self-inflicted injury by the Tamaranehs.

"The ancestral spirits are simply angry with that family," an elder, whose own father was among those whose advice Grandpa Amidu Tamaraneh had defied on the chieftaincy issue, said while recounting events.

Only the pastor's wife, Mary – with the support of her husband, an unassuming, quiet and reticent man – stood by them while in hiding. The fact that Pastor Dumbuya and his wife never themselves had children of their own was a tool they used in consoling Teacher Paul and Rosemarie.

"The Lord giveth and the Lord has taken away," the pastor said, while conducting a short burial-in-absentia service in the bush for the twins whom he again pronounced – as he did many years ago when he christened them – as Amidu Stephen Tamaraneh and Amadu Samson Tamaraneh.

The Roboli people were still in the bush when Sarah Fergusson, through Vicar Andrew Decker, got the British military in Sierra Leone to check for the Tamaranehs and they could not be traced. But now they had returned to their houses. The junta had made practical efforts at bringing people out of the bushes following the signing of the Banjul Peace Accord (although the Roboli people made sure they hadn't heard the sound of an Alfa jet for several days before feeling convinced enough to return). But life was still hard – very hard. The embargo stayed on – it would only be lifted after the return of President Kargbo Ndomahina, the pro-democracy radio had stated. But at least the fear of the jets had gone from Roboli.

At the national front, the news of High Commissioner Mark Fergusson's sacking didn't mean much for the people of Roboli. But it meant worse for the Tamaranehs. The twins (who used to interpret political events for them through their newspaper, which, to its very last edition, found its way to Roboli via military and rebel routes) were no more. And even worse for Teacher Paul and Rosemarie, their hope for a continued physical connection to their grandson Joel (left behind by their son) had been shattered by the withdrawal of Mark Fergusson.

National events were no longer the cup of tea of the one-time current affairs icon of Roboli, Teacher Paul. In one of those moments when he tried to open up from his grief, he told Pastor Dumbuya, "Post-independence African politicians are a mess of porridge. And African soldiers are a baggage of mess. Thank you for providing this opium for the masses to have some hope." To which the pastor merely nodded.

With schools indefinitely closed due to the fluid military situation in the country, Teacher Paul had joined his wife Rosemarie (whom he admired for having shown more resilience and gracefulness in her time of grief) in subsistence farming for their daily survival.

And that was all that mattered for now, Teacher Paul believed.

29

Less than two weeks after the dismissal of High Commissioner Mark Fergusson, they did the deed. Mallam Musa Odofo and President Kargbo Ndomahina – unbeknown to any other leader – authorised and announced to the world that a full-scale military operation involving ten thousand Nigerian soldiers had been effectively launched to remove the military junta from power in Freetown. And five days later – with the help of the civil militia, armed to the teeth with the new weapons from the British mercenary firm – the mission was all but accomplished.

***

In fact, the operation had started three days earlier. The moment he had put down the phone that evening after speaking to President Ndomahina, Mallam Musa Odofo summoned the head of the Nigerian Army and instructed him to send additional troops to Sierra Leone immediately and to put those already on the ground on red alert. "We are ready for immediate action," he had snapped. In addition, Aso Rock also announced the appointment of five-star General Victor Adekera to immediately replace Colonel

Baiblos Adeyemi as head of the Sierra Leone Military Expedition (SLEOMEX). Two days later, Nigerian soldiers and civil militia stealthily arrived at the outskirts of Freetown, using bush paths late in the night, and took positions on top of the hills overlooking the city – one squadron with heavy weaponry was based at Mount Aureol University, as all educational institutions had closed. Nigerian military chiefs – meeting deep into the night at Aso Rock – code-named it 'Operation Octopus'.

* * *

For Mallam Musa Odofo, this was a real-life do-or-die battle. He had as much at stake in it as President Ndomahina. Perhaps, even more. In fact, even more. If SLEOMEX failed, if Operation Octopus did not succeed, the worst that could happen to the Liberia-based Sierra Leone President was to stay in exile. But a worse fate awaited Mallam Odofo. The international community's spotlight would immediately be turned back to his own military junta. And that would be it. He would not escape: for crimes against humanity at home in Nigeria; for war crimes abroad in Sierra Leone. No, for Mallam Odofo, Operation Octopus must succeed. President Ndomahina must be returned to Freetown. To hell with UN Resolution 1347. To hell with Britain.

* * *

He was Major Musa Odofo when he and eight other middle-ranked officers overthrew the civilian government of President George Obafemi fifteen years ago. The group of middle-age military officers formed the 'Council for the Prosperity of Nigeria' (CPN) led by Colonel Mahmoud Mahmoud.

Just a year later, Major Musa Odofo staged a palace coup, accusing Mahmoud Mahmoud of 'deviating from the revolution's ideology by appointing corrupt civilians in the revolutionary council'. Musa Odofo renamed it the Reformed Council for the Prosperity of Nigeria (RCPN) and, true to his word, appointed no civilian in his cabinet. As the new Head of State, and to have full leverage over the military, he rapidly promoted himself and his colleagues to General – retiring all former senior officers.

They did very well in the first five years. A new sense of 'Nigerianness' was instilled in the population, as the new government bandied patriotism and nationalism around. They overhauled the oil industry and started getting huge revenues from selected companies. Regular electricity supply was restored to cities that had only known blackout for decades. So also was the water supply system improved across cities, towns and even villages. The RCPN built a new capital city in Abuja, moving the administrate hub of government from the old decrepit city of Lagos.

But soon, media reports started popping up about members of the council building lavish mansions and owning extravagant bank accounts abroad, that they were feeding fat from the nation's resources through fraudulent kickbacks from contracts given to cronies. Nigeria's crusading *Nation First* newspaper traced General Musa Odofo's wife, Gracie's name to a string of multi-million multiple-currency accounts in a Swiss Bank. She was nicknamed 'Mama Gucci' by the Nigerian press for her love for an ostentatiously extravagant life. She owned fifteen private vehicles – using one twice a month. Her flamboyance, with a retinue of ladies-in-waiting, was known in hotels across Europe, where she did her shopping.

The RCPN reacted to the media reports with a wave of suppression and repression. Journalists were arrested, beaten and jailed. Some simply disappeared – to eternity. Media houses were closed, some burnt down. Even mere activists of freedom of expression were clamped down; some escaped into exile and started piling pressure on the international community to restore democracy in Nigeria. More kidnappings, more disappearances, more killings.

But it was only after General Odofo refused to grant pardon to the human rights activist, British-educated Professor Ken Sawyer, after he and nine others were found guilty of subversion and treason by what some sections of the Nigerian media called 'an RCPN kangaroo court', and got them executed by firing squad, that the world woke up to the horror of what was happening in Nigeria.

The new British government of Prime Minister Ed McInroy, having committed to an 'ethical foreign policy', had felt obliged as the former colonial power to lead the efforts at restoring democracy in Nigeria. Another 'wanted' Nigerian writer, Prof. Kelly Olambo, had escaped and sought asylum in Britain. He granted extensive interviews, piling pressure and gaining sympathy for the world to do something about 'burning Nigeria'. The British government consequently championed UN resolutions placing sanctions on petroleum products from Nigeria and a travel ban on all the officials of the RCPN. The council was forced to come up with a date for elections for a return to civilian rule, excluding 'all members of the RCPN and their family members from contesting in the forthcoming elections, while granting all of them general amnesty from prosecution'.

In-between, General Odofo had tried a public relations campaign by getting RCPN supporters – some said they were forced – to organise a demonstration to show that 'the people of Nigeria are happy with the government of General Odofo'. It was during this time that he got the Munir Religions Council to bestow on him the title of 'Mallam', which he decreed to be his official title henceforth. The guest of honour at the ceremony was his 'friend and brother', the Libyan Dictator, who had defied the international community's pariah sanctions and flew into Abuja with 300 Philistine security personnel.

But when the international community remained resolute, with Britain sending a frigate to Nigerian waters, Mallam Odofo realised he could not stop the tide. He conducted the elections, almost entirely sponsored by the international community, with observers coming from all over the world. But Mallam Odofo's preferred candidate lost. He grudgingly accepted the results, as all observers declared them 'free and fair'. He then set a two-week date for the official handing over ceremony to the elected President, Buhari Okonkwo. Just after the international election observers had left, Mallam Odofo arrested the President-elect. He claimed to have not only unearthed massive electoral fraud but that the intelligence services had got sufficient evidence to prove that President-elect Buhari Okonkwo was planning to arrest and execute all the members of the RCPN.

The international community felt betrayed and conned by Mallam Odofo. Britain was at the forefront of tightening the sanctions screws. The Foreign Secretary announced and placed 'an immediate freeze on all assets, liquid or otherwise, belonging to officials of the Nigerian government anywhere in the world until the democratically-elected President Buhari Okonkwo is inaugurated'. There were some rumblings within the Nigerian army too. The RCPN arrested several officers on allegations of 'working with outside forces to subvert the ideology of the revolution'.

The tightened sanctions soon started biting hard. Nigeria was officially a pariah nation through UN Resolution 5954. (The sanctions on petroleum products were somehow bypassed by some Russian, Iranian and Ukrainian vessels anchoring offshore and using small boats to do their deals.) Life became very difficult for the ordinary Nigerian as prices of commodities skyrocketed. Some resorted to a policy of 'non-cooperation with the government of Mallam Musa Odofo'. Civil servants refused to go to work; even some drivers of government buses didn't turn up.

None of the RCPN leaders could travel out of the country and Mallam Musa Odofo had vowed not to cave in to the demand of handing over to the democratically-elected Buhari Okonkwo. "It would be like putting your own neck on the slaughter lab in the presence of your enemy holding a cutlass," he had summed it up. From all intelligence, Buhari Okonkwo, if given power, was poised to take revenge for his cousin Prof. Sawyer's execution, irrespective of public assurances that the amnesty on RCPN members would be respected. Odofo had recordings of meetings where Okonkwo's senior supporters were plotting and saying these things. The British – and the rest of the world – didn't find that credible. While Mallam Odofo weighed his options for a way (any way) out, he heartily welcomed any development that would sway the international community's attention away from Nigeria. Even if just for a little while. "One step at a time," he kept telling his Chief Security Officer, Mamadu Gowon. He knew he was in a bind. He had to find a way of wriggling his way out – if that was possible.

Some happenings in another West African country made it possible. Almost suddenly, there was a coup in Sierra Leone, overthrowing the government of President Kargbo Ndomahina. With the British government's commitment to its ethical foreign policy – and more so for the emotional personal ties that Prime Minister Ed McInroy had for Sierra Leone – the immediate focus for the restoration of democracy was shifted from Abuja to Freetown. Sierra Leone was the apple of the eye of British foreign policy in Africa, in Prime Minister Ed McInroy's rulebook, in his eyes. Britain had to act quickly. The royal frigate off the shores of Nigeria was ordered to leave immediately for Sierra Leone waters on the very night that the British naval vessel left Freetown with President Ndomahina.

And, ironically, Britain would have to work with Mallam Musa Odofo in solving the Sierra Leone crisis, wrote High Commissioner Mark Fergusson in his report to London in the aftermath of the coup. He had underlined 'the inexplicable and extremely intimate personal affinity between President Ndomahina and the Nigerian dictator, a relationship which, to all intents and purposes, the former is obviously incapable of doing without'. And the High Commissioner, who himself had a personal dislike for the Nigerian dictator on top of the official line, also noted that 'Mallam Musa Odofo already has boots on the ground as a potent counterforce to the Freetown military junta if it came to having to use raw military prowess to restore the legitimate President'.

So they worked together. They had to work together. Britain's strategy was that a swift mission of restoration of democracy was to be done in Sierra Leone and then would turn to the showdown being played out in the Nigerian scenario; that, after the junta in Sierra Leone would be the junta in Nigeria. In the meantime, the junta in Nigeria was needed. "Talk about a necessary evil," the British Foreign Secretary had exclaimed after the Cobra meeting held for the purpose – to dislodge the junta in Sierra Leone. And the junta in Nigeria exhibited 'unrestrained overzealousness by not waiting on any one's orders, neither consulting anyone, to start bombing Sierra Leone using military jets', High Commissioner Fergusson wrote a few days later when it was decided he also had to decamp to Liberia as 'the security situation is deteriorating and worsening by the hour'.

In Liberia, High Commissioner Mark Fergusson's personal recommendation had got the UN to initiate peace talks with the junta in Freetown 'in the interest of the suffering masses'. Though he had failed during that first week of the coup to get the military junta to immediately go back to the barracks, Mark Fergusson came away feeling that the junta leader himself was willing and able to convince his men to give up power if their 'legitimate concerns' were addressed. The junta leader had emphasised during their meeting that President Ndomahina had hastily left the territory of Sierra Leone, which effectively meant he had abdicated and abandoned the people; and that there was no room for a vacuum – making Mark himself feel guilty for the 'hasty' bit.

'Stampeding President Ndomahina back to power could worsen an already volatile situation,' Mark Fergusson had written in a subsequent dispatch to London for the attention of the British representative to the UN. 'If we can resolve the situation through peaceful diplomatic means, without having to shed blood unnecessarily, that would be the most ethical route to take.'

President Ndomahina was never comfortable with this. When he communicated to Mallam Odofo his doubts over 'so-called peace talks with the Freetown military junta', the Nigerian dictator calmed the President down and encouraged him to co-operate. "You should only always insist that the military option remains open, even if a last option," Mallam Odofo had emphasised.

The diplomatic route would endear the exiled President to the international community and the spotlight would continue to be on Sierra Leone, giving some breathing space to Mallam Odofo's RCPN to weigh its options out of its own imbroglio. President Ndomahina's situation had provided the needed respite. Nigerian officials, on the insistence of President Ndomahina, were to be allowed to sit in planning meetings in Monrovia with British officials, including High Commissioner Mark Fergusson.

Soon the idea of hiring a British mercenary firm was hatched and bought and executed. A secret American diplomatic cable had stated: 'The contract was paid for by Aso Rock through diamonds that President Kargbo Ndomahina had been allegedly depositing with his friend in the course of the last decade.' Invariably, Mallam Odofo had scored a diplomatic goal: the sanctions on Nigeria had to be eased for 'essential activities geared towards the restoration of democracy in Sierra Leone'.

Limited petroleum supplies were allowed, authorised flights started operations. Personnel of the British mercenary firm, Jungle Boys International, flew in and out of Nigeria in tying the knots of the contract. Invariably, Clause Three of the Banjul Peace Accord clearly stated that 'the military option will be used if the Freetown junta refuses to cooperate with the efforts to restore the civilian government of President Kargbo Ndomahina'.

And then Britain had suddenly withdrawn High Commissioner Mark Fergusson without informing Mallam Musa Odofo and President Ndomahina. Worse still, it had to do with the contract with Jungle Boys International. Mallam Odofo felt betrayed, and even trapped, by the British antics. The pending investigations on the issue by the parliamentary sub-committee would mean High Commissioner Mark Fergusson, and any other witness that might be called, would detail the role of Aso Rock in the whole deal. And the international spotlight would automatically turn to the Odofo regime again. He would do all in his power to prevent this – if he could!

So after getting the consent of, or after giving his consent to (it was hard to tell which was which), President Ndomahina, Mallam Odofo was also now going to act in total spite of the British. He would rather die trying to survive. He would rather try. He would rather survive – not die. That had always been the way of men who had found themselves in a situation as his. One thing the Nigerian dictator was absolutely sure of was that he would never hand power over to the imprisoned President-elect Buhari Okonkwo, who was a cousin of the executed Professor Ken Sawyer. Mallam Odofo had underrated and dismissed the chances of Okonkwo during the elections. 'Buhari Okonkwo is planning a bloody revenge for his countryman', an intelligence report from Mallam Odofo's trusted and fearsome Chief Security Officer underlined. Things were looking terribly bad for him: if he handed over power, the noose might be waiting for him; if he did not hand over, the British were ready to force him out. He had to find a way – if there was one. Maybe there was only one left now.

To Mallam Odofo, therefore, if SLEOMEX succeeded – if Operation Octopus went as planned – he would have created much-needed breathing space for himself, some political oxygen for the RCPN. Sierra Leone would become his satellite state under President Ndomahina. If things came to the worst for him in Nigeria, he would have created a haven to possibly hide; and President Ndomahina would readily protect his friend and restorer. Both agreed to go for the jugular.

Mallam Odofo was therefore inwardly beaming, with smiles hidden behind the rugged face of the soldier, as he announced to the world from Aso Rock, "The Nigerian Army has today launched Operation Octopus in Sierra Leone because the Freetown military junta has shown utter disrespect for the Banjul Peace Accord by attacking Nigerian bases in the past couple of days in the country. They have breached the Accord. Therefore, the last option – the military option – is now being implemented as authorised by the elected President of Sierra Leone, President Kargbo Ndomahina."

* * *

Prime Minister Ed McInroy was utterly shocked. He knew Mallam Odofo was a maverick – Mark Fergusson never spared a moment repeatedly underlining in his reports the 'unholy leverage the Nigerian dictator has over the President'. But the British Prime Minister had underestimated how far Mallam Odofo could go to display it. To Britain, by this military action, Nigeria had literally invaded Sierra Leone. There was no international law that supported the Nigerian operation. No UN Resolution. "This is an aggression, pure and simple," the Prime Minister told a hurriedly convened Cobra meeting. And the Foreign Secretary was immediately mandated to instruct the British UN representative in New York to raise the alarm that 'Britain unequivocally condemns the violation of Sierra Leone's sovereignty and territorial integrity'. Downing Street further felt impelled to issue a statement demanding Mallam Odofo to 'immediately halt the Nigerian military action, as the diplomatic option is still open through the Banjul Peace Accord'.

***

Apart from – or over and above – the Prime Minister's trumpeted 'ethical foreign policy' was his deep-seated sentimental personal attachment to Sierra Leone stemming from his father's colonial work there, his mother's services to Mount Aureol University, his own birth there, his continuing affection for the country since his university gap year, and then his determination to help the struggling country out of the doldrums – with a politico-military nemesis staring in its face. He had just sacrificed his best friend, Mark Fergusson – whom he had originally specifically chosen to 'save the country'. The Prime Minister was normally a man who hardly showed emotion under any circumstances, but he hit the table twice during the Cobra meeting.

Similarly, apart from – over and above – the personal affinity he had with President Ndomahina, Mallam Musa Odofo had his own sentimental personal attachments to Sierra Leone. True, the two had immediately struck a relationship when they met at Britain's Sandhurst Military Academy as officer cadets from former colonies of British West Africa. And when Major Musa Odofo staged the palace coup against Colonel Mahmoud Mahmoud, Sierra Leone (under the-then newly inaugurated President Ndomahina) was among the first to congratulate and recognise the RCPN junta. It was true also that the relationship went deeper and too personal when President Ndomahina, according to *The True Light* newspaper, turned Mallam Musa Odofo 'into his secret personal diamond banker, stashing away to Aso Rock uncountable and innumerable amounts of gem stones from the fields of Tongo and Kono'.

But, beyond that, Mallam Musa Odofo had more personal and historical reasons. So when he had consolidated his authority in Nigeria and started doling out 'technical and expertise support' to Sierra Leone – especially for the security forces, to the extent of providing a presidential elite force to protect the presidency – Mallam Odofo saw it as much a support for President Ndomahina as it was for 'the sister country on its own merit'. Mallam Odofo had said in several forums that even if it were not President Ndomahina in power, he would have still supported Sierra Leone. What was questionable – when it became known to the public – was whether the support would have been on the same scale if the Sierra Leone leader had not deposited diamonds with the Nigerian leader. 'Maybe with the absolute power he has garnered as the man in charge of "the superpower of West Africa", Mallam Odofo would have created a puppet for Sierra Leone anyway. But he couldn't have asked for a better puppet than President Ndomahina', *The True Light* had stated in an editorial.

By size and military might, Nigeria had become the Big Brother of the West African sub-region and even beyond. General Odofo's regime made that status more resonant and fearsome. Being the single most generous contributor to the finances of the West Africa Heads of State Group, Mallam Odofo wielded power above his colleague Heads of State. And once or twice – advertently or inadvertently – Mallam Odofo had even publicly said he was willing to sacrifice President Ndomahina for the good of Sierra Leone. It never went down well with the Sierra Leonean leader – though he knew it was meant to be a joke. He only expressed his dissatisfaction to Femi Cole, behind closed doors. She had laughed it off as 'the usual boys' bluff'. He agreed.

* * *

But Mallam Odofo had meant what he said about loving Sierra Leone more than its President. He regarded Freetown as his fatherland. Justifiably so, history said so.

Hand-in-hand with the pre-colonial founding of Freetown (then called the 'Province of Freedom') by British philanthropists for the repatriation of freed slaves (among whom were white wives, including High Commissioner Mark Fergusson's great-great-grandmother), British naval boats were also deployed at Freetown's natural harbour to enforce the abolition of the slave trade. It had emerged that unscrupulous British and other European slave traders were still engaged in the human trade after the British Parliament had proscribed it. The Freetown-based British Navy arrested the traders' ships at the high seas and offloaded the human cargo in the 'province of freedom'. These new arrivals – who never reached the slave plantations in the Americas and thus were not actually freed slaves like those brought from Britain, Nova Scotia and other places – were called 'liberated Africans'. They consisted of all types of assorted tribes and peoples from the West African coast.

Among them was Adesanya Odofo – the grandfather of Mallam Musa Odofo! A young, muscular Adesanya was captured and torn from his family during a midnight raid in Yoriboland and sold as a slave. They had covered a considerable part of the sea journey under harsh conditions (they were packed like sardines in tins on the ship's decks; with those who died on the way, including his only brother, thrown overboard into the deep sea) when a British naval boat intercepted them and dragged them to Freetown. They were all freed and given makeshift shelter by the Black Star Liner Philanthropy Mission, which was running the affairs of the 'Province'.

Adesanya learnt carpentry and was soon employed as a building support worker by the Mission. He got married to another liberated African, Muskuda, a Fulani lady captured from Benin. Their only son was Clifford Odofo, the father of Mallam Musa Odofo.

It was a strict policy of the Philanthropy Mission that all the children of freed slaves and liberated Africans must attend the 'schooling services' provided. Clifford Odofo made good use of it and soon became one of the first students enrolled at the new tertiary institution. He was trained as a catechist. When the British Crown took over and turned the 'Province of Freedom' into a colony, eventually extending its administration to Nigeria, Ghana and The Gambia, Clifford Odofo became an itinerant catechist with the Philanthropy Mission, which had extended its services to the 'British-administered areas'. He ended up being a full-time catechist in Yoriboland, the area where his father (who passed away while Clifford was still in training) had told him he came from. Clifford only came back to Freetown briefly for his mother Muskuda Odofo's funeral. He sold his father's house and permanently relocated to Nigeria, having found a wife there and already with three children, the first of whom was Musa Odofo. Clifford used to tell fantastic stories about the beauty of Freetown to his children. "I'm sure one day I'll take you there," he used to tell them. As young Musa Odofo grew up, he had liked asking further questions about the land where his grandfather and grandmother were buried. Which languages did the people speak? How did they dress? What did they eat? And Clifford was delighted to talk about it. "A whole street was named after your grandfather – Adesanya Street. It is there. As a carpenter, he worked hard to build Freetown. You will one day go and see it," the father had told the inquisitive Musa Odofo. "Two things I don't like about that country though – too much tribal politics and the Lebanese shadow state. It saddens my heart."

So, despite their integration into the Nigerian society, the Odofos were always identified as Sierra Leoneans in Yoriboland. Musa's father was referred to as 'Clifford Odofo from Sierra Leone'. Despite having been born in Nigeria and speaking Yoribo like all other kids, Musa Odofo would here and there be told about his Sierra Leonean roots. Though it all died down later, he never forgot about those reminders. He had a longing for Sierra Leone. He would like to know there. There was a room in his heart for that place – while he still loved Nigeria.

The Yoriboland people's reference to the Odofos as Sierra Leoneans was not borne out of negativity, but out of admiration. In those days, Sierra Leoneans on such missions as Clifford's, abroad in the British-administered areas, were seen as 'the black people who speak on equal terms with the white man'. This was a time – not too long after the slave trade – when white people were either feared or loathed by other Africans. Freetown was, as Clifford Odofo himself had insisted, 'the seat of the white man, the melting pot of Westernisation and the cradle of civilisation' in the sub-continent. So people from Sierra Leone were seen as 'wise and educated' and were treated with deference by their fellow Africans – hence 'Clifford Odofo from Sierra Leonean' in Yoriboland, which only made a young Musa Odofo crave more 'the Athens of West Africa'.

When a youthful Lt. Musa Odofo of the Nigerian Army got a slot to be further trained in Britain and met with his Sierra Leonean counterpart, Lt. Kargbo Ndomahina, it was the beginning of the realisation of the dream of his father – even his own dream – of physically reconnecting with the 'land of the free' – or of the freed. For Lt. Odofo, the Sandhurst encounter with Lt. Ndomahina was just a part of the jigsaw; but the big picture was Sierra Leone and, as it turned out, himself!

And that was the picture General Musa Odofo, the Nigerian military dictator, had displayed when he took the singular decision – after speaking to President Ndomahina – of authorising and announcing the launch of Operation Octopus.

As far as Mallam Musa Odofo was concerned, he was doing a duty for his fatherland – as much as he was doing it to save his own skin in the motherland. And he was convinced his action was justified in the Banjul Peace Accord, in the crafting of which Nigerian diplomats led by his Foreign Minister played a key role, with the British, the UN, the Americans and other West African leaders acting as moral guarantors. The Nigerian delegation to Banjul – just as the Freetown junta delegation – had only been allowed to travel to The Gambian capital for the purpose of the peace talks. Both countries' de facto leaderships were on international travel bans.

***

It was hard or impossible to know Nigeria's exact foreign policy towards Sierra Leone under the Odofo regime. It was at best a double-tongued one – not mere diplomatic double-speak. It was a policy that sought the interests and fed the ego of one man alone – Mallam Musa Odofo – even if it led to double jeopardy for the Freetown military junta, or even if he had to sacrifice President Ndomahina. Whatever worked for Odofo! There were flying rumours that he had an initial hand in the coup against his friend, President Ndomahina. Explanations or rationalisations were given.

It was said that the Sierra Leonean coup-makers at least had the feeling – actually some conviction – that they had the initial support and backing of the Nigerian military leader. Some members of the public had pointed at the inaction of the Nigerian soldiers on the ground – apart from those in the presidential guard participating in escaping with the President from State House on the day of the coup – as a signal of tacit Nigerian support for the Sierra Leone soldiers. *Esprit de corps*?

But it even went further than that. When Sierra Leonean military personnel had initially started complaining about lack of resources and about the nonchalant behaviour of the politicians towards their plight, they got more than sympathy from their Nigerian counterparts on the ground. They got encouragement – perhaps urgings and nudgings – to act. A senior Nigerian bomb instructor openly said during training at Bengeuma barracks in the outskirts of Freetown that eliminating corrupt politicians – as the Army had done in Nigeria – was one step forward for Africa. "I took part in the public executions of those corrupt politicians in Lagos," Major Bolobolo told the Sierra Leonean soldiers. He had quickly added, "Anyway, I am just trying to tell you how I moved from being a firing squad marksman to a bomb expert." Soldiers were expected to decode messages.

And when the young Sierra Leonean officers succeeded in capturing State House and arrested all the top military brass present at the meeting that day at State House and the news reached Nigeria, a top military aide to Mallam Musa Odofo, claiming to speak on behalf his boss, actually called and congratulated the Freetown coup-makers. "General Odofo will speak to you tomorrow," the Aso Rock voice had crackled to the Sierra Leone coup leader.

* * *

The rumour that Mallam Musa Odofo surreptitiously instigated the Sierra Leone coup through some Nigerian military agents in Freetown was further embellished by a story within the Sierra Leone Army. It was said that, on the day of the coup, when escaping with President Ndomahina via the back gate of State House, there was initial confusion between the Sierra Leonean security and the Nigerian soldiers embedded within the presidential guard with regards where to take him.

According to this story, what happened was that when the President briefly spoke to Mallam Musa Odofo following his unceremonious evacuation from State House, the thoroughly shaken Sierra Leone leader merely told the Nigerian dictator that he was safe with the presidential guard – which, to Mallam Odofo, meant the President was in the hands of the Nigerian elite guard. But in reality, on the ground, the Nigerian soldiers within the presidential guard were outnumbered by a ratio of three to one

– thanks to the constant nudging of British High Commissioner Mark Fergusson, who had vehemently protested that even the presence of Nigerian soldiers within the presidential guard was abhorrent enough, let alone fulfil Mallam Odofo's wish to make it an all-Nigerian squad.

So, that day of the coup in Freetown, the Nigerian personnel's wish of taking President Ndomahina to their unit base at Newton barracks outside Freetown was countered by the Sierra Leonean ADC who stood his ground that the President had already instructed them to go to the British High Commission.

Indeed, when Mallam Odofo later learnt that the British had escaped with President Ndomahina to Liberia without his knowledge, he was very furious. "Scouts, they are. These Freetown boys are not soldiers. They are scouts," he exploded in front of his Chief Security Officer who was updating him. As far as the Nigerian coup-making rulebook was concerned, soldiers never staged a coup and let the President escape. He immediately slammed the door on the Freetown junta. Even the RCPN military aide who had earlier called to congratulate the coup leaders refused to communicate with 'the scouts' any longer. The Freetown junta leader had ended up concluding that the initial call was itself a ruse.

There were too many strands to the story – to the rumours. But what was clear was that the elimination or arrest of President Ndomahina would have put Sierra Leone in virtually the same juxtaposition as Nigeria. And Mallam Odofo knew only too well that the British were more interested in Sierra Leone than in Nigeria. The historical ties were one; the large-scale donor support per capita and safeguarding the investment or vested interests of British companies were two; Prime Minister Ed McInroy's outspoken attachment to the country was three; High Commissioner Mark Fergusson was four – Mallam Odofo would later learn. And if President Ndomahina was gone for good,

Mallam Odofo would have had a stash of diamonds all by himself. But the Freetown 'scouts' had bungled the operation. Whether Odofo instigated it or not, allowing a toppled politician to escape was not soldierly behaviour in the eyes of even the average Nigerian soldier.

Therefore, when President Kargbo Ndomahina contacted Mallam Odofo from Liberia the next day, explaining that the situation was so desperate that there was no chance to inform his 'big brother' about the evacuation, but that the plan of the British was to restore him back to power, the Nigerian dictator unequivocally pledged and committed himself to the enterprise. In fact he would lead it 'at all cost' – for their friendship's sake.

"Rest assured, Kargbo, I'll take care of those scouts and their foot of state," he said, a phrase the Sierra Leonean leader had ever since picked from the Nigerian leader, maximised and expanded on it in all the international conferences that he would attend as 'the legitimate Head of State of Sierra Leone'.

Since then, Mallam Odofo did not waiver in his devotion to restore President Ndomahina back to power. And now he had beaten the British and the UN and the rest of the international community to it – through Operation Octopus.

30

British Prime Minister Ed McInroy was thoroughly incensed about Mallam Odofo's Operation Octopus. And he had believed the Nigerian leader had finally pressed the self-destruct button. Not only was the aggression untenable in international law, but Ed McInroy was sure an all-out battle with the Sierra Leonean forces would only result to a protracted war and would in fact delay, if not totally upend, the planned return of President Kargbo Ndomahina.

As far as the Prime Minister knew, records of the Royal West African Regiment's participation in the two world wars showed that Sierra Leonean soldiers were braver and more gallant than the Nigerians. In infantry, Sierra Leone, perhaps by virtue of being the first colony, was the best in British West Africa. To the British government, therefore, it was foolhardy for the Nigerian leader to commit troops on the ground in Sierra Leone to take on the Freetown junta.

Downing Street was consequently totally opposed to Operation Octopus. A swift press statement from the Prime Minister's communications director called on 'the entire civilised world to condemn this brazen Nigerian aggression in Sierra Leone.

General Musa Odofo has crossed a red line'. At the urgings of the British Ambassador to the UN, Secretary General Kirikiri released a statement expressing 'concern over unfortunate unfolding developments in Sierra Leone', and called for a 'peaceful resolution of the crisis'.

There was friendship, and concealed connivances, in diplomatic circles too, even at the highest level, which former British High Commissioner Mark Fergusson would later learn from covert sources while researching for his planned book writing.

Secretary General Kirikiri had secretly assured his former UN-colleague-turned-exiled-President that he would turn a blind eye to Operation Octopus. He would delay convening a Security Council meeting for a UN Resolution on the development – as long as Mallam Odofo's assurance of a 'swift, short, sharp' operation was carried out.

Two days earlier, Mrs. Memunatu Ndomahina had actually boarded an internal Rynair flight from her New Jersey residence to visit Mrs. Nana Kirikiri in New York. They tied bolts and nuts in their relationship, recalling their UN days and how time flew. The President's wife (his first wife; Femi Cole being the other) had earlier received a courier with a huge package from her husband (their husband) for onward delivery to 10 UN Boulevard, New York – the Kirikiris' residence. She had delivered the package and returned to New Jersey.

***

The Freetown military junta was totally caught off-guard. Caught unawares. Scouts.

But if Operation Octopus had happened in the first few months after the coup, the Sierra Leonean soldiers wouldn't have been caught unawares. They were prepared 'to fight for our country till the last drop of blood', as junta leader Captain Matthew Thomas had put it, following President Ndomahina's first announcement from Liberia that he would be returned to power 'very very soon'.

"Sierra Leone will never be returned to those days of unbridled corruption at the detriment of the poor people of this country. We are able, willing, determined, committed and ready to lay down our lives in defence of this nation against any foreign military," Captain Thomas had threatened.

The rank and file of the Army – and even some of the disillusioned people, tired of the Ndomahina days or coerced – came out in support of the junta. When Nigerian jets started unleashing bombs in Freetown, ordinary soldiers climbed up high-rise buildings, firing at them with rocket launchers and rocket-propelled grenades. The soldiers were fired up! In high morale! They had boasted of having succeeded in downing two jets into the sea – which the Nigerians dismissed as 'blatantly false propaganda'. There were also a couple of incidences in the Lungi Airport area where the Nigerians were based. Though the Sierra Leonean fighters couldn't overrun the base, they succeeded in capturing a good number of Nigerian soldiers in a ratio of three to one vice versa. Top-level negotiations led to an exchange of prisoners.

Eventually, the British, through High Commissioner Fergusson, initiated peace talks under the banner of the UN, which culminated to the Banjul Peace Accord.

By then, the Freetown military junta had not only been sucked into the complacency and serenity of diplomacy, but the soldiers' will to fight had actually been sapped almost entirely by the air, land and sea blockade. The country had stagnated – actually, strangulated. The morale in the rank and file of the army was at its lowest ebb, not least because for three months running, their normal monthly supply of rice could not be delivered because no ship ventured to berth at the Queen Elizabeth Quay since the Ukrainian experience. Even their salaries could now only buy one-third of what they used to buy, as the prices of commodities had sky-rocketed. Some commodities were even no longer available in the market. Bread and salt had become a luxury.

Meanwhile, as per directives from Aso Rock, the Nigerian soldiers and their civil militia affiliates had secretly smuggled themselves in the middle of the night into the bushes of the hills overlooking Freetown with their new heavy artillery weapons from Britain's Jungle Boys International. When they descended on Freetown first thing in the morning, going straight to State House even before Captain Thomas could wake up from his bed – let alone come to the office – the Freetown junta was in disarray from the word go. Freetown residents trembled and wailed to the sound of the apocalyptic bombardment – backed by more airstrikes. Incessant for five consecutive days – day and night.

But the Freetown junta were an army, and that morning they tried to do what they could to prove it. They immediately issued a statement from the military headquarters (because State House had already fallen) calling on the attention of 'the moral guarantors of the Banjul Peace Accord to the fact that the Nigerians have launched an unprovoked and unwarranted attack, which will be resisted to the last' – without blood being mentioned this time. Indeed, they resisted. Street battles ensued.

Not for long. Just days later, all their defence lines had been broken. The junta leaders fled to the provinces, some of their civilian collaborators and a few middle-level officers were arrested. Most rank and file soldiers merely surrendered. Reprisals and counter-reprisals, neighbours versus neighbours, were prevalent before the dust settled. There were huge civilian, as well as military, casualties on both sides.

Operation Octopus was complete and over, Mallam Musa Odofo announced from Aso Rock, and President Kargbo Ndomahina would be returned to Sierra Leone in a month's time after 'mopping up' operations.

* * *

The excitement in Liberia was out of this world. The joy, jubilation and jollifications were surreal. President Ndomahina immediately released a statement, stating, among other things: "I am honoured and also humbled to congratulate my big brother, friend and colleague Head of State, the venerable Mallam General Musa Odofo, for doing an impossible job for me… I also thank the Nigerian military as a whole for saving Sierra Leone." He asked the people of Sierra Leone to 'exercise patience just a little bit longer for my long-awaited, people-deserved return'.

"Your President is on his way back. Stay calm and stay blessed. I'll see you all soon," the statement triumphantly concluded.

That evening, Femi Cole made sure she brought a combined team of Liberian and Sierra Leonean newsmen and cameramen to the 'presidential lodge' for President Kargbo Ndomahina to grant interviews. She sat by his side, beaming, wearing some gorgeous African attire – in conformity, actually uniformity, with the President's own outfit. Couplet attire. *Ashobe.* She had prepared everything for this day!

A lot of partying went on afterwards as exiled ministers, parliamentarians, party functionaries and all the other lackeys flocked the presidential residence. Femi Cole was now actually unhesitatingly being referred to, by all and sundry, as Madam First Lady.

* * *

It was a tricky and ironic situation for the international community. Britain had to find an explanation for that. The British representative at the UN quoted Shakespeare when a journalist threw a question at him in the lobby of UN HQ in New York about the British government's immediate policy u-turn on Nigeria's role in the Sierra Leone crisis: "All is well that ends well."

With the Freetown junta out so shockingly quick, the British government concluded it would be 'unethical and undiplomatic' not to congratulate President Kargbo Ndomahina on the certain prospects of his imminent return. It was about returning the civilian President, or rather about restoring democracy – though not the way Britain had planned or envisaged.

The American government, having been a major (even if comparatively passive) stakeholder all along, urged Prime Minister Ed McInroy to continue to take the lead by acknowledging the 'success story of a clear path to the return of democracy in Sierra Leone'. Downing Street consequently issued a well-crafted message commending 'the willpower of the Sierra Leonean people to stand up for democracy' and appreciated the fact that 'the operation was carried out with minimal loss of life and property, a worthy price for democracy' – without mentioning Nigeria or Mallam Odofo or Operation Octopus in any of it.

During Prime Minister's Questions in the British Parliament, the Opposition Leader asked with tongue in cheek, "Mr. Speaker, how many more embarrassing u-turns is my right honourable friend ready to plunge Britain into before he comes down to earth and realises that he is not a Sierra Leonean? Hard-earned British taxpayers' money is being wasted and the reputation of our country is being torn apart just for personal ego. Will he tell this House what is going on? Are there more diamond deals that we are yet to know about?"

This brought uproar in Parliament, with both sides of the House heckling and shouting at each other before the Prime Minister rose up to respond: "Mr. Speaker, I will not go down the road of personal attacks. The whole country knows how I got here, and why he is on the other side. But what I would say to him, Mr. Speaker, is that there is no price tag for democracy. The protection of democracy, no matter where – which is a core part of British values – is priceless." There were triumphant shouts from his parliamentary majority, drowning the Opposition.

The Prime Minister immediately pledged a £500 million recovery package for the damaged Sierra Leone economy 'after the return of the democratically-elected President Kargbo Ndomahina'.

On their part, the Americans – according to sidelines chit-chat at the UN in New York – now felt on level terms with the British, who had previously said 'might is not right' in relation to the Panama 'democracy saving' operation, in which America militarily removed Dictator Manuel Noriega and restored President-elect Guillarmo Endara. 'We have always supported democracy everywhere', the White House Press Secretary subsequently stated on the Sierra Leone crisis.

In Aso Rock, Abuja, Nigeria – commended by the British or not – Mallam Musa Odofo felt on top of the world.

31

In his new sedentary life, Mark Fergusson was today readjusting in his mind the oft-used saying that 'a week is a long time in politics'. From his experience, it was an understatement. To him, time in politics could be as fleeting as the twinkling of an eye. In the twinkling of an eye, Mark was a diplomat; and in the twinkling of an eye, he was no longer British High Commissioner to Sierra Leone. In the twinkling of an eye, President Ndomahina had been overthrown; and in the twinkling of an eye, the sanctions on Mallam Odofo had been eased.

'In the twinkling of an eye' was recurring in Mark's head even as he pored over hundreds of files and documents relating to his entire tenure in Sierra Leone, with particular reference to the British mercenary firm deal, in preparation for his defence at the parliamentary sub-committee hearings. Mark was a very meticulous man, everyone knew. But he was upping his game because this was actually a battle for his integrity, for his future, for his life.

"I did not do anything fraudulent, Rachael," he had further assured his wife that night when they could not go for the dinner at the Ritz Hotel. "I informed the Foreign Office every step of the way. There are letters. There are documents. There are minutes of meetings."

Rachael had refrained from asking any questions. She was just listening. And when she did that, her husband knew she believed him. "I have all the correspondences with official letterheads. We held meetings at the Foreign Office. If, therefore, the outcome is deemed illegal – or however they have coined it – as a contravention of a UN Resolution, the Foreign Office should take responsibility for clearly giving 'no objection'."

Mark had also emphasised that all the meetings held at the Foreign Office with middle-level officials together with executives of Jungle Boys International were called at the behest of the Secretary of State for Foreign Affairs. There were correspondences to that effect.

The Prime Minister knew that – later. Ed McInroy's contention during the Downing Street meeting was that Mark did not personally inform him about the mercenary arrangement at inception. He had looked his friend straight in the eye and said, "And a diplomatic cable states that diamond kickbacks were received on behalf of the British High Commission."

Mark was shocked beyond explanation. "And you believe that, Ed… ehm… Prime Minister?"

"It is not about me believing. It's about what the Americans have reported in the cable. It's out there at the UN. And this is a government. Britain's image has to be protected."

"I know. But you know me, Ed. You know me better. You know this is false. A blatant lie."

"Nothing much I can do now, Mark. I am your friend to the last. But you have to clear your name. Clear your name before the sub-committee."

Mark had acknowledged that the mercenary deal was done in exchange for diamonds. But he said he merely facilitated the connections and that the diamonds were handed over directly to the firm by Mallam Musa Odofo on the official request of President Kargbo Ndomahina, 'who is the legitimate President of Sierra Leone'. He had all the documents to the effect – minutes of meetings, details of transactions, the contract itself. Mark had argued that the Foreign Office position, the official British position, was that President Kargbo Ndomahina – despite having been overthrown physically and now being based in neighbouring Liberia – was still the legitimate President and was thus recognised by the international community. President Ndomahina had been representing Sierra Leone as Head of State in all international forums – including the UN General Assembly. He had been signing treaties on behalf of the country. He was therefore acting as thus when he went into the Jungle Boys deal, of which the Foreign Office 'was more than aware'.

"I am a small piece in this diplomatic jigsaw. If there has been any breach on UN Resolution 1347, I believe the responsibility lies at the feet of the Foreign Office. Not me. Let's be fair," good old Mark – the 'Political Fergie' from his university days – asserted.

He continued to explain – as if the Prime Minister did not know – that virtually all diplomatic offices had moved from Freetown to Monrovia in recognition of President Ndomahina. It was logical and legitimate that the President could enter into a contract with a private mercenary firm in defence of his authority and the territory of Sierra Leone. They – all the parties involved, including the Foreign Office – didn't read UN Resolution 1347 otherwise. And Mark had thought that, as per protocol, the Secretary of State had been regularly updating the Prime Minister from the very beginning.

"I'm really sorry for not personally informing you. But you know how the Foreign Secretary perceives my friendship with you and how he is wary of me bypassing him on official matters. Perhaps I should have ignored him. It's a genuine mistake. I'm really sorry."

It was too late.

The Prime Minister had felt thoroughly embarrassed when UN Secretary General John Kirikiri had shared the diplomatic cable with him. He had to take an immediate action before the news could reach the media and burn his ethical foreign policy to ashes. A scapegoat was needed to be roasted. The Secretary of State for Foreign Affairs was too big a fish, too key a pillar in the party hierarchy. Sacking or suspending him would tear the party apart at a time when their parliamentary majority was needed to approve the pending invasion of the Middle East to remove the Worst Dictator, in what promised to be the acid test of the Prime Minister's ethical foreign policy.

So the lot fell on Mark Fergusson.

Ed couldn't look at his long-time friend in the face again when bringing the hammer down. His eyes seemed concentrated on some new information he had just discovered in the documents on his desk (the very desk chosen by Mark after his friend swept his way into Downing Street about three years ago). And then he said, slowly but firmly, still looking down, "I'm sorry, Mark, but you have to go with immediate effect."

Mark's head had whirled. He was stunned. But he had accepted the decision without any protest. He had only asked for 'one last favour' – to use the back door of Number 10 Downing Street to avoid the prying, preying cameras of the journalists outside. Mark had granted the request.

It had all happened in the twinkling of an eye.

So presently, in his study at his North London home, even as he devotedly perused the documents from Liberia in preparation for his defence – taking notes copiously – Mark wondered why 'in the twinkling of an eye' was recurring in his mind.

* * *

The date for the first hearing had been set for May 25. Though the official summons itself said it would be an investigation of his tenure in Sierra Leone, Mark knew only too well that it was by and large only about the so-called 'Arms to Africa Affair' (the AAA, as per his notes). He had therefore used the first days to solely concentrate on that issue.

On the first day, he had read the one hundred and fifty-page contract document itself, signed in Monrovia by President Ndomahina and the Chief Executive of Jungle Boys International, Sylvanus Attenboro. On the second day, Mark had marked out some clauses for particular attention, laboriously taking notes, while looking for the metaphorical devil in the detail. He had finished that late in the evening. On the third day, he was back in his downstairs office early in the morning, sipping his coffee after extracting the letter he wrote to the Foreign Office about the deal and the acknowledgment signed by the head of the Africa Desk at the Foreign Office, John Coleson, on behalf of the Secretary of State. Things were looking easier than he had thought. He even found a photograph of one of the group meetings at the Foreign and Commonwealth Office – it didn't now matter to him that he had no minutes for that particular meeting.

He found minutes of the meetings with middle-level officials of the Foreign Office. He also found minutes of the Abuja and Monrovia meetings. He was savouring the moment. In fact, he was now eagerly looking forward to the first hearing of the parliamentary sub-committee investigations. "Bring it on," he said to himself, as he remembered the promise he had made to Rachael, Sarah and Ben that he would defend his name and save the family's reputation. He might have lost his friend, but he had not lost himself, he concluded.

Mark had just now picked up the minutes of the final meeting at Aso Rock (attended by the British High Commission's political attaché – because Mark himself had personal dislike for dictators and wouldn't meet the Nigerian dictator – Jungle Boys International representatives, President Kargbo Ndomahina, and chaired by Mallam Musa Odofo) when the door to his office opened. Rachael had never interrupted him since he started his preparation. She must have good reason for doing so now. Exactly so: there was an urgent phone call from Exeter. James Fergusson, Mark's father, had been taken ill into hospital.

In the twinkling of an eye.

32

James Fergusson had returned to Britain from his two-week trip to Sierra Leone a boisterous and happy fellow. His friends at the local pub at Exeter noticed the difference. Not that he had originally been the gloomy type, but that was nearly what he had become since Mark's mother disappeared from their lives. James would go to the pub and grab a pint or two to drown his sorrows. He had a couple of friends, but he didn't like talking much with them. He would sit in a far corner with his pint, sipping away, and then would quietly slip away. He liked coming there as much for the pint as for the name of the pub itself: 'The Duke of Edindurgh'. He liked the man whose name it bore. His friends knew that. And, behind his back, they called him 'The Duke', also in tacit reference to his solitary fortitude.

James was at that time more or less a lone man. Except that he was also known for his devotion to the welfare of his son as he made sure he took Mark to and from school every school day. When the son eventually pulled through life and went to university, James became an enlivened and re-energised man again. He would now have discussions with his friends at the pub and he would take a pint to 'water my joy' – to the laughter and clinging of bottles. He would now even chat with female fellow customers – though he had the reputation of a man who kept his private life private. He was a happy man.

But James Fergusson became happier and chattier when he came back from Sierra Leone. He would go to the pub, tell everyone who cared to listen how his son's career path had helped him find his maternal family tree. He told them about the adventurous journey his great-grandmother made to Sierra Leone 'as a wife', how she worked closely with British abolitionist William Wilberforce in the establishment of 'the province of freedom', and how the country was beautiful with white-sand beaches ("But there's a lot of corruption," he would whisper). He talked about his granddaughter Sarah's writings, especially the groundbreaking article about his great-grandmother in a local newspaper in Sierra Leone. His pub friends now openly called him 'The Duke' – to which he would at times respond, "Yes, I am the Duke" – to boisterous laughter.

It was in one of those discussions in the pub that James met Raphael, a reporter for the local *Exeter Times* newspaper. Raphael developed an interest in the story, especially when James said he brought from Sierra Leone ten copies of that edition of *The True Light.* He promised to come with a copy for Raphael at the pub the next day. The reporter was so impressed with Sarah's article that he took it to his editor. They got Sarah's consent through James and re-published the article in the *Exeter Times*. They made a front-page story out of it with the headline, 'LOCAL GRANDPA JOYFUL FOR GRANDDAUGHTER'S BREAKTHROUGH RESEARCH ON BRITISH EXPLOITS IN SIERRA LEONE, LEADING TO FINDING OF GREAT-GRANDMA'S GRAVE'. James Fergusson's face was splashed alongside the story. He suddenly became a local celebrity in his own right.

Soon, national newspapers picked up Sarah's article from the *Exeter Times*, with one sceptically asking 'Where on Earth is Sierra Leone Located? Exeter Man Discovers History'. James Fergusson therefore became the story. The regional BBC television interviewed him, then followed the other British television channels. They had found an incredible human interest story in James – his feeling of fulfilment after his trip to Sierra Leone.

No other British man had ever tried so much to tell the British public about Sierra Leone since the days of William Wilberforce. As his son was the British High Commissioner to Sierra Leone, James Fergusson had now unwittingly created himself as 'Sierra Leone Ambassador to Exeter'.

Many of his long-lost former schoolmates and workmates were thrilled and surprised to see their man in the news. Some reconnected with him through the media houses. Among them were his two best friends in secondary school: James Baldwin, who was now managing the Exeter branch of Tesco supermarket; and Gabriel Williamson, born of an Indian mother and a British father, who confused James when he told him he had become a vicar. Life could be a rollercoaster; in secondary school, Gabriel Williamson was a strong advocate of atheism.

Though he had still refused to leave the flat where Mark was born, James Fergusson believed he had lived a fulfilled life.

***

The last time Sierra Leone got such publicity in the British media and the attendant attention from the British public was when the small West African nation joined hands with Albania as an emerging radical wing of the world in championing support for the recognition of China (the People's Republic of China – PRC) as against Taiwan (the Republic of China – ROC) at the UN. Kargbo Ndomahina was a Sierra Leonean diplomat at the UN in New York then.

That time, President Kargbo Ndomahina's predecessor, President Daymia Turay, came under the British media spotlight for not toeing the line of Britain on the China/Taiwan issue. Though Britain later took up a lead on the side of China when the wind against Taiwan grew stronger, British officials noticed Sierra Leone's unwillingness to follow British timing on the matter. It was an unwillingness that bordered on a total break. Sierra Leone, of all? Just a few years ago she was one of the Queen's most loved colonies – the jewel (some said diamond) on the Crown. The story was all over Freetown 'that the only other man the Queen ever danced with' apart from her husband was Sierra Leone's first Prime Minister.

Diplomat Kargbo Ndomahina, then speaking for President Daymia Turay, had said in New York on the China issue: "We know the Queen loves our country. And we thank her for that. She certainly has some soft spot for Sierra Leone. For good reason. But we are talking of a new world order. We are no longer a British colony. We are now a non-aligned nation. And that has to be accepted and respected as well." This quote had got extensive reportage in the British press at the time.

But that was a few decades ago. The People's Republic of China was now ensconced with Britain, America, France and Russia as a permanent member of the UN Security Council. And Sierra Leone had become unknown in the world's geo-political melee. A new generation of British people had emerged and had hardly heard of Sierra Leone. Even the war in the country, for the most part, did not get attention from either the British media or from the British general population.

Therefore, James Fergusson's new media flurry about Sierra Leone was replaying history in another form. He had unwittingly touched a nerve in the old establishment.

The Queen had fond memories when she watched his interview on television. That night, she called her granddaughter Rachael (who was still then in Sierra Leone) to tell her just that. Sierra Leone had somehow taken centre-stage again in Britain –

even if at the same time making the world know it was one of the poorest nations on Earth with a knife-on-edge life expectancy and a simmering war.

Prime Minister Ed McInroy was also particularly elated about it – knowing that this would not have happened if he had not appointed Mark Fergusson as High Commissioner to Sierra Leone.

***

But all changed when the 'Arms to Africa' story broke and High Commissioner Mark Fergusson's photograph and story dominated the front pages of British tabloids and carried the headlines in television networks. James Fergusson only got to know that his son had arrived in London the previous day when he had cause to call his daughter-in-law, Rachael, to know 'what this breaking news about Mark is all about'.

Mark was not available to speak to him at the time – he had gone for a walk with Sarah. Rachael lovingly assured her father-in-law (they had always liked each other) that everything would be fine, and that Mark was in good spirits. She had promised to tell Mark to call him back.

But James Fergusson was not in good spirits ever since. He could not believe that Prime Minister Ed McInroy could 'publicly disgrace his best friend for any reason whatsoever'. James withdrew to his former self – as he was in the years just after Mark's mother disappeared. Reclusive. Reserved. Introverted. This time he actually stopped going to the pub. He preferred buying his pint at the off-licence shop of his Pakistani neighbour and having a drink at home – to now drown his joy or water his sorrows.

Day in and day out, James expected his son to call him back. Mark had actually wanted to since the day Rachael told him, but he kept postponing it. He had convinced himself that Rachael's assurances to the father were at least enough for now. He wanted to concentrate on re-shaping Sarah and preparing his defence. And after that, call his father.

This was not good enough for James as the news had spread in Exeter. He rebuffed several attempts by the local press to interview him. He became really irritable when local reporters waylaid him at the Pakistani off-license and asked him whether he still believed in 'the Sierra Leone dream'. He told them to respect his privacy. The next day, the *Exeter Voice* newspaper splashed James Fergusson's face on the front page with the headline, 'LOCAL GRANDPA'S FAIRYTALE STORY ABOUT SIERRA LEONE ENDS IN NIGHTMARE – AND HE WOULDN'T TALK ABOUT IT'. The *Exeter Voice* was a local rival of the *Exeter Times*, which had broken the original story of James Fergusson's trip to Sierra Leone – the former anti-McInroy, the latter pro-McInroy.

James Fergusson knew how to endure suffering in silence and alone. But it was his welfare officer who made the phone call to his son in London that day.

One of Mark Fergusson's landmarks as chairman of the Exeter local council was to have added to the benefit system welfare officers for all over-seventies living alone. The welfare officer would support and check on his or her clients twice a day. James Fergusson's was Brian Collins, whose functions now included going to the Pakistani off-license since the incident with the *Exeter Voice* reporters.

It was Brian who had found James Fergusson poorly in his flat that morning and had called the paramedics. He had checked on the next-of-kin bio data and called the home of Mark Fergusson in London. The phone was answered by Rachael, who presently told Brian to hold on.

It was actually the doctor who had asked Brian to call. He was calling from Exeter hospital. So when Mark came on the line, Brian passed the receiver to Dr. Robinson. Good old Dr. Robinson, the very obstetrician who supervised the pregnancy and delivery of

Sarah and got Rachael's wrath for the gender mix-up some two decades or so ago (How time flew! Or how time rotated, as the frank-talking doctor would always put it! Definitely an old man now, but he sounded unmistakable.) Mark recognised the voice immediately. But he didn't want Rachael to know right now. He only wanted to know about his father's health.

It had happened that, just about a month after that baby gender scandal, Dr. Robinson was moved from the obstetrics department to first the infants ward and then the general ward, and now to the 'ward for the aged' where James Fergusson had been brought with 'serious – but not life-threatening at the moment – respiratory problems'.

"He needs several days of examination and observation here," the doctor said.

"I am very grateful, doc," Mark said.

"You'll be regularly updated through the welfare officer."

"Grateful."

Mark had barely put the phone down when it rang again.

It was not the hospital. It was Andrew Decker. Even though the vicar had this special and secret telephone relationship with Sarah, he continued to have an open one with her mother and would usually call. He had already known from Sarah that her father was in town (and of course he had already heard the news), but Andrew Decker did not expect Mark to answer the phone. The vicar was pleasantly surprised when the male 'hello' came on the line.

"Oh, I'm sorry for the intrusion, my diplomat."

Mark immediately recognised the voice and the signatory title the vicar had been calling him ever since he became High Commissioner; and retorted, "Oh, my vicar."

"I… I… I just wanted to talk to Mrs. Fergusson…'

Mark was going to call Rachael, covering the speaking part of the receiver, when Vicar Andrew added, "I just wanted to know whether she is watching the news."

Mark quickly uncovered the receiver. "Which news?"

"About the new High Commissioner to Sierra Leone, sir."

"No. What do you mean?"

"It's on television. It's there as we speak. That's all I wanted to tell her."

"Ok. Thank you, vicar."

"Most welcome. Please tell her I'll call later, my diplomat."

They both hung up at the same time.

Mark's fingers first missed the power button of the remote control. When he pressed it, the breaking news stared in his face: 'JOHN COLESON OF THE FOREIGN OFFICE IS NEW HIGH COMMISSIONER TO SIERRA LEONE'.

Mark's first reaction was consternation. And then full realisation. "So this was what John was fighting for all along," he sighed to himself.

Rachael had decided to go upstairs while Mark was speaking to the hospital about his father. On hearing Mark call out 'Rachael, Rachael', she thought there was something he needed her to say to Brian or to her father-in-law. But she found Mark standing in front of the television.

"What, darling?" she asked as she descended the stairs.

"The traitor has got it," he said, pointing to the screen.

He moved away from the front of the TV screen for his wife to see. And presently the presenter repeated, "This is a breaking story from Downing Street. The head of the Africa Desk at the Foreign Office, John Coleson, has been appointed as the new High Commissioner to Sierra Leone following very dramatic developments in the small West African country, where the military junta has been removed by an intervention force for the reinstatement of the exiled democratically elected President."

"Wow," Sarah muttered. "Was he not the one briefing the Secretary of State on your issue?"

"He was the one who wrote an anecdote that I got diamonds

from the arms deal, referencing sources at the British Embassy in Monrovia. He was spoon-fed by those disgruntled Foreign Office personnel who felt sidelined ever since we relocated to Monrovia. He put all the lies together and fed them to Ed through the Foreign Secretary. Worse still, they fed the same lies to the Americans, who went ahead to put them in a diplomatic cable."

"Well, he's got what he wanted. Let him take it all. We'll be fine. Let him go get his own diamonds now," Rachael said, as she came nearer to her husband and put her right hand round his side.

Mark responded by putting his own hand round her side. They held each other for a while. He pecked her and then requested, "Please, darling, let me go finish what I was doing."

"How about grandpa?" Rachael asked about her father-in-law.

"Oh, yes," Mark jolted back, as if the news about his father was long time ago. "It's not very serious. But they are keeping him in for observation." He had slowly loosened himself from her embrace while talking and was on his way to his study room by the end of the last word. Left on her own, Rachael now had an intuition that the informant at the British Embassy in Liberia who had called to tell her about Mark becoming too close to Femi Cole in Monrovia must have been one of John Coleson's people. Mark's traitors. Rachael had planned to raise the issue with Mark after the botched Ritz hotel dinner… And now she was thankful that events prevented her from doing so.

One and a half hours later, Rachael came in the study again.

"Another call?" he asked.

"No. A dispatch came for you," she said as she handed the envelope to him.

It was from the chairman of the parliamentary sub-committee. It was a short and sharp note addressed to Mark: 'The Office of the Prime Minister has ordered the investigations into the alleged breach of UN Resolution 1347 to be suspended immediately as the lead witness has been appointed High Commissioner to Sierra Leone.'

Mark didn't know how to react: whether to laugh or to cry; whether to shout or to remain silent; whether to jump or to remain seated. In the end, he just handed the note back to Rachael. She was still lingering there out of curiosity, knowing the dispatch must have had something of great import the moment she saw the Westminster stamp on the envelope when signing for it.

Rachael shouted 'Thank God' after reading it, throwing herself on her husband with showers of kisses.

And now, suddenly, Mark realised that all had changed, or was changing again. He wouldn't need this office now. He might not need it soon. He might never need it for this issue again (except that he had always planned to write a book about his career as a diplomat). But all he needed now was this beautiful lady wrapped around him...

In the twinkling of an eye.

Rachael was happier to know from her husband that it was Vicar Andrew who called to inform about the breaking news. "He has always been in touch," she reported as they left the office to have some champagne (it didn't matter what time of the day it was) for the first time since Mark came. He didn't tell her yet about Dr. Robinson. It was not a time to open old wounds.

* * *

Mark himself had initially thought Operation Octopus was foolhardiness, if not a terrible blunder. He had believed it would only exacerbate the situation, and his situation. Because the military intervention would only cause the international spotlight to continue to focus on Sierra Leone; and the mercenary arms deal issue would have to be brought into perspective. President Ndomahina had not spoken to him since. He and Mallam Odofo were desperate. No man could stop them.

But now, as things had turned out, Mark was having a rethink too – if Operation Octopus was an evil, it was a necessary evil, he concluded. The same words the Foreign Secretary had used.

Mark sipped his champagne.

33

Even Rachael was now surprised at the fast-paced manner by which her daughter was moving on. At last reasoning had overcome emotion, she said to herself.

Like every good mother, Rachael believed Sarah deserved a better life, a better future, or what she normally called 'a second chance'. In Rachael's innermost thoughts, her daughter was responsible for her own predicament. *If only she had listened to me about the relationship with Stephen,* she kept reminding herself. But she would definitely not gloat over it. She was a mother. The mother. She must bear it all. *All I always wanted is my daughter's happiness,* she affirmed to herself. And now her dream was coming true. Sarah was moving on.

The joy of Rachael. The joy of a mother.

* * *

That morning after the night she accepted to move on without Stephen, Sarah woke up feeling like she had just thrown off a huge burden off her shoulders. She had just discovered – re-discovered – freedom. Freedom from the past; freedom for the future.

That night, pondering on Vicar Andrew Decker's words, she had lain in her bed supine, eyes wide open, as it all happened. The ceiling had disappeared before her eyes – or she could not see the ceiling, or she felt she could not see the ceiling – when all the reminiscences came flooding in.

But now, this morning – let Stephen be with his Aslan wherever they were. She was now willing to move on with, or for, her family. And, she suddenly felt convinced, for herself. Feeling unburdened, the last act she would do for him was say a prayer. She felt morally compelled to say a prayer; she couldn't remember ever saying a prayer all by herself before.

"Wherever Stephen and Aslan might be, let them be in peace," she tried to structure the words in her mind.

* * *

It was deep into their relationship, Sarah already pregnant with Joel, that Stephen told her about a fanciful bond he had with a lion. He had said it all started in his primary school days when an English teacher taught them the poem, 'Pussy cat, pussy cat, where have you been? I have been to London to visit the Queen.' Stephen had told Sarah that on that very night he actually dreamt of a cat taking him to London to see the Queen in a big palace. But when he had told his parents, they had said it was just a dream. It had happened a second time and was dismissed as a dream again.

He had said it happened again, and again, and again – this cat would come in his dream and take him to places. At times it would show him coming events.

"It would say 'the French teacher will not come to school tomorrow', and when I went to school, the French teacher did not come."

Sarah's head was on his chest, him caressing her hair on the white sands of River Number Two Beach – just an outing for two. She was rapt in attention.

"Nobody else believed me except Samson. They said it's the way of twins to fancy things. But I know you will believe me."

Sarah's eyes were closed and she didn't say a word. He knew she was listening. He continued that, as he matured, he realised it was not actually a cat in his dream. It was a lion. It was a lion who went to London to see the Queen. It was a lion who, in the dream, took him to London to visit the Queen.

Sarah immediately jerked, opened her eyes and sat up straight.

"Maybe it was also a baby lion when I was a child. But as time passed, the line between dream and reality became thin between me and him. Even during the day, I could fancy seeing this lion acting as a guide or something. He even appeared to me – well, in my dream – in prison."

Then Sarah had interjected: "It's like Aslan."

"Who is Aslan?" Stephen had asked.

"You don't know Aslan?"

"No."

"It's like him in your dreams."

"Ehm ehm ehm…"

"That means you haven't read the Narnia books."

Stephen had felt a bit embarrassed and had wanted to say those books were never in his school or university curriculum; but he had conceded, "Man doesn't know everything," which sent Sarah cracking with laughter. She then went on to tell him about Aslan the lion in British author C.S. Lewis' books.

"So, Aslan was the one who guided and protected Peter, Susan, Edmund and Lucy from the White Witch in Narnia. He also would appear and speak to them just as he does with you," Sarah concluded.

Stephen was more than satisfied that Sarah believed him. "Maybe it is Aslan," he said, as they burst out laughing.

He had gone on to tell her how, when he was in prison with five other journalists at one time, Aslan appeared in his dream and told him they would be released the next day. He had told his colleagues that night. And they had marvelled when it happened.

Now in London, Sarah believed it was all fantasy. "Fantastical and fanciful. That was what it was," she thought to herself. After all, why did Aslan not tell Stephen that the bomb was going to be dropped on their offices? Where was Aslan?

But whatever it was, it was now over. She was moving on.

So, that decision night before the morning, Sarah had properly structured the words in her mind. Her only prayer – her last prayer for him, which was her first ever prayer alone – was: "May Stephen and Samson and Aslan be at peace wherever they are – whether in our world or in Aslan's world. Amen." She found herself involuntarily closing her eyes when she said it.

***

So in the morning, Sarah immediately jumped out of bed, went to the bathroom and did her etiquette. Back in the room, Joel was still fast asleep. She took off her black pyjamas – for the last time. She donned her white Adidas tracksuit with her trademark Union Jack cap and Clarke's trainers. She was going jogging alone. But before leaving, she picked up all her black stuff (pyjamas, dresses, underwear and gowns – all the black stuff she had been using as her mourning adornment for Stephen) and put them in a big plastic bag. Everybody else in the house was still asleep, or at least in their rooms – her parents upstairs, her brother downstairs. She took the plastic bag outside and dumped it in the bin. She came in again, knocked on her parents' door and loudly said, "Mum, please have an eye on Joel. I'm going jogging." She was off before Rachael could come to the door.

And Sarah actually went jogging. She went to the same park and did twice the usual rounds of her teenage years. She was full of energy this morning. She felt sprightly and just kept on exercising until she realised she had done more than three hours. She returned home using the old route through Sunfield Road. She reached the telephone booth. She looked at it, hesitated a bit, and then walked towards it. She went for the door handle. And then she pulled back. She didn't open the door. She was not making a call. She didn't want to call Vicar Andrew Decker again. "It's over," she said, and walked away. She then ran – jogged – towards home.

She found her mother holding Joel in the living room. Rachael didn't believe what she saw: no black on Sarah.

"You are looking so cute, darling. Come here, come here, come here," she said, holding Joel in one hand close to the chest and using the other to gesticulate to her daughter to come for a hug.

"Thank you, Mum." Grandmother/mother, daughter/mother, son/grandson in one full embrace. The two were all smiles. And they had a lively chat on food – what they would eat today.

The moving on was for real.

Two days later, Sarah presented an itinerary to her parents. She had got in touch with her cousin Lynn, the Earl of Durham's daughter. Lynn's parents were away in Spain for two weeks and she was all by herself at Durham Castle with the servants. Sarah wanted to go and spend some time with her, she requested. At the same time, she would go to Durham University for her transcript – because, although she eventually graduated from Mount Aureol University in Sierra Leone, her degree was actually Durham-awarded.

Rachael was over the moon. "Of course, of course, darling. You need it. You need the reconnections. Go and have fun. I'll have fun with Joel." Mark had no objection.

A few days into Sarah's new socialite life at Durham Castle

(organising daily parties and dinners and cocktails, inviting old friends), her father phoned her up to tell her Grandpa James had been admitted at Exeter hospital. "It would be good if you could check on him, since it's just a few miles away from Durham."

"Sure, Daddy."

"And then I have some good news."

Sarah's heart leapt. "What good news, Daddy?" *About Stephen?* she nearly asked.

"The investigation on me has been suspended indefinitely."

"Oh Daddy, that's really good news. I'm so happy. Congratulations."

He told her the case was as good as closed – because the man who should have led the evidence against him would now take his position in Monrovia, bound for Sierra Leone ("Because the military junta has been overthrown and President Ndomahina is going back."). She had had no time for news at Durham Castle. No time for television – just partying and music.

But the news of Grandpa's illness ruffled her a bit. She liked the old man, and he loved her. She was carrying his wife's name, Sarah, the mother of her father. James Fergusson therefore doted on Sarah – he always called her 'my wife'. Sarah promised her father she would visit Grandpa in hospital.

* * *

James Fergusson recognised her immediately. The nurses had told her he was poorly, and the recovery could take time, but that his brain was still sharp. Yet she didn't expect it to be this sharp.

"What are you doing here, my wife?"

"I am here to look for my husband," she found herself replying appropriately, as they both laughed out loud in the presence of the male nurse who had just ushered her in. He left them on their own immediately.

James Fergusson dominated the conversation. He was asking all types of questions, mainly about Sierra Leone and vividly pinpointing on events.

"My trip to Sierra Leone *is* the most fulfilling moment of my life."

Sarah wanted to divert him and change the subject matter. But Grandpa would have none of that.

And then he asked about Stephen, 'my good friend'.

"Oh, he is fine."

He had never been told that Stephen was killed in the war (Mark had said he would find the right time for that) and Sarah didn't want to tell him now. Not now, of all times. So she again said, "He is fine."

"When is he coming?"

"Maybe soon… You see, Grandpa… Ehm, how are you feeling right now? Have the doctors told you how long you are staying for?"

"No, no, no… Forget about the doctors, my wife. Forget about me. Tell me about Amidu."

He could even remember that name! Sarah was thoroughly amazed.

"He is a lovely lad. Not many lads are like that, even here. He took me to places. I saw the other side of life."

"I know, Grandpa, but you need to rest."

"I have been resting all this while, my wife."

"You need more rest, the nurse told me," she made up.

"Ok. Well… please tell him to come quickly."

"Who?" Sarah thought he was now referring to the nurse.

"Stephen or Amidu," he laughed croakily.

"Oh, Grandpa." *He remembered all that*, she thought.

"Whichever. Whichever name. The good lad."

It was her turn to tell him that his son's, her father's, case had been suspended.

James Fergusson brightened: "Oh yeah? I knew it. I knew it. Ed made a big mistake."

***

Sarah returned to Durham Castle with a lot of sobriety. The past few days had been a totally different world from what she had recently known – and worlds apart they were. Night in and night out, they had been in this continuous revelry – boys and girls, or ladies and gentlemen, as they called themselves, all by themselves – in Durham Castle, doing stuff. A lot of water passed under the bridge. That was what moving on involved. And not for once did she think of Stephen – she was not even sure she thought of Joel, as he was her little secret from her friends. Not even Lynn knew about Joel; it was still a secret within senior royal circles. It was all going good for Sarah.

And now a visit to Grandpa in hospital had torpedoed all of it. Stephen's name had come up in her life again. And it lingered. The Stephen story was persisting.

She called her father to tell him she had visited Grandpa and she had found him in good spirits. She said the doctor was not in, but that a friend of Grandpa's called Gabriel Williamson met her there.

"He introduced me to him. He was an old schoolmate of his. He is the local vicar at Exeter. He says he visits him every day."

Mark Fergusson was pleased with his daughter.

"Thank you for doing that for me. I remember that name – Gabriel Williamson. He used to tell me a lot about him. He is now a vicar?"

"Yes, Daddy. He was so lovely. He sends his regards to you."

But when she put the phone down, it was what Grandpa had said to her about Stephen that continued to linger. She was poised to shake it off.

That night, even though there was another party organised by Lynn, Sarah said she could not join because she was having a headache. She retired to the less raucous wing of the castle. She needed some rest. It was she who needed some rest perhaps more than Grandpa. Or at least, just like Grandpa – who had suddenly forced reality back on her.

But she wouldn't – she was not prepared to – give it too much consideration. The past could come popping up now and again; but it would not stop her decision to move on. All she wanted now was some quietness, some rest, some good sleep. And tomorrow would be a brighter day, she believed.

34

But something happened before tomorrow came. In her sleep. In the quieter wing in Durham Castle.

That very night, Sarah dreamt about Stephen for the first time since she'd left Freetown. It was not like that daydream she had had in London with her eyes open, the ceiling disappearing, gazing into the open skies from her bed. In Durham, she had slept. And then she dreamt. It was about them, their love story retold, with some embellishment in the end. About how they fell in love with each other; about… about…

At last, a dream came indeed. In full. Or in over-full. When she least wanted it. So the hot zone of her brain had all along been waiting for Grandpa's words?

* * *

It was the nudging of the News Editor, Edwina Campbell, that had got Sarah to loosen up and open a social window away from the tight grip of her diplomatic circles. Edwina and Sarah had become both professional and personal friends. Their relationship became tighter and closer since they jointly researched and wrote the celebratory article on the 'Freedom Journey from Britain to Sierra Leone' of their great-great-great-grandparents – one black, one white. In the article, they had even fictionalised some conversations that might have taken place, and written how 'it was possible that our great-great-great-grandparents knew each other and indeed had a chat either on that boat or on arrival at the land that they were all looking forward to. But, whether they met or not, they came together on the same boat. And they were both interred in Freetown. And we, their great-great-great-grandchildren, have met by the most unusual of routes at *The True Light* newspaper…'

'Krio girl' Edwina (Krio meaning a descendant of freed slaves in Sierra Leone) was on top of her game. She was a jovial and outgoing lady who struck a chord with Sarah immediately. As News Editor, Edwina did not believe in desk journalism.

"We go out and get our stories. The stories of the ordinary man. Human-interest stories. And we put them side by side, in perspective, with the stories of the powerful. We hold the powerful to account through the people," Edwina had told Sarah on the second day of internship. The News Editor had asked her out for lunch at the Rumours Restaurant in central Freetown, three streets away from their office.

It resonated with Sarah. She had always been at the posh restaurants on the beaches or at hotels in western Freetown, or at diplomatic dinners and cocktails and lunches. The high-class life. At Rumours Restaurant, she found a totally different picture. It was the hub of the average man: men in suits, ladies in linen dresses, guys in jeans, girls in tights; the refined and the loud; people talking freely in high tones, laughter here, shouts there; men drinking beer during lunch before going back to work. Sarah liked the atmosphere. It was good seeing another part of Freetown life (apart from having seen a glimpse of it from the comfort of an air-conditioned vehicle). There were beggars waiting for them for 'small change' at the door as they departed; and on the streets, there was a half-naked man pushing an *omolanke* (a locally-created four-wheel push cart) full of assorted commodities, shouting his way through the traffic; another man was toting a full 100kg bag of rice on his head, sweating profusely as if water had been poured on him; a woman was selling wares on the side of the road, assisted by two young girls who should have been in school; and boys of school-going age were selling sweets, biscuits, water, cakes, and the popular locally-prepared cake *beanch akara*; while others swirled around Edwina and Sarah to try to sell some wares, and Edwina would stave them off by shouting, "We nor dae buy. We nor get money." And they burst out laughing.

So, Rumours Restaurant became their rendezvous after spending the earlier part of the day looking for stories. They reviewed their work there over lunch.

It was in one of those sessions that Sarah told Edwina about the story of her great-great-great-grandmother – and how she would be happy to actually know what happened to her.

"It will be interesting to know. The family never knew anything else about her apart from a sole letter she had written and given to a sailor about how she had reached 'the province of freedom' and did not regret coming," Sarah explained.

Edwina was immediately enticed. This was her story as well. She had always wanted to put into writing the folklore of the 'return voyage' she had heard from her parents and grandparents and other people in the Krio community: "It will be more than interesting to know. I am in for it." She then told Sarah the story of the freed slaves, of whom she was a descendant.

They agreed to do a joint research and article. Their research took them to the Sierra Leone museum (which, it turned out, was the original land where the first office of William Wilberforce, the abolitionist, was located), the State House archives, the university library, and to a basement in a store at the British High Commission. And it turned out that Sarah's great-great-

great-grandmother was Wilberforce's Personal Secretary. She was married to a freed slave who became the first teacher of the arrivals' children. She died of 'unexplained causes' only three years later and was buried on abolitionist land, as was the practice then. (Sarah and Edwina posited in the article that she could have died of malaria: 'No wonder Sierra Leone was nicknamed "the white man's grave".'). They found her tombstone: 'Mary Fergusson – Wife, Mother, Personal Secretary to William Wilberforce; Died 10th day of March in the year of Our Lord 1799'. Sarah had wondered why no age was stated.

So they wrote and published the article, establishing that 'the white women who came from Britain to Sierra Leone with the abolitionists and the freed slaves were never near being prostitutes; but were responsible, reasonable, rational and respectable ladies who looked beyond colour and status as forbears and epitomes of the beauty and inevitability of multiracialism.' As the two grew closer together, Sarah's diplomatic social circle noticed and complained. She had tried to balance her time between the two circles. But the imminent transfer of the American Ambassador – meaning the departure of her closest friend, Celia, the ambassador's daughter – snapped everything on the diplomatic circle. It left Sarah hanging on her new relationship with her News Editor – which she was enjoying and loving. They were even hanging out on weekends – and Sarah had kept saying how she would miss this place when she would leave in a few months' time.

It was this closeness and fondness with Edwina that caused Sarah to agree to attend the newspaper's monthly 'outing to the beach'. It was actually Accountant Samson's original idea or version of 'all work and no play makes Jack a dull boy'. On the last Saturday of each month, they took the newspaper staff to an outing in one of the Freetown peninsula beaches. While the recurring event was incorporated as a professional function to balance the newspaper's account books, it was actually a no-holds-barred social gathering. Staff hardly interacted with each other in the office if they were not working in the same department, so the monthly social gathering was a moment to meet and share ideas as well. Everybody attended, including the editors. Staff looked forward to it – they ate, drank, and swam. Sarah had seen the monthly 'notice to all staff' about the outing but had ignored it. She had rejected Edwina's personal invitation several times.

But Edwina was never one to give up. Sarah was the one to give in. The News Editor reminded the intern there was now only a few months remaining before her return to Britain and she would not be able to write a full report about her experience in *The True Light* if the monthly outing were not included. "You need to see everybody as their most casual self," Edwina had implored, and Sarah had responded, "I'll give it a thought and let you know." The next day, Sarah told Edwina she would attend – but that it should be a secret between them until it happened.

***

All these details were being relayed in Sarah's dream as she lay sleeping in Durham Castle, while her cousin, Lynn, was having a party in the east wing with other girls and the invited boys.

And the dream continued… The details continued to pour in.

Sarah's change of mind – or rather consent – for the monthly beach meeting was accelerated by two factors, or maybe three. 'Or four? But the first two felt like an obligation to me', she had written in her journal – still relayed in the dream.

***

After the office scandal about her editorial encounter with Editor Amidu, Sarah didn't leave things lying. She had actually gone ahead and asked her father to include in the next diplomatic dispatch a letter she had written to Vicar Andrew Decker (after enquiring from her dad about the vicar who made her read scripture at Westminster Abbey during the Second World War commemorations on Remembrance Day). She had written to cross-check the Editor's claims about the origins of the Church of England. Alas, when the response came, it confirmed all what Editor Amidu had said and written in the editorial. She had already personally gone into his office to say sorry for the misunderstanding. ("I'm sorry, I got it wrong," she had said. "Never mind. We are all learning," he had said). Staff had seen how conciliatory she had become with the Editor. But now she thought attending the monthly outing was a great moment to counter any further claims of remnants of a misunderstanding.

The second thing that made Sarah feel obliged to attend the outing – as she had written in her diary – was similarly editorial-wise. Editor Tamaraneh was very much involved in putting together the article about the black and white great-great-great-grandparents who sailed from Britain to Sierra Leone. He was supportive ever since News Editor Edwina Campbell sought his endorsement of it – what they called 'commissioning' in the newspaper world. He gave them some tips and leads here and there, and of course thoroughly edited the final version. Not only that, he went on to do an editorial on the subject matter. Even Sarah's former friends in diplomatic circles admired and celebrated the article (even her former critic at the British High Commission, John Davenport, congratulated her). She now believed going to the newspaper's outing would be a show of gratitude and camaraderie.

Apart from that – Sarah had further written in her diary – she felt she owed it to her friendship with Edwina to now do a valedictory bonding. 'The final act of friends about to separate who could never meet again.' And Sarah also thought it would be good to be in a social gathering with all those people she had been seeing in the office and didn't have time to speak with, and say goodbye to them somehow. 'I agree with Edwina that indeed my experience at *The True Light* newspaper, my internship story, will not be complete if the monthly outing bit is left out!'

And everybody – not least the Tamaraneh twins – was surprised when Edwina turned up at Tokeh Beach with her friend (that's how she introduced her amidst laughter; not workmate, not an intern), Sarah Fergusson.

There were lots of activities that day: loud music was playing in the background, eating and drinking, dancing and walking on the beach, swimming and singing. The façade of officialdom had disappeared; even the secretary, who had always seemed to have an inexplicable reverence for her boss in the office, was now talking freely and even took Editor Amidu to dance. Sarah laughed aloud. She at first kept an observatory eye, but she soon found herself in the thick of it after a few drinks. First to take her to dance was Samson, the Editor's accountant twin brother. Edwina took the Editor.

It was fun. Sarah ended up dancing with almost everybody, male or female. Soon she was face to face with Editor Amidu, who, instead of dancing, rather asked her if she minded a walk on the beach. She hadn't thought about it and was saying "Ehm, ehm, ehm… I, I, I…' when he interrupted with "Come on, you need a break," holding and slightly pulling her hand. She saw herself following.

They didn't walk for long – didn't even talk much – but she found it absolutely appropriate. The sea breeze was refreshing and the sun was now going down, reflecting itself in full amber on the far end of the Atlantic Ocean. They both saw the sun going into the sea.

"I have never beheld such a beautiful sight before. Not even in movies," she confessed.

"Oh lucky me, what a first!" he said, laughing.

They were on their way back when Sarah said she was wholeheartedly grateful for the time that she had spent with the newspaper: "My father didn't make a mistake in recommending you… I mean the newspaper. I couldn't have found a better place to start. Thank you for the opportunity. And thank you for being a forbearing and tolerant Editor."

"Please don't mention it. The pleasure is mine. We should thank you instead for agreeing to do your internship with our newspaper. You have given us more glamour and credibility. And I want to personally thank you, because I have not been arrested or invited to the CID since you came. They are afraid." They both started laughing again.

"You think they'll come once I'm gone?"

"Maybe. Maybe not. They may be afraid of your dad; but they are unpredictable."

Meanwhile, Edwina soon wondered where Sarah had gone; and she discovered that Editor Amidu was also absent.

"Where did you go?" she confronted her friend when she returned.

"I was talking with your Editor."

"You were not only talking; you were walking."

"Ok. We were walking."

"Know that there's no Editor at the outing. We are all the same. Today, you are my friend, and I brought you here. I should know each of your movements."

They both burst out laughing.

It was all fun, and Sarah returned home satisfied that it was worth it. Attending the newspaper's monthly outing had given her a wholesome picture. It was a Saturday, she had noted in her diary.

Next Monday, as they were having their usual lunch at the Rumours Restaurant, Sarah found herself asking Edwina questions about the Tamaraneh twins: how long she had been working with them, how much she knew them, what he knew about them. She was generally enquiring about the twin brothers.

"I think they are a brilliant duo who could go places with the dedication I have seen in them."

"Of course they are," Edwina said. "You wouldn't have found me here if they weren't."

Two days later, after discussing a front-page story in his office, Editor Amidu asked News Editor Edwina how her new friend was doing.

"She is ok. We were just talking about *you* the other day."

"About me? About what?"

"Just general talk… ehm… about your devotion to duty."

She did not clarify that Sarah was enquiring about the Tamaraneh twins. She liked polishing or embellishing stories; she liked saying things as she interpreted them.

The next day, Edwina wouldn't come to the office because she was doing a day trip with an NGO to the provinces. Editor Amidu wanted to fill some vacuum and asked Sarah out for lunch. She obliged. He took her not to Rumours, but to the popular Breaking News Restaurant owned by media mogul, Baba Maddieu. It was also in central Freetown, but in a class between the posh beach restaurants and the melting-pot Rumours. This was by and large a middle-class restaurant – only men in suits and ladies in high heels were seen here.

The Editor and the intern had a wide-ranging discussion: family, history, politics, literature – any idea or topic that popped up (they delved on *The Canterbury Tales* when hilariously discussing their former 'dispute' over the Church of England editorial). And within an hour, each had been able to form an intellectual opinion of the other. But perhaps what caught Sarah's curiosity the most was Amidu's story about his name – that it was the name of his grandfather, who fought in the Second World War. Sarah was surprised – actually shocked – but didn't outwardly show it.

"What do you mean?"

"My grandfather's name was Amidu."

"I know you said that. But what do you mean by he fought in the Second World War?"

Never had it occurred to Sarah that Africans had participated in the Second World War. She knew that black people who were already based in Britain or America or Jamaica or in Europe at the time – anywhere outside Africa – could have participated in the War, but she never knew that the British government recruited soldiers from its former colonies. This was another shock information, or revelation, from Editor Amidu. She never knew this information when, as a teenager, she was reading the Scripture on Remembrance Day at Westminster Abbey – in remembrance of those who fought on the side of the British, on the side of the Allies.

"So your grandfather actually fought for my great-grandmother to still be Queen," she muttered.

"What do you mean? Is the Queen your great-grandmother?" The information-shocker pendulum swung the other way.

She waved it off with, "I wouldn't have told you. Or maybe I shouldn't have said. But that's not the point. Look, I am kind of surprised about this Second World War issue of your grandfather."

Not only that, Sarah became more than wowed when Editor Amidu further revealed that after demobilisation in Jamaica, his grandfather was actually one of the Windrush generation, shipped to Britain to help rebuild the country through manual labour.

"That is so interesting. Honestly, our family is indebted to your family," Sarah acceded.

What Stephen got from the lunch was that she didn't have a boyfriend waiting for her in London. Not directly.

"I know you are longing to see London soon. You must have missed it."

"Ehm… not really. I love the weather here."

"Obviously."

"And the *only* person I long to see is my brother."

He *noted* that.

As they walked down the stairs of the Breaking News Restaurant, Editor Amidu asked, "How about us four hanging out this weekend?"

"Us four who?"

"Edwina, Samson, you, me."

"Oh, I don't think…"

"Come on, we need a better way of saying goodbye to you."

"I'll have to ask Edwina then."

"Sure."

Edwina was head over heals when Sarah told her. The quartet drank and danced the night away that Friday at the Seaview night club on Lumley Beach. Returning home, they were to drop off Sarah first, and then Edwina. When they reached the High Commissioner's residence at Hill Station, Editor Amidu felt obliged to walk Sarah to the door. As they were going, she, tipsy, leaned a bit on his shoulder and said, "You see, I am taller than you," laughing.

He also laughed and said, "All my grandfather's three wives were taller than him. And he always told us that an okra tree will never be taller than the farmer, because he knows how to bend it to get its produce."

That was hilarious for Sarah; and it got her laughing loudly, saying: "That's funny, that's really funny." As they reached the door, she said, "Hey, let me warn you. I think my friend fancies you."

"Which friend?" he asked doubtfully.

"Edwina, of course. I saw the way she was dancing with you tonight."

He now held her by the side and said, "Another misrepresentation of facts."

They burst out laughing.

And holding her tighter by the side, he said, "I think I fancy someone else."

"And who could that be?"

"She is right here with me."

She raised her left hand up and covered one part of her face, while saying, "What are you talking about?"

"I mean it," he said.

"You are drunk."

"Not at all."

And there was silence. Pitch silence for a few seconds. She had now uncovered the other part of her face as her hand dropped to find herself in both his hands. They just looked at each other. Faces very close. Thoughts rushed through her mind. He just suddenly withdrew and said, "I'll remind you tomorrow."

She quickly opened the door as she said goodnight. She closed it behind her, her back leaned to it, and sighed, "Ahh."

When he came back to the vehicle, Edwina retorted, "That was long."

"Was it?" he asked.

Samson, on the wheel, laughed.

* * *

Newspapers in Sierra Leone didn't come out on weekends. But journalists worked on Saturday for the Monday edition. They would come in between 11:00am and 3:00pm. All of them – the quartet last night – were in the office again the afternoon after. It was normally one of the busiest days of the News Editor; and Edwina, ever devoted to duty, never went out for lunch on Saturdays (time for some Krio food in the office).

Editor Amidu broke his tradition of sending his secretary. He walked into the newsroom and found Edwina, Sarah and a couple of others there. They were all surprised. He asked for a minute with Sarah – another lunch date this afternoon at the Breaking News Restaurant. Everything went so fast. Sarah thought it was crazy. But she was giving it a go. There was nothing to lose. Just the friendship was worth it.

Sitting at the same table as the first time they were there, she found herself indulgent after Editor Amidu repeated the sentiments, and said he was not drunk last night at all.

"I think I like you…"

"You think?" she found herself asking.

"I feel it."

"I also like you."

"No… I mean, I love you. I've never felt this way before."

"Do you also want to marry three wives like your grandfather?" she found herself asking. They both burst out laughing.

"Never."

Deep within her, she thought she felt the same way about him too. But she was not sure she actually did. However, she decided she would go out with him to pass the short time remaining.

"By the way, what does the 'S' stand for in your name?" she found herself asking again.

"Stephen."

"I've got it. That's what I'll be calling you from now on."

"I don't remember anybody calling me that for a long time."

"Well, I'm re-starting it, *Stephen.*"

Laughter.

***

Both were very civil and gentle in their relationship. It blossomed bud by bud. They didn't rush at anything. She gradually became convinced and grounded, and believed she should inform her parents. He was at first even against it, saying maybe they should give it more time. She said she didn't want her parents to keep guessing about what was going on in her life. So she picked the day and the place to tell them at Lakka Beach that Saturday. There was nothing to worry about. She had simply fallen in love, she had told her parents.

Sarah had no greater confirmation of this than when her grandfather, James Fergusson, visited Sierra Leone. The old man fell in love with 'the lovely lad' the moment they met. They went to different places of touristic value – they went to see the chimpanzees and the hippos, they climbed the hills of Roboli and had lobsters on the beaches. "I think he is a good lad. He deserves my granddaughter's love in my great-grandmother's country," James Fergusson had told Mark in confidence at Hill Station while the two of them had a drink on the boys' quarters' veranda the day before his departure back to Exeter. He sealed it.

The plan was that Sarah would return to Britain; and if they both continued to feel the same way for each other, then Stephen would be invited for a visit. They would then take it from there.

And it was all going as planned. Sarah believed she had won over her parents, especially her mother, who had eventually seemed comfortable. Until Sarah heard, rather overheard, that conversation that night of the farewell party for the American Ambassador's wife.

***

Sarah was obviously in deep sleep at Durham Castle. The dream was so cinematic and detailed, choreographing all the major events in her relationship with Stephen. But if anyone had come to the room in the west wing of the castle, they would have had no idea about what was going on in the soul of her motionless body. She was curled up in bed, a pillow between her legs, snoring. The loud music coming from the other side of the castle – as cousin Lynn and the girls and the boys were slaying the night away – didn't affect her at all. Presently, her body moved, and she turned, inadvertently throwing off the pillow from between her legs…

Her dreaming continued… Just that now the events were not just being relayed as they happened. In the dream, she now saw what actually never happened – or what she didn't see – in real life. And she could now even read the minds of others, like that of her mother – just like a narrator.

And so that Saturday night, at Hill Station in Freetown, Stephen attended the farewell party for the American Ambassador's wife organised by Mrs. Rachael Fergusson in her capacity as head of the diplomats' wives' association. It was a three-pronged event for Rachael – Sarah could now see in the dream.

Apart from the purpose for which the party was being organised, Rachael also had several things in mind. They were double-edged, if not self-contrasting: image-laundering by getting her daughter and Stephen present; and explaining the plan to her friend to talk Sarah out of 'a conundrum'.

By that time, Rachael's mind had become confused. She felt she had lost the plot – especially after speaking to her grandmother, the Queen; and during the visit of James Fergusson. She felt like someone who was mid-air, holding on to a parachute whose balloon had burst. Unless she landed before all the air was out, or some other parachutes came to the rescue, or some kind of miracle happened, she was sure to fall hard on the ground or in the sea or in the bush or on top of a roof or wherever. And she was looking for any object to aid her – whether a tree branch or a huge bird. *If a fish swallowed Jonah from nowhere, then anything is possible,* she had found herself finding consolation in some biblical reference.

Rachael knew that by inviting Stephen to the dinner, she was putting paid to the rumours within the diplomatic community that her family had been torn apart by a rebellious Sarah. The daughter's presence with her boyfriend was a bid to silence the critics. Let it be, while she weighed other options. All along, Rachael believed deep within her but without saying it that Stephen was very good at public relations and that he came out well at conversations. Beyond colour, he was a standard gentleman in every civil gathering, which she was sure he would now prove to anyone who could have a chat with him at the farewell dinner.

At the same time, Rachael had to get Sarah present in order to create an opportunity for her daughter to have a discussion with her friend, Celia, the American Ambassador's daughter. Celia had promised she would have a word with Sarah on Stephen's relationship if she had the opportunity. Rachael created the opportunity through the farewell dinner.

And then – perhaps above all – Rachael was looking forward to emptying her gut feelings to her friend, Christine, the American Ambassador's wife. They were very close. Not just because of the name-dropping 'historic special relationship' between their two countries, and not merely because of their common native language, English. But ever since they knew that Florida was Christine's home, and it was where Rachael had Ben, they really became friends. They used to joke that they might have bumped into each other on a Miami beach at that time.

So, the Freetown Hill Station residence of the British High Commissioner was full and boisterous that Saturday evening – or night. The sprawling carpet-grassed back garden with its swimming pool and water fountains, with dimmed lights, was the venue: each wife with her diplomat husband. Government ministers' wives were also invited – but most of their husbands didn't turn up. (The excuses varied, but High Commissioner Mark Fergusson was not the most liked diplomat in the government of President Kargbo Ndomahina. The British envoy had introduced financial aid reforms that had 'removed bread' from Ministers' mouths; and they hated him – for want of a better or worse phrase – for that.) The wives didn't mind. It was their own moment to peer-review their household affairs.

And so the farewell dinner went on well according to Rachael's plans. She saw inquisitive diplomats having a discussion with Stephen and she knew he was wowing them on Sierra Leone issues. She also saw Sarah having a conversation with Celia, obviously dissecting the folly of the relationship with Stephen. And then she ensured she had her heart-to-heart chat about her plans with her friend Christine in her bedroom.

So, Sarah's dream at Durham Castle now replayed that moment, that night, in her parents' room.

After much had gone on, as the night wore on, Stephen told Sarah he was leaving. He had had a good time with Grandpa James Fergusson, who had himself retired early to the boys' quarters after having a few pints 'to water my joy', and having been earlier introduced as 'the other guest of honour' at the dinner.

Stephen only wanted to sneak away and needn't say goodbye even to Sarah's parents: "You'll tell them goodbye for me later." Sarah acquiesced and decided to escort him outside. Coming back to the house, she remembered that she had planned to call her brother, Ben, for an update chat. However, it was impossible to do it in the living room, as it was also full of guests. The only option was her parents' room, which had the other telephone. She knew they were busy with the guests and would not come there soon.

She was mistaken. Just a few moments after she entered the large, spacious room, and having to walk to the far end of the room where the phone was installed by the bedside, Sarah heard some laughter in the hallway resembling the voice of her mother. She stood still. And now she heard two voices conversing, coming nearer, by the door of the room. There was another round of laughter. That was unmistakably her mother's voice.

Sarah had an instinctive thought and an intuitive reaction – definitely not wanting her mother to find her in the room. Not that Rachael would be mad about Sarah breaking the rules by using the private phone, especially if she explained that she was going to call Ben. But, instinctively, Sarah just didn't want her mother to find her in the room. She didn't want to start explaining – especially when there was a third person. *Avoid the scene if you can,* she concluded instantly. And, automatically, Sarah just dashed into the big wardrobe – the side which was her father's compartment – and stood in the middle of the coats and suits.

Already in, she thought maybe she had overreacted. Maybe her mother was just showing someone around the house, which she normally did, retelling the history of the place from the days of the abolitionists to the colonialists to today. But Sarah was prepared to stay in the wardrobe until the lingering voices went away – then she would sneak out and abandon the idea of calling Ben tonight and wait till tomorrow. They normally spoke on Sunday anyway. She had only wanted to call him tonight so she could give him a feel of the 'happy life' in Sierra Leone: to have told him who was present at the party while they were still present – except for Stephen who had left, which was why she was having the time to make the call.

But alas, Sarah heard the door opening and the two voices were now much clearer – it was her mother and Celia's mother, Christine. Rachael had never brought anyone else into this room. It was un-British to take non-relatives to one's bedroom. But her relationship with Christine had virtually transcended mere friendship. Indeed, it had gone beyond the diplomatic façade. Christine herself once said she never had a relationship beyond the official with Rachael's predecessor, the former British High Commissioner's wife, Margaret, 'who still behaved like we were in the days of Empire'.

Rachael and Christine had the Florida connection. And Christine had previously taken Rachael to her own bedroom anyway (it was not un-American to take friends to one's bedroom). So there was nothing wrong in returning the courtesy.

Just that Rachael was doing it for her own personal interest. There was nowhere else in the house to have this discussion except in the bedroom. And whatever impressions Christine might have about the room would not matter now anyway, because she was leaving.

Rachael did not want anybody else to hear this conversation – not even her husband. So she had made sure that Mark was deep in discussion with other diplomats. She also had an eye or two around but didn't see Sarah and concluded that she was somewhere in a corner with Stephen, or perhaps still with Celia. But that wouldn't matter much to Rachael because the only other person to come into their bedroom would be her husband, Mark. And he was busy. So, she had asked Christine to come with her to the room.

The American Ambassador's wife was amazed at how spacious the room was – it was the biggest room she had ever been into, with its king-size (or queen-size) bed. She light-heartedly said she thought the British normally accused the Americans of loving big things. Rachael explained the history of the place – most of which Christine already knew anyway (she only didn't know before that the Queen had slept in that very room). Rachael walked her friend to the settee in the other corner of the room, away from the bed but within hearing distance of the wardrobe.

"You have really spoilt me tonight, Rachael," Sarah heard the American Ambassador's wife saying. "I am forever indebted to you."

"Oh don't mention it, Christine. We are more than friends now. We are sisters now," she found herself saying exactly what Maria, her Mexican friend at university, once said to her.

"I'll certainly invite you to Israel," Christine made reference to the new diplomatic station her husband had been posted to. And then she posited, "So, to what do I owe this extra honour of bringing me into the Queen's bedroom?"

Laughter.

Christine had thought maybe her friend had some special farewell gift for her, apart from the one already presented openly.

"My dear, it's about Sarah."

It was like a psychological circuit-breaker to Sarah in the wardrobe. Her train of thought froze. She immediately held her breath on hearing her name. For an instant, she thought breathing – the normal act of inhaling and exhaling air – would make a sound that could be heard by the two and cut short the conversation. Sarah held her breath until Christine asked, "What about her?"

"Come on, Christine, you know so well that things are not good about this her relationship with this African boy. Everybody is talking about it."

"Oh, that?"

Sarah could not hold her breath anymore, and she was now realistic enough to know her breathing in the wardrobe would not be heard outside. She would do it slowly and gently – while listening.

As the details of the conversation were churned out – well, it was Rachael actually doing all the talking – Sarah at one point thought she should just come out and spoil everything. Her emotions were eating her away – she was becoming red in there and tears started running down her cheeks. But her reasoning came to the rescue – listen to the end, she resolved. And that she did. So her mother's new-found likeability for Stephen was all a ruse, a smokescreen to hide her true intentions of bringing the relationship to an end? And she was recruiting others to accomplish her goal?

What tortured Sarah's soul most was hearing that Celia was acting on Rachael's behalf when they had a conversation about Stephen earlier. Sarah had thought it was the normal friendship chatter. Knowing that her friend was about to leave, she had opened up to her about her feelings, her plans, her love for Stephen. There was no indication that Celia was doing Rachael's bidding. This was classic betrayal by someone she had called a friend all this while, Sarah concluded. And she was furious that all their conversation would be relayed to Christine, and then to Rachael.

Celia had always wanted Sarah to have a relationship with the German Ambassador's son – as Celia herself was doing with the Italian Ambassador's son – just for casual reasons. But she never thought the opposition to her relationship with Stephen would reach such heights.

But Sarah got two consolations from the discussion. Even though Christine had agreed to get the full details of the conversation with Celia, she cautioned Rachael, "Try to be very careful about the tactics you use in handling the matter. Be careful not to end up hurting your own daughter." But, on the balance of probabilities, what impressed Sarah most was Christine's statement that Stephen was held in high esteem by the diplomatic community. "He is respected even by my husband, of all people – choosy and picky as he is, if you know what I mean. He thinks that lad seems to be a different breed. Though with these Africans, you never can really tell." Christine seemed to have added the last sentence as a second thought to make her friend comfortable.

Sarah allowed a full five minutes after they had left before she came out of the wardrobe. She was sweating profusely. Her parents normally put the air-conditioner on just before going to bed. She walked to the door and listened again. There were no voices, no footsteps. She opened and closed the door behind her gently. She headed straight to her own room, jumped into bed, not bothering to change clothes, sobbing rapidly and allowing the tears to flow as much as they could. Ben didn't even come to her thoughts again. She couldn't even remember she was going to make a call at all. It was now about her battle with her mother over Stephen all over again.

It was an hour or so later, when most guests had gone and Celia herself was about to leave but didn't know where Sarah had gone with Stephen or when they left, that Rachael confronted Mark to complain about 'the disgusting and disrespectful behaviour' of the two leaving all the guests and 'going to do their thing'.

"I told you this boy was never good for our girl, but you don't believe me. Now, you have the evidence. Publicly." She said the last word with the motive of sticking a knife where one could.

Mark himself was incensed now. He raged inside. But he didn't say a word. Only his instinct led him straight to Sarah's room. He found her fast asleep. Still, Rachael didn't take back her words, but justified them. "But why wouldn't she tell anybody, even her friend, what she was doing? It's still the same thing."

Mark just retorted: "We better just leave everything for now. It's been a long night."

* * *

Sarah wouldn't have known all this if it were not for the all-knowing nature of dreams. Because her parents had never told her about this part of what happened that night; and it would only be later that she would corroborate its truthfulness. But now, as she clawed on the pillows under the quilt in her sleep at Durham Castle almost two years after the events, her body moved. As she turned from her left side to the right side again, she unconsciously placed another pillow between her legs. And then she became motionless again. But she stopped snoring. Back to deep sleep. And back to the dream…

The next morning at Hill Station in Freetown, Sarah woke up to follow her mother's footsteps. 'Like mother, like daughter' had never been so quickly adopted and adapted. After the crying and sobbing and pouring out of her heart for a while following the wardrobe experience, Sarah reached a serene mental equilibrium and just kept silent. Then suddenly a thought fell on her: to behave exactly as her mother had behaved; that is, act with pretence while executing Plan B. It was the belief that she had found a solution – that it would be the only way to teach her mother a lesson (*I'll give her a dose of her own medicine*) – which made her sleep eventually. That was when her father came to the room and found her asleep.

Sarah acted normal that morning in Freetown. She was the first to wake up. Her mother found her having breakfast in the dining room. Sarah was the first to speak.

"Good morning, Mum."

"Good morning, dear." She didn't show any anger.

"Sorry, Mum, I was so tired last night and had to sneak to bed."

"Never mind, dear. It was only your father who was a bit concerned about not seeing you, only for him to rush into your room to find you sleeping."

Sarah smiled and added, "Stephen had to leave early and didn't want to disturb you when you were busy with the guests. He asked me to say goodnight, but I was so tired."

"I perfectly understand. He did so well to stay that long."

"Thanks, Mum. He said he enjoyed the company."

"If you are happy, I am happy."

Sarah said she would be going to see him in a few hours. There was no objection from Rachael, apart from the oft-repeated admonition, "Just follow the rules."

Sarah was totally disappointed to have gone to Stephen's residence only to find he was not in. She was petrified. Where had he gone? All types of thoughts started flooding her mind (including Christine's words to her mum last night: 'Though with these Africans, you never can really tell'). Her first instinct was to go back home. But she wanted to prove a point, and pinpoint a fact. So she decided that there was nothing she could do with her time now but to wait for at least one hour and see if Stephen would return and explain to her. She took out her novel (she always had something to read) from her bag, sat on the veranda, and started to read *Harry Potter and the Philosopher's Stone*.

Thirty minutes later, she raised her head and saw Stephen approaching her. He was in a suit. He was the first to speak, as much as he was surprised.

"Oh my dear Sarah, what happened? You didn't tell me you were coming. So sorry you have had to wait outside."

"Ehm… ehm, never mind. I just wanted to surprise you. It's ok. I was passing the time reading while waiting," she said, smiling, and then got up. She now obviously realised it was a Sunday and Stephen had gone to church. She saw the Bible in his hand.

"You are lucky I didn't go to my traditional church, where we could stay for hours," Stephen explained, laughing and taking her by the hand. "Anglican services are shorter."

"You went to the Church of England?" Sarah picked it up immediately. "I thought you don't like them."

"Oh Sarah, I never said I don't like them. I was invited anyway."

"Invited to the church of that Anglican priest you wrote about?"

"Yes, it doesn't matter. I don't worship men or the church. God can be worshipped anywhere, everywhere. If you remember, that editorial was titled 'Even The Church Cannot Save Itself: Only One Can'."

"Oh come on, Stephen, spare me another lecture. I'm not here for that. I am here for *you*…"

They both laughed as they entered the apartment. She spent the whole day there. She came to not follow the rules – her mother would learn later, unfortunately.

"I'm going to make you a meal," she had said.

"Oh, that will be lovely."

They went to the nearby Indian supermarket and bought noodles and spaghetti. This was food Sarah had introduced to Stephen from the outset. At first, he was reluctant to be contented with eating it without adding his favourite cassava leaves or potato leaves with rice. But as time went on, he had grown to love it all by itself due to the frequency with which Sarah prepared it when she came.

"It's really lovely. I enjoyed it as always," he said after they finished eating from the same plate.

"Thank you." Sarah then suggested they should watch a movie and have some more wine.

"Ok. Just before we do that, I would like to read you a poem in appreciation of the nice food."

"Wow. A poem? I'm all yours."

Stephen dashed into the living room and came back with a book. "Don't say anything until I finish reading it."

"Ok."

"How beautiful your sandaled feet, O prince's daughter! Your graceful legs are like jewels, the work of an artist's hands.

Your navel is a rounded goblet that never lacks blended wine. Your waist is a mound of wheat encircled by lilies.

Your breasts are like two fawns, like twin fawns of a gazelle.

Your neck is like an ivory tower. Your eyes are the pools of Heshbon by the gate of Bath Rabbim. Your nose is like the tower of Lebanon looking toward Damascus.

Your head crowns you like Mount Carmel. Your hair is like royal tapestry; the king is held captive by its tresses.

How beautiful you are and how pleasing, my love, with your delights!

Your stature is like that of the palm tree, and your breasts like clusters of fruit.

I said, "I will climb the palm tree; I will take hold of its fruit." May your breasts be like clusters of grapes on the vine, the fragrance of your breath like apples…"

Sarah had held her peace to the end – albeit with gasps and spurting 'wow, wow' in-between. She was blushing all the way. But now, it was not so much the poem that had amazed her as what she noticed.

"Thank you, thank you, thank you, love. But what's that?" she asked, pointing her finger.

"It's a poem for you."

"I know. Thanks again. But where are you reading it from?"

"From the book I'm holding."

"The Bible?"

"Sure. From the *Song of Songs*."

"You mean the Bible has poems? Love stories?"

"Many, many love stories. I mean, the Bible itself is the mother of all love stories. The love story."

"I see. But please spare me some preaching today... I really, really love the poem. That's so nice... And you deserve a special reward for that..."

She pulled him by the hand and dragged him towards the bedroom (she had long since known that she was actually not taller without her high heels). They had forgotten about the movie. Last night's resolution took over her: she had taken the decision not to follow her mother's rules anymore! And Stephen – willingly, excitedly, romantically – swam across the Rubicon with Sarah in conjugal we've-both-been-longing-for-this youthful zest.

***

It was more than a shock to Rachael when a month or so later, her daughter said she was pregnant – well, that she had missed her cycle and could be pregnant.

"How could you do this, Sarah, how could you?" a very mad Rachael kept repeating as she paced up and down the living room.

"These things happen, Mum."

"They don't just happen. Why did you flout my rules? Why didn't you at least use contraceptives?"

"I really don't know, Mum." She knew very well she was lying and she knew her mother also knew, but she didn't mind. She had executed her Plan B as a response to her mother's Plan A. She would rather anger her mother than be cut off from Stephen.

It was then that Rachael suggested an alternative: to abort. Sarah was shocked. And said she had already told Stephen about it.

Rachael burst out, "It doesn't matter. It's about our name, Sarah. You can tell him you had a miscarriage."

It only made matters worse. The situation went out of control.

Mark Fergusson returned home from his trip to the war-support conference in London with President Kargbo Ndomahina only to find out his daughter had moved away from home to stay with Stephen.

* * *

The dream at Durham Castle now took Sarah on a blitzkrieg round of major events in her relationship with Stephen: how they had promised to love each other forever, the trip to Roboli where she discovered that Stephen was from a royal family, and how she loved the traditional reception of dancing and singing she was accorded that time, how she was treated like a princess, their visit to the cinema where they watched an Indian movie, *Ghazab*, about twins who embarked on a frolic of revenge when the one was killed but his ghost came back to collaborate with his living brother in identifying the perpetrators, their visit to the chimpanzees and the hippos when Grandpa James Fergusson visited (which actually happened before her pregnancy but was now being presented in the dream as if it came after that).

And now, in the dream, there was this elaborate wedding between her and Stephen at Westminster Abbey. She was in her all-white bridal dress – just like that day when she read scripture in this very cathedral. Their son, Joel, about seven years old, was the page boy – also dressed in white. The bridegroom, Stephen, in a black suit, had come forward and given a bouquet of flowers to the page boy to pass on to the bride. And just at that moment, as she bent down to receive the flowers, Sarah woke up from her sleep.

She jumped out of bed and went straight to look at where Joel's cot was standing. It was not there. Only then did she realise she was in Durham Castle. Not in London, where Joel was with his grandmother, Rachael Fergusson.

It was still too early to check on them, but she knew they were okay. It was all a dream. What a dream. *How come dreams can put together a person's history in such a condensed way?* she thought. *Well, it even added what never happened; and omitted what really happened: instead of Stephen's funeral, it was a wedding.*

It was just a dream. It couldn't change anything. It wouldn't change her resolve to move on, Sarah concluded.

She decided that she would go to Durham University today to collect her transcript. She could not stop the dreams of the past, but they would not stop her dreams for the future. She was poised to move on.

35

Hardly could there have been another much-talked-about send-off party within the diplomatic community in London that year. It was held at the Nigerian High Commission premises at Trafalgar Square. That evening, diplomats and their spouses ate and drank in honour of the pending departure to duty-post in Monrovia, Liberia, of the newly appointed British High Commissioner *for* Sierra Leone, John Coleson.

* * *

Even though, all this while, back in Nigeria – and in the eyes of the world – the government of Mallam Musa Odofo was a pariah that had plunged the country into sanctions biting the ordinary man on the streets, the Nigerian High Commission in London had remained a thriving and influential stakeholder in the diplomatic community.

Britain had robustly led the international community in condemning, sanctioning and closing diplomatic missions in Nigeria since the plea for a stay of the execution of human rights activist Prof. Ken Sawyer fell on the deaf ears of Mallam Musa

Odofo. The killing of the British-educated activist, coupled with the similarly, if not more, confrontational imprisonment of the man who had apparently won an election bankrolled by the self-same British-led international community, directly undermined the ethical foreign policy efforts of Prime Minister Ed McInroy's administration. Britain had therefore tightened the screws on the beleaguered government of Mallam Musa Odofo. The British High Commission in Nigeria was effectively shut down; and other Western countries, including the US, had followed suit.

But the Nigerian High Commission in Britain was alive and kicking. Officially recognised. Functional.

Two things were explained – the third was self-explanatory – by the Foreign and Commonwealth Office. While Britain could easily pack its bags and order its officials to leave Nigeria, it was not that simple to tell Nigeria to pack its baggage out of Britain. The Commonwealth status of Nigeria was crucial, and the fight was not against the country but its leaders who had been banned from travelling outside Nigeria.

"We don't have problems with the Nigerian High Commission in Britain. We don't have issues with the High Commissioner to Britain," John Coleson, then as head of the Africa Desk in the Foreign Office, had told a curious British press. He had further explained that even if the High Commissioner were to be declared *persona non grata* and asked to leave Britain in the worst-case scenario, the Nigerian High Commission could not be ordered to shut down. "Britain is a great respecter of international laws and treaties. And the land on which the Nigerian High Commission premises stands is Nigerian property, if anybody needs reminding. It is apparently the Republic Of Nigeria. Not Her Majesty's land. Not Crown land. Sorry."

On the issue of the resurgent relationship between British officials and Nigerian officials in Monrovia, the Foreign and Commonwealth Office spokesperson had said it was 'the inevitable though uncomfortable route in trying to restore democracy in Sierra Leone, even as the commitment to restore same to Nigeria remains unwavering'. He had accepted that meetings had taken place in Abuja between Nigerian and Sierra Leonean and British officials, but couldn't say if Mallam Musa Odofo himself was present at such meetings.

"We are working with the devil – and even eating with him, but with a very long spoon. We know when to call the party off and overturn the tables. The Nigerian dictatorship will be brought to account eventually. For now, we will work with them to bring sanity to Sierra Leone, which we all know was Britain's first colony in that part of the world and therefore we have a moral responsibility to jealously protect it. As things stand, the situation in Sierra Leone requires more urgency due to the rebel war that has been compounded by a military takeover. We must not allow democracy to fail there, by all means necessary."

And the unofficial self-explanatory justification was how much the Sierra Leone project was close to Prime Minister Ed McInroy's heart – he had felt morally obliged to save democracy in the country where he was born and had such strong emotional ties with. It was no secret.

And now, Mallam Musa Odofo (well, Nigeria) had virtually singlehandedly done, through Operation Octopus, what the whole international community was struggling to achieve – removing the military junta in Freetown for the return of the democratically elected government of Sierra Leone.

Yes, Britain was initially opposed to the methods used, as the British Ambassador to the UN had made it categorically clear that 'the Nigerian action does not have the mandate of international law and protocols; and we have asked Nigeria to explain why it has taken such brazen aggression'. But before Nigeria could explain – beyond everybody's imagination, perhaps even beyond the expectations of Mallam Musa Odofo and President Kargbo

Ndomahina – events had happened in rapid succession. Within days, the Freetown junta had been dislodged – its soldiers had been defeated (some surrendered, some disappeared into the countryside) and its leaders were on the run. Democracy had won the day. Might was right. What had been achieved was what Britain was desirous to achieve anyway. So be it. Britain was now prepared to jump on the bandwagon and lead the way.

In a dramatic change of diplomatic course, in line with Downing Street's new posture, the British Ambassador to the UN told a *New York Times* reporter: "It would be foolhardy to leave the affairs of Sierra Leone entirely in the hands of Nigeria. Now, it is about working closer with the devil to monitor his every step and then overtake, overthrow, or overpower him. The Freetown junta has been forced out. The Abuja junta would also be forced out. But first things first – work with Nigeria to solve Sierra Leone before turning on Nigeria again. That's the British policy as at now."

When the Sierra Leone High Commission in Britain therefore apparently breached protocol by organising a send-off dinner for the new British High Commissioner to Sierra Leone at the Trafalgar Square premises of the Nigerian High Commission in London, the Foreign and Commonwealth Office – though initially a bit surprised and had thought matters were being taken too far – acquiesced. Not only was the new High Commissioner John Coleson (together with his newly-wedded Israeli-born wife, of course) in attendance, the Foreign Secretary briefly graced the occasion too – 'to underline how Britain is passionate about the Sierra Leone project', irrespective of where it led them.

"It was a memorable dinner," the Secretary General of the Commonwealth Secretariat, Nigerian-born Dele Dulu, who chaired the proceedings, said to reporters later. When asked why the press was not invited, he quipped, "It was a family meeting." Virtually all the African ambassadors in Britain were in full attendance. The vote of thanks was given by the Bugandan High

Commissioner, who inadvertently praised their citizen, John Kirikiri (the current UN Secretary General), for his role in the process of giving the Freetown junta false hopes that lured the Sierra Leonean soldiers from security alertness. "We used the double-edged sword of democracy," he said to applause. Even the American Ambassador in Britain attended the ceremony. It appeared they all agreed that all was well that had ended well. Why not flow with the tide then? Conspicuously, Ghana was not represented!

***

John Coleson left his wife, Mia Coleson, in London and flew to Monrovia to lead the efforts on the smooth return of President Kargbo Ndomahina to Freetown. She would eventually join him in Sierra Leone, the couple had agreed.

John Coleson had one major strategy in mind in getting his job done – dismantling 'the cabal' left behind by his predecessor, Mark Fergusson. His first pronounced action towards that was when he swapped British officials of the twin Sierra Leone and Liberia missions working in the same building in Monrovia. An internal memo from the new High Commissioner stated that the top three officials of the Sierra Leone mission were being replaced by their counterparts in the Liberia mission. It turned out that these officials in the Liberia mission now taking over the Sierra Leone mission had been closely working with John Coleson all along when he was head of the Africa Desk at the Foreign and Commonwealth Office. They were aggrieved about having been sidelined in their own turf: they used to supply information to John Coleson about the activities of Mark Fergusson. They had reported to him that the British High Commission benefited from diamond kickbacks in the 'Jungle Boys arms deal'. These were the officials John Coleson was comfortable to work with:

they were the ones to lead the relocation process from Monrovia to Freetown.

Meanwhile, Prime Minister McInroy had immediately dispatched hundreds of British troops to Sierra Leone as forerunners to an emergency UN-Resolution-mandated multinational force 'to disarm the warring factions and maintain the peace'. Another British frigate with arms, ammunition and Chinook helicopters went down south the Atlantic to Freetown to boost up the security ahead of the arrival of President Kargbo Ndomahina.

Soon, the British official and media language or tenor changed from a unilateral Nigerian intervention in Sierra Leone to a British exemplar of fighting for democracy around the world. The British forces were restoring democracy in Sierra Leone. Prime Minister Ed McInroy's ethical foreign policy was at work.

* * *

Having been seen – and portraying herself – as the engine that had been propelling President Kargbo Ndomahina's political vehicle in exile, Femi Cole would love, or would have loved, to jointly share the glare, glamour and glory of flying together with the President on the day of returning to Sierra Leone.

It was no longer a secret; it was no longer a mere rumour that Femi Cole was officially or unofficially but certainly the recognised partner (if not actually a wife) of President Ndomahina. There could be no better moment of underlining this than returning home as a couple after their harrowing, struggling days in exile. But the option of her going ahead to prepare the ground for the coming President was also mouth-watering and attractive. There was sense in it, there was a lot to prepare in advance at home, and nobody else could do the job better, she accepted.

She would have to travel by road from Liberia with a long convoy of vehicles that included all the British officials of the *new* Sierra Leone High Commission, plus diplomats from other foreign missions who had relocated to Monrovia and would now re-relocate to Freetown, guarded by Nigerian soldiers and a few British paratroopers as well. It sounded and felt presidential in itself, Femi Cole concluded.

It was a long journey. But Femi Cole – quintessential Miss Sierra Leone – saw it as an opportunity to warm herself into the hearts of the people. She made intermittent stops in towns and villages – waving, shaking hands, speaking to the people about the pending return of the President. In certain instances, in the towns and villages where the convoy did not stop, some people even argued that President Ndomahina himself was in the vehicle with the 'P1' license plate.

Femi Cole explained to the people that President Ndomahina had stayed behind in Monrovia, waiting to return on the very day of the new inauguration (the people clapped); that he would return home on a helicopter provided by the UN (the people clapped again); and that Mallam Musa Odofo of Nigeria (the people clapped at the mention of the name) would join him in Monrovia from Aso Rock and the two would fly together to Freetown on D-Day (the rapturous, continuous clapping would not stop until Femi Cole left the gathering).

President Ndomahina had actually originally insisted that Femi Cole should fly with him. But High Commissioner John Coleson – stoutly supported by the three newly-appointed officials who were not fans of Femi Cole – persuaded him on the need to fly together with Sierra Leone's Opposition Leader (whom *The True Light* newspaper once called 'the rubber-stamper who is as culpable as the government in not putting the interests of the people centre-stage' in the pre-coup days) in order to present a public relations united front. Travelling with the Opposition Leader, John Coleson had insisted, would send a message to the public and the international community in particular that what had happened in Sierra Leone had the full support of all and sundry across the political divide. The President had agreed after Femi Cole herself had jumped on the opportunity of – as High Commissioner Coleson put it – 'being a kind of interim President before the President himself returns'. Femi Cole – with her OSLEWIL ladies, of course – would be in charge of organising the whole Freetown return programme until inauguration day. She would be reporting daily to President Ndomahina until his arrival. *A one-day king is a king. I'll be president until the President returns,* Femi Cole had thought to herself.

And she did the job very well with an extra touch. Her journalism and PR skills had never been so effectively employed. The media spotlight couldn't go away from her, as she was constantly in the news with her daily press briefings regarding preparations for President Ndomahina's return. Even the new British diplomats, once they arrived in Freetown, and as far as inauguration preparations were concerned, found themselves reporting to her.

So, it was Femi Cole who actually changed the date of the President's return – adding another week to the original scheduled date – citing that, among others, there were still pending mopping up operations, vetting of personnel and purchasing of relevant stage materials for the occasion. The change of date was accepted by President Ndomahina. And by all.

36

There could possibly not be a happier grandmother in Britain at this time than Rachael Fergusson. All her prayers of late were being answered. Well, she didn't really do prayers in the traditional way. She had wishes, not prayers – and these wishes were lately coming to pass for Rachael. Her wishes in Sierra Leone were butchered; now her wishes in Britain were flowering.

Stephen had thwarted her wishes in Sierra Leone. Now there was no Stephen. Her daughter had agreed to move on. Actually more than that: Sarah had already moved on. After all, Sarah was right now in Durham Castle living her life away, Rachael thought to herself. Plus, her husband was all hers again. And she had an extra bonus in Joel, as she believed this bundle of joy had also become all hers.

***

Since Sarah left for Durham Castle, Rachael felt like a nursing mother all over again with Joel in her care 24/7. To the consolidating grandmother, this was a glimpse of how it was going to be after Sarah decided what she wanted to do with her new life – either to do further studies or to work. Rachael herself didn't need to work – didn't want to work. She was getting more than enough from the Royal Fund. She would be just happy doing this job of taking care of Baby Joel. She would raise him up – bring him up as a Fergusson.

And that thought just raced Rachael's mind back to that day at Exeter Hospital when she had expected to give birth to a baby boy and ended up getting a girl, a 'miracle baby,' Sarah Fergusson. It now seemed to Rachael another replacement was taking place. In the place of Sarah Fergusson – her daughter – was now Joel Fergusson. Ok, he was Joel Tamaraneh on paper, as written on the birth certificate, she acknowledged. But at least he was going to be raised up the Fergusson way – the Rachael Fergusson way. Why wouldn't she be happy right now?

And why wouldn't she be happier when she took into consideration the way things were turning out for her husband. She knew that the 'Arms to Africa Affair' was as good as dead. John Coleson had got what he wanted and had taken the place of her husband in Monrovia. "Good for him. That's politics for some people," Rachael had remarked to Mark on the day the news broke. But what was certain was that she had got her husband back in one piece. A big wish had come to pass – though not the way she would have particularly liked.

And Rachael believed and knew that Mark Fergusson was capable of bouncing back in a different way. She had never seen a more self-created man, who would never feel sorry for himself in any situation. Mark knew how to be down and then up and then down again. And then up again: he was on his way up right now – if not up already. As the parliamentary sub-committee investigation had vanished, he would be getting a sumptuous pension. At this age, they really didn't need more than what they already got. So Rachael was Britain's happiest grandmother – and also mother – at this time. And the news from her daughter Sarah that her father-in-law, James Fergusson, was in high spirits in hospital also further raised Rachael's spirits that morning when she was looking at Baby Joel – just about the same time Sarah jolted from her long dream at Durham Castle.

***

It didn't take Mark Fergusson long to know exactly what he was going to do next. He was going to write a book – on his life as a diplomat; with particular reference to the so-called 'Arms to Africa Affair' (he referred to it as the 'AAA' in all his notes). He was already musing over it. He would use all the documents he had gathered for the botched parliamentary sub-committee hearing to inform his book. He would tell it all as he knew it. No holds barred. He was going to tell the story – the true story – about his sacrifice for the now-acclaimed British success story. He had always wanted to write a book. But these events had ignited the desire. And there couldn't have been a better time as now. The press would certainly be interested in his story. He had inadvertently been thrown into the limelight; and now he would use that limelight to tell the true story. He would particularly put in the book that he had never even seen a diamond with his naked eyes!

But one thing Mark planned to do first was to visit his father. When Sarah had told him about James Fergusson's high spirits, she also informed him that Grandpa expressed a desire for his son to visit. He wanted Mark to meet with his former-schoolmate-turned-vicar, Gabriel Williamson. Mark therefore decided to get the filial visit out of the way before settling down to his book-writing.

***

Later that day, the Fergussons couldn't thank their stars enough when they got a call from Sarah saying she had been offered the position of Research Assistant at the Mass Communications Department of Durham University. Rachael's prayers – wishes – could not have come to pass more quickly. Silent prayers, or unspoken wishes, could also be answered or fulfilled, she believed.

Earlier that day – the morning after the long dream (the one and only dream thus far about Stephen) – Sarah was so desperate to move on that she left Durham Castle while her cousin Lynn was still sleeping (apparently with a hangover from the previous night's partying). Sarah went by taxi to Durham University to collect her transcript.

Professor Craig McAlister, the head of the Mass Communications Department at Durham University, described Sarah's visit as 'a miraculous coincidence'. He was her personal tutor two years ago and was stoutly opposed to her going away to Sierra Leone to complete her studies. Sarah had agreed with him until Uncle Ed McInroy intervened and convinced her. Now she was back for her transcript and she found her former personal tutor as head of the department. In addition, Professor McAlister told Sarah that the department had been looking in the past year, without success, for a Research Assistant to boost the university's twinning programme. And the candidate must have had some experience in one of the twinning universities abroad – which immediately qualified Sarah for the job. Consequently, in retrospect, it was really a good thing, in relation to this job, that Sarah listened to Uncle Ed and went away to complete her studies at Sierra Leone's Mount Aureol University, which was twinned with Durham University.

"If you are willing to leave London to come to stay at the university quarters, it's a five-figure salary, the job is all yours," the professor said in his usual carefree manner. Sarah could not believe her ears. What better way to start her new journey without looking back – without having Joel as a constant reminder.

Her parents were all the more excited when she broke the news to them. Sarah was now back at Durham Castle, and cousin Lynn also came on the line to tell Uncle Mark and Aunty Rachael how happy she would be with Sarah in the Durham neighbourhood again (they had only met once at the university cafe when Sarah was studying there). After breaking the big news, Sarah informed her parents that she was coming to London the next day to pack and leave, as the job was to start with immediate effect. She had asked the professor to give her a few days.

This just met Mark's own plans – or prayers, or wishes. He would kill two birds with one stone: he would wait for Sarah to come, and then he would drive her to Durham, so that he would see his father at the same time.

And when it actually happened, it was much more than what Mark had really hoped for. The whole family decided to come along. Not only that – or much more than that – they would meet Dr. Robinson (Rachael had become all the more excited when Mark had disclosed to her the remarkable coincidence about the doctor), meaning that he was going to see Sarah for the first time since the hospital mix-up many years ago.

"As the whole family is going, we should go with April 17 and April 18 as well," an excited Rachael ventured.

"Spot on, Mum. I want them to come see my place," Sarah remarked, all smiles.

"Of course, they are part of this family," Mark agreed.

Ben didn't say anything.

It was such fun in the car – with Ben driving, Mark in the front seat, Rachael and Sarah in the back seat (the mother holding Joel, the daughter playing with the lovebirds as their cage was strapped to the window handle on her side). All was well.

So, at the Exeter Hospital café, the Fergussons converged with Dr. Robinson and Gabriel Williamson. Today, Mark and Rachael decided to tell Sarah the story about the birth mix-up. And it all turned out so poignant and hilarious and reconciliatory.

"So you even hid this story from me all these years," James Fergusson said, laughing loudly.

But it was Sarah who responded: "No wonder at times I feel like a boy."

More laughter.

"There you go, there you go. I might not have been totally wrong," Dr. Robinson was hitting the table as he laughed along.

"God had long planned it this way," Gabriel Williamson preached.

"Well, He took a long time to put it right," Rachael declared with laughter again.

"None of us thought this moment would ever come," her husband said.

Mark had thought he would take his father back to his Exeter home but Dr. Robinson said the old man had not fully recovered. James Fergusson himself said he felt more comfortable at the hospital, as long as Gabriel Williamson was visiting.

There are no prying reporters here, James Fergusson thought to himself.

So, from the hospital, the Fergussons drove to Durham University to drop off Sarah – the Research Assistant. Her quaint self-contained two-room apartment was all ready. They all liked it. And the lovebirds seemed to like it too.

"Maybe they want to stay with you," Rachael said.

"Maybe next time," Sarah replied, as she hung the cage back on the window handle of the car before kissing Joel goodbye.

"Goodbye, Miracle Baby," came from Ben, prompting spontaneous laughter from all (well, except Joel and the lovebirds). They left Sarah and took the journey back to London without any major incidence. In their hearts, the family had regained its equilibrium.

Book Three

Son-in-Law

"...worthy to escape all these things that will come to pass..."

37

It was not the international community only – or alone – that had overwhelmingly wanted the Freetown military junta out. Even the majority (but certainly not all) of Sierra Leoneans wanted the ill-fated regime out too. As the British led the way, all the pro-democrats had been praying and hoping and wishing that the long nightmare would come to an end. The only problem was that they were not unanimous in the methods to employ.

Britain and the UN – at least at the official level – had wanted a smoother round-table solution. Mallam Musa Odofo and President Kargbo Ndomahina had seen it in another light and used the short-cut military method. And now everybody was on board. The people were now fully on board – if they had not been on board all along.

* * *

Several months ago – on the day of the coup against President Ndomahina and the days following – the people did not know whether to dance or to cry, whether to come out to the streets or to stay locked up in their houses. They were not sure of what had happened: perhaps it was still one of the 'ninety-nine survival tactics' of President Kargbo Ndomahina.

The Ndomahina government had quelled several insurrections and forestalled many military coups (imaginary or real). And the 'perpetrators' had paid the penalties: some were publicly executed by a firing squad 'to teach others not to try the government of President Kargbo Ndomahina again', according to the ever-ready-to-defend spokesman, Minister of Information Bai Sankoh. The government had ruled with an iron fist. It was a police state: critics, journalists and other activists were silenced through random arrests and disappearances without any trace. The economy was sinking – as corruption ruled the day, embodied in the President's chief financier, Lebanese businessman Amza Alie (who plotted against fellow Lebanese rivals and got them deported). He got virtually all the government contracts – delivering nothing, except to the President.

And so, to the people, it had felt like the Ndomahina government would never come to an end. The so-called Opposition was in fact an ally: four of its leaders were members of President Ndomahina's Cabinet. That's why the press called Sierra Leone a 'pseudo one-party state; the country of *usai den tie cow nar dae e dae eat*'. It was the status quo.

And the people had resigned to fate. That everything should be left in God's hands.

***

Even when the rebel war had started, with its leader, Retired Major Kalu Brima, announcing that they had taken up arms to remove the government of President Kargbo Ndomahina ('because the unpatriotic cabal of Ndomahina can never be removed by democratic means, as thuggery during campaigns and stuffing of ballot boxes during elections has been the order of the day'), no one took the rebels seriously. Government officials were still living the lavish life with family members shopping abroad, driving around town in expensive cars, dressing extravagantly and spoiling each other in weekly partying – while the soldiers who had been sent to end the rebellion were suffering serious casualties.

It was worse for the civilians, especially women and children, caught up in the war-affected areas. There were harrowing reports of massacres, burnings, lootings in towns and villages. There was a lack of political will. The soldiers complained about lack of material support to prosecute the war. A mutiny to that effect ballooned into a full-blown coup, sending President Kargbo Ndomahina packing into exile in Liberia.

***

But even when the trembling voice of Captain Matthew Thomas had announced on state radio that night that the sixteen-year administration of 'the corrupt and wicked Ndomahina misrule has come to an end', most Sierra Leoneans didn't believe – couldn't believe. It was simply unbelievable – in the sense that no one thought it was ever possible.

"It could be a set-up by the Ndomahina government to execute more political opponents," a former Sierra Leone colonel, wanted for treason in Freetown who had escaped to Guinea Bissau three years ago, had told the BBC immediately after the coup.

All had only believed it was a real coup when they heard President Ndomahina's counter broadcast from Liberia.

But then the people's troubles had just begun.

On the day of the coup itself, there was a lot of looting, shop breaking, beatings and even killings. By the afternoon of the next day, the situation had been brought under control, according to the military high command. But it changed nothing because what had been lost had been lost, and no one was asked to give an account of anything. Soldiers took the law into their hands here and there, even in family disputes or to settle old personal scores – sometimes leading to deaths.

On their part, the rebels had immediately announced a ceasefire, 'welcoming the overthrow of the most corrupt and killer government of the wicked President Ndomahina, while we wait to hear from our military brothers who are now in charge'. Within days, they had reached an agreement, naming rebel leaders in the Cabinet – negotiated by the Libyan Dictator, who was their chief sponsor (all the top rebel commanders had received training in Tripoli).

* * *

The response from Nigeria had been swift, in an obvious fall-out between Mallam Musa Odofo and his friend, the Libyan Dictator. Odofo had hated the North African's meddling into West African affairs. Besides, the Nigerian dictator was in a battle for survival – a life-and-death matter. The Libyan Dictator was in his own world.

The sudden appearance and activities of Nigerian Alfa jets, dropping bombs here and there, had caught the people in the middle. There was more lamentation across the land. The military junta had tried to do some self-promoting public relations stunts by conducting what they had called 'commissions of inquiry in absentia' for President Kargbo Ndomahina and his henchmen. No one knew where these trials were held, but within a week, 'Ali Baba and his forty thieves' (as the junta spokesman had called President Ndomahina and his government) have been found guilty of massive corruption, egregious embezzlement and state kleptocracy!' The junta released documents showing the deep-seated corruption that was going on. They had then announced an 'official end to the war with the rebels'.

But Mallam Odofo would have none of that. The bombs kept falling. And Mark Fergusson and Co decamped to Liberia.

* * *

And soon, it was found out that the Freetown junta leaders were perhaps more corrupt, with their girlfriends taking centre-stage in businesses and contracts. Some snatched other men's wives! Diamonds were being smuggled by new Lebanese magnates – Amza Alie having escaped via helicopter on the night of the coup. And the junta deal with the rebels, which brought the fighters from the bushes to the towns and cities, only meant another yoke on the necks of the people. The rebels were practically a law to themselves: beating people, killing some; and even challenging the authority of soldiers, as fights between the two broke out here and there.

When will this nightmare ever come to an end? was the question uppermost on the people's minds in a country shut down by air, land and sea.

* * *

The people of Roboli, the hometown of the Tamaraneh twins, were no exception. They had also borne the brunt of the excesses of the Ndomahina government (in fact, two of the soldiers publicly executed by firing squad 'on trumped-up charges' after a two-day trial were natives of Roboli). They knew very well how their kith-and-kin journalist, Amidu Tamaraneh, was jailed several times and harassed by the Ndomahina government. And they knew how 'education is a privilege and not a right', as had been declared by President Ndomahina himself.

And the people of Roboli also knew that – despite the Ndomahina repression – Editor Amidu Tamaraneh was not in support of the Freetown junta. His father, Teacher Paul, had always talked about his son's 'sincerity of purpose, and putting the nation first'. He had explained to the people of Roboli that his son's newspaper's stance against the Nigerian military bombardment was not to be interpreted as either hatred for the Ndomahina government or love for the Freetown junta.

"My boys stood for the truth. They died for the truth. That's how I brought them up," Teacher Paul had kept consoling himself among his friends. "Even though I lost my twins through a bomb from a Nigerian jet, I bear no grudge, and I have no regrets that *The True Light* newspaper stood for the truth." Teacher Paul had said the nation would not have suffered this much if all sides had listened to the newspaper's editorial stance of a commitment to a peaceful resolution of the conflict. He had always said this to anybody that cared to listen – after they came out of hiding following the signing of the Banjul Peace Accord.

But now Teacher Paul was not averse to what had happened through Operation Octopus. "The junta has been kicked out; and it is good in our eyes. All we want is peace. It is welcome news – if that is going to end our nightmare." After all, he had lost his sons. And, on top of that, the rebels had chopped off the hands of his good friend, Alieu Vascular Bundles.

* * *

Due to Alieu Vascular Bundles' affluence, influence and networking within the cobweb of rebels and soldiers that made him travel to Freetown and other places to do his business, the flamboyant businessman had been able to help many people at his hometown of Roboli. Even on the day he had brought the news of the killing of the Tamaraneh twins, Alieu Vascular Bundles had given a bag of rice and some condiments to Teacher Paul and Rosemarie.

"Things are tough for the ordinary man, but not for Vascular Bundles," he usually boasted, while lending a helping hand where he could. And he was appreciated in the community for that. But the people of Roboli were shocked and horrified when about two months later, Vascular Bundles was brought and dumped in the town centre with his hands chopped off.

It had happened that one of the most monstrous methods adopted by the rebels was cutting off people's limbs – even children were not spared. The true story of why Vascular Bundles suffered this fate would never be known (his own versions varied). But it was a dispute over something. Some rumour said it was over money. Another rumour said it had to do with missing diamonds. Yet another said a woman was involved – that she dated both Alieu Vascular Bundles and a rebel commando. The bottom line was that his former allies had turned against him, took all he had, and cut his hands off. A sympathetic faction had brought him to Roboli with the wounds still fresh – though the 'sympathetic faction' looted everything he had at Roboli in 'self-payment'. He was treated by a native doctor (an herbalist, to be more appropriate) – a job that had left a permanent monthly recurring pain in the parts where the bones and the flesh met. Vascular Bundles now relied on the generosity of others. He had never had time to settle with, or for, one woman; those who had been coming and going had gone and weren't coming again. His friend, Teacher Paul, was doing his best to help from their farm produce.

So, they were all happy to see the back of the junta – whether the correct procedure or the correct law had been followed or not in removing them, they didn't care.

"As long as they are gone, that is what matters," Vascular Bundles said in low whispery tones to Teacher Paul who had come over to share the news of Operation Octopus. Vascular Bundles now spoke with a lisp. There were now big gaps in his cavity because his former-friends-turned-enemies even took away his golden teeth – not to talk of the gold or gold-plated chains and rings which went away with the hands.

Therefore, when the news about Femi Cole having

triumphantly entered Sierra Leone with the longest motorcade ever seen – with the British, the Nigerians, the Sierra Leoneans from Liberia; convoy following convoy – heralding the pending return of President Kargbo Ndomahina went round, the people of Roboli were not less excited at the prospects for their country.

"At last, this nightmare is coming to an end," Teacher Paul had told Vascular Bundles.

Everybody was looking forward to the set date for the President's return.

38

There had never been – and there would never again be – a day like the day set for the return of President Kargbo Ndomahina to take over power again as the legitimate Sierra Leone Head of State in Freetown. Pomp, pageantry and power at their apex. There was mirth everywhere. The people simply went agog.

They had been preparing for this day for the past few weeks. The mopping-up operations had been done; thousands of junta collaborators had been arrested (some were killed with tyres hung over their necks, pouring petrol and lighting a match, justifying it with 'the evil that men do burns with them'). Femi Cole had been on top of the situation in terms of preparations. The national stadium, the venue for the re-inauguration, was painted afresh; even streets were washed, and some people also re-painted their houses with President Ndomahina's party's colour – pink.

The whole of Sierra Leone woke up to dancing, drumming, drinking and jubilation – except for the small conclave where the three countries met, to where the remnants of rebels and soldiers had retreated.

* * *

The rebel leader, Rtd. Major Kalu Brima, in response to Operation Octopus, had declared that they would re-start the war 'for the betrayal of trust by Nigeria and the international community'. When retreating, the renegade soldiers and rebels had written graffiti on houses and abandoned vehicles like 'we will be back' and 'Ndomahina is a thief'. They had declared Operation Pay Yourself (which meant they looted anything they could carry on their way back to the jungles). The rebel leader hated President Kargbo Ndomahina to his guts. They were squad-mates in the military.

"Ndomahina was the greatest army traitor who sold out his colleagues and many civilians on false allegations about coups. After doing the dirty job, the former President sent him to the UN for fear that he would himself have staged a coup. I could have been killed myself like the many others because Ndomahina got me arrested for a coup I never knew about. I had to escape," the rebel leader once told the BBC. So there were certainly no celebrations in the rebel junta's holed-up base for the President's return.

***

But in Freetown, before even the cocks crowed, there were already scores of overloaded vehicles – with some passengers in the boots, honking their horns away, and the locally produced 'pegapak' liquor being the drink of the occasion – taking over the streets. Politicians who had returned from exile ahead of time had solicited the support of youth and women's groups with bags of money and liquor, to display banners of these politicians' support 'for President Ndomahina and democracy'. Some hired open trucks and placed musical sets with big speakers playing loud music across the streets. Some had their own musical equipment set up at home, doing the same. It was a day of joy, a day when the people

– or their wishes – had prevailed. Since around 5:00am, streams of people had been pouring into the national stadium.

This very stadium, in the last few months, until the return of Femi Cole, was a theatre of agony and misery hosting thousands of malnourished displaced persons from all around the country. The 'inauguration committee' moved them to makeshift camps in the outskirts of the city with the promise of building houses for them after the return of President Ndomahina.

***

President Kargbo Ndomahina woke up in Monrovia not believing that this day had finally come. Well, not quite. He was just saying to himself, "So this day has finally come." What seemed impossible was becoming possible – had become possible, he noted, as he smiled in bed and wished Femi Cole were here. Never mind; he would see her soon anyway – in a matter of hours. They spoke last night, and she gave him all the details of the preparations and how the whole nation was going to receive him 'like a king' today. He thought it would be more than that – to be accompanied by Nigeria's Mallam Musa Odofo on a helicopter and landing in majestic fashion at the national stadium amidst cheering crowds was more than just royalty – it was supernatural. Mallam Musa Odofo would soon arrive from Abuja, and off they would go to Freetown to seal their accomplishment – the President relished, still in bed.

***

Mallam Musa Odofo knew this was as much his day as it was President Ndomahina's – if not more. If ever Africa had come close to proving to the neo-colonialists that it could solve its own problems – that the continent had its own way of solving its problems – this was what he had delivered through Operation Octopus, which had led to this day's celebrations. The British could go ahead and try to take the glory from him for all they wanted, but he knew he had dealt them a heavy blow – a double punch; actually a triple punch. They had grudgingly accepted his military mission in Sierra Leone, and they had also reluctantly lifted his travel ban and permitted him to travel with President Kargbo Ndomahina to Freetown.

Initially, the British had categorically opposed the lifting of the travel ban. Mallam Musa Odofo might have militarily outsmarted them through Operation Octopus (they didn't call it that: they called it 'a maverick dictatorial idiosyncrasy'), but they were not willing to lift the travel ban until power was handed over to the imprisoned democratically-elected President of Nigeria, Buhari Okonkwo.

"Operation Octopus breached UN sanctions, and Mallam Odofo should not be further accorded the unethical privilege of what will be a breach of the sanctions imposed on his regime," new British High Commissioner John Coleson had stated his government's position during a meeting for that purpose in Liberia. But the British lost out again. President Kargbo Ndomahina had insisted that he would not feel safe to return – in fact he would never go back – without Mallam Musa Odofo. He pleaded with John Coleson to understand, but the latter had responded that his government's ethical foreign policy had no room for a dictator like Mallam Musa Odofo. It was then that President Ndomahina went ahead to plead with the Americans to prevail on the British.

* * *

All along, the Americans had been part and parcel of the 'return project' processes. They were strategic partners and were included in most of the meetings – they were stakeholders of democracy, and they also had vested interests in Sierra Leone through several American companies operating in the country. But the British had always taken the lead in lieu of Sierra Leone being a former British colony – 'as per the partition of Africa over tea and coffee in Berlin', Teacher Paul would say. And so, in Monrovia, in many ways, the Americans were mere observers and did not particularly influence decision-making. Even in terms of the response to diplomatic dislocations and relocations, the Americans had done it differently.

While the British and many other diplomatic missions in Sierra Leone had relocated to Monrovia with President Kargbo Ndomahina, the Americans neither totally shut their Freetown embassy nor did their Ambassador relocate to Monrovia. Instead, while leaving behind a small team of essential staff and its consular section open throughout the junta interregnum, the American government had evacuated the American Ambassador and the embassy's senior officials and their families back to the United States, instead of to Liberia. They had explained that they had a fully functional embassy in Liberia and the Ambassador there was given the added function of acting as American Ambassador *for* Sierra Leone for as long as President Kargbo Ndomahina was based in Monrovia. Ghana had done the same.

In terms of policy, the Americans had from the outset publicly stated their 'full and unequivocal support for the British-led efforts to restore democracy in Sierra Leone'. But they were not taking the lead. If what befell Sierra Leone had befallen Liberia, it would have been a different story. Liberia was a former American colony – if it even qualified to be called that. Liberian, American; Sierra Leonean, British. Consequently, in the present scenario of preparations for the return of President Kargbo Ndomahina to Sierra Leone, it was by and large an all-British affair.

* * *

Ambassador Tom Hopkins was therefore more than a bit surprised when President Ndomahina requested him to intervene in pleading with the British to lift the travel ban on Mallam Musa Odofo. "If only for a day, to allow him to travel from Abuja to Monrovia to Freetown and back, to witness and demonstrate his stamp of approval for my leadership on re-inauguration day." President Ndomahina's argument, apart from gratitude to Mallam Odofo, was that the Nigerian dictator's presence at the ceremony would send a message to the renegade soldiers and rebels that continuous Nigerian military presence in Sierra Leone was assured. "And it can only make the right impact and send the needed signals to those inhuman imbeciles if the pronouncement comes from Mallam Odofo himself in Freetown."

The Americans would never miss an opportunity that gave them leverage over the British. It was something they loved – something they always wished for. And once Ambassador Hopkins saw how determined President Ndomahina was on the issue, he knew this diplomatic edge was also in the American bag. Downing Street reluctantly gave the green light following several meetings between President Ndomahina, Ambassador Hopkins and High Commissioner John Coleson. It was a last-minute intervention that perhaps the Americans wouldn't have had to make if the British had not been too regimental in following their ethical foreign policy. But this made the Americans feel within themselves that their contribution towards making the final occasion a success was as well their victory. However, Ambassador Tom Hopkins did not have to travel to Freetown with the others. The American government had merely sent back to Sierra Leone all the officials, including the Ambassador, who had earlier been relocated to America. They had arrived in Freetown in time for the inauguration ceremony. They knew they had pulled off another last-minute interventionist glory like the Hiroshima and Nagasaki intervention did in ending the Second World War. On different scales of course. But it was the pep talk at the American Embassy in Monrovia afterwards.

* * *

Prime Minister Ed McInroy did not care how others termed or twisted it. What he knew was that this was generally a British victory – his ethical foreign policy had prevailed over dictatorship; democracy was being rescued in Sierra Leone. It was the dedicated work of British officials that had brought this great accomplishment. He now even started to see again the good side, the better side, the sterling side that he had always known of his friend, former High Commissioner Mark Fergusson. If not for Mark's untiring efforts in evacuating President Kargbo Ndomahina, if not for the former High Commissioner's establishment of a radio station that constantly broadcast messages from and for the exiled government, and definitely if not for his role in getting a private British mercenary firm to supply not only the weapons but its personnel actually taking part in the operations, this victory wouldn't have come to pass. It was the British knack for success that had seen this through. And the Prime Minister was happy for that. How he would have loved to be present at the inauguration in person. But he now really had more pressing issues to attend to in person – particularly with regards canvassing parliamentary support against the Worst Dictator in the Middle East. Despite that, as long as Mallam Odofo was going to be there, the Prime Minister would never attend.

"It will be diplomatic suicide for the British Prime Minister to share a table or podium with a dictator his government has declared illegitimate and has imposed sanctions on," John Coleson had swiped at President Ndomahina when the latter enquired whether the Prime Minister would attend the ceremony. "Downing Street, through the Foreign Office, has directed that I aptly represent the Prime Minister." He went on to state that,

"The Prime Minister remains unwavering in his support for the government and democracy." That was why Downing Street had further directed that John Coleson should fly on the same helicopter with President Ndomahina and Mallam Musa Odofo from Monrovia to Freetown on D-Day.

The Prime Minister's office was even now not enthusiastic about refuting claims from some sections of the British press that in actual fact British military officers based in Sierra Leone participated in Operation Octopus. What the Prime Minister knew was that he would soon do a state visit to Sierra Leone and underline the victory of his ethical foreign policy. Till then, today (D-Day) was worth celebrating at Downing Street as well. He would organise a small dinner for a selected few in the evening. He was giving a thought as to whether it would be politically expedient to include former High Commissioner Mark Fergusson on the list of invitees. Or whether Mark, the man he knew so well, would not turn the invitation down.

***

The Nigerian press was livid. Amnesty International, which had been championing the advocacy against human rights violations in Nigeria, was irate. So were human rights activists in Nigeria and the exiled Nigerian writer based in Britain. 'The double standards of the international community led by Britain, as far as the handling of the dictatorship of Mallam Musa Odofo is concerned, are hereby roundly denounced and condemned', an Amnesty International statement declared.

Scathing headlines about British self-interests sprang up and dominated in Nigerian newspapers. *The Morning Standard* was succinct: 'The same way the British dealt with Africans through the divide and rule indirect system during colonialism is the same way they are now doing things in a neo-colonialist fashion.' Prime

Minister Ed McInroy came in for particular denunciation for 'his flip-flopping foreign policy'. The editorials riled that he was 'over-vociferous about removing the junta in Sierra Leone while he has not done the same with the junta in Nigeria, which is more ruthless and preceded the Freetown junta'.

Not only that, another editorial from *The Nigerian Star* stated that the British government had swiftly made a u-turn, moved from condemning Nigeria's military escapade in Sierra Leone to embracing it. Beyond that, the British government was now working hand-in-gloves with Mallam Musa Odofo, 'who has refused to hand over power to the man that Nigerians have elected but was instead arrested and is now rotting in jail. And the British have the effrontery to overlook the concerns of the majority of Nigerians by lifting the travel ban on Mallam Odofo, for him to travel to Sierra Leone. Is it because there are no diamonds in Nigeria?'

The Nigerian media didn't mention, or didn't care, whether the lifting of the ban was just for a day or just for a few hours. To them, it was betrayal. It was the nature of the neo-colonialist. British selfish interests first – was the editorial line in most Nigerian newsrooms. 'Britain has sold out. The people of Nigeria must brace themselves to continue to suffer under the ignoble regime of Mallam Musa Odofo', one lamented.

On the contrary, the Sierra Leonean media was exuberant and triumphant, feeling vindicated. They hailed the British position in the same breath as the Nigerian action. 'Democracy has prevailed, and it is worth celebrating. No ifs, no buts', *The Freetown Standard*, in the same vein as all others, declared.

Interestingly, the D-Day return of President Ndomahina did not make it in the British press – except if perhaps one took the BBC Focus on Africa radio programme and an anecdotal report on BBC World Service radio as part of the British press. But, clearly, the British taxpayers wouldn't normally listen to those.

* * *

And so that morning, when Mallam Odofo left Nigeria for the first time in two years, the atmosphere in Abuja – though not as pompous and widespread as that in Sierra Leone – was not less exhilarating and fulfilling. Praise-singers of Mallam Odofo's invincibility were not in short supply. There was singing and drumming at the Aso Rock helipad.

"The talk of handing over power to the so-called democratically-elected President is as good as dumped. Mallam Musa Odofo will continue to rule Nigeria in the foreseeable future," a die-hard civilian supporter boasted on Lagos radio after the Nigerian dictator had left for Monrovia. The supporter had said there was nothing the world could do about the Nigerian status quo.

Apparently, Mallam Odofo was now dictating for the world. He had carved out a 'new Sierra Leone' for himself, and the world was cheering him on, he thought to himself. That's why he was now free to leave Nigeria to attend the inauguration of his protégé, President Ndomahina. He thought of the diamonds he already had in safe-keeping; and he thought of the prospects of having many more now that they had taken control of Sierra Leone again. The world was under his feet, he thought.

* * *

The major thing that Mallam Odofo did that morning before boarding the helicopter for Monrovia was to hand over a note to his most trusted lieutenant, Chief Security Officer Colonel Mamadu Gowon (who was by and large the most powerful man after the dictator, on top of the other Generals in the Council, and he was notorious about being the hatchet-man of the regime in carrying out kidnappings, raids, and killings). Col. Gowon took anything that his boss told him to do seriously – and had always acted on it promptly. And he loved it when his boss gave him such honour in the presence of the other council members – instilling fear in them.

Mallam Odofo landed in Monrovia amid another round of fanfare. Although most of the exiled Sierra Leoneans had returned with Femi Cole, the Liberia-based Sierra Leoneans (that is, those who had been living there before President Ndomahina's overthrow) did not want to be left out of the melee of triumphant festivities. There were also some who had come after President Ndomahina relocated there but were not yet willing to return to Sierra Leone for a variety of reasons. They all therefore organised special celebrations for the departing President. So when the helicopter carrying Mallam Musa Odofo landed at the back of the British Embassy compound in Monrovia, it was greeted with dancing, drumming and singing.

It was not to be a long stopover. The two leaders would just have a short briefing and then off they would go to Freetown. Apart from that, all President Ndomahina did was to ask his 'big brother' to speak to his wife in the USA (who could not come for health reasons officially, but was not needed really), Mrs. Memunatu Ndomahina; and also to their great friend, UN Secretary General Kirikiri, for his support as well. Mallam Odofo acquiesced to both. The only thing President Ndomahina added to the talk with Kirikiri was asking the UN man to twist open the head of the carved statue Mrs. Ndomahina had earlier delivered, to see 'the real gift I sent you as a form of gratitude'.

***

Meanwhile, in Freetown, by midday the national stadium and its environs were all full beyond capacity. The skies were dominated by eight Alfa jets displaying flying acrobatics that had never been seen before. Any time a dramatic stunt was pulled off – like one jet pretending to fall off the skies and then picking up flight again

– the people in and around the stadium would cheer loudly, the current cheering louder than the previous one.

The Master of Ceremonies was the Minister of Information, Bai Sankoh, who was handpicked by Femi Cole over and above the Minister of Justice whom President Ndomahina himself would have preferred. But Femi Cole was in charge of the ceremony and her word prevailed. She preferred Bai Sankoh because he had been her unofficial Personal Assistant during the exile days in Monrovia, he was also the one who first brought her to State House as a correspondent, and he also singlehandedly wrote the first draft of the speech to be delivered today by President Ndomahina (the Justice Minister had merely made minor legalistic inputs to the speech; and Femi Cole didn't like him because his father was an 'alfa man' – an herbalistic soothsayer – who was 'eating too much of the President's money' through *juju*). And, in reality, Bai Sankoh was a better choice due to his mastery of not only the art of public speaking but also in being down-to-earth with the people. So the Information Minister did a riveting running commentary in very colourful and descriptive language as events unfolded at the national stadium, even making those absent to feel they were not missing much.

39

Apart from being the practical host of the Sierra Leone government-in-exile, the Liberian government had never been practically involved in the high-level deliberations on the fate of President Kargbo Ndomahina since his arrival.

A few reasons were explained by Liberian government spokesmen on different occasions. Just as the British had leverage on Sierra Leone in lieu of colonial ties, so did America on Liberia – perhaps much more; actually much more. The Americans had a special relationship with Liberia. The freed slaves that were transported from America to Liberia were more of a triumphant bunch because they had just been on the winning side in defeating the British forces during the American war of independence – in sharp contrast to the Sierra Leonean freed slaves who had fought on the side of the defeated British forces.

In fact, Liberia was never a colony per se. The Americans had quickly put structures in place on arrival to make Liberia the first African country to be granted independence. And by way of compensation, the leadership of the nation was handed over to the freed slaves – as against the natives. The Americo-Liberians – as they came to be called – were in charge of Liberia's affairs. The ties with America therefore also remained strong. The American dollar was a quasi-national currency alongside the Liberian dollar, as the Liberian economy was inextricably linked to the American financial system. American Presidents – irrespective of their party – had over the years shown great interest in the affairs of Liberia, with a couple or so actually visiting Monrovia. To every Americo-Liberian leader (from the short-lived colony status to the current administration), the White House was familiar terrain.

The reverse had happened in Sierra Leone, as the British did not only rule as a colonial power for long, but they actually fell out with the descendents of the freed slaves, the Krios. Britain had eventually bypassed its former allies and handed over power to the natives at independence several decades later. Not only that: the British determination to dislodge the Krios (for allegedly supporting an insurrection and having anti-colonial views by calling for the 'total freedom of the people of the province of freedom and immediate independence as had been done in neighbouring Liberia') was demonstrated in a deliberate policy targeted at Krio businesses and investments. The economy ended up in the hands of the Lebanese at independence, as Krio businesses were squeezed out when bank loans were made unreachable for 'people of negro origins'. Most of the government contracts went to the Lebanese (a trend continued down to the generation of Lebanese businessman Amza Alie, the personal friend and financier of President Ndomahina). On the political front, the Krios were squeezed out when it was open to 'all people of negro origins' – knowing that the freed slaves and their descendants were a minority. No British Prime Minister had ever visited Sierra Leone before Ed McInroy! Just as both President Kargbo Ndomahina and his predecessor Daymia Turay had never been invited to Downing Street!

Ultimately, while the Liberian economy was relatively booming, the Sierra Leone society was at its tether. Sierra Leoneans were streaming into Monrovia to buy cheap merchandise to sell in Sierra Leone. Others went there for jobs.

The Liberian spokespeople's line of explanation (going into history and all that) about their government's lack of enthusiasm to be part of the 'return project' of the exiled Sierra Leone government was that of 'we warned him, but he didn't listen'. It had happened that when President Ndomahina was still in charge in Sierra Leone, he got some 'advice' from the Americo-Liberian President, Robert Lawson, on how to adopt sound economic policies, fight against corruption and stem the tide. The Sierra Leone President was not pleased about this – and had called his counterpart 'a black man pretending to be a white man'. Relations between the two were at best frosty – at one point, Liberia closed its part of the border for several days until the Americans mediated.

Therefore, when President Ndomahina was overthrown, his Liberian colleague (who had had a better relationship with President Ndomahina's predecessor, as they visited each other) was not that surprised. He was only surprised that President Ndomahina had agreed to seek sanctuary in Liberia. So he left his guest to his own devices with the British. And, obviously, President Ndomahina himself would have been uncomfortable, if not irritable, to have been discussing his fate in the presence of President Lawson.

However, the Liberian spokespersons had always insisted that, "Liberia unreservedly supports the efforts of the international community to restore democracy in Sierra Leone, and hosting President Ndomahina until the situation is resolved is the least the Liberian government can do." But it was clear this was more a gesture of respect for the international community than love for a neighbour whose house was on fire.

The Americans knew all this. And they saved the day by agreeing to the dual role of the American Ambassador to Liberia as a de jure representative of Liberian interests in the 'presidential return committee' meetings as well as having a mainly observer status for America. He would share Liberia's concerns through back-and-forth briefings – security, policy review, inauguration– at 'return committee' meetings and could take decisions on behalf of the Liberian government, it was agreed.

Therefore, apart from meeting at international conferences like those for ECOWAS, AU, and UN, which President Ndomahina had been attending in exile as the recognised Head of State of Sierra Leone, and at times having to fly on the same aircraft to and from Monrovia, the two leaders never officially met inside Liberia. President Lawson never visited President Ndomahina at his residence or office. Reciprocally, President Ndomahina had never been to Liberia's State House or at the 'real' presidential lodge. The diplomats were their go-betweens (Mark Fergusson was an expert in that).

But today, on the departure day, President Lawson was visiting President Ndomahina to bid him farewell – and the Americo-Liberian would be included in the briefing. The brief stopover in Monrovia by Nigeria's Mallam Musa Odofo had changed everything – even if just for today, the last day of President Ndomahina in exile. It's a day to say goodbye. Or good riddance. Whichever. But the Americo-Liberian President was obliged, by protocol, to meet Mallam Musa Odofo – a visiting Head of State, even if just in transit, even if just off the travel ban hook for a day, even if the Nigerian dictator were not here for Liberian matters, even if the host did not actually like to be in the company of the other party in the room or vice versa.

Mallam Musa Odofo liked playing the 'big brother' role whenever the opportunity arose. He liked the fact that he was being 'adored' by his colleague Heads of State. Nigeria, the big brother in West Africa. Mallam Odofo was currently presiding over the affairs of two colleagues in Monrovia, and about eight others were waiting in Freetown's national stadium for *his* arrival.

So in the briefing room at the 'other' presidential lodge – or what were actually the British Embassy premises in Liberia – were Mallam Musa Odofo, President Ndomahina, President Lawson, British High Commissioner John Coleson, and American Ambassador Tom Hopkins. The briefing was being done by the Nigerian commander in Sierra Leone, General Victor Adekera, who had executed Operation Octopus. He was flown into Monrovia from Freetown yesterday by the UN helicopter that would soon take them all, except the American Ambassador and the Liberian President, to the ecstatic ceremony in Freetown.

It was therefore a short briefing. General Adekera told them how the whole of Sierra Leone was now "virtually under the full control of the pro-government forces led by the Nigerian Army – except at the place where the three countries meet, where the defeated soldiers and rebels are reported to be holed up, digging diamonds and gold for their godfathers as they have been doing all along. We will soon flush them out." He explained that 'the junta remnants' were being protected by Guinean dissidents (Guinea was also currently under military rule, following the death of their long-time ruler. The dissidents now hosting the Freetown junta were supporters of the former President who felt persecuted by the military regime in Conakry. Unlike the British, the French said they would not interfere in the internal affairs of its former colony). "Notwithstanding," said General Adekera, "not a single shot has been fired in the whole territory of Sierra Leone for over two weeks now. The security situation is therefore hundred per cent under control, Your Excellencies, sirs."

After he did an elaborate salute in front of the three heads of state and two ambassadors, General Adekera called on the Russian pilot of the UN helicopter to debrief on the route they would take from Monrovia to Freetown. The arrangement was that the presidential helicopter that brought Mallam Musa Odofo from Abuja would go back to Nigeria. The Nigerian leader would have to be flown into the territory of Sierra Leone by a UN helicopter.

The British had put their foot down on that particular issue and would never give up or give in on it, after the American Ambassador had succeeded in getting them to lift the travel ban. As far as they were concerned, Mallam Musa Odofo was only temporarily off the hook on the travel ban due to the precarious situation in Sierra Leone. And this only came about due to multi-national and multi-agency efforts. It did not mean the bilateral issues had been overlooked. Britain had therefore only agreed to lift the ban 'for just this day', and had insisted that the official Nigerian helicopter would not be allowed in Sierra Leone territory. The Americans had therefore granted that they would – acting on behalf of the Liberian government – allow the Nigerian helicopter in Monrovia for five hours. UN Secretary General Kirikiri was very much involved in the deliberations and had offered the UN helicopter to fly Mallam Odofo, President Ndomahina and entourage to Freetown. And the same helicopter would later in the day take back Mallam Odofo direct to Abuja after the inauguration ceremony in Freetown. Agreed.

Mikhail Kurtosky, a veteran Russian pilot who had worked with the UN in different crisis zones for over twenty years, therefore gave a detailed description of the route they would take from Monrovia to Freetown: how, on this side of the border, they would mainly fly over marsh lands and rivers before going by the Atlantic Ocean; then over to Sierra Leone maritime territory before going over Sierra Leone land, mainly swamps at first and then the rainforests; before going back by the Atlantic Ocean on approaching Freetown. He said, in his broken English, "This is the safest route we have been using to tumble between Freetown and Monrovia and back."

"Tumble or travel?" asked the American Ambassador.

"Yes, yes sir… travel sir." Everybody burst into laughter. And the pilot went on to say that it was the same route the American mining company, Leone Rutile, had been using non-stop throughout the crisis with its helicopters shuttling between Sierra Leone and Liberia without any incidence. It was just a forty-five-minute flight.

In his deep Russian accent, Mikhail Kurtosky asked to be forgiven for being panicky and for mixing up his words. He said this was because, in all his years of flying, this would be the first time he was having a Head of State on board: "Not only one, but two at one go. I want to retire immediately I drop you all off."

The room burst into roaring laughter. Even Mallam Odofo, who was never a man of laughter, laughed along loudly.

40

As all this was going on in Monrovia, the merry-making ecstasy continued in Freetown. The national stadium was by now practically full to the brim – in fact beyond the brim. Throngs of people were revelling on the stands and outside the perimeter of the stadium. Some youths climbed up the poles of the flood lights.

And Information Minister Bai Sankoh never tired in his running commentary. Rehearsed or not, he did it very well. He would call out the banners proclaiming welcome messages for President Ndomahina by such and such a politician from such and such a town or village. And, in-between, having been privy to the speech to be delivered by the President, Bai Sankoh would drop hints here and there about "no negotiations with the defeated junta… no collaborators of the junta will be given jobs in this government… in fact all of them deserve jail… an inquiry into all civil servants who worked with the military junta will be instituted…"

Whenever a politician arrived at the stadium, Minister Bai Sankoh would chant his or her name, giving a brief history of him or her until he or she took their seat. Sankoh did the same for the four other Heads of State that attended (eight were expected, but they sent apologies with middle-level officials (Ghana sent none, saying her High Commissioner would relocate at a later date) – to the chagrin of Mallam Odofo when he learnt about it just before boarding the helicopter in Monrovia).

But Minister Bai Sankoh reserved the best of his descriptive powers and praises for "the one who actually made this day happen, who placed everything on the line to ensure success, who was there when no one else was, none other than the woman among women, our dearest First Lady, Her Excellency Femi Cole." Cheers and cheers, continuous cheers from the crowds.

Just as she had done when entering Sierra Leone from Liberia, Femi Cole entered the national stadium with a longish convoy of vehicles – heavily guarded by Nigerian soldiers. She was still, as expected, riding the presidential vehicle, P1. When President Ndomahina would arrive and the whole ceremony came to an end, both of them would ride on the same vehicle through the streets of Freetown to their Juba Hill residence, where she still preferred to stay instead of State Lodge 'until it is meticulously checked for landmines that could have been left behind by the junta boys'.

A local musician had got his bread buttered when he was selected to do a song titled 'No Woman Like Femi Cole'. The music burst into the speakers the moment Bai Sankoh pronounced her name; and the stadium became more euphoric. She was dressed in a white flowing Africana gown with multicoloured embroidery at the chest, with a head-tie to match and a handkerchief for the same effect. She ordered her steps as per the rhythm of the music and would stop and turn from one side to the other, waving her white handkerchief to the cheering crowds. Some women wished they were the mother of Femi Cole. But she was now an orphan (her mother had died of heart attack a week after the coup and buried in her absence). But not for today. Today, Femi Cole had many mothers. She was the daughter every mother would want to have in Sierra Leone at this moment. Such were the lyrics of the local musician's song.

The moment she had gracefully walked up the stairs to go take her seat at the presidential pavilion, the music stopped. The police musical band took over with a signatory tune. Everybody stood up. Then she majestically walked to her seat; but not before shaking the hands of all the dignitaries present, including the four Heads of State, the representatives of those absent, the American Ambassador to Sierra Leone, the German Ambassador, the leader of the EU delegation, and the special envoy of the UN Secretary General (as Kirikiri himself could not make it in person due to 'currently more pressing matters in the Middle East').

* * *

Apart from Femi Cole (who felt more than compensated in the end), two other people had lost out in the slots for the helicopter ride from Monrovia to Freetown – the substantive BBC Freetown correspondent who had ever since relocated to Monrovia and Anglican priest Olumendi Metzeger (the one in the editorial of *The True Light*), both of whom were very close to Femi Cole in Monrovia. Before the change of plans, they had been promised seats on the helicopter. But the British decision that forced Mallam Musa Odofo to fly on the same helicopter with President Ndomahina meant the two could not be accommodated again – as per order of priority. They had to travel with Femi Cole – which the BBC man eventually found compensatory, having to do a running commentary of their journey, thereby dominating the airwaves that day with live interviews with Bush House on Focus on Africa.

Unfortunately for the Anglican priest, while fleeing from Sierra Leone to Liberia, his young wife had been abducted by a gang of civil militias. It had happened just before they crossed the border into Liberia. The militia, who were actually fighting on the side of President Ndomahina, had asked the priest to choose between his beautiful wife and his life. The lady pleaded with him to take his life.

The priest was at the time in the company of an assorted group of fleeing Sierra Leoneans who suffered similar fates on the way. Some saw their friends and relatives abducted. Others saw their loved ones tragically killed in front of their eyes 'for looking like rebels'. Once in Monrovia, the Anglican priest overcame his sorrow and became an adviser to Femi Cole. He always gave her ideas.

To make up for his troubles, Femi Cole insisted that Olumendi Metzeger would lead the prayers today at the inauguration ceremony, instead of the Catholic priest President Ndomahina would have preferred. Femi Cole knew that the President's parents were Muslim and he was brought up that way – he had only changed religions to meet the strict requirement of marrying Memunatu Kallon, a Catholic priest's daughter. Femi Cole was determined to erase anything relating to Mrs. Ndomahina! Invariably, the Anglican priest was actually not in the good books of President Ndomahina because Metzeger (no relative of Sierra Leone's first Prime Minister, Tuboku Metzeger) used to condemn 'the prevalence of fetish beliefs in presidential circles, especially promoted by the head of the civil militia'. A close aide of President Ndomahina had remarked that the priest was foolhardy to have left his first wife for his captured second wife, and 'he should stop crying over spilt milk'. Femi Cole didn't take kindly to that. The aide was fired. But the President never had anything to do with the Anglican priest. He worked solely for Femi Cole. So he was all dressed up for today's ceremony, in priestly regalia, sitting on the right hand side of 'the First Lady'.

* * *

Therefore, to board the UN helicopter from Monrovia were the Russian pilot and his co-pilot (another Russian who had worked with the UN for six years), Mallam Musa Odofo, President Kargbo Ndomahina, the two ADCs of both, British High Commissioner

John Coleson, Nigerian Commander General Adekera, Opposition Leader Dauda Kabia (who was excluded from the briefing), and Lebanese businessman/presidential financier Amza Alie (President Ndomahina had insisted he must travel with them, even though Amza himself had tried to show humility or hypocrisy by offering to go ahead by road).

The same pomp and pageantry that welcomed Mallam Odofo earlier was the same pomp and pageantry now seeing them off. But the Nigerian dictator was not now in a very good mood after learning that four Heads of State did not go to Freetown. He believed in the more, the merrier. He had planned to use the occasion to invoke African unity by calling on colleague African leaders to stand up to the neo-colonialists and condemn the sanctions that had been slammed on Nigeria, seeking a united front in calling for non-interference in the internal affairs of nation-states by the British, just as the French were doing with neighbouring Guinea. The Guinean military leader himself was one of those who did not come to Freetown for the ceremony, as the balance of power was still very shaky in Conakry.

After the briefing, the Americo-Liberian President didn't see his colleagues off at the back of the compound where the UN helicopter was waiting. But Mallam Odofo was satisfied that he had presided over 'a brotherly truce', by which he was able to elicit a pledge from President Robert Lawson to make an official visit to Sierra Leone in a month's time.

But Mallam Odofo was happier – and that was what was uppermost on his mind – when he thought of the task he had entrusted to Chief Security Officer Col. Mamadu Gowon in Abuja through the note he had handed over to his subordinate in the presence of the other Generals. That was how to show that Mamadu was in charge while Odofo was away.

They boarded the helicopter just about the time Bai Sankoh was telling the waiting crowds in Freetown, "Now that the First

Lady is here, you will soon see your beloved President Ndomahina arriving here, in this stadium, by helicopter." Loud shouts and cheers came from the crowds. Through the Nigerian intelligence officers attached to her, Femi Cole had known exactly when President Ndomahina would board the helicopter. And she had informed Minister Bai Sankoh that she would arrive at the stadium just about the time the President and others were boarding the UN helicopter in Monrovia. It was all good on both sides.

When taking off, the helicopter scattered dust and debris, sending the revelling praise-singers helter-skelter to take cover. They couldn't do those final waves they had wished for. President Kargbo Ndomahina had finally left Monrovia for Freetown after several months in exile.

One of the organisers of the Liberia farewell, Patrick Monjama (who had spent so many years in Liberia that only the relocation of President Ndomahina to Monrovia had jolted him back to his nationality), said, "There has never been a more blessed man than President Kargbo Ndomahina. He has succeeded where all the others have failed, where the Kwame Nkurumahs of this world failed – to have been overthrown and then restored back to power." Monjama hid behind a tree from the scattering debris, but still ensured he took a long look, immediately after, of the helicopter as it disappeared from view. And most of the other revellers were now waving to the empty skies before they went out to the streets of Monrovia, continuing with their dancing and singing.

41

It was a French-made high-radar twin-engine helicopter – an AS532 Cougar. The UN had just acquired one hundred customised of that brand – to be specifically sent to top hotspots in the Middle East, Somalia and Sudan. So, Sierra Leone was originally not on the list of recipients.

But then Operation Octopus had occurred. And UN Secretary General John Kirikiri immediately inserted Sierra Leone in the 'top hotspots' list. Ten of the helicopters were immediately dispatched with a small multinational team that would in due course become the Sierra Leone UN Military Mission (SLUNMIS). The aircrafts were all white, with 'UN' boldly emblazoned in black on both sides and under the belly of each.

***

It was while they were on board the helicopter that they realised how they had distinctively dressed, as if they had consulted each other. For the soldiers, it was understandable; for the civilians, maybe also understandable.

Airborne, it was British High Commissioner John Coleson who picked it up and broke the ice. He had to shout due to the sound of the aircraft's engine. "So the soldiers have dressed soldierly, and we the civilians are all in black suits." Everybody started looking at everybody else. They had sat facing each other in a semi-circle form as the helicopter's sitting arrangement was designed. And then they all started laughing.

Mallam Musa Odofo retorted, "Yes, yes... You are men in black, and we are men in uniform." Another round of laughter.

"I am a man in black and also a man in uniform at heart," President Ndomahina came in. "Once a soldier, always a soldier."

"Yes, old soja never die," Mallam Odofo endorsed.

It was during that discussion that High Commissioner John Coleson knew that both Mallam Musa Odofo and President Ndomahina were military colleagues at Sandhurst. He was wowed by their sharp remembrance of particular places in Britain. He felt pleasant about it.

So, except for the differences in the colours of the neckties, the four civilians (President Kargbo Ndomahina, Opposition Leader Dauda Kabia, Lebanese businessman Amza Alie, and High Commissioner John Coleson) were all in white shirts and black suits. While, except for the differences in rank and the epaulettes showing on the shoulders of the wearers, all the soldiers (General Musa Odofo, General Victor Adekera, ADC to Mallam Musa Odofo Major General Hydara Ahmadu, and ADC to President Ndomahina newly-promoted Colonel Brima Antumani) were in combat military fatigues, the green-brown-and-black-splattered ones they normally wore in battle – the camouflage ones. There was no better way of underlining the key factor of the Nigerian military's prowess in the 'presidential return' project.

* * *

Meanwhile, in Freetown, it was again the turn of the Nigerian Alfa jets to display their skyline dominance. The timing was well coordinated. After their first display in the morning, they had returned to base in Lagos (from where they had been conducting their operations in Sierra Leone throughout these past few months).

Despite Nigerian soldiers being in control of Sierra Leone's airport, it was deemed impossible for the jets to operate from there due to security, refuelling and maintenance concerns. That was one major reason why it was reported that the Nigerian government was spending approximately one million dollars a day on Sierra Leone. The cries of some Nigerians about wasting money on 'a senseless pot-calling-the-kettle-black war' were ignored. Mallam Musa Odofo knew better where the money was coming from; President Ndomahina knew the operation was not short of resources. And now their mission had gone according to plan – *the end justifies the means.* And so the Nigerian Alfa jets could display as much as they liked, having played a key role in the success of Operation Octopus.

And the people cheered every time a flying stunt was displayed.

It was all timed. The jets left Lagos about twenty minutes before the UN helicopter took off from Monrovia, and they arrived or flew past the national stadium just about the time Minister of Information Bai Sankoh had finished speaking about First Lady Femi Cole and about the imminent arrival of President Ndomahina, with Mallam Musa Odofo. So, it was stage-managed to look like the Alfa jets interrupted Bai Sankoh's speech, as he led the chorus of shouts on the microphone. The jets (now ten in number) rowed and roared in different directions in the sky back and forth around the national stadium.

The people continued to cheer.

And by now, Information Minister Bai Sankoh had created a theatrical rendition with the people: he asked questions, and they responded accordingly.

"Who do the white people want to rule Sierra Leone?"

"President Ndomahina," the people answered.

"Who is going to rule Sierra Leone for the next twenty years?"

"President Ndomahina."

"Who do you, the people, want to rule Sierra Leone?"

"President Ndomahina."

"For whom has the wicked junta been removed?"

"President Ndomahina."

***

The security communications system was all centralised and set in a multi-way mode. Therefore, the pilots of the UN helicopter, the pilots of the jets, the military aircraft control room in Lagos, the Abuja airforce intelligence monitoring room, the quickly established SLUNMIS headquarters in Freetown (where Britain, America, Sierra Leone and Nigeria each had representatives) were all in communication with each other even before Mallam Odofo left Nigeria this morning.

And Mikhail Kurtosky, the UN Russian pilot, had presently reported that they had crossed over from Liberia and were now in Sierra Leone airspace. The jets swerved and swaggered to the cheering crowds in response.

42

Maybe Mark Fergusson was the only British man closely following events in Sierra Leone that day from Britain. He was doing so through an email forum, set up by a former American Peace Corps who had been consistently posting daily updates on developments in Sierra Leone since the war began. Today the updates were being done on an hourly basis, basically summarising what Information Minister Bai Sankoh was saying at the stadium. Mark was also religiously checking his emails on his Macintosh computer every hour.

President Ndomahina had actually specially invited the former High Commissioner to the Freetown ceremony 'at the expense of the Government of Sierra Leone', but Mark Fergusson had turned it down. For obvious reasons – though he promised to visit at a later time, 'because Sierra Leone is my motherland too'.

And Mark had just now read the email update stating that Minister Bai Sankoh had said at the national stadium that President Ndomahina had now entered the territory of Sierra Leone by helicopter.

Mark just sighed to himself and went back to reading some documents while waiting for the next update.

* * *

Deep into Sierra Leone territory, by the marshlands of Tomabom in the east, the airborne passengers had naturally retreated into splinter groups. Mallam Musa Odofo and President Ndomahina, seated next to each other with an in-built table in front of them with files, were now in a tête-à-tête in tones that they alone could hear and understand. John Coleson, via the proximity of sitting, also naturally struck up a conversation with Lebanese businessman Amza Alie, who said he was a fourth generation resident of Sierra Leone, and that he could not even trace any relative in Lebanon, and brandished his Sierra Leonean passport. "Sierra Leone is the only place I know as home." The three serving military personnel (the Operation Octopus Commander and the two ADCs) seated at the tail end, with the junior officers flanking the senior officer, also engaged in military pep talk. The only lone man was the Opposition Leader, who, to be fair enough, felt contented with himself, looking blank – looking lost.

Soon, they came by the Atlantic, and John Coleson peeped through the window to see the lush vegetation and general beauty of the coastline. Amza Alie seemed to know each of these places, or even everything about Sierra Leone. He was excited to meet the new British High Commissioner. He hoped he would be of help to the new envoy, as he described himself as a confidant of President Ndomahina (and indeed John Coleson earlier saw in Monrovia Amza Alie receiving a bag from the President). On the day of the coup, Amza Alie first escaped by helicopter to Lebanon before joining the President in Liberia, where the once-ubiquitous businessman largely remained in the shadows – though still in control of 'the resources'. So now, air-borne on their way back, he was most excited as he conversed with the new British High Commissioner. "But we would get to know each other better as time goes on," his voice rising higher, even though the helicopter's engine was now not so noisy after gaining serenity in the air.

That very moment, President Ndomahina quickly turned from Mallam Odofo to the talking duo and said something in a native language that the Lebanese businessman seemed to immediately understand. Amza Alie was famous – or infamous – for being the man controlling the President's wealth, especially the diamond network. Stories abound as to how he (with the Minister of Mines his chosen lackey) caused many genuine diamonds to be declared as 'mere stones' – only for him to sell them secretly in the black market in Antwerp. Amza Alie was very powerful. He even had two Cabinet Ministers dismissed for disagreeing with him. He knew too much about President Ndomahina. *The True Light* once described him as 'the only man who knows where and when President Ndomahina sleeps every day'. For Amza Alie to now start talking freely with John Coleson, the new British High Commissioner, was unacceptable to the President.

The Lebanese tycoon could be in charge of the shadow state, but Ndomahina was still the President.

Amza Alie stopped talking instantly and would not respond to John Coleson's questions anymore beyond 'Yes', 'No', 'I really don't know'. The High Commissioner noticed the change and therefore went into his briefcase for some documents to read.

Definitely, President Ndomahina had still not forgiven anybody for the unceremonious withdrawal of his ally during the struggle, former High Commissioner Mark Fergusson. Not least the person glaringly symbolising that action, John Coleson. The President had not yet thought out how his relationship with the new British High Commissioner would pan out. And so he did not expect Amza Alie to jump ahead of him about getting to know each other better.

President Ndomahina immediately returned to his low-toned conversation with Mallam Musa Odofo, who seemed to have caught the drift. The Nigerian dictator's mind was immediately drifted to what his father, Clifford Odofo, had once told him about 'too much ethnic politics and too much Lebanese influence in the economy of Freetown'. And, presently, he took his pen from the front pocket of his military jacket and scribbled on the pad on the table before them for President Ndomahina to read: 'Remind me about the Lebanese when we reach in Freetown.'

43

Paul McIntyre, the American General Manager of Leone Rutile, had been in Sierra Leone for ten years. And his company's operations did not grind to halt, despite the upheavals in the country. A former marine himself, Paul came to the country first as Deputy General Manager and two years later he became the top man of the thriving mining company. He had fallen in love with Sierra Leone – he couldn't have thought of a better place to act as an antidote to his former hardcore military life.

Paul had liked it when, before the security situation deteriorated, he used to go to Freetown and hobnob with many other westerners. But he also liked it at Leone Rutile itself. Sierra Leoneans nicknamed it New York, not so much in comparison to skyscrapers (there was no really tall building at Leone Rutile) but to affluence and modernity. Leone Rutile was an oasis of luxury in a tumbling country – a blossoming flower in a wasteland. Based in the southern heart of Sierra Leone, the company was exporting millions of tonnes of Rutile every week. Ships berthed at a special port at Leone Rutile to transport the precious mineral for the manufacturing of valuable ceramic and titanium materials in America and Europe – to be sold to the rest of the world.

The American company had secured a leasehold of one hundred and ten years (subject to further extensions) ever since the precious mineral was discovered. They had then built a self-sufficient 'city' – so that all the over-five hundred workers, expatriate and local, were living there in exquisite quarters. There was a constant supply of water and electricity from generator plants shipped from America. There was a fuel station, a cinema, a night club, bars, buses, primary and secondary schools, conference centres – and everybody was asked to pray privately. Workers were paid in dollars, ten times above the average Sierra Leone salary. It was the place almost everybody wanted to work. A perimeter fence was built around the two hundred and fifty-acre land, and it was secured by both foreign and well-vetted local security personnel (mostly ex-servicemen). The rumour around Sierra Leone was that American marines were guarding Leone Rutile – maybe since it was known that Paul McIntyre was a former US marine. In reality, the foreign personne l at Leone Rutile were former volunteers of the National Guards of America. However, they actually got further training from quasi-military schools that had former American marines as instructors. It was from one of those that Paul McIntyre, backed by his business degree, applied and got the job.

As his company was still running and doing its shipments (albeit at a smaller scale due to an increase in insurance and some vessels citing security concerns for cutting down on trips to Sierra Leone), Paul McIntyre had witnessed the recent political upheavals of Sierra Leone. He was angry that a country with such valuable minerals could be so poor and so ignorant and so fateful. He used to wonder what type of food African politicians ate – and, during his moments, he would tell his Sierra Leonean employees to their faces: "I hate African politicians to my guts and to my bones. You can go tell them that Paul McIntyre said so."

The General Manager even condemned Sierra Leonean politicians for the selfish deal they signed with his company in which the landowners were paid pittance, 'while huge kickbacks went into the politicians' pockets'. When the villagers would once in a while organise themselves to demonstrate 'for our stolen land', Paul McIntyre would appease them by sending emissaries with money and some basic commodities like soap, salt and sugar. But he would always also send a message: "They should go demonstrate against their politicians and not against this company." And he would add, loudly, "In the abundance of water, a fool is thirsty." He would immediately go to his back veranda to light a cigarette, and then snuff it out in the ashtray almost immediately after. But the people knew better. They had naturally learnt how to survive President Ndomahina's ruthless regime. They knew where to demonstrate and get some daily bread instead of daily beatings.

***

Paul McIntyre knew that President Kargbo Ndomahina would be re-inaugurated today. It was a holiday throughout Sierra Leone. Except, of course, at Leone Rutile, where work was going on almost normally. They didn't recognise Sierra Leonean national holidays – only American ones. It was New York, of course.

But as he sat in his dainty third-floor office at Leone Rutile, Paul couldn't help but entertain a thought on the occasion. He thought President Ndomahina was an extremely lucky man; and he hoped the President had learnt his lessons and would, on his second chance, now work in the interest of the people. It was a forlorn hope, he believed. *African politicians didn't have the capacity to improve their lot. A greedy cancer had eaten up their mentality and taken over their whole being,* he thought to himself.

Paul decided to shake off these thoughts: he went out to his balcony, overlooking the forest, and lit a cigarette. The clouds were bright and some cool breeze was blowing. He had barely exhaled the third puff of smoke when he heard a humming sound from a distance. It was obviously the sound of a helicopter. His company's two helicopters were grounded today (they observed the holiday) – except in the event of an emergency. And he didn't know of any emergency. So it must be another helicopter.

44

In Abuja, the motorcade of Mallam Odofo's Chief Security Officer, Mamadu Gowon, who by all means was appropriately calling himself 'Acting Head of State', swept through the streets at breakneck speed – siren-led, flashing lights and all – and headed straight for the maximum prison.

He had read the message handed to him by his boss before leaving, and he would carry it out to the letter as always. He savoured the moment. This was possibly the greatest mission he had ever carried out. He said loudly, to the hearing of his driver and personal security, "Our regime's reign has just begun," followed by some dry laughter that the other two knew they shouldn't join in.

* * *

Just about that time in Freetown, the Nigerian Captain in charge of the air control room dashed into his British supervisor's office at SLUNMIS headquarters to report that he seemed to have lost signal from the UN helicopter, and that his calls could not go through as well.

"You may have touched a wrong button," Major Tom McNeil

said as he left his desk to follow the Nigerian officer to the control room.

***

In New York (the original New York), UN Secretary General John Kirikiri didn't go to work today. He had spoken to both President Ndomahina and Mallam Odofo when they were about to leave Monrovia from his home phone. He had, first thing in the morning, called the President to wish him well and inform him about his day off. He had not played any direct role, he believed, in getting President Ndomahina back to power, but he was happy for his old friend, whom he also hoped had learnt some hard lessons. Mrs. Nana Kirikiri was happy her husband had called a day off. She was preparing his favourite *egusi* for lunch. After the phone call, he had gone back to bed to read a novel he had got halfway with about a year ago. And now – after gruelling through a few chapters – he had just remembered what President Ndomahina had told him about opening the gift statue 'on this our day' to see 'the real gift inside'. He was still in his sleeping gown. He put the book down, came off the bed, and strolled to the living room. It was now almost lunchtime, and Mrs. Kirikiri was busy in the kitchen.

John Kirikiri took the gift lion statue from the living room to the bedroom. He sat on the bed and placed the statue between his legs as he twisted the top, as directed by President Ndomahina. It was screw-like, and it opened. In the trunk was a package wrapped in a white cloth. He dipped his hand inside, took it out, unwrapped it and saw a Gucci perfume box.

"Why would Ndomahina send me a perfume from Liberia?" he asked himself. He remembered how back in the day, when they were together in the UN, they used to go to downtown Manhattan to buy expensive perfume. But he didn't need a perfume gift now – certainly not from Africa.

Kirikiri was tempted to just put the box away. On second thoughts, he decided to open it. There was no bottle inside. There was another cloth pouch instead. He pulled it out with its contents. His fingers felt some hard substances like stones. He opened the mouth of the pouch. He put his hand inside and brought out some pebbles. Indeed it was stones – precious stones.

Diamonds!

Kirikiri couldn't believe his eyes. And he sincerely couldn't believe Ndomahina would do this. He felt like rushing to the kitchen to inform his wife how foolish Ndomahina could be. He would never accept such a gift. These diamonds could be used to develop Sierra Leone, not as gifts to friends, he immediately concluded. There and then, he decided, though he would be the last to spoil their day with an unpleasant phone call, he would immediately return the diamonds to President Ndomahina, with strong advice. And that was final. He didn't even have to inform his wife about it again; he wouldn't want her to influence his decision. *Affluent women and their love affair with diamonds – he had never even bought one for Nana. Why open Pandora's box?*

So he put the pouch back into the box, and wrapped it with the white cloth again. But he now put it in his personal briefcase. He screwed back the head of the lion statue and returned it to its place in the living room – he lingered and wondered and wandered in his own living room. And now Mrs. Kirikiri came through from the kitchen.

"Oh darling, you are here. I was going to inform you lunch would be ready soon."

"Thank you, honey. Whenever you are ready, I'm ready."

"Is everything ok?" Nana had instantaneously read her husband's body language. He normally called her 'professor of psychology' for her uncanny ability to read minds and situations.

But he was the 'chancellor of psychology'. "Oh yes, I was just having a look at this statue from our friend."

"It's such a lovely gift. You know how much I like lions. And having a statue of that in the house is so refreshing," Mrs. Kirikiri said. The husband recalled how she used to drag him to the Safari Park in Kenya to see lions while on holidays. But not ever since he became UN Secretary General, Nana noted.

45

The sound of the helicopter's engine came nearer and louder and clearer from the forests of Leone Rutile. It had used the same route from Freetown to Monrovia last evening; but by then Paul McIntyre was ensconced in his posh apartment with his Sierra Leonean girlfriend, far away from the operations area. He could never hear the sound of a passing helicopter from there.

But presently, from his office balcony, Paul knew he would soon see the helicopter flying overhead. He knew of the UN helicopters and the British Chinook helicopters that were in-country, and he knew they could use any route to fly around Sierra Leone and the sub-region – except obviously at the place where three countries met, where the rebel forces were suspected to be having surface-to-air missiles and rocket-propelled grenade-launchers.

Paul was halfway through his cigarette – 'this bad habit', as he called it himself – when he heard what he thought was the sound of a gunshot. But in that same instant he heard a loud explosion. *A small sound preceded a big sound*, his military head noted. The humming sound also immediately stopped. And he didn't see the expected helicopter. He raised his head up, only to see a pall of smoke billowing above the forest. He dashed back into the office for the telephone to alert security.

That was about the same time as the Nigerian Captain at SLUNMIS headquarters in Freetown noticed a loss of signal from the UN helicopter and tried to place a call to the pilot. It didn't go through, and he decided to inform his British superior.

***

The moment the two officers entered the control room at SLUNMIS headquarters, a call came through from Lagos. Major McNeil, the British official, answered it himself. It was about the same issue: Lagos had lost contact with the UN helicopter pilot. What was happening?

Only then did Major McNeil know it was beyond a mere tampering with buttons by his junior Nigerian officer. He suggested Lagos gave an order to two of the displaying Alfa jets to do a quick reconnaissance of the route of the helicopter from Monrovia to Freetown – or rather from Freetown to Monrovia and back. The order was given immediately. The Alfa jets pilots were listening in to the conversation anyway, and the designated two flew off, away to their mission to look for the helicopter.

"Maybe it's in a foggy area," Major McNeil said, not really sure why he said that, because he knew this was not a foggy season in Sierra Leone.

***

Meanwhile, at the national stadium in Freetown, Information Minister Bai Sankoh was becoming more and more exuberant in his oratory snippets, in his name-calling of who had come to grace the occasion. As far as he was concerned, President Ndomahina was now on the outskirts of Freetown – according to the timing he had memorised about the helicopter's landing at the stadium. And when the two Alfa jets dashed off (leaving the rest behind), Bai Sankoh drew his audience's attention to that, saying the two had left to go escort the helicopter into the stadium. More cheers – more jubilation – from the ecstatic crowds.

* * *

Thirty minutes later, the helicopter had still not arrived. The crowds were a bit restless. Even when Bai Sankoh called on the local artist to entertain them with another live performance of the 'Femi Cole music', many were less enthuasistic now.

Bai Sankoh sprang to his feet, grabbed the mike, and stopped the performance when he saw the Military Attaché at the American Embassy going up the stairs to the presidential pavilion. The Information Minister started, "Oh yes, the time we were waiting for has now come. You can all see the neatly dressed American military officer has arrived and is now approaching the presidential pavilion, and up he comes, up he comes, taking his time, taking his steps… in a dignified and graceful manner… he is here now… Coming up… up, up, up…"

And the people cheered louder and louder.

But the American Military Attaché was shaking his head all the way up the stairs, as he marched on towards where the American Ambassador was seated. The Military Attaché was not supposed to come here. The American Ambassador suspected something was amiss. He could even see it from the officer's stern look below the beret.

* * *

The pilots of the two Alfa jets had reported that they had scoured not only the agreed route but all other possible alternative routes

– even going deep into maritime territory in the hope that the Russian pilots had decided to use the ocean route, which was actually shorter. But there was no sign of the helicopter. They did the reconnaissance several times over. After all, Sierra Leone was a small country; even Lagos was bigger than this whole country.

But the Lagos operator, his heart now in his mouth, said they should do it all over again – even when the pilots added that there was no fog and it was therefore a mystery that the helicopter was missing. The Lagos operator did not like that word; and he had shouted back, "It's not missing."

At SLUNMIS headquarters in Freetown, Major Tom McNeil and the Nigerian Captain were listening to the multiway conversation in consternation. They absolutely didn't know what to say – or what to do – apart from stare at each other and wait for the unknown.

46

So, at the national stadium in Freetown, by the time the American Military Attaché reached where the American Ambassador was seated, Information Minister Bai Sankoh had fallen back to his rendition of rhetorical questions, to which the crowds obligingly responded.

"Who do the white people want to rule Sierra Leone?"

"President Ndomahina."

"Who is going to rule Sierra Leone for the next twenty years?"

"President Ndomahina."

"Who do you, the people, want to rule Sierra Leone?"

"President Ndomahina."

"For whom has the wicked junta been removed?"

"President Ndomahina."

* * *

Walking right behind the American Military Attaché was the Deputy Commander of Operation Octopus, another Nigerian General who was in charge while his boss was away to Monrovia to escort President Ndomahina back to Freetown. But Information

Minister Bai Sankoh did not mention the Deputy Commander. Maybe he was too excited about the American Military Attaché's presence. Maybe it was just an oversight. Maybe he didn't even know it was the Deputy Commander. Maybe he was waiting to do that later.

And now the two officers reached the American Ambassador's seat. The Military Attaché did a salute and handed a note to his boss. It was succinct and to the point, military-style writing. After reading it, the American Ambassador suddenly turned pale, and then red. Transfixed.

He jolted back to reality with, "What?" The other VIPs sitting nearby heard that.

* * *

By now the top hierarchy of the web of security and 'peace mission' players in the Sierra Leone project had all got the news (SLUNMIS headquarters in Freetown, Lagos, Abuja, Downing Street in London; and UN headquarters in New York) – the tragic news about what had happened in Sierra Leone's 'New York'.

* * *

UN Secretary General John Kirikiri had earlier told his staff not to contact him today, as he wanted to have some quiet time at home. He was in the middle of the lunch with his wife when the telephone rang. Mrs. Nana Kirikiri went to pick it up, as she sighed with, "Who is disturbing us now?"

"Hellooo."

And then she told her husband it was for him – from the office.

"But I told these people not to disturb me today!" he protested, as he reluctantly went to the phone. His own "What?"

after getting the news was louder than the American Ambassador's at the national stadium in Freetown. Mrs. Kirikiri immediately stopped in her tracks on her way to the dining table, turned to her husband, and asked "What is it, darling?"

And, presently, her husband repeated the information being relayed to him in the form of questions back to the informant – so that Nana could get the gist of the conversation.

"You mean it has been confirmed that the UN helicopter carrying President Ndomahina has been involved in an accident?"

"And there are only two possible survivors?"

"And the others are in critical life-threatening situations?"

"They are now being treated in an American-run hospital at this Leone Rutile place, where the aircraft came down?"

Mr. and Mrs. Kirikiri couldn't believe it.

Neither could British Prime Minister Ed McInroy, who would describe it as 'one of the saddest days, if not the saddest day, of my life' in his memoirs five years later.

The Nigerian Generals in Abuja and Lagos were equally stunned. It was hard for anyone to know how to react to the news. But all agreed that the most immediate steps were to treat the casualties, and to manage the situation at the national stadium in Freetown; to get the crowds out without immediately revealing what had happened to avoid a violent backlash or chaotic scenes.

That was why the lot fell on the American Military Attaché (who was the first to be informed from Leone Rutile – as was the protocol for all American companies operating in Sierra Leone to inform the American Embassy of any emergency – and he had broken the news to all the security stakeholders). That was how it was agreed that he should be accompanied by the Nigerian Deputy Commander to the national stadium to do just that.

47

Earlier, at Leone Rutile, when Paul McIntyre had phoned up Chief Security Officer David Macarthy about the sounds he had heard and the smoke he had seen, it was not news to the retired American National Guards Officer. CSO David – as he was popularly known in 'New York' and at post for over a decade now – had responded that he was also just about to call and inform the General Manager.

***

The moment it had happened, the security sentry (a Leone Rutile designation) manning one of the high-rise outposts had immediately reported to the CSO via VHF security radio that he had seen a UN helicopter coming down.

"SOS… SOS… SOS… Over."

And CSO David had immediately responded: "Please report… Over."

"Passing UN aircraft blast… In flames… Down north-east of outpost, forest near golf course… Running to scene now… Over."

"Make haste… Over."

* * *

So CSO David told Paul McIntyre that he was also just about to call him, and that he was going to the scene with emergency services immediately. Paul McIntyre just slammed back the receiver after saying, "Keep me updated." He slumped in his chair and now took the 'bad habit' to another level: he lit a cigarette inside his office. He had always previously gone to the veranda, even during the rainy season.

When CSO David and the emergency team arrived at the scene with their fire engines and ambulances, it was a sorry site to behold.

"My God," Paul McIntyre retorted when CSO David informed him it was the helicopter carrying President Ndomahina and entourage. Paul had – as per the existing protocol of being an American company in Sierra Leone – immediately informed the American Embassy in Freetown. At hand was the Military Attaché, who in turn ramped up coordination by informing the Nigerian Deputy Commander and SLUNMIS headquarters.

There was a platoon of Nigerian soldiers twenty miles away from Leone Rutile sent there just about a week ago as part of the nationwide deployment of personnel after the defeat of the Freetown military junta. The Nigerian Deputy Commander immediately ordered the platoon commander to head for Leone Rutile with the medical personnel of his team.

"I mean immediately. Ok?"

"Yes, sir."

By the time the soldiers arrived, the CSO-David-led Leone Rutile staff had already conveyed the victims to the company hospital being run by Dr. Peter Winterbottom, an American multidisciplinary surgeon.

* * *

The moment it had happened – the moment he realised the enormity of what had happened – security sentry Abdulai Kablai, a Sierra Leonean ex-serviceman, knew what to do immediately. He, like all other security sentries recruited at Leone Rutile, knew the standards and procedures as taught at training and in refresher courses by the former American National Guards. Kablai was one of the best in training and he had earned a reputation for diligence.

The moment he had seen the UN helicopter falling from the skies in smoke, he had taken out his walkie-talkie and called CSO David, in accordance with the Leone Rutile security network code of practice. And when CSO David had said, "Make haste… Over," Kablai had immediately switched off the phone, dropped the gun and raced down the stairs of his sentry post to the scene.

***

The way the helicopter had spun in the air before nose-diving within seconds, Abdulai Kablai had expected a heavy impact on the ground and a bursting into flames. It was in flames. But it did not burst into flames. It had happened that, on its way down, the aircraft first landed on the branches of one of the huge cotton trees planted around the golf course, and then it was sprung to an oak tree (which was originally brought from America) before it finally reached the ground, turned upside-down. The smoke and the flames were coming from the area between the tail boom and the engine of the helicopter. The engine had ceased.

As he came closer, Kablai could hear loud groans and cries and banging. The helicopter was shaking on its rotor blades, the smoke engulfing the scene. He tried to go round the aircraft, but the smoke kept on billowing, with the wind playing its own part in it. He was heartened to hear the approaching siren sounds. They came in full force – four fire engines and three ambulances (the full capacity of Leone Rutile).

When the flames were doused and the smoke subsided thirty minutes later, the greater task of having access into the helicopter to rescue the victims began. Its having landed upside-down made matters worse. In the end, ladders and axes (thankfully – if there was anything thankful in such a scene of horror – the fire fighters had come with ladders and axes) were used to climb and force the doors open.

There was blood and burns and debris, amid some groans from voices in trapped bodies. Others were completely silent. Some were still strapped to their seats, turned upside-down, in a waist-hanging position. The fire-fighters used razor-sharp knives to cut off the belts. They didn't know who was who. One seemed to have been burnt beyond recognition. Another's leg had been cut off by what seemed like shrapnel.

The fire fighters had to improvise by wrapping each victim with a fire blanket, padding it, tying it with nylon ropes and lowering it slowly down to the waiting medicos, who immediately took each victim to an ambulance, administering first-aid and trying to see who was alive and who was not; who needed more attention and who did not need attention anymore.

***

When they reached with the victims at the Leone Rutile Hospital, Dr. Winterbottom immediately realised there was not much he could do in 'this seemingly hopeless situation'.

General Manager Paul McIntyre was already there waiting. He couldn't remember having cried his entire adult life – even when he had lost a close friend in the Middle East while serving in the US Army. But Paul shed a tear or two after he saw the burnt body of Amza Alie, saw blood oozing from the mouth of President Kargbo Ndomahina, and heard the continual groans of British High Commissioner John Coleson.

48

At the national stadium in Freetown, Femi Cole was approached by the American Ambassador and he whispered to her, "Madam, we are being asked to leave quietly, because there's a developing security situation." She brusquely retorted, "What security situation, Ambassador? I've not been informed about any security situation."

The American Ambassador knew how to handle the situation; that's why he had offered to do it when the American Military Attaché and the Nigerian Deputy Commander had wondered how to tell her to leave. So the American Ambassador calmly replied, "I am informing you now, madam. We would have to leave now."

Femi Cole got the message fully and obliged immediately when she saw the visiting Heads of State and other VIPs being led from their seats by the American Military Attaché and the Nigerian Deputy Commander. She clutched on to the top sleeve of the American Ambassador's coat all the way down the stairs – head down, without a word.

***

The moment Information Minister Bai Sankoh saw this activity (the authorities had agreed he was going to be managed last) – when he saw the VIPs, including Femi Cole, rising from their seats and going down the stairs – his excitement reached its crescendo.

He took to the mike and told the crowds, "Now, now, now, now, the moment has come… Now, you can all see for yourselves. You can all see that the President is near. Now all the big men are being led by our great First Lady, Her Excellency Femi Cole, coming down to receive our beloved President."

By now, a group of Nigerian soldiers had come up the presidential pavilion, and each VIP was being guarded or actually ushered away. It was only after all the VIPs had been taken away that the Nigerian Deputy Commander approached Information Minister Bai Sankoh and informed him – with directives to 'find a way of telling the crowds' that, due to unforeseen circumstances, the re-inauguration of President Ndomahina had been postponed; that they should all go home and stay tuned to their radios as they would be informed about the details later. Bai Sankoh wanted to ask questions; but the Nigerian Deputy Commander had no time for that. He militarily turned away. He had an emergency security meeting to attend immediately.

Minister Bai Sankoh was not himself, expectedly. He summed up enough courage and delivered the message. This was a hard message to deliver – perhaps the hardest message to deliver, even for its briskness and no details. It took him about five minutes to compose himself. He wanted to know what had happened. He needed to know what had happened. He was desirous to know what had caused the cancellation or, as they put it, 'postponement' of the ceremony at this crucial last minute. It must be something very very important. But he did not know. He had not been told. He was not even given an opportunity to ask. All he was told was to tell the people to go home and details would be supplied later. He had to find a better way of putting it. He must still rise to the occasion!

So, after he had composed himself, he also recovered his oratory powers. He started with the rendition of, "Who does the white man want to rule Sierra Leone at this time?"; and the crowds shouted back, "President Ndomahina." And so on and so forth, just as before.

"Well, now, I have some good news and a bit of bad news."

There were murmurs.

"Sorry, not bad news. I have some good news and not-so-good news."

And in varied discordant voices, the people shouted back what summed up as, "Tell us, tell us, we want to hear it all."

And he yelled back, "Who do you, the people, want to rule Sierra Leone for the next twenty years?"

They responded, of course, "President Ndomahina."

"Ok, let me start with the very good news. Nothing can stop the re-inauguration of our beloved President. We love him, and the white people love him. Everybody loves him – except for those heartless rebels and people with bad hearts. Not so?"

And the people shouted back, "Yeahhh."

"So the white people love our President so much that they are having an emergency meeting with him today."

"Yeahhh," the crowd shouted back; but some did not shout as previously, not knowing where this talk was leading.

"And so, inside that good news is the not-so-good news."

"Tell us, tell us," came from not so many voices this time.

"Because of the emergency meeting, the President is going there right now…"

Some gasps came from the stands. Knowing how long they had been waiting, they feared more delay. But, of course, it was worse than that; worse than they would ever have feared, worse than their present pessimism.

"And so, because the President is going there as I speak, I have just been informed to tell you all, his beloved people, that the waiting will not be much longer…"

"We will wait... We will wait... We will wait," became a chorus.

It was hard for Bai Sankoh to stop them now. "Wait, wait..."

"We will wait... We will wait..."

"No wait, wait, please wait for *me*. I am not done yet."

"We will wait."

"Helloooo."

"Hiiiiiii."

"Who does the white man want to rule Sierra Leone?"

"President Ndomahina." He just managed to get some less enthusiastic voices. But there was some relative calmness again, with the murmurs continuing.

Bai Sankoh knew he could not delay anymore. He said it in the soberest and solemnest of tones. "What I am trying to tell you is that, because our beloved President has to attend that emergency meeting, I am sorry, this ceremony, unfortunately, has to be postponed."

"Hmmmmmmm."

"Let us all go home and wait for the new date for our President's return."

There was consternation. An atmosphere of enveloped silence briefly took over. Bai Sankoh himself had paused and got enveloped in it. And then the silence suddenly broke into a mixture of wailings and shouts and yelling. It became a roused rabble – in a political muddle.

It took some time before Bai Sankoh could be able to somehow get their attention again – haphazardly – and told them he understood how they felt; but that it was just a short delay. "Let us all go home quietly and listen to the radio for the details of the next inauguration ceremony date."

They didn't go quietly. Some shops were looted. The Nigerian soldiers turned a blind eye to it.

All the Alfa jets had since disappeared!

***

At Leone Rutile, Dr. Winterbottom had emerged from the operating theatre to tell General Manager Paul McIntyre that there was 'a possibility of only two people surviving' – one of whom was the British High Commissioner, whose leg had been cut off. The medico said he had applied some rudimentary treatment and bandaged the limb of John Coleson, "but both or one of them could make it if they are to be flown immediately to a better facility."

The other possible survivor was President Kargbo Ndomahina's ADC, who seemed to have some internal bleeding.

"Everybody else is dead?" was the immediate question from Paul McIntyre, who only got to know in hospital that Mallam Musa Odofo and Opposition Leader Dauda Kabia were also on board.

"I'm sorry," Dr. Winterbottom said.

Paul knew what to do in the circumstance. The royal frigates off the shores of Sierra Leone had modern hi-tech medical facilities. Taking the casualties there was the only option. Dr. Winterbottom himself would fly with the two on one of the Leone Rutile helicopters. It was just a twenty-five-minute flight.

The Nigerian soldiers from the nearby platoon had arrived just in time for the airlifting of the two. The bodies of the rest were deposited at the Leone Rutile morgue awaiting instructions from Freetown. While waiting for that, the Nigerian soldiers were now tasked with guarding the hospital premises – guarding the authorities, the former authorities, the bodies of the late authorities.

***

Femi Cole had kept asking "What's going on? What is happening?" without getting an answer as she was being driven at breakneck speed back to her Juba Hill residence – the residence of President Ndomahina. The Nigerian Deputy Commander had given to Femi Cole's personal bodyguard (a Nigerian soldier, of course) a copy of the same note the American Military Attaché had given to the American Ambassador at the stadium. The bodyguard was instructed to hand it to her when they reached home.

Femi Cole fainted in her living room immediately after reading the military-style-written note: *'The UN helicopter carrying President Ndomahina, Mallam Musa Odofo and British High Commissioner John Coleson came down around Leone Rutile. Emergency services immediately dispatched to help Rutile Staff who reported the incidence to us. Unfortunately, we've lost the two Heads of State. We are here to evacuate all VIPs before the crowds are told to disperse.'*

Her personal doctor had to revive her to face the stark reality. But she felt numb about it when she regained full consciousness. She couldn't even cry. A blank inexplicable spirit took over her. Perhaps she still didn't believe it had happened, that it *could* happen: President Ndomahina and Mallam Musa Odofo in one fell swoop? How could that be possible?

It was simply unbelievable for Femi Cole. Her heart was palpitating and throbbing in intermittent contractions.

49

Perhaps it was more unbelievable in Abuja.

The signals operator at Aso Rock was a Mallam Odofo loyalist, answerable only to him and, in his absence, to Chief Security Officer Mamadu Gowon – not to the Deputy Head of State. The moment they first lost contact with the UN helicopter, the signaller had immediately informed the Chief Security Officer. Thirty minutes or so later, it emerged there was an accident; and then it was confirmed that Mallam Musa Odofo was a fatality. Was dead. Chief Security Officer Gowon was terrified – a sharp belly ache suddenly struck him. But he was a soldier – a gallant soldier, with men under his command.

He had earlier carried out the deed as per the instructions in the note from Mallam Musa Odofo. And now this. He knew he was in a bind – an almost impossible situation. He knew the other members of the ruling council hated him. He only answered 'Sir' to Mallam Odofo and nobody else. And now this. But he was a gallant soldier. He had to move quickly with the men under his command. He had to stage his own coup and take over power before it was too late. He sprang into action.

The only snag was that, as the communications system was interconnected, the signals operators in Lagos were also privy to the information. And while those operators were as well loyal to Mallam Odofo, they were not actually political loyalists – for they were at the same time committed to their military career. They were reporting through the chain of command, and not directly to the Chief Security Officer. And so, almost simultaneously, the news reached the Nigerian Military High Command and the Deputy Head of State (the actual number two man in the Reformed Council for the Prosperity of Nigeria – RCPN).

They took action before anybody could know it. When Chief Security Officer Mamadu Gowon and his motorcade of assorted bodyguards swooped into Aso Rock, they merely entered into a trap. He was immediately arrested and detained. All his bodyguards were disarmed and sent to Abuja's 'quarter-deck for re-training'. Military tanks were rolled on the streets of Abuja and Lagos. Nigerians became more confused. There was no information on what was going on. *Mallam Musa Odofo must be up to something again,* many thought.

* * *

In London, Mark Fergusson raised his eyebrows when he saw the email update from the former American Peace Corps stating that Information Minister Bai Sankoh had informed the crowds that the ceremony had been postponed. "What could that mean?" Mark asked himself.

The answer didn't take long to come. His friend, or rather his former friend, Prime Minister Ed McInroy, had decided that the British people must be informed immediately because High Commissioner John Coleson was 'in active public service' when the accident happened. Coleson's newly wedded wife, Mia, who was away in Israel (her home country) to say goodbye to her parents in anticipation of her relocation to Sierra Leone, was officially informed first. And then the breaking news came from Downing

Street that the British High Commissioner to Sierra Leone was involved in a helicopter accident, that he was now being treated in a royal frigate off the shores of Sierra Leone, and that efforts were being marshalled to evacuate him to Britain immediately.

Mark muttered, "What? Wow, wow, wow," before calling Rachael to come and see what was on television. She was stunned.

"Wow… Mark, darling, this could have been you," she said, as she fell into his embrace. They were not happy. They were serene.

* * *

As the full story quickly unfolded on British television networks, it was Sierra Leoneans and Nigerians living in Britain who called their compatriots back home and informed them about what was being reported: that both President Ndomahina and Mallam Musa Odofo had died in a helicopter accident.

That was about two hours after the crowds had left the national stadium in Freetown, with some force applied by the Nigerian soldiers in dispersing the reluctant ones from the stands. Soon, the local news networks in the two countries picked up the story before there was any official announcement to the effect.

* * *

The people in both countries were shocked beyond belief. But maybe the Nigerians ended up being more shocked.

As the news was now confirmed, some Nigerians openly celebrated: drumming, dancing, and drinking 'to the healthy death of the dictator', as one put it. They believed it was an answer to their prayers for the end of the repressive Mallam Odofo regime.

"Now the military has no choice but to hand power over to the imprisoned democratically elected President, Buhari Okonkwo," was the refrain that took over the streets of Nigerian towns and cities.

But their hopes were soon dashed on a rock when the Nigerian Military High Command released a statement saying that the Deputy Head of State, another General, was taking over. The statement insisted that indeed it was the plan of the RCPN to hand over the reins of government to the democratically elected President.

"But we regret to inform all Nigerians, at home and abroad, that, unfortunately, on the instructions of Mallam Musa Odofo, who is now late, before he departed Abuja earlier in the day, the democratically elected President, Buhari Okonkwo, has been executed in prison by Mallam Odofo's Chief Security Officer, Col. Mamadu Gowon. He is now under arrest and has confessed to the crime in what has now turned out to be a vain attempt to further consolidate Odofo's stranglehold on power. The Military High Command hereby appeals for calm. We hereby pledge to conduct fresh free and fair elections within a year, and we are committed to handing over power to whoever emerges as winner. Let it be known to all and sundry that, with immediate effect, all bank accounts, assets and properties both local and international belonging to Mallam Musa Odofo and his immediate family members are hereby put on freeze. A commission of inquiry is being set up to investigate these assets and every single *kobo* belonging to the state will be returned to the people. We hereby declare thirty days of mourning for the late democratically-elected President, His Excellency Buhari Okonkwo. We will update you on any further developments. Thank you all. Long live Nigeria."

The Nigerian national anthem followed the broadcast.

* * *

In Freetown, the Nigerian Deputy Commander, in collaboration with SLUNMIS, issued a statement at about the same time, imposing a dusk-to-dawn curfew, calling on the people of Sierra Leone to show understanding 'as we collaborate with the international community to find a way out of the tragic events that occurred today'. He declared a three-month period of prayer and mourning for President Ndomahina, and that more details would be released later.

Meanwhile, following the news, there were celebrations in a small part of Sierra Leone, at the place where three countries met, as the remnant rebel junta forces fired shots all night – according to nearby villagers who fled overnight, thinking an attack was being launched.

***

That night, Leone Rutile General Manager Paul McIntyre did not sleep at all. He wondered why. He never liked African politicians, he never liked President Ndomahina, and he utterly despised Mallam Musa Odofo. But why was he being tormented by their deaths? Just earlier, he was forced to shed tears. And now he could not sleep. Was it because he virtually witnessed the accident occurring live? Was it because it had happened in the territory he was in charge of? Was it because…

When he woke up in the morning after a brief sleep, the first thing Paul McIntyre asked CSO David to do was to check all the ammunition in the hands of the sentries. As far as Paul was concerned, he thought – in fact, he believed – he first heard a shot before the helicopter's explosion.

CSO David did all the ammunition checks meticulously but there was no missing bullet. Still not really satisfied, Paul McIntyre asked for sentry Abdulai Kablai to see him in the office. The General Manager asked the guard if he, while at the sentry outpost yesterday, did not first hear the sound of a gunshot before the explosion and the helicopter's fall from the skies.

Kablai's response, in his trademark hoarse voice, left the General Manager with more questions than answers. "Sir, the rebels have never ventured near Leone Rutile because they know there is always tight security in place. They know we are American-trained, sir."

Paul McIntyre's doubts did not therefore go away. He was a soldier, he was a former marine. He knew the sound of a gunshot. He was sure he heard one that moment of the accident. Or was it just his mind playing on him? Was it not 'this bad habit' taking its toll on his brain? He was now not sure.

He would have to wait for the forensic report that would be given by the UN experts who would come to assess the accident, assess the helicopter – its carcass, rather.

* * *

The newspapers in Sierra Leone were even more suspicious of the 'so-called accident', calling for 'a swift and thorough investigation of the disaster in order to expose and bring to justice all those responsible, *no matter where they are*'.

The headlines were unequivocal: 'Democracy Massacred', 'Who Murdered Our Democracy?', 'It Was Not An Accident'. But the one that was more confrontational was the ruling party's mouthpiece, with the headline, 'Britain's Got Blood On Its Hands!'. The paper went at length to hypothetically connect the events, starting from the 'window-dressing breach of a UN Resolution', to the impromptu sacking of 'the real friend of Sierra Leone' High Commissioner Mark Fergusson, to 'the British hatred for Mallam Odofo', to the refusal to allow 'the Nigerian Head of State to use his own helicopter to come with President Ndomahina to Freetown'. In summary: it was all planned to assassinate the two. The British-donated radio, *Voice of di Pipul*, echoed and magnified the same sentiments.

But the question they refused to answer was: why would Britain get its own High Commissioner on the same aircraft if they had planned to murder the Africans? Cannon fodder? *Britain does not do suicide bombing.*

Everything now hinged on the forensic examination of the accident.

***

The Nigerian media was not so enthusiastic anymore about the post-mortem. There was nothing retrospectively palatable for news consumption, as one commentator put it. The Nigerian journalists were now purposefully forward-looking, calling on the new military rulers to keep to their word of returning the country to 'genuine democracy within a year', reminding the international community not to rest on their oars 'to avoid *déjà vu*'.

50

One month later, the Nigerian Deputy Commander was firmly in charge of the affairs of Sierra Leone. He was now holding what he called consultative meetings with all the country's stakeholders. Religious leaders, political parties, women's groups, youth organisations, community development associations and all sorts of assorted groups were consulted 'in trying to find a way forward for Sierra Leone'.

Naturally and constitutionally, the Vice President should take over under such circumstances, but President Ndomahina had got his deputy executed 'for treason'. He had never announced a formal replacement thereafter.

Meanwhile, under the banner of SLUNMIS, more countries – including Ivory Coast, India, Pakistan, Kenya, Ghana, Bangladesh and Malaysia – had sent troops for 'the peace-keeping force', in accordance with a British-engineered UN Resolution. Arriving with the peace-keepers were the multinational forensic experts who had come to examine the UN helicopter carcass at Leone Rutile and would put out their report within a month.

***

Femi Cole's services were no longer required – no longer requested – in the scheme of things. Despite her protestations, she was not included in any of the consultations anymore. Not to talk of reporting to her about anything. In fact, the new Nigerian commanders had withdrawn all her security, save one personnel who was actually a surrendered Sierra Leone Army private and deployed at the late President's property 'not for the protection of any particular person'.

Femi Cole's company was only kept these days by OSLEWIL cheerleader Adama Mankhantel, Information Minister Bai Sankoh and Anglican priest Olumendi Metzeger. And presently, Femi Cole had just received a letter from lawyers acting on behalf of Mrs. Memunatu Ndomahina asking her to 'vacate the Ndomahina property or legal action will be taken against your person within fourteen days'.

But Femi Cole had expected it. And she was ready for it. She was continuing to occupy the property on the grounds that President Ndomahina left her there. But her firmer grounds were that she was pregnant for the late President and she had only suffered a miscarriage after hearing the news of his tragic death. The family doctor, Dr. Mustapha Ferenkeh (who had travelled with her from Liberia), was witness. She therefore asked her own lawyers to reply.

* * *

It was a similar state of affairs that prevailed in Nigeria under the Military High Command (the new Generals were shying away from using the RCPN name). Nigerians were sceptical, but they had been undone by the killing of the democratically elected President. They had no choice but to cooperate in finding a way out. Though some doubted whether the pledge would be carried out, many were heartened about freezing the assets of Mallam Musa Odofo and his immediate family.

The new Nigerian junta further placed a travel ban on named friends, business associates and some members of the Odofo family. Many Nigerians therefore decided they would give the new regime a try, out of necessity. There was no alternative. Consequently, the new junta was also holding consultative meetings with various stakeholder groups.

* * *

The international community also toed the line. Britain announced a partial lifting of the travel ban on RCPN members 'for essential official travel only'. It also eased some of the sanctions on petroleum products 'as a relief for the suffering masses', while insisting that 'elections must be held and power transferred to a civilian government within one year as pledged by the new Nigerian leaders'.

For Sierra Leone also, the air, land and sea blockade was lifted with immediate effect. Britain particularly urged international aid agencies to go in immediately, as there was an emerging humanitarian crisis in Sierra Leone.

Meanwhile, British High Commissioner John Coleson was recuperating at London's St. Thomas' Hospital, as he had been evacuated on the night of the accident. And Prime Minister Ed McInroy was reluctant to announce a replacement just as yet.

John Coleson's co-evacuee, President Ndomahina's ADC, didn't make it: he had succumbed on board the Leone Rutile helicopter before it landed on the royal frigate. Dr. Winterbottom could do nothing about it.

* * *

It was within this same period that Teacher Paul and Rosemarie received a visitor at Roboli. It was Rosemarie's younger brother,

Sowa, from the south-east. He had decided to come and check on his sister after the roads were declared open and safe by the Nigerian military. Everybody seemed to have forgotten about President Ndomahina – the country engulfed in Easter holiday euphoria. Even the usually rugged, hardened-face Nigerian soldiers were smiling at checkpoints, wishing passengers a 'Happy Easter'. Sowa gave a wry smile in one of the villages on the highway when he saw that the beaten and battered effigy of Judas was still on display (in Sierra Leone, it was a tradition for children to make an effigy of Judas and then give it a thorough public flogging on Good Friday for his infamous betrayal of Jesus).

The moment Rosemarie saw her brother, she burst out crying. This was the first time she was actually crying out loud for her beloved twins. However, Sowa thought it was only a cry for the joy of seeing him, until Teacher Paul told him they had lost the twins.

"When?" Sowa asked.

"In Freetown, months ago."

"No. It didn't happen."

"What do you mean by it didn't happen? A Nigerian jet killed them," Teacher Paul confusedly asserted.

"No, it didn't."

"What are you talking about, Sowa?" Rosemarie now had some strength to interject.

Sowa said that in fact the main reason for his coming was because Stephen and Samson (those were the names Rosemarie gave when she used to take the twins for holiday to the south-east) had given him a letter for the parents.

Teacher Paul and Rosemarie couldn't believe what they were hearing. Sowa was now getting his rucksack off his back to look for the letter, while still talking.

According to him, the boys were out for lunch with some humanitarian workers on the day that the bomb was dropped on their offices. It happened that those 'foreign friends' were leaving the country that very day; and that when the cataclysmic events happened, the twins were offered an opportunity to come along out of the country (even before the coup, ever since the rebels captured the diamond-rich city of Kono a year before and internally displaced people started pouring into other towns and cities, everybody who had a passport and important documents was carrying them everywhere in readiness for any eventuality). Since Roboli was cut off, Sowa's narration continued, the twins had asked their friends to pass through the south-east so that they would send a letter to their parents. That was how they came to find him.

"I saw them with my own eyes. I spoke to them with my own mouth. I heard them speak with my own ears," he said. He had now removed the letter from the bag. "Here, here it is." He passed it to Teacher Paul. It was not in an envelope. It was just folded.

Teacher Paul unfolded the note and exclaimed, "It's true. It's them, no doubt. This is my son's handwriting."

Rosemarie shouted "Thank you, Lord" as she snatched the letter to see.

Indeed, it's true.

"But that's several months ago. Where would they be now? How would we know they crossed the border at all?" Teacher Paul asked.

"We continue to hope and pray," Rosemarie, now tear-dry, said, as she ushered her brother inside the house to have some rest and some food. Only then did she say 'Happy Easter' to him.

But Teacher Paul was neither happy nor hopeful. It made him brood more. He could recall that there had been reports of rebels abducting aid workers, missionaries and nuns (for whatever reason was hard to say, because they never asked for ransom like it was done in other conflict situations in Africa). Apparently, Teacher Paul brooded on his veranda, the twins must have been abducted along with their foreign friends. And he knew if the rebels or even the civil militia got to know who they were, it meant death. *The True Light* had been vociferously critical of both groups' treatment of civilians in the course of the war.

Teacher Paul thought it would perhaps have been better the initial story were true: that the twins were killed by a Nigerian jet. Instant death from a bomb was better than death at the hands of an enemy, who must have applied some interrogation and torture first. Teacher Paul wished Sowa had not brought this information. He wished Sowa had not come at all. Strangely, he wished his brother-in-law had been abducted on the way coming to prevent him from reaching with this message. The Tamaranehs were already healing and accepting the reality of having lost the twins. Sowa's coming had now opened an old wound even wider. For him.

***

In Britain, the Queen breathed fresh air into the Fergussons when she awarded knighthood – not so surprisingly – to James Fergusson, Mark's father, for the role he played in 're-enacting the historic connection between Britain and its former Sierra Leone colony'. Sir James Fergusson MBE. He got it while still in hospital and celebrated quietly with his friend Gabriel Williamson and Dr. Robinson.

"I would never in a thousand years have dreamt of this," James crackled, after reading the *Exeter Times* with its scintillating lead, 'Queen Honours Exeter Man'. They all burst out laughing and cheering in the hospital cafe. James was okay with staying in the hospital as long as Dr. Robinson allowed, and the latter was also more comfortable with that in order to keep a constant eye on his patient. "Here is more than a hotel," James had relished.

***

It was Rachael who came up with the idea of celebrating the MBE honour accorded to her father-in-law by organising a party in their North London home – though the guest of honour himself would not be present. Mark agreed.

And what better time to organise the party than Easter Sunday evening, just a week away. Easter was a big thing – if not *the* big thing – in Britain. Everybody looked forward to it, though nobody really cared much about what it was about. Just a time for surplus shopping – and to eat and share eggs as never before with friends and family. It was just the best British holiday – Good Friday, Great Saturday, Easter Sunday, and Easter Monday in that order every year. Good weather most times. It heralded summer time: there would be some sunshine – unlike the Christmas winter period. Rachael was over the moon about who to invite, knowing that Sarah would certainly come for the holiday.

Rachael knew some of her proposed guests would be with the Queen in their traditional Church of England ceremonies that day. She would have them over for the night – Monday would be a bank holiday.

Rachael phoned up Sarah and told her about it; and said that there were also "several letters waiting for you". Sarah was excited about her grandfather's honour and praised her mother for coming up with the Easter party idea. She was not sure about the letters, because they could just be responses to the job applications she had written and posted the day before she left for Durham Castle. But now she had got a job.

"I am inviting a selected number of our royal relatives," Rachael told Sarah. "Do you have any in mind?"

"No, Mum, just go ahead. I'll just flow with whoever is present."

Rachael got it. Or thought she got it. Her plan was to invite mainly bachelor royals, from whom Sarah could find a pick and move on for good.

***

On the day of the party, it was all bustling at the Fergussons' North London residence. The last time they had such high-level guests was at the farewell party they organised before leaving for Sierra Leone. This one was even better. Many more royals were in attendance. It was Easter.

It all went well through the evening to late night. After her well-received 'Happy Easter' speech to now-almost-raucous guests, Rachael, dressed in flamboyant glittering royal regalia, made a lengthy midnight telephone call to her long-time Mexican friend, Maria de Sanchez (it was just early evening in Mexico City). She gave her details of what was going on: eating and drinking and 'royal networking with Sarah'. Maria said she would be in London in two weeks. She had already planned the trip with her Jamaican partner; the news had just ignited her desire to come and join in her friend's joy belatedly.

"You know we are sisters now."

"You know we are sisters now."

Both hung up laughing.

And Rachael was happy with what she saw at the party itself, as Sarah was chatty with the boys. That was a good beginning. Good prospects. And nothing made her surer than seeing Sarah escort the Earl of Leicester to his car when he was leaving. They were childhood friends; they could be rekindling something, Rachael thought to herself. *All was working according to plan.*

Sarah and the Earl had actually met earlier at the Queen's Easter church service at Westminster Abbey when Sarah attended with her father, Mark. It was Mr. and Mrs. Fergusson who were invited, but Rachael was too busy with the preparations for the party tonight. And she had other ideas (among which was taking Joel away to his great-grandparents, the Duke and Duchess of Lancaster, to be with them for Easter).

Sarah had embraced and cherished the idea of being at Westminster Abbey again after such a long time. When she passed by the tomb of 'the unknown warrior' interred at the Abbey, she had a quick reflection as to why 'he' was never identified. *Could he have been an African soldier like Joel's great-grandfather? Or was it that…?* She shook off the thought. It's not really necessary to dwell on it now. It was not important in the circumstances. She turned her eyes up to deliberately re-admire the centuries-old Gothic architecture of the Abbey. She had moved on… Inside the church, her heart sank a bit seeing Vicar Andrew Decker, in gorgeous flowing priestly robes and a biretta to match, conducting the service. It was in post-service chit-chat that the Earl of Leicester and some other royals had confirmed to her father they would be present at the party. The moment Rachael got the information, she organised the sitting arrangement for their sprawling back gardens accordingly.

***

When all had been said and done, the Fergusson family acknowledged it was a great night and retired to their respective rooms. Sarah – the new Sarah – went back to her old room again. She missed Joel but was satisfied that he was in good hands in Lancaster Castle. She was exhausted and just going to sleep now; but then she saw the letters her mother told her about. She would like to skim through them quickly and get them out of the way. Out of the way before her date with the Earl of Leicester tomorrow evening.

About ten minutes later, Sarah rushed out of her room shouting, "Dad, Dad… Mum, Mum… Dad, Dad," and was now hitting her parents' door.

"What is it, darling?" Mark asked as he opened the door.

"He is alive, Daddy, he is alive." She brandished a paper before him. "Here's the letter, Daddy – Stephen is alive. He wrote this letter himself."

By now Rachael had also come to the door. She was the one who took the letter from Sarah. But Mark also held a part of it to see, and he said: "Yes, I recognise the handwriting."

Rachael was perplexed, holding the letter but not reading it. But she was showing some interest and some excitement as well. "Where did he write from?" she asked.

"It says Casablanca. From a refugee camp in Casablanca."

And then Rachael asked a more pertinent question. "But why has he not called since? He has this house's telephone number."

Sarah somehow tended to agree with her mum: "Yeah, I don't know why. But he said he tried to reach us by phone or something."

Mark was quickly perusing the letter. He smiled briefly when he read, *'My dear lovebird'*. And he saw the part where Stephen wrote, *'To no avail, I have tried to reach you by telephone on this number…'*

"Oh, I see the problem."

"Which problem, Daddy?"

"About the telephone number. Remember that the British telephone coding system changed seven months ago. You would have to add another '0' in front when calling from abroad. He didn't know this; that's why he has written the number in its old form."

"Oh yes, that's it, Daddy, that's it."

Rachael let go of the letter, and she was falling. Mark immediately grabbed her.

"Rachael, Rachael, Rachael."

"Mum, Mum, Mum."

She had passed out.

"Call 999," Mark told Sarah. "While I tend to her."

* * *

The North London neighbourhood gossip the next morning was that someone over-enjoyed at the Easter celebrations last night so much that they had to be taken away by an ambulance.

For the Fergussons, for now, while there was so much to try to unravel about this somewhat mystery letter from Stephen, Rachael's health had to be dealt with first.

* * *

Meanwhile, UN Secretary General John Kirikiri now knew what to do with the diamonds. As far as he was concerned, there was certainly nobody to hand them back to now. He had decided that he would use them – rather, the proceeds from them – to build an international centre in his home country where young African leaders could be trained on the importance of democracy. What a retirement package, coming in the penultimate year of his term as Secretary General! After a lot of eating and drinking, he had an Easter Sunday surprise for his wife. He floated the idea to Nana, but only told her an unnamed organisation was going to sponsor the project. He just wanted them to agree on the name to be given to the centre.

"Let's call it the Kirikiri International Centre for Democracy," an exhilarated Mrs. Kirikiri said.

"That's right. That's why I love you, honey." On second thought, he added, "I think we should include good governance in it: the Kirikiri International Centre for Democracy and Good Governance."

"I agree. It sounds better, darling."

"And the motto shall be: 'Democracy will not survive without good governance'."

That night, the two lovebirds, holding hands, smiled all the way from the living room to their bedroom – but not before the top UN man stroked the head of the gift lion statue on the way.

His briefcase was by his bedside – to be seen and touched at every waking moment.

***

That bank holiday Monday morning in London, as Mark was rushing to go to his wife in hospital – while Sarah and Ben (who, maybe stirred by the American in him, spent the night with his friends at a Camden Town carnival and came home to find his mother had been taken away) were still sleeping – April 17 and April 18 were fluttering and flapping their wings alongside what seemed like intelligible voices coming from them. Mark clearly noticed this.

While driving to the hospital, he gave a serious thought to it. Indeed he remembered his ornithology lessons in school about lovebirds also being parrots, but not the naturally talking type. However, though his intuitive reason for buying April 18 was just out of a desire for April 17 to have company, Mark could now recall that his teacher once said if a couple of lovebirds were caged together, they had the capacity to develop language.

Mark thought – actually believed – that he had heard something like, 'The wind that is blowing is the wind that is blowing'. Not as a pairing chorus from the lovebirds, but in cantata fashion: one bird saying 'The wind that is blowing' and the other responding 'is the wind that is blowing'.

"But why have they not been speaking like this ever since… until this morning, after last night's events?" Mark asked himself as he reached at the car park of St. Thomas's Hospital – the same hospital where doctors were currently in the process of fixing a prosthetic leg onto British High Commissioner John Coleson, whose wife, Mia, had also just driven into the same car park.

***

By now, Sarah had woken up. It should be one of the happiest days – if not the happiest day thus far – in her life. It should have been. But she was feeling as if some heavy weight had been placed on her body and she couldn't move a single fibre. She was despondent. Not because her mother was in hospital (she was sure doctors would take care of her); not because of the Earl of Leicester (he didn't even cross her mind again); not about scepticisms over Stephen's actual whereabouts right now (the letter was written three months ago as per its date and it had stated that they were on the move).

It was all about Edwina Campbell.

After Rachael had been taken away to the hospital, Sarah went back to her room and read the full six-page letter. She was full of excitement and smiles when reading Stephen's narration of events from Sierra Leone to Morocco. But the part that struck her like a thunderbolt was where Stephen had written: 'I am sorry to inform you – if you've not already heard – that your friend, our friend, Edwina Campbell, was among the fatalities when the bomb was dropped on our offices. In my place, she died… Heartbroken on many fronts… Your lovebird, Stephen (Amidu).'

Sarah lay in bed wanting to go to the bathroom, but she couldn't; she wanted to have breakfast, but she couldn't; she wanted to inform either her father or her brother, but she couldn't. Immobilised. Some heavy weight was pressing her body to the bed. She saw the letter – the papers – lying by her in bed. She tried to sum up strength. She struggled with attuning her mind to some movement. And then she was able to move her fingers in the right hand. And she shook her hand. Some kind of sensation came slowly into her tissues. She summoned more strength, and she was able to raise her hand up and take her bedside pen. She picked up the last page of Stephen's letter. And then she wrote on the margins adjacent to the lines about Edwina: "Dear God, if there's life after death, please make Edwina Campbell my guardian angel. Amen."

And she slipped back into sleep…

About the Author

Sheka Tarawalie was a print journalist in Sierra Leone during its war. He later sought asylum in the UK before being called back to serve in governance (most notably as Press Secretary to the President). His autobiography, *Pope Francis, Politics and the Mabanta Boy* (Matador), was published in 2019. Now back in Oldham, UK, he is a member of the Society of Authors and the National Union of Journalists.